Home
— *at* —
Last

WILLIAM A. FRANCIS

Author of Lucky Jack!

HOME AT LAST

iUniverse books may be ordered through booksellers or by contacting:

iUniverse
1663 Liberty Drive
Bloomington, IN 47403
www.iuniverse.com
1-800-Authors (1-800-288-4677)

ISBN: 978-1-5320-6760-0 (sc)
ISBN: 978-1-5320-6759-4 (e)

Print information available on the last page.

iUniverse rev. date: 02/07/2019

For Karen, Bill and Jim

Contents

Part Two
"All Aboard!"

Part One

The Adventures Begin

Know'st thou the excellent joys of youth? Joys of the dear companions and of the merry word and laughing face?

—Walt Whitman

A Pennsylvania Pastoral
(1950-1951)

Ben Warren lived in a corner of postwar Pennsylvania where struggling Depression-era Pittsburgh families settled. This was the scrubby, shale-lined landscape of rolling hills called Allegheny Acres. There was once wealth beneath those hills—twisting vaults of coal—but no more; the mines closed in the late forties, all deposits expired. Above those invisible tunnels that collapsed slowly and quietly there were spotty cinder block basement houses capped by flat, tar-papered roofs. In time, however, first floors were built above basements and the happy families moved above ground.

"Do not mock them, for they live in their own homes. *Own* as in possess. *Own* is an adjective—their *own* home, you see." So said Albert, Ben's father, poor but proud.

Although miles of tunnels deep under the land were all but forgotten, there were reminders of them for those who knew where to look, such as the yellow sulfur creeks pooling at the base of Coal Mine Hill. In the spirit of Tom and Huck, boys knew where to look.

"They got bodies in that mine, 'djaknow?" Ned waited for their shock.

"Naaa—ain't no bodies in there. What you sayin'?" That was the chorus of little kids, easily scared kids.

"It caved in, that's what. Miners stuck in there. That's true."

"Awwww. Hey, huh? You kiddin'."

1

"Lots of bodies," Ned said. "Now you know, huh? That's why it's sealed up. It's a graveyard, see? Boooo." Ned's graveyard.

Boys swam in this putrid yellow water on hot summer days. Health warnings went unheeded even when there was talk of another polio outbreak. It was a rite of passage on an August morning for little boys to be thrown naked into the ponds by older boys. Ben got it last year. You got it only once, or "onced," as some said. Dunked over and over, the boys held their breaths and pinched their noses until their lungs seemed to burst. But back on land, after much crying and choking on sulfur water—it was difficult to distinguish sobs from gasps—the boys were allowed to pull on their dry clothes hanging on tree limbs and slouching over berry bushes. Soon, however, they joked and laughed, for they were newly baptized members of the stinky-water club. Arm-in-arm, feigning punches, trading mincing blows, the newly-bathed staggered home on cinder paths. An older boy, the leader of the ritual, held a headlock on a kid for half a mile. The exhausted fraternity was home for lunch by noon.

Ben loved it all—his father's comical little farm; the primitive schoolhouse with two outhouses down the hill (boys and girls and their six teachers all used them); riding sleds down Burger Road hill; and playing Robin Hood, actually being Robin, when his sister would let him. Sally played Robin, and she could be bossy. There was no place else he wanted to be, no place. It was home, his own home.

Up and down the twisting, crushed-cinder roads were little struggle-farms with their comical outhouses and sagging sheds; salad gardens were planted with small rows of summer lettuce, radishes, and fall potatoes. Corn grew tall and spindly. It was fed to the occasional cow or goat. Chickens wandered free with their jerky strut; above them hawks floated. From the chickens came brown eggs for Sunday breakfasts and legs and wings for Sunday suppers. Goats were tethered to iron posts driven in the hard soil, the posts moved around the scrub yards every few days to fresh grass and weeds for the goats. Some families raised pigs out back—if the property was deep enough to separate the pigs from the kitchen. The awful smell on hot summer days lingered through the night. Chicken remains were fed to pigs whenever an occasion called for it.

On either side of Burger Road were shallow gutters. The most devastating storms filled them to overflowing; angry currents leaped across the cinder road, mining deep channels. The rainwater churned the mud-stuck trash from the last monsoon. And when a rainbow finally appeared against the dark sky and the sun turned the bristling water to copper-gold, the road was little more than a rutted path. In an hour or so, sluggish township trucks loaded with tons of cinders made their way up the road for yet another repair. Kids followed the trucks, breathing in their dust through colorful bandannas. They explored the trenches for novelties and bottles for refunds, Hardly audible under the rumble of trucks, they shouted to one another—"Lookit what I got! I'm takin' it home!"

"Wowwee! Geeze. What is it?"

"I seen it first, I'm keepin' it."

A prize was a prize.

★ ★ ★ ★ ★

One chilly October evening, with the pleasant scent of burning leaves and the sweet fragrance of fireplace logs, an old farmer in bib overalls appeared with a large black pipe between his teeth. Ben watched Albert, his father, standing in the pen where a young pig, named King Midas by bookish Sally, rooted peacefully. The old farmer opened a long switchblade and stropped the sharp blade on his cotton sleeve. Albert quickly gripped the now-angry pig and lifted him toward the knife. It was over in one flash of the blade followed by a *bon voyage* spank of salt ripped from the farmer's hind pocket and slapped on the red mess of the pig's rump. The pig squealed so loud its voice choked as it kicked its hind legs to rid itself of the salted pain. "*Soo-ee*" shouted the farmer as he folded his knife. The pig bounded and kicked his way to the comforts of the hog trough and gulped the slop that had been dumped there for him. The cost for this service was two dollars. Then silence enveloped them, along with the scent of sweet smoke from burning logs and leaves. Ben watched with his mouth open. He sniffed the air for change. So this is farming? Fix a pig, puff your pipe, and pocket four quarters and a dirty dollar bill.

He winced at the raw pain and the fistful of salt and the jocular remark that followed: "That'll make you some fine, sweet bacon someday! Yes siree." He could not understand what happened, and he hoped he would never have to eat the bacon from Sally's pet. How quickly the excitement of witnessing the pain, blood, and agony turned to sadness and guilt. He vowed to be kinder to Albert's menagerie: Snowball, Diego, Bessie, King Midas, and the Sunday chickens without names. As night fell under a full moon, a quiet peace gathered on Albert's comical little farm. The animals were fed and they were very quiet. King Midas, fixed for life, snored peacefully on yellow straw in the cool, embracing mud by the feeding trough.

Cecilia cornered her husband in the kitchen, a smile still on his face after the successful procedure. "I have *never* heard a more grotesque sound in my life. And me, with only one good ear. The sound! I can still hear that squeal, that snort, that guttural groan of poor King Midas. Horr-i-ble."

Albert's smile having become a smirk, he nevertheless rose to the occasion. "Perhaps we should have named him Silence? That's a Puritan name, you know. But given to girls, appropriately."

"Pigs didn't have Puritans!"

Oh, I'm sure pigs did have Puritans." He laughed at the absurdity, and Cecilia saw it, too.

"Albert, I leave you to explain all of this to Sally. You wordsmith. Is there anything I can do to make King Midas feel better? Anything?"

He thought about the question. "Not that I'm aware of at the moment. Let time do its job."

"Please, Albert. No more bloodshed on this hallowed land!" But her plea was unheeded.

★ ★ ★ ★ ★

The back two acres of Albert's gentleman's farm were surrounded by an electric fence, its wires carelessly threaded among tree branches and tough, bushy stems. To test whether the fence was really working, Ben and George, his older brother, took turns gripping the wire. As often as not an electric jolt was merely like another pulse, like the peaceful pulse on the cow's neck when the sun fell on it right. So, Bessie ignored the mild shocks when she touched the wire. The boys walked along the fence wire to remove branches that fell in a recent storm. Then the wires were potent again. Ben felt the shocks down to his ankles. Then, after luring Bessie to the wire with a taste of hay, they cast streams of water across the fence and onto the cow's back. There was a great roar from the startled cow, and with it came a message: don't touch the fence. He remembered his promise of kindness to the animals, and here he had failed. In a spirit of penance he uttered a little prayer.

Twice a day Bessie's warm, pungent milk was poured into the separator that divided the cream and pale milk that were then boiled and chilled. But the milk tasted like the shed the cow slept in with the goats. Raw nature. The goats were named Snowball, who was all white, and Diego, who had a dark cross covering its back and flanks. Bessie had a heifer, a cute little thing with a perpetually wet nose and pleading eyes. The heifer came about because Albert had walked with Bessie to a neighbor's scratch farm and mated her with Toro, a very old and very surprised bull. The cost for this service was two dollars.

★ ★ ★ ★ ★

This need for farming was imbedded in Albert's romantic brain. Man was meant to live on the land, he would say, while downing a raw egg in a glass of cheap port wine. Cecilia, if she could have her way, would have nothing to do with the farm. She was raised in an elegant Pittsburgh setting by a prosperous importer of wines and spirits from all parts of Europe. She had attended a convent school in Albany and then she graduated from the University of Pittsburgh years before Chancellor Bowman had the dream of building the forty-two story Cathedral of Learning on Pitt's broad Oakland campus.

Cecilia, of necessity, made little compromises. She once was told by a child that Bessie was loose and ruining her mother's "salad garden." Please come and fetch her, she was told. So, she removed her apron, found a spare piece of clothesline some fifteen feet long, and trudged up Burger Road hill to the Skipper "farm." She apologized to Mrs. Skipper, looped the clothesline around Bessie's neck, and, at the odd distance of twelve feet, led the polite cud-chewing cow very slowly down the steep road. She sang a little school song in French to calm Bessie and she prayed to prevent Bessie's sliding on the cinders and rolling over her. Between verses of a sweet song she interposed the word *merde,* a word not heard in prayers or in the little song about dancers on the bridge in Avignon, France.

One Sunday, Cecilia served a stringy chicken that had been sacrificed on Albert's workbench in the name of rustic celebration. The chewy meat was flavorless. The boiled lima beans were not well received by the children, but the mashed potatoes, laced with store-bought butter and iodized salt from the shelf above the refrigerator, were a delight. Red Jell-O wiggled and squirmed in a dish like exotic fish.

Albert could not be trusted when he shopped in Carnegie. His weakness was looking for real bargains, any bargains. The most unwelcomed bargain came from a butcher shop where the butcher's favorite customer had ordered beef tripe, a white, carpet-like meat of a cow's stomach. The customer had failed to claim it by closing time. Albert got the unclaimed meat for a fraction of the cost and presented it triumphantly to Cecilia. But she had never seen the lining of a cow's stomach. She tried her best to cook the new bargain meat in her new pressure cooker, but the meat came out of the cooker tough and tasteless. At the end of the unfortunate dinner, Cecilia tried not to laugh when the children made jokes about it. But she laughed, too. Albert fumed and stewed for the rest of the evening: women should be able to cook, shouldn't they? He knew that tripe was eaten on almost every continent. It's a delicacy for many. He ate it first in northern England. It was served with onions. It was not his favorite, he admitted, but the tripe in South America—so many great Asian cooks—was enriched with superb spices, curry, onions, and beans. His lips and mouth were numb for an hour. Excellent! He smoked his Prince Albert in deep frustration.

Before going to bed, hungry Ben stuffed himself with graham cracker sandwiches mortared with store-bought butter. George joined him with toasted shredded wheat buttered on both sides with cinnamon sprinkled on it. Sally had disappeared by then with one of her Wizard of Oz books.

On yet another Sunday, the chicken served was very suspicious. The bones were too large and quite noisy when tapped on the serving plate. The large-boned "chicken" turned out to be goat meat. The truth about it unfolded painfully—Snowball's stall was empty. Did he run away? Diego seemed to be longing for his companionship. And then the truth was revealed, and Ben was furious with his father—"You killed Snowball! How could you? "Why . . . ?"

"Well," Albert said with cool detachment, "there are children in Europe and China who would give anything for a meal of goat meat. Have you thought of that? By then he was growing passionate. "Have you ever given that a moment's thought? Have you?"

Cecilia calmed him as best she could. "Albert," she said, "perhaps you meant to do what you thought was right, but can't you see that we are not in China or bombed-out Berlin? Really now, Albert. Snowball was the favorite of the children. Try to understand. Oh, please spare Diego, Albert, if you have a heart!" Diego was spared.

★ ★ ★ ★ ★

On sunny Saturday mornings there was a weekly ritual. The children polished their shoes for church as they listened to a radio program just for kids—*Smilin' Ed's Buster Brown Gang*. When it was over, they would drive to Dithridge Street in Oakland, to visit their aunts, and go to a movie on Centre Avenue, and then they'd have a nice dinner in the elegant dining room. But if Albert's aged Pontiac would not start, or if the children had colds owing to the frequent rain, of if they had been really naughty the week before, they spent Saturdays at home in small remorse: the boys went to the woods behind the house and pretended they were Indians or cowboys, their little dramas depending on the last movie they saw on Centre Avenue. Sally, as usual, sat in the dining room with her illustrated book of famous opera stories listening to the Metropolitan Opera broadcast on the old Zenith radio. She knew the stories by heart. She lost herself in Italian operas as her brothers lost themselves in the woods hiding behind trees and firing pretend arrows at each other.

On rainy Saturdays at home, with little to do, Ben listened to the opera with Sally and tried to understand the strange-sounding words. Some of the arias were familiar: they heard them so often on their aunts' wind-up RCA playing 78 rpm records of Caruso. George mocked the music by twirling and singing "la Donny mobile lays." Sally told him to shut up if he knew what was good for him. George shut up, but his mock dancing did not stop. On a particular rainy Saturday, Ben stood at the base of the stairway from which he could spy into the kitchen and living room. He saw his father looking wistfully through the large window into the streaming rain, like sheets of slate, while he packed his pipe with Prince Albert tobacco from a narrow can; he saw Cecilia waiting for water to boil to make Jell-O, water from the well beneath the house, a distant look in her eyes, to some future she might be denied; he saw mysterious and silent George snoozing on the lumpy sofa; and he saw Sally nodding off to radio static and a Wagner passage from *Die Meistersinger*. He wondered whether their five lives intersected and were strung to one another in a special bond. He worried: was something happening, was something about to change, was something collapsing? Such was Saturday on the rain-driven afternoon: Albert's pipe, held in his palm, smoke curling meditatively; George slumbering deeply on the sofa; Sally's sleeping foot twitching in harmony with violin music; and Cecilia, that distant look in her eyes, stirring and stirring and stirring lemon Jell-O in a glass bowl. Yes, Ben concluded, something was about to change, some secret was being withheld from him, the youngest of the family and the most in need of protection. But what, and when? The barometer fell slightly and thunder rolled over Allegheny Acres.

They all had ways of escaping from Burger Road now and then, but Ben was always happy to get back to it, to the unlimited variety of adventures, play, and sport. In the summer, there was baseball on the field above their little house. The boys wore Pittsburgh Pirates uniforms their aunts had bought them. There were two or three on a team. Rules were made up on the spot. They did away with second base when only two were on a team. If Ben was on third and George got a hit, then Ben could trot home to bat. But with runners stuck on first and third, the inning was over. That was the rule. If George was on base and Ben hit a little fly ball toward him, he had to catch it, and Ben was out. If he didn't try to catch it, or intentionally dropped it, or pretended to be tying his laces, Ben was out. That was the rule.

Ben tried hard to hit the ball for a double or triple, but almost always the ball shot up into the sky, paused, and came down with a dull *thunk* a few feet from home. He heard the jeering chorus—"Look, up in the sky, it's a bird, it's a plane, it's . . . *Ben!*"

Rules changed from week to week, but only after heated arguments. It was decided that a batter could run from third to first and home if he was sure he'd hit a home run. But getting stuck on first was an out. That was a rule. The first team to score twelve runs was the winner. The visiting team usually won the game in the top of the first inning. The home team seldom got to bat. Then a new game began. The afternoon soon dissolved into comedy when players were required to run the bases backward—as in a movie played backward—while reciting *Casey at the Bat* or *The Boy Stood on the Burning Deck*. It was allowed by the rules to merge the two poems. And on and on it went.

★ ★ ★ ★ ★

As Halloween approached, its mysteries began to appear. Nights grew shorter. The orange moon in its early phase was already setting. Darkness and a spirit of mischief possessed them. Fireplace smoke perfumed the air. At school Ben drew pumpkins and witches on lined paper meant for homework. He colored them with crayons and hung them around his bed. As he got better and better at capturing the mood of the season, he tore off feeble early pictures and replaced them with richly detailed scenes of smoky nights, foggy mornings, black cats screaming on window sills, and the Headless Horseman racing through a graveyard that tilted left and right with ancient tombstones. Oranges, reds, blacks, blues, grays, yellows, and greens blended to make bold hues. Blue and yellow made a watery green. Orange and yellow made chimney smoke at dusk just after sunset. Red and orange with some black made the witches' blaze at midnight. And the Headless Horseman's jagged neck, where the cannonball had blasted his head, was a mix of red and yellow. His head was tucked under his left elbow, his white mouth gaping, and his pupils turned into his brow. His nostrils ran with gray gore. The blue-black horse under him rose in fury to protect the rider against the shot, but too late, its eyes casting furious dark-yellow light.

He could not have known how much his artwork resembled Goya's mad, diabolical paintings. All he knew about Goya was a picture of a little Spanish boy dressed in red, as red as tomato soup, and the boy looked happy in his odd costume. The boy held a bird on a string, and the nearby birdcage door was open. But Ben was bothered by the two cats in the foreground. They seemed ready to pounce on the bird. What was this all about? Was the boy being sadistic? Did he even know that the pet cats might attack the defenseless bird? What was Goya up to? The little reproduction was on a wall above his Aunt Helen's bed. Surely she would not have allowed the little boy's idle pleasure to hang above her bed unless she approved of the painting. Each time he saw it, he became suspicious of Goya. What was he up to?

But drawings were not enough. George, Ben, Sally, and Bob Bain—called BB—soaped windows with cakes of Ivory soap and rattled windows with notched thread spools spun on a pencil by a long piece of string. This instrument was the devil's yo-yo, fiercely loud and house-shaking. There followed the sprint to trees or sheds to hide and watch for tired farmer-miners and their rotund wives, who wore their gray hair in buns and never removed their aprons. They peered out windows into the dark, or stood in doorways listening for any sound. But there was only silence until an annoyed farmer's wife shouted: "Now you boys have had your fun and need to go home and stay there, you hear? I know you're listening, and I think I know where you live. So . . . no more, you hear!" They never tricked the same house twice.

On a cold Halloween night, they knocked on their victims' doors and politely extended their opened pillowcases or flour sacks. A good-natured farmer commented on their costumes: "What are you, anyway, Indians? My word! Does your ma know you painted her lipstick all over your face? Where'd you get them chicken feathers? Don't look under them birds for eggs for a week!" From his palm he dropped something into the bags, perhaps candy, perhaps pennies.

They happened to knock on the door of the old farmer with the black pipe. He said, "Well, goblins and ghosts have come out of the caves, have they?" Puff, puff, puff. "Seems like I got me some sweets here for Indian chiefs making the rounds. Yes sir." He dropped a Baby Ruth bar into each sack. Ben noticed the leather switchblade case on his belt. "Thanks," they called over their shoulders and then whooped up and down the dark road and through the trailer park by the yellow creek. They stopped often to eat candy from their shoulder-deep sacks.

They had had their Halloween and were very satisfied.

School

When Cecilia first saw the Bairdford School building her three children had to attend, she burst into tears. Ben did not understand why she was so upset. He waited for her in the car for a very long hour (by the little clock in the dashboard) while she and Albert were inside signing papers. When they returned she cried again, tears of resignation. "This is so unacceptable," she said, "so primitive." She turned to him and said, "We should have done better by you."

"Isn't that true, Albert?" He nodded his head slightly in response. Cecilia had not finished: "We'll try to make better provisions for the children's education. I'll think of solutions every day. But one solution I think I already know." She looked at Albert, but he did not look back at her. They drove away silently through wintery Bairdford, the little ghost town that looked like an abandoned movie set for westerns.

Was she crying because the school building was made of sooty wood? There were many windows, which was good. But what he could not see from where Albert had parked on the county road were outhouses below a hill, one for girls and one for boys. She must have gasped at the sight of them. There was a water pump with a child-friendly, extra-long handle for tall boys to pump buckets of water for the water dispensers in the rear of the classrooms. A large pile of coal was nearby. "Coal, coal, coal," she complained. "So much coal, everywhere." He would soon learn that each morning in the cold weather strong boys carried buckets of coal up the many steps to the classrooms. A potbelly stove in each room was kept glowing throughout the day. A custodian kept the stoves lit during the night. Smaller boys or girls in winter coats took erasers outside to the pump in the late afternoon to clap them, causing momentary white clouds. It was a treat to take a turn clapping erasers. The trick was to read the wind, which never stopped, and to keep the mouth shut and the eyes tightly closed. He quickly learned to love the school's antiquated features and bizarre culture. Why was mother so upset? What was her "solution?"

On the far side of the school was a large play area for recess and a wooded lot. Boys would go into the scrub woods and chase each other. They played marbles in circles cut deeply into the dirt. Their bags of marbles were protected as though they were gems from the king's treasury. Girls had jump ropes, some so long that three or four girls could jump together. They sang songs as they jumped: "Mary had a puppy dog, she loved it like a brother, she asked her mother could she please, please have another, p-l-e-a-s-e, p-l-e-a-s-e, p-l-e-a-s-e!" Whether the plea was for another puppy or another brother was never clear.

Up and down the hill boys would run at recess and they would slide on the icy snow right into the outhouse walls, shocking girls, who shrieked and laughed. Recesses were often longer than fifteen minutes, but, however long or short, there was groaning when a teacher rang the brass bell. They all lined up and struggled silently up the ten steps into the building. The cloakroom was crowded. Pushing and shoving, the boys and girls removed coats, hats, and galoshes.

The cloakroom was the setting of numerous paddlings of naughty boys who were fighting at recess, or cursing, or cheating, or stealing. While the teacher applied the paddle in the cloakroom, boys and girls all sat nervously in the excited air. The paddled boy sobbed and went directly to his desk. All was forgotten before the day ended. But there was one case that required the principal to come to the room and lead a boy named Eddie into the cloakroom for an especially hardy paddling. What happened was this. The teacher had left the room for a few seconds, but that was enough time for Eddie to jump up from his seat, grab the yardstick, and pretend he was a pirate. He waved the yardstick, thrusting it, fending off imagined blows. What he forgot was that the brand new movie screen had been opened and extended for a film they were about to see. The yardstick cut into the screen, tearing it badly. There was no movie that afternoon.

When he could not sleep at night, Ben was caught up in a half-dream about the boys who were so painfully paddled in the cloakroom. The teachers administered four smacks, and then they resumed teaching geography or arithmetic just like nothing unusual had happened, but there was a boy in the last row trying to sob quietly, his head in his arms, his face on the old desk. Ben had heard his father's stories about boys being whipped and caned in his school near London. Does anything ever change? A boy had to be brave to be a boy. It wasn't enough to be a clown or a trickster. He worried that he was not a brave boy. And then he slept, and when he woke, the fears were in the distant past. But they returned like ghosts now and again.

There was no cafeteria. Each noon in the classroom they ate lunches and drank from little boxes of chocolate or white milk. Candy bars were sold for a nickel. Baby Ruth bars went first. Sandwiches were traded, apples were bartered for, and fruit pies in a cardboard-like crust were especially prized. The most common sandwiches were egg salad. They filled the room with a pungent odor all afternoon. Before afternoon classes started, girls drew pictures on the board, or wrote "Annie loves Steve," with heart-shaped decorations around the announcement. Annie, laughing, ran to the board and ended the courtship with a few swipes of the eraser.

For Thanksgiving, their teacher, Miss Miller, wrote a little play about Indians and Pilgrims to be performed on Wednesday night before the holiday. He was to play an Indian wrapped in George's purple bathrobe with its zigzag arrow decorations. His one line was, "We bring turkey for feast." The turkey was made of bundled ears of corn on which feathers were glued. Pilgrim men wore black robes and had tinfoil buckles laced in their shoes. William Bradford, an important Pilgrim leader, wore a tall hat with lace at his neck and wrists. Eddie the pirate played Bradford, but he protested wearing lace; he was teased about it. Girls wore bonnets and long aprons over their mothers' housedresses that dragged on the schoolroom floor. Pilgrim men shouldered muskets made of broom handles with brown fabric wrapping and black cardboard funnels for nozzles. Annie, with her gold curls, bright blue eyes, and eager smile, was the star. She played a woman named Dorothy Bradford, William's wife. Her best line was: "The Lord has blessed our long crossing to this land of Freedom. Let us all make Thanksgiving prayers for His bountiful Grace." Indians fell to their knees and held their hands to the paper moon hanging from thread. Ringing applause and hearty shouts followed her words. Then Miss Miller entered from the cloakroom with her violin and bow in her left hand. She played *America the Beautiful* with such feeling that tearful men and women who had emigrated from war-torn Poland dried their eyes on handkerchiefs and colorful babushkas. Ben had been in one of their homes on a winter morning when the classroom stove mysteriously went cold. He walked home with a local boy who lived in a mining company house on a cinder street. He played for an hour or so, ate a delicious potato-filled pie, and walked back to school and a warm classroom.

After Miss Miller played the violin, there was a treat of cinnamon cider and little donuts. George asked how the donuts could be made so small. Sally poked him. "Such a genius," she said. The lights were low. The stove, already banked for the four-day holiday, shone blue-orange through the narrow draft control. But through the windows they saw snow falling. The snow covered the ancient Fords and Chevrolets in the parking lot. The men churned and churned the motors to start them, but some of the batteries had died in the cold. The men and boys pushed the cars to the hill to let them coast before engaging the clutch to wake up the motor. The cars rattled off to the mining town and its crushed-cinder streets covered with snow.

Cecilia tried to be cheerful. "You like history, don't you?" she asked with hope in her voice. "Don't you?" she asked again. He tried to see her eyes, but the car was dark in the falling snow. She told him that if he liked history he would learn someday that the woman played by beautiful Annie, Dorothy Bradford, jumped to her death into the bay. "It must have been simply awful," she said, in a voice that was so personal, as though she were Dorothy. "Oh, so awful! She missed her home, would never . . ."

In the cold, dark Pontiac sliding in the deepening snow, Ben feared that he had just learned what his mother's solution was. Could it be true that she might take the path of this woman named Dorothy, an Englishwoman who saw the barren, cold land of the New World, the Promised Land of the Pilgrims, with so many godless, terrifying Indians, as though it were modern Bairdford, coal-scented and tunnel-holed, with its own primitive customs? There were no longer any Indians, true, but wasn't Albert's mean little car called Pontiac, an Indian name? And didn't he and George play Indians in their woods? And wasn't he just recently a bathrobe-Indian, his faced streaked with lipstick? Were they the new Indians?

"Oh, Albert, you drive on bald tires, even in winter, and here we are in the dark inching our way home. What if we have an accident?"

"I'm not going to stop to put on the chains. It's so dark, and so cold. So, sit quietly; let me navigate the currents of the snow path, and if we slip a little and slide left or right, I will steer us safely and get us home to hot chocolate and warm beds. Now, don't you feel better already?"

"Things must change, Albert. They must. For the children. For their future."

"We'll see, we'll see. Here's our turn, and then into the driveway. Thank heavens I don't have to drive up Burger Road hill."

Ben listened in fear, and then he remembered that tomorrow was a free day and the boys could ride their sleds all day down Burger hill, unless the county had spread cinders on the steep road. But it's a holiday, so why would they spread cinders? Get out early, just in case. Get out early.

Skating in Winter Woods

After Thanksgiving, winter settled in for a long three months. Puddles froze in the yard, and ruts in the crushed-cinder road became little skating ponds. Cars struggled to climb Burger Road hill, even with tire chains. Sled riding was thrilling but perilous. If a car began to climb when sled riders were racing down, three abreast, two sleds had to go into the gutters, and the third rider rolled off his sled, which might run under the car, its engine racing and tires throwing ash and snow. The sharp left turn at the bottom of the hill was managed by experienced riders, but careless or inexperienced riders who missed the turn slammed into a mud embankment, as Sally learned one day on her short sled. She was dazed for hours. The true test of championship prowess was making the turn and keeping up speed all the way to Saxonburg Road. Double riders, either sitting together or piled on top of one another, rarely made the curve before they fell off, their sleds bouncing on, skimming the bumpy surface of the rutted snow with a high-pitched musical note.

They could sled ride for an hour after school and all day on the weekend. But when there was no new snow to cover the township's ashes, they staggered through Albert's woods to the farmer's pond where they cleared the snow and put on their skates. They played rough games of hockey using a crushed soup can and tree limbs bent to resemble hockey sticks. It was very cold on the pond that was on a windy high point of land. Their lips turned blue. Gloves gave little protection as they were always wet. They tried building a fire, but the farmer came out of his house and said "no fires," and threatened to chase them back through the woods.

Some boys had real skates like hockey players wore. But Ben's skates were ancient leather ones worn by one of his aunts when she was in school in Albany. She used to say, "Brrrr, it was too cold to pray!" His pinched feet ached in the narrow skates. He was teased about them every time. After a few minutes on the ice, his feet were numb from the fit and the cold, and his weak ankles ached. He skated as well as he could to keep warm but falling often and sliding on his back until he stopped. He felt a little better sliding on his back, but getting up was difficult, causing more falls. He was covered with bruises he was too cold to feel. Still, nothing would keep him off the ice, for his friends were there.

Night came on quickly, often taking them by surprise. He was told to be home in time for dinner, without fail. When the dark came, he knew he had about ten minutes to take off the skates, put on his boots, and stumble as fast as he could across the floor of the woods that was covered by fallen branches and large rocks that surfaced over the years of freeze-and-thaw. When George was with him, they held one another up as they staggered comically through the woods. It was a kind of game. But when he was alone, he often fell in the dark. His face was slashed by thin branches. These winter woods where he loved to play Robin Hood in the summer now frightened him. The first lesson he learned was never to be alone in the dark, frozen woods. The second lesson was that it was almost impossible to walk home through the dark woods while wearing skates.

On a windy freezing afternoon he began skating. He waited for others to come, but they did not. So the pond was all his. He raced from one end to another, braking in snow banks up to his shins and then turning for a race back. He explored every corner, tried to skate backwards, and made awkward turns. He never felt better on the ice. As dusk fell, he was reminded of his mother's edict to be on time for dinner, as if a can of Campbell's soup couldn't wait. He pulled his scarf tighter and fastened his borrowed bombardier's fleece-lined hat around his chin. On he flew. If only Annie were there to cheer him on, to laugh at his clowning. And then it was dark, so fast, except for the light that the snow and ice still seemed to hold. He sat on the little bench, removed his wet gloves from his frozen fingers, and began to loosen the laces. But he couldn't. They were frozen stiff. He tried and tried, but his fingers were too cold to feel the laces. He began to lose hope, to become frightened.

He had no choice but to stagger home through the woods, his blades snagging on fallen branches. He stumbled across the snow to the edge of the woods. On his knees, he crawled like a grounded acrobat under the electric fence wires, tearing his jacket and pants. Fortunately, his father had turned off the electricity for the winter. And then the long clumsy and dangerous journey began, an adventure in blindness and foolishness. His boots flew from his fingers as he tumbled over a fallen tree. Branches cut his cheeks. For a moment he steadied himself on trunks of small trees, but he had to go on, across the ice on the little stream, and around boulders that banged against his knees in the dark. He kept hooking his blades on branches that he had to snap with sudden upward pulls of his aching legs. How long the folly continued was lost on him. But there, in the distance, finally, was a single light bulb burning like a lighthouse for the wayward and lost. Beyond the shed was the lawn. He was so exhausted and sore that he just turned his ankles inward, and, half-skiing and half-jogging, he fell with a thud against the kitchen door. Home was the skater home from the pond . . . . "JesusMaryandJoseph," Cecilia cried when she saw him. "What has happened?" She took his head in her hands; she studied his face as though he were a stranger, a waif. "Blue lips, and you're all scratched and cut. It's a wonder you're still . . . ."

"I know," he said. "I had to walk back from the pond with my skates on."

"Of all the. . . ." she began to say. "Sit down." She used a long slender knife like a saw, holding each foot in her lap; she began sawing away at the laces. When she finally opened the skate boots to pull them off, she was even angrier.

"Look at you! No socks! Skating in this weather with no socks!"

"I had socks," he pleaded, "but they're frozen to the leather. "See?" He demonstrated by ripping them out of the skates. His little victory.

"You march up to the bathroom and fill the tub with hot water. Albert, please put more coal in the furnace."

Albert, roused from his sleep by the commotion and shouting in the kitchen, stumbled half-asleep to the basement. Sounds of iron-on-iron followed, along with mild oaths as he burned himself on the furnace's door handle.

"George, please come down here this instant! I want you to put a pile of warm clothes by the bathroom door, his pajamas, robe, and slipper socks. And don't forget a plushy towel, too."

She called up the stairs to him: "Lifebuoy all over, and then I'll put some salve on your cuts."

"But Lifebuoy stinks," he whined.

Sally watched from the sofa. "It's so Italian," she said, not quite sure what she meant by it.

The water felt so good, the Lifebuoy finding each cut and bruise. He dozed in the hot water. Reluctantly, hearing Cecilia's voice calling from the kitchen, he allowed himself to be coaxed from the tub. Slippery and naked, he reached for the towel and warm clothes George had dumped on the furnace grate. Their touch was warm and welcoming. Mother put salve on his cuts and scratches and gave him two aspirin tablets. "Take these now," she said, "and come down to dinner. We had tomato soup, which I'm reheating, and grilled Swiss cheese sandwiches, your favorite. But I really ought to send you to bed without dinner. Really!"

Cecilia relented when she learned that *The Lone Ranger* was about to begin on the old Zenith radio. This was his favorite cowboy program. "Please, please," he begged.

"Well, all right. Listen to the program if you can stay awake. But let's be clear: please, please," she said, kindly mocking him: "No more stunts like this one! My hair is already gray!"

The hot tomato soup was thickened with standing in the pot and rich with milk; the grilled Swiss cheese was salty and chewy, and the bread crispy. Was this Heaven? he thought.

The Lone Ranger theme began. It was time. Over his shoulder he asked his mother for another red bowl of Jell-O. "Please, please."

"Now, would you like another red bowl of Jell-O, or a bowl of red

Jell-O?" mother asked in her measured voice, calmed now by a return to the ordinary.

"Yes." he answered, his attention fixed on the music.

He felt great. He felt safe. The story was about Silver and the Lone Ranger getting lost in the desert. How warm that must feel. The Masked Man fired silver bullets into the air to signal Tonto, but Tonto never came. Hours passed in the hot sun; their water was all gone.

"Well, big fellow," the Lone Ranger said to Silver. "You have been my constant companion. No one else can ride you. I have saved the last bullet for you, my friend." That's what friends do? he thought. And then the Cheerio commercial began.

He never learned what happened, for he fell asleep holding the antenna wire high enough for the static to stop. How he got into bed he could not say. In the morning, at six o'clock, he smelled the sweet aroma of cocoa warming in a big pan and he heard his mother's gentle stirring, wooden spoon on metal pot. Comforting. He ached everywhere. The scratches and cuts burned. Bruises throbbed with every motion. He sniffed his hands for the medicinal, carbolic scent of curative Lifebuoy soap. Yes, he thought, he would live!

Yesterday. That was the best day of his life—and the bravest, too!

The Honeymoon Express

The boys campaigned for three very special Christmas presents: new Flexible Flyer sleds; BB guns; and real ice skates.

"Boys, boys, Santa has a small sleigh," mother said.

They begged for BB guns, promising never to turn them toward people, animals, or passing cars, and, especially, toward each other, whether in jest or anger.

"Well, we'll see about *that*. You are both responsible and I trust you, but what if something happened. What if one of your friends takes a gun and shoots a chicken or a dog, or a person? You would have to be supervised. There would have to be a target shooting area behind the house or in the woods."

They promised to be responsible. They begged over and over. As Christmas approached, they discovered sleds in a basement storage area under the steps. They were long, shiny with shellac, with red metal parts and the Flexible Flyer decal. All that was needed was new clothesline rope they could pull them with. And snow. Sally would have the old, short sled, which still had embankment mud embedded in the failed steering that had caused her to wreck a few weeks earlier. She asked for skis, Wizard of Oz books, and wool plaid shirts.

They never tired of begging for Red Ryder BB guns—"Pleeease, we'll be good," they promised morning, noon, and night. "Please, please, please."

Mother told them that there's a book called *Penrod Jashber.* "In it a boy wants his father to give him money for a squirt gun. His father says no, over and over, but the boy keeps pestering with 'please, please, please,' just like you."

"Did he get the squirt gun?"

"As I recall, his father finally gave in."

"Please, can we have BB guns," they begged.

"You never know," she answered. "Santa is watching!"

They searched the house for hidden BB guns, but without success.

At the Bairdford School, Miss Miller gave the children well-worn Christmas song books, and if they were good in the half hour before the busses arrived, they could sing their favorites. For a week before the holiday recess they sang *Joy to the World, Hark the Herald Angels Sing,* and many other carols in a loud chorus. They were lost in their separate Christmas dreams. After lunch, messages on the blackboard were about Christmas, with artwork of candy canes, wreaths, and perfectly symmetrical Christmas trees with large stars on top. Angel faces resembled Annie's yellow curls and blue eyes. At lunch they painted the windows with Santa scenes on a snowy background. Viewed from the playground they looked real, like the department store windows in the city. On the last day before the holiday vacation, they gave Miss Miller little gifts: collar pins, a pen set, note paper with pictures of dogs and cats, and candies of all sorts. Some of the boys ate the candy intended for Miss Miller, but there were still little boxes of chocolates with red ribbons from girls and the timid boys who could be trusted with such responsibilities as not shooting BB guns at animals, people, cars, and, most important, each other.

Two days before Christmas the kitchen windows steamed as Cecilia baked sugar cookies and her famous bread. They traced snowmen in the window mist and watched them melt in narrow streams falling onto the sill. They slurped tomato soup, downed little triangle-shaped sandwiches, and finished their meal with lime Jell-O in which mother stood red candy canes. Bread was tasty hot with melting butter from the Clover Farm store at the end of the road. They listened to radio programs of symphonic music from New York, adventure programs about the Klondike, and tales from the African jungle about lions crossing boiling waters to attack safari hunters napping after their long and, regretfully, final meals. The Lone Ranger, Tonto, Silver, and nephew Dan Reid rode beneath the purple sky. (So, Tonto *had* rescued the Lone Ranger and Silver after all, while he slept in his warm clothes on the big couch after the skating episode in the dark.)

On Christmas Eve they drove to Dithridge Street to visit the aunts. They ate a festive dinner of chilled salmon, quivering tomato aspic, and warm apple pie with a slice of cheddar cheese. They were teased about what Santa would bring (George and Sally rolled their eyes). But Ben kept the spirit alive with an excited "oh, boy," and, "is Santa watching us right now?" Sally rolled her eyes.

"Absolutely," said mother. "There he is, in fact, behind the curtain."

"Where? I don't see him!" His glasses nearly flew from his face when he spun his head around until his neck hurt. "Where?" he shouted.

"Too slow, I'm afraid." She nipped the edge of her cheese and tilted her head affectionately. "Oh, you have to be very, very good to see him, I'm afraid. But there's still time."

He didn't know when his father left the gathering in the living room. He just slipped out to the car with bags of gifts from their four aunts, all single ladies who spoiled the children on birthdays and, especially, at Christmas. The old Pontiac was freezing cold, but they were full of excitement and cared little for comfort. The drive back to Burger Road was long and tedious. Pittsburgh's streets ran up and down hills. They crossed a long bridge. The ride put him to sleep, as it usually did.

Early on Christmas morning, before the sun came up, the tree's magical lights of red, green, yellow, blue, and white mixed and reflected on colorful balls and tinsel strands tossed lazily here and there. Many decorations were decades old, some scratched, some chipped, but they belonged on that tree.

Below the tree were many packages of odd shapes, all wrapped in festive green, blue, and red and tied with gold ribbons. The sleds were missing, however, and there were no boxes that might have held BB guns. In his stack of presents he found clothes (underwear, socks, and a shirt); two brand-new books wrapped in bright jackets (*Tom Sawyer* and *Black Beauty*); a View-Master with the price tag on the box ($2.00,

Kaufmann's) and three-dimensional disks of Haiti, pineapple fields in Hawaii, Northwest National Parks, and Banff National Park. He loaded a disc. The colors in 3-D jumped out at him, and the view over mountain rims gave him vertigo. He also got a Honeymoon Express, a little wind-up train that ran without stopping around a colorful track, through a tunnel, and across a bridge, over and over again. What this frantic circling had to do with a honeymoon and marriage he never learned. Perhaps a lesson for life?

Then there was a gun-and-holster set unlike any he had ever seen: two metal cowboy cap guns painted bright red in leatherette holsters with wooden bullets that could be removed from little loops.

"That's from your Aunt Helen," mother said. "She knows you like pistols. There's a cowboy shirt that goes with it."

He put the guns aside because they needed to be studied. How could he put a roll of caps in the things if there was no part that opened? Was this a trick? Were these pistols a life lesson, too? Yes, perhaps women should not buy pistols.

There were coloring books and a box of eight serviceable crayons for a world without silver, gold, and white. There was a *Red Ryder* comic book and a subscription notice for a year of issues. There was a snug, fleece-lined bombardier hat with plastic goggles (no longer would he wear George's), and a real army-green knapsack containing leather gloves and a red wool scarf. He loved Army-Navy stores as much as he loved five-and-ten-cent stores on Penn Avenue in East Liberty. What he always dreamed of was a pair of high boots with hooks for lacing and a small pocket at the calf for a penknife. All the boys had them at school, but knives were forbidden. They tucked their pants into the tops of their boots and swaggered like big shots. He was jealous.

"Now here's a present you overlooked," mother said, handing him a small package.

"Wow, a harmonica!"

"Santa said it was either that or a drum set. I think he made the right decision!"

He laughed.

"Listen," she said. "Do you hear that? Someone is out back. Quick! Run and see." Sally, who knew what was up, just watched them.

The boys pushed and shoved each other as they ran to the kitchen and pulled the door open, but they saw nothing. George turned on the light. And then they saw two sleds leaning against the wall under the window. One had a red bow, the other green.

"My, my, well look at that! Santa must have forgotten. He came all the way back with the sleds. Now who wants to be red and who wants to be green?" The sleds had safely travelled from the basement closet just in time.

Beautiful Flexible Flyers. They promised to ride them from morning to night. They promised to pray for snow at Christmas Mass. The skates didn't matter. He would fly on the bright runners of his aunt's skates from long ago.

The children collected the remaining dimes and quarters from their occasional allowances to buy Albert a large can of Prince Albert pipe tobacco. For Cecilia there were four kites of blue, red, yellow, and purple—one for each mood that took her to the top of the hill behind the house in spring's windy, threatening weather. (Last spring, Sally helped Cecilia to climb the steep and slippery path, and on the boys' ballfield she joined her mother in contesting with the wind as long as the cheap paper held together. They laughed like girls in the chilly wind and bursts of rain. Then, kites shattered, they slid down the steep path holding on to shrub trees like ski poles. They left their muddy shoes on the porch to dry.) In March, they would climb the hill once more; the kites above their craning necks would twist together, spinning, then halting, in a frenzied aerial tango.

Two days after Christmas George was going to have his thirteenth birthday. "There's an early birthday present for you in the closet by the stairs," mother told him. It was a BB gun. Just like that. Then he was given copper-colored BB's to fire, but under supervision until he knew just how to use it. He loved the oil smell when he fired it without ammo. After each shot he sniffed the barrel. The wisps of smoke were intoxicating.

Ben looked at his mother. She understood. "Oh, how could I forget? If you look under the sofa, you might find a special box waiting for you."

And there it was—a Red Ryder BB gun, a carbine, with a container of BB's that resembled a shotgun shell. Just like that.

A perfect Christmas, and it was only eight o'clock in the morning. The whole day spread before them, time-frozen, and they could see that snow was falling fast, an unspoken prayer already answered. They could ride their bright new sleds.

Sally already had her nose in an Oz book. Ben asked her what the Tin Woodsman was up to.

No answer.

"Sally, what's the Tin Woodsman doing?"

"What? Nothing right now."

"Let me know when he starts rattling around, OK?"

"Uh-huh."

Sally wanted to take the Oz book to Mass with her, just this one time.

"Of course not, dear, that would be disrespectful. The book will be waiting for you when we return."

Sally wasn't happy. She could be bossy.

Just for fun, Ben asked whether he could take his BB gun to Mass. "Of course you can," she replied. "Just don't aim it at the altar boys, because one of them will be George."

Saint Victor's was built on a slag pile close by their school. To get up the hill, Albert had to take a run at a narrow turning road made of slag and ashes, hardly wide enough for two cars. He hugged the side of the makeshift road, but coming home after Mass, the right side of the car was so close to the edge that Ben almost felt it falling off the path to the road below, a drop of twenty feet at the top. The road was called temporary years before. With snow on the road Ben's fear was even greater.

Cecilia pleaded on the curve coming down the hill after Mass. "Oh, Albert, do be careful, please. This road will kill somebody someday soon."

The rural poverty of Bairdford was apparent everywhere, but especially at the grade school and the church.

"Why did we move here? Was it smart?" she said. "We simply have to make plans to move, to take the children out of that cold institution woefully serving as a school." Why, Ben asked himself. Why?

Her remark was sharpened to reach Albert's heart. They had moved to Allegheny Acres so that Albert could have his dream to live off the land, grow vegetables, and keep animals—cows, pigs, goats, and chickens.

"Oh, just think on the bright side," he answered. Ben had no idea what he meant.

"I'm going to talk to my sisters about moving back to the city, to find a little house in Sacred Heart parish where the schools are new, modern, and forward looking. I'll ask them for my share of Papa's estate. It won't be much, but we can do it. Please get us off this coal pile! No more school *sur le* sewer. Pardon my bad French, but you get my drift. Albert, make a gift of this for me and for the children."

"I would have to sell the cow, the pigs, and the goat. Who is going to buy them? No one has any money."

"Just let them go, Albert, let them go free. Let *them* live off the land for a change!"

"Cecilia, you'll feel much better once April comes, when it's warm and the fruit trees are in blossom."

"And the children will track in gobs of mud every time they come into the house. And guess who will wash it and sweep it? And besides, we don't have fruit trees."

"Put them to work, then. They aren't infants."

Silence followed, and then Albert said the words that made Cecilia cry, those fate-filled words that promised to change Ben's young life so wonderfully. (*They would stay, they would stay!*)—"We need to be here in the spring because my parents are coming for a month's visit from British Guiana, and my brother Willie will meet them here. He's just retired from the textile mill in India."

Cecilia did not utter the Irish prayer of desperation, "JesusMaryandJoseph." No, instead, she uttered the French convict's prayer just after the prison door slammed shut. *Merde!*

"Sorry, sorry, so sorry," she whispered to the children in the back seat. Rarely did she apologize twice in a day for her French.

And then they were home.

As unhappy as Cecilia was with the disturbing news of a prolonged visit by three very fussy people with British accents and odd culinary tastes, she put on a brave face and saw the rest of the day pass with good spirits. The boys carried their sleds up Burger Road hill that was already scored with sled trails. They met BB Bain, Skipper, with his comical goat face, and Kenny Horst. BB Bain said "Hi," and then ran down the hill as fast as he could and fell upon his sled. He made a fast run, turned the sharp corner at a tilt to avoid sliding over the culvert into the creek, and coasted to a stop at the highway. Ben looked at George for a signal, but George just plopped the sled, gave it a push, and was off on a slow ride on runners coated with red paint. He left a telltale smear of red behind him. Ben followed. But after a few runs the metal blades were bright and sharp. They answered Skipper's plea to ride their new sleds with an insincere "in a minute." He was forever borrowing things. His own sled, old and battered, was not good enough. It occurred to Ben that Skipper would soon be begging to let him shoot their BB guns. Whatever their cautions would be, he knew Skipper would fire at the first car he saw on Burger Road. If he let him have the gun for another minute, a dog or chicken would be next. That's the way he was: it was what Cecilia called "genetic."

Sally was finishing her Oz book by the living room window. Curled comfortably in an old chair and wearing her new plaid shirt, she held the borders of the book as though it were the ship's wheel in a growing storm. George left a trail of wet clothes on the floor. The windows were steamed with mother's cooking and baking. The house was comfortably damp, and the coal heat coming from the registers assured an evening of quiet happiness.

"Albert, are you still napping?" No answer.

"I guess he is, and having dreams of English school days and visits from his parents every summer. Well, let's see how nostalgic he is when his parents and Willie show up on our doorstep in May or June. George, please call your father to dinner. *Merci*, and give Sally a shake, too. Tell her it's time to come home from the Emerald City."

To herself, just loud enough for those who wanted to hear, she prayed, "Where did I go wrong, please tell me."

That must have been the cue to wind up the Honeymoon Express and send it careening around perpetual curves until the engine died of inertia. What was the rush, anyway? Why did he ever petition so long for this little diabolical choo-choo from the Sears and Roebuck toy catalog?

"Please, please tell me," she sighed, and then she straightened her back, ready for what came next.

Snow fell silently from a darkened sky, the underlid of Heaven as far as Ben was concerned. And he *was* concerned, selfishly, of course, but it was Christmas, and he loved it passionately. Who could blame him? After all, he was just a kid.

Ice Fishing

George complained that anyone having a birthday two days after Christmas was going to miss out on some nice things, especially presents. Doubling up on presents—"here's a Christmas/birthday present for you"—was just unfair. As a result of his frequent complaints, extra care was taken to separate the two events, although George's "early birthday present" of a BB gun on Christmas morning was suspicious. So as not to forget his special day, his birthday was celebrated on December 27, at Dithridge Street. Their cousin, Little Barbara, George's age, came from Green Tree, along with her mother, known as Big Barbara, and her parents, Erhard and Frances. Little Barbara was beautiful and mannerly. George really liked her. There would be an afternoon of games, a special lunch of his favorite dishes, a trip to the museum or to a movie, a birthday dinner with cake and ice cream, and presents to open. There were also special party favors for them.

And, as the evening came to a close, there was an exciting event: ice fishing in December. This was an old family favorite that must have come from the Victorian age, a parlor game to entertain children.

But Cecilia was still upset with the news that her in-laws and Willie were coming for a long visit. Ben sensed her deep unhappiness. Her mind was not on fishing. He thought about the woman named Dorothy who must have looked long and hard at the harbor water before she made her decision to drown rather than to start a new life in the New World.

Big Barbara, who could sense the tension in her Aunt Cecilia's voice, observed that it would be wonderful to see Albert's parents and Willie after so many years.

Albert said, "How true. We haven't seen them for many years. The children will hardly remember them, and they have never met Willie, my older brother."

Cecilia admitted that she thought Willie was a very handsome bachelor. Her lady friends would be swooning, and that promised to be entertaining. She smiled, and the party resumed.

Fishing was supervised by adults, who provided long pieces of fishing line, usually string. The lines were passed over the top of a hall door, which was then closed. Behind the door, their aunts tied gifts to the string. The birthday boy held a string. When he felt a tug it was time to reel in the catch. The door was discreetly open just enough to allow the fish to be landed and then closed again. But it was not easy for George to pull in this gift because his aunts teased the line and the "fisherman" from behind the door. "I've got one," George shouted.

"Well, reel it in. Where is it?"

"It's a whopper," he said. "Do we need a bigger hole in the ice?"

"And I've got one too," Little Barbara called politely. Her gift came quickly as the door was open just enough to allow the tiny little package to rise over the top.

"Oh, throw it back and let it grow some more," George said.

"It's a silver dollar," Little Barbara exclaimed. "It's so heavy!"

"Well, well," Sally said, "the silver dollars are running!"

Sally's catch was a Wizard of Oz pen and pencil set.

When George finally landed his whopper there were cheers. He unrolled three comic books tied tightly together with ribbon.

"Wow, these are great," he yelled. He handed them to Ben, who sniffed the fragrant pages.

Then George was allowed to fish again because it was his day.

This time, he again struggled with the catch. "The boat's tipping, the boat's tipping!" he shouted.

"Pull, pull." They all shouted.

Sally dryly reminded them that this was to be ice fishing, and you don't ice fish from a boat.

Finally, with his feet planted against the door, he reeled in a big box.

"It's a book," George was thrilled. He ripped the paper from the box. "It's called *Wild Animals I Have Known*. I'll bet there's a fish story."

Ben's line went slack. He guessed the prizes were all gone, but after some whispering he felt a tug. He reeled in a tightly wrapped dollar bill smelling like the perfume that saturated everything in Aunt Frances' purse. He knew because she often asked him to fish out one of her Bugler cigarettes and a book of matches.

Their aunts laughed behind the door. Then the strings were collected and wound tight for the next birthday.

Winter Rain

Albert thought: if spring must come early to Allegheny Acres, it should never come this early. Temperatures during the day reached the high forties. Snow began to melt, first in the southern and eastern exposures and then, slowly, to the north and west. Icicles ran like open faucets from the roof gutters. At night the cold returned, and in the morning the icicles were long and hard again. From the west, storm clouds appeared, low and dark. Down the rain came with springtime fury. Strong wind drove the rain into the side of the house. Icicles dissolved. Roof gutters overflowed, their twisting streams of water now liquid icicles. The noise was constant and a little frightening. Large islands of snow slid down the pitched roof and crashed into the bushes below. The bushes sprawled under the weight of the snow. In the distance weak lightning was followed by low rumbles of thunder. The late February storm lasted for days. Sally looked out the picture window in awe. "It's operatic," she sang out, "right out of Wagner—the creation of Valhalla! The gods are in battle!" Cecilia replied, half amused: "Yes, dear, Valhalla."

The coal pile by the garage door glistened in the gray light. In the furnace the coal smoldered. The house reeked of damp smoke.

"Albert, can't you shut off the furnace for a while. We'll wear sweaters."

"Don't you understand," he answered, "that the house will be cold, damp cold at that, and the walls will run with dampness? We don't want mold."

The children enjoyed the indoor life on Saturday and Sunday. They read, colored pictures, begged mother to make bread, slept at odd hours, and listen to the opera from New York City. Christmas presents were still new. The Honeymoon Express ran around and around on its track, hurrying somewhere, never arriving. Ben read an Oz book, with Sally's permission. The daylight was a little weak for the View Master, but the three-dimensional pictures were still fresh and wonderful. He strapped on his red pistols, which slung low on gunslinger hips. But who was he then, Roy Rogers, Gene Autry, or Red Ryder? He needed to be more exotic. Perhaps the Durango Kid or the Diego Kid, something South of the Border. *Kid* sounded right, so he was the Kid, lightning fast on the draw—he announced his new name throughout the house. But ironically, sadly, he couldn't get the guns to fire without rolls of caps. There was no way to get a roll *into* the guns. He pulled, pushed, and shook them, but with no success. But while drawing and twirling the guns in the basement, he dropped one on the hard concrete floor.

"Oh, no, I broke it!"

The gun split open like a butterfly in flight, exposing the firing parts. There was a small hinge running along the inside of the barrel and a little snap-clip at the base of the handle. Elated, he ran to his room, got a box of caps, and jumped down the basement stairs two at a time. He loaded a roll and pulled the strip up and under the little lever that automatically advanced the roll after each shot. Slowly he closed the two halves and heard the snap that locked the gun together.

Bang, bang, the gun sounded. The wonderful powder burn filled his nostrils.

"What's going on down there," Cecilia called. "Is something wrong with the furnace? Albert, there must be something wrong with the coal you bought. It's popping."

"It's only me," the Kid shouted. "My cap gun *works!*"

"Oh, is that all?" She turned to find Albert with hands on his hips. "Albert, the house is not on fire now. I am sorry if I alarmed you, but you never know, do you, with the coal mine tunnels underneath the house and the gasses that seem to escape up the well lining."

"I admire your caution," he said. "All alarms are welcome."

Typically British, Cecilia thought, and then she offered him a cup of tea as a sign of truce.

Meanwhile, Ben fired all the caps on the roll and reloaded it for more shots. The other gun was still clamped shut, but he would open it, somehow. The Kid needs two guns to fight the crooked rustlers. Christmas! Its spirit was alive. It hadn't been washed away by the torrential rain that turned the snow to soup and covered the frozen ground in deep swales. Above him, an orchestra pounded through the basement floor. Sally turned up the volume. *Bang, bang*, the syncopated shots were followed by screams from the Met stage. The Kid pointed his weapon and fired shots between hammer blows.

"Are you ever going to stop that commotion?" Albert shouted from the top step, his teacup saucer steadied between two fingers.

He boldly replied, "Never!"

"Albert, let the Kid alone! He's cleaning up the basement. In an hour all crime below the living room will have been defeated. Weren't you ever a child yourself?" Albert did not answer. "More tea?" she asked.

The shootout upstairs and the romping orchestra became more interesting than plugging imagined varmints. He holstered his pistols, which he would call Red Fire. He went upstairs. The light in the living room brightened, but the rain still drove down.

"Hey, Dad," he called boldly. "What kind of games did English kids play?"

"If you must know," he answered, "we did constructive chores for entertainment. Try to imagine that. 'Make yourself useful,' your grandmother would say to me. So I made myself useful, and that was that. Your Uncle Willie just made himself scarce when grandmother was peeved. Grandfather had little more to say than 'humph' and 'yes, yes, quite right'!"

Ben began to reminisce. "I remember grandfather when we lived in Ruthfred Acres. I was three, I think. He was brushing the steps with a dust brush and pan. He backed down the stairs banging the brush against the walls as he swept. I watched him come down, rear first. He was muttering something. When he came to the lowest step, I reached out and poked him in the bum. 'Nemina' I said, and laughed. That was my word for enema. He was furious, but he still laughed."

"Old Woman," he shouted, "Humph, humph, I have just been attacked by an aborigine!" He remembered this as though it happened yesterday.

Mother was listening. She laughed, saying she vividly remembered that moment.

"Now, young man, when your grandparents come, and Willie comes a few days later, please be kind, considerate, and respectful. After all, you know, Santa is *always* watching you. Keep your pistol pointed far away from grandfather. He has a long memory, too."

"What's Uncle Willie like?" Ben asked.

"He's much like your father," she said, "and just as handsome. He's elegant and refined. He has lived in India, 'Inja,' you see. He does not know baseball, and football is somehow not really football. He'll explain. He's quiet, keeps to himself, reads novels, probably mutters to himself frequently, as bachelors do, and probably receives bank statements every week from Barclays Bank in London. I feel certain that while reading them he whispers words like 'rascal' and 'bedevil.' This much is true, however: he calls his mother 'Tibbens.' Don't ask me why. He will probably wear tropical white clothes that are common in what he calls 'the colonies.' You must all do your best to entertain him. He will call it 'distracting him,' but that's what he'll need—distracting."

"This is going to be fun," Ben said. "When are they coming?"

"When are they coming?" she asked. "Too soon, I fear, too soon."

"Be brave!" she said to him, but she was really talking to herself.

She then called to their father: "Albert, the boys and I are going to take the table scraps to the shed and the bag of cans and bottles to the garbage pit." Silence. "Did you hear what I've just said?"

Sally called to them, saying that he was probably napping.

Mother rolled her eyes, and told them to wear jackets and galoshes because the water on the ice and snow was about an inch deep. They were to make sure that she didn't slip and fall.

The trio left by the kitchen door. Mother had the scraps, which she called "slop," and George carried the cans and bottles. Ben held mother's arm tightly. They half-slid and half-tiptoed across the icy water. He wasn't surprised to see the garbage pit filled with water. Bottles bobbed on the surface.

"What do I do?" George asked mother.

"Just dump it and let nature take its course, like everything else around here. Now, just hold your breath in the shed and I'll be quick. 'Pig, here's your dinner.' Ugh, it stinks here."

The rain was falling lightly, and the wind was quiet. On the way back to the kitchen, Ben asked his mother why she was so unhappy about the visit of his grandparents and his uncle. He'd never heard anything unkind said about them.

"That's true," mother said, "but they were thousands of miles away. We wrote occasionally, and that's all."

George asked why she felt the way she did about them. "Weren't they relatives? What did they do wrong a few years ago?"

"We're getting soaked out here. But you deserve an answer. Have you ever played that cruel game called 'the man in the middle'? Surely you have. Two players throw a ball back and forth, and the man in the middle, who is usually younger, or smaller, infirm, or female, has to try to intercept the ball."

"We play it sometimes, but it's just for fun," Ben said.

"Well, I felt like I was the man in the middle when your grandparents lived with us. I'm sure it's fun when you play it, but it was not fun for me, let me tell you."

They stood under the little roof over the kitchen door to hear more.

"It's more than either of you can understand, but I know Sally understands. She's the oldest, and she's been stuck in the middle at times. The last time your grandparents lived with us was on that dreadful little farm in Ruthfred Acres near Bethel Park. You must remember something about it, Ben. Remember falling off the horse? Enema?"

Ben remembered napping in bed with grandmother before dinner, and he remembered grandfather coming down the stairs backward. And there was a train behind the house. The train was kind of up on a high track and all it did was go back and forth. He realized at that moment that it was a big noisy Honeymoon Express. It just didn't seem to go anywhere, and mother explained that it was a "measuring train" that just went back and forth on a short service track. She could not explain why this was so.

"A train should *go* somewhere, shouldn't it?" she said. "I'd forgotten about that train! So, your grandmother and I listened to soap operas in the afternoon and talked about what we would do for dinner. I had a wonderful time with her. She's sweet and loving. But when your father came home at night from his studio in Carnegie, something strange happened. The two of them got into some kind of an unpleasant scene. She became bossy and very critical of what I was doing. Your father was no help. He just accepted what she said as the truth. I felt a little betrayed. I was younger, then, and, after all, she was his mother and our guest. Oh, I hope I'm not making too much of this. But I am so afraid that when she comes she will pick up immediately and become critical and bossy. Then your father will have to come to my aid, which will be difficult for him."

"So, you're the man in the middle," he said.

"If I had known this would be a long conversation, I would have brought umbrellas," she said with a laugh.

"Your grandmother is a lovely person. Grandfather has always been aloof, but that never bothered me. I should have stood my ground then! I was the woman of the house. I just didn't stand my ground, and I'm afraid I won't be able to this summer. But with Willie here—I have always gotten along famously with Willie—I hope he'll be a buffer for me. Do you know what a buffer is? Well, a buffer would protect and defend me."

Ben tried to cheer her up. He said he remembered the cat, Bootblack, and he remembered asking his father if the manure he was spreading around the tomato bushes got into the tomatoes. Albert said not to worry about that, and then, because it was cold out, he wiped Ben's nose on the corner of his handkerchief.

"And I remember that horse he kept, the one the three of us sat on, and I was over the tail, and I fell off?" He realized again that he talked a little too much.

"Treasure all of your memories," she said. "Remembering is a sign of superior intelligence. But, watch out, because memory also leads to revenge. I know."

In the kitchen they realized that they were all soaked through. Albert came into the room. He thought they got lost in a blizzard, and he would have to release Alpine dogs to find them.

"Now that you mentioned it, Albert, a little whiskey would taste good right now. With a thimbleful of water. While we change, would you please pour me a little?"

"I can pour you a little," he said, "and I can pour you a little more, too!"

"Oh, Albert," she said in a cheery way, "sometimes you can be the perfect gentleman, like Cary Grant and Joseph Cotton all in one."

"Do George and I get any whiskey?" Sally asked.

"A few drops in water, but no more."

"Wow," George said. "He's in a good mood. I wonder why?"

"I think it's because he's going to have some whiskey," Ben said.

"And he didn't have to take the garbage out in the rain."

"Don't forget me," Sally called from the couch. "I'd like mine with a thimbleful of water."

The next morning Albert went to the shed to check, "to count heads," as he put it. Ben heard the crack, crack, crack of his footsteps on the thin ice. Overnight, the bottles and cans had floated out of the garbage pit and settled in a fragile layer of ice that held them in place. He thought his father would be furious, but he wasn't at all. Instead, he rushed back to the house, sliding and slipping, shouting "whoops" and "well, that was nice." He got his two-and-a-quarter format camera and retraced his treacherous path so that he could photograph the bizarre scene of bottles and cans trapped higgledy-piggledy in the ice. When he returned, elated, his smile was robust. You would have thought he had come from an exotic country. Seldom had he seemed so happy. Actually, *his* was a picture worth taking!

A Python from India

Uncle Willie was preparing for his trip to the colonies. His bungalow in Punalur, Travancore, India, where a large paper mill was situated, had to be emptied. Houseboys must have taken a hundred pounds of ancient wicker junk to a bonfire, sorted through his old clothes for items that fit them, and dumped his various dying plants on a junk pile. For a man of impeccable dress, he left behind him a sorry waste of trash. "You see," he said in his letter to Ben, addressed to him as 'Master', "This section of India is damp much of the year, hot all the time, and dusty. Nothing lasts long. Paper curls, turns brown, attracts insects, and falls apart. Corpses, whether animals or humans, are crudely burned on scant mounds of wood, and the unconsumed remains are carried off by semi-wild dogs, which complete the ritual." He loved that letter because it was written to a child-adult. Uncle Willie could not temper his vivid images for the Kid with red pistols. He did not understand children, which was wonderful, because Ben then became an adult. His uncle was polite, sometimes humorous, and always British.

But one item he did not destroy was a snakeskin—thirteen-feet long. It was sent in a shoebox, tightly wrapped to fit the box and covered with tissue. A note was included containing a half rupee with the head of George VI King Emperor and an Indian tiger on the reverse. He told the children that it was common for long snakes to be run over on the narrow roads during rainy season. He had one of the snakes "treated" to preserve the skin from nose to tip of tail, if snakes have tails. He said that the snake was a python, now "perpetually in hibernation." This kind of snake wraps itself around its prey, which might be a dog or a deer, squeezes tighter and tighter, suffocating the victim. Then, he said, the snake unlocks its jaw and slowly takes the prey into its mouth head first, slowly moving it through a series of strong muscles until the last-to-be-seen tail passes into the jaws, and then the mouth shuts. The digestive process takes days and days. The python rests, sleeps, and then, at the end of the process, regurgitates what could not be digested. Then jovial Uncle Willie wrote that if it had experienced an especially good meal, the python lets out a long belch and slithers off somewhere to say its "grace after meals."

In geography class they were learning about India. They began class with a reading from Rudyard Kipling's *The Jungle Book*. They loved the exotic tales and complained when it was time to stop. Please, just another page, please? They heard another story. After she finished reading, Miss Miller urged the boys and girls to save their nickels and dimes so they can go into town with their parents and see the marvelous new movie, *Kim*—actually made in India. Men would be dressed in fashionable red and gold costumes and women in brightly colored *saris;* they would ride on the backs of enormous elephants in Delhi. Imagine that! How exciting!

Skipper waved his hand. "What if they fell off?"

"Why, Jackie Skipper, you have such a vivid imagination. Let's see. . . ." Then Eddie shouted, "Look out below!"

Miss Miller laughed and shook a kind finger in Eddie's direction: "Eddie knows something about movies, isn't that right, Eddie?" Eddie—the pirate with a yardstick who once attacked a movie screen.

Skipper and Eddie, always buddies, smiled happily as they relished the minor chaos they had just created in Kim's chaotic India.

And then they looked at maps of India. Sometimes they drew maps or solved map problems. They learned about the rivers, the crops, family life, and religion. Near the end of the India unit, they were asked to bring in something connected to India, such as a picture of the Taj Mahal or of sacred cows in the city streets. He sat up in his seat as he imagined Bessie in Bombay. Mother would love to send her there.

Josephine, who wanted so much to be good, asked, "Miss Miller, am I allowed to feed a cow in India? I mean, they look so hungry."

"Of course you may, perhaps a slice of apple after breakfast. That would be very nice."

On Monday, he brought the python skin knowing it would frighten the girls and excite the imagination of adventuresome boys.

"All right," Miss Miller said, while clapping her hands. "Who wants to touch a python?"

"Ooooh," said the girls. "It's creepy!"

Since it was his show, he could ask for help.

"Annie," he said, "will you please hold the head of the python skin and I'll hold the tail."

"Yuck," she said. "Do I have to?" She appealed to Miss Miller.

"The rules are the rules, you know. Don't worry, the python won't bite you."

They stretched the python skin to its full length so everyone in the class could run a finger from one end to the other. Danny said that he liked snakes, especially big ones like they have at the zoo. Surprisingly, some of the tougher boys faked touching the skin. Their fingers were a quarter inch above it. Others touched it while looking at the ceiling. Ben had it set up so that the kids began at the tail and ended at Annie's curls, which the boys liked. Eddie got back in line again. Then Steve did the same. Annie smiled and shook her curls in appreciation. Miss Miller smiled in satisfaction. The India lessons were a success.

And then she read a story of natives hiding in a tree waiting for a lion to come and feed on a dead goat. The lion approached cautiously, sniffed and licked the carcass, and settled down to its meal. Meanwhile, the natives in the tree branches above the lion dropped a sharp stake weighted with a heavy stone. The lion was impaled. It roared, turned, and tried to flee, but the wound was too much. The natives swung from the trees with knives drawn and had revenge upon the lion that had attacked the village. The boys clapped. Ben rolled the python skin tightly and returned it to the box.

"Next week, students, we will begin lessons on mysterious Japan. Do you know what a samurai does? Well, be prepared for some exciting facts about the Japanese and the islands they live on. I'll bring in silk for you to feel and a special tea you can sip. And special sticks used for eating rice. Yes, sticks! And I'll have pictures of warriors in ancient costumes and women with their faces painted white. And pictures of pink cherry blossoms. And we'll learn a few Japanese words, too. And, who knows, maybe someone will bring in a reptile monster. Wouldn't that be fine? And we'll learn how to bow to each other and how to sit on the floor in a special way. So, say goodbye to India, children, and hello to Japan." She bowed, and then announced it was time for lunch.

Remembering

Easter was near. Ben remembered Easters past:

Easter is yellow-gold, blushing-pink, lavender-blue, and paradise-green. Easter is candy hidden in bushes or stuffy closets. The season of denial called Lent disappeared at noon on Holy Saturday. The children counted down the seconds knowing that the three of them would race off in different directions toward suspected hiding places for chocolate and jelly beans.

"You are getting closer, but not yet! Try to think like an old bunny. Not house-broken, mind you! Where would he hide it?" Cecilia enjoyed the moment as much as her children did.

She made them work to find their treasures.

"Hot, hot, cold, cold, getting warmer!" She cheered them on, laughing.

Albert was amused for a minute, but he soon became impatient with the fuss.

"Cecilia, just tell them where it is," he said.

What he did not understand was their complicity, for they knowingly looked in the most ridiculous places, the obvious places remembered from the year before—upstairs under beds, in the basement coal pile, in dusty galoshes, in the oven, under sofa cushions, and behind cereal boxes in the kitchen.

Ben began to go outside.

"Now you are getting hot, blazing hot!" she said.

Under the porch he found a paper bag painted with a bunny's face. George and Sally followed him, blinking in the noon sun. Behind the single tree in the center of what they called the front yard, George found a little nest of colored Easter eggs covered with dry leaves.

"I'm going to the shed," Sally called over her shoulder. *"I'll bet she put some there."*

She ran back holding a bag of smelly jelly beans that had picked up the goat's odor overnight.

Cecilia laughed and laughed.

"There's one more. Where do you think it is? Look, look!"

Her hand was moving in the large pocket of her apron. What was she holding?

Sally got to her first and untied the apron strings. The weight of the pocket made the apron fall with a clunk on the little wooden porch.

"It's a chocolate Easter egg from Reymer's, and it's not hollow, either. Wow!"

Cecilia then said what parents were supposed to say: "Now, no candy until you've had your lunch!"

"We're not hungry," George said. *"We just want candy."*

"You would pass up Campbell's tomato soup and tuna fish sandwiches?" she said. *"What kind of children are you, might I ask?"*

"Cecilia, I've told you often, you spoil them. Well, let's not let the soup and sandwiches go to waste. You and I can have lunch—set an example. There are children in poor countries who would like soup and sandwiches." Ben's long reverie ended. The new Easter was upon them.

★ ★ ★ ★ ★

But for all of the colors of Easter that pleased the eye and soul on Holy Saturday, there was the long monotonous gray season of Lent, with the sacrifices, the fish on Fridays, the endless Stations of the Cross, the dark purple and black vestments, and the feeling of emptiness these all brought. Ash Wednesday, when they got the smudge of ashes on their foreheads, was usually cold, snowy, and dark by five o'clock. There were no Mardi Gras celebrations in Allegheny Acres, Culmerville, or mythical Red Hot, or the other ghost towns linked by Saxonburg Road, no drumbeats and no men and women hiding behind masks and dancing with rum or whiskey in their bellies. Recesses at school were not so wonderful, with the cold and snow and the icy path down the hill to the outhouses claiming victims who fell, rolled in the mud, and brought back swollen lips and cut knees.

Cecilia invited Sally to fly the kites standing in a corner by the stairs since December. "Would you like to?" she asked. "We still have the tails, remember? There are things we need to talk about, too, like going to the city for eighth grade at the Cathedral school. If we stay here, of course. You could be in the Cathedral's Confirmation class. That is my hope." And so Cecilia asked Albert to drive them over the cinder roads leading to the boys' baseball field, but she did not invite him to fly a kite. "Today it's just for girls," she said.

"I understand," said Albert. "I will now go fly a kite! Bye-bye."

"I'll make a nice dinner when we return."

George asked what would be in this nice dinner.

"We'll have goose, or pheasant, or quail, or even robin stew, if enough robins have come back from Florida. Whatever we can snag. Fishing in the sky has no guarantees!" She winked.

George, pleased with Cecilia's wry humor, said that a mess of robins would be tasty after the long winter of dried cod and soft potatoes.

Between winter and spring, with the bodily insults of Lent and failed promises of warm weather, their foolish conversations were not unusual. Cecilia promised to write them down for posterity, but when posterity came there were no little dramas after all. Such was life.

Surprises

And so he understood mother's feelings, and he understood them even more when she announced on Holy Thursday that they would all drive to the city for Easter Mass at a lovely church called Sacred Heart in a neighborhood called Shadyside.

"Your father will drive us there for Solemn High Mass. We will sit near the front where we can see and hear the splendid choir. The organ is one of the finest in the country. The vestments, the flowers, and the stained-glass windows will be spectacular. You will think you are in a splendid cathedral with the King of France in attendance. After Mass, we can walk around the church to see side altars and artwork. And then we will walk around the block to see the modern grammar school and the girls' high school. Now, you'll need to use your imagination because the girls are taught on a temporary basis in a Quonset hut, but the new high school is being built and will open next September. It will be the finest school building in Pittsburgh."

"I have another surprise for you. After Mass you will meet my cousin, your cousin, too. She joined the order of the Sisters of Charity many years ago. She and a companion will come in from Seton Hill College, where she teaches. She was always a fun-loving girl, the life of the party."

"So why did she become a nun?" Ben asked.

"She had a vocation, a special calling, you see. Don't try to figure it out. Just be thankful for her decision to answer the calling."

"Does she have one of those weird names," George wanted to know, "like Sister Cumberbund, or something?"

"It's 'cummerbund', I believe. But, no, she is called Sister Thecla, after an old saint. Just say her name ten times and you won't have any problem saying, 'Good afternoon, Sister Thecla.' You will absolutely love her!"

"Are there any more surprises?" Sally asked, with her eye on the radio, where she hoped to hear opera music from New York.

"I don't have any more surprises. Do you have any surprises for me?"

"No, but just a question," Ben said. "Does Dad know all of this?"

"Probably not," she said. "He's best with one thing at a time. I'll tell him this afternoon. Not a word, do you understand?"

He suspected there were other things Dad didn't know. He would have to wait for them to be revealed.

George invited Ben to go to the woods to shoot Easter bunnies with their BB guns.

"Maybe we can wing a chicken on the way," he answered. "What was our cousin's name again?"

"Uh, I think it was Sister, uh Sister, what was it, like Sister Thing?"

"There's no one named Thing. Did you ever hear of a church called Saint Thing?"

"No, but I think we're close."

Ben held his rifle at the ready, walked toward the shed, and spied a tin can—an enemy sniper—bobbing in the flooded dump. He cocked his rifle, aimed, and fired. The BB knocked the can on its side, but it popped up again—a tough commando! George picked another target, a ketchup bottle floating like a buoy. It took him four shots to shatter the bottle's neck from only fifteen feet.

"Nice shots," Ben said sarcastically.

"Not bad with the sun in my eyes," he answered.

"You had fifty-three more chances to hit it."

"Why's that?"

"It's a Heinz 57 ketchup bottle, that's why. It's the favorite target of nearsighted kids. Everyone knows that!"

"OK," he said, "put some ketchup on this knuckle sandwich!"

Minor ouch.

Then they ran in the mud to the woods where they fired at stones in the creek. Between shots, the accuracy of which they disputed, George told him that Sister Thing's name was Thecla. He said he knew it all along. They shouted the name ten times: "Good afternoon, Sister Thecla."

They agreed that mother had something up her sleeve because she was just too happy. Their aunts and new-found cousin, Little Barbara, were probably in on it.

"Now it looks like Dad's the man in the middle," Ben said.

"This'll be something to watch, won't it?" George answered.

"Yeah, Hawkeye, something to watch!"

When they went back through the kitchen, mother and father were huddled over cold bowls of tomato soup. Tuna fish, by now the bane of Lent, filled the air with its pungent aroma. Sally's opera music filled the house with German passion.

"So, that's the story," mother said. "I think it's best for us all."

"Well, it may be and it may not be. I am not a fortune teller," he answered.

"It's good that you said 'fortune.' If we move now, I'll have three thousand dollars to put down on a house. It's from my share in Dithridge Street."

"So moving to Shadyside and Sacred Heart parish is good for the children. True, but living in Shadyside puts us only ten minutes from your sisters, who have never liked me. In fact, except for Frances, who is a good egg, they seem to despise me."

"That's a little strong, but it's not your fault, believe me, Albert. They are all single women, and when you married me, their youngest sister, when I was already thirty-five, they felt a deep resentment. You already know that my father never approved of any young men who came to court his daughters. He was born in 1843, a different time and a different world. For heaven's sake, he met President Lincoln in Washington. Another world!"

Albert agreed without seeming to understand what it meant to have another world in America.

"Do you remember that safe in the third floor hallway at Dithridge?" she asked.

"Yes, I've often wondered about it."

"Well, it's a symbol for us both," she said. "Why? Because it contains a mystery, but no one remembers the combination. It's my guess that it contains inconsequential stuff, perhaps an old watch, and some old bank papers—pre-Depression. My sisters are like that safe. They've hidden their secrets. They learned never to talk about their feelings. What's inside them is rarely revealed. You've seen them at their best, just looking away when there's tension and conflict. But you know the combination to my safe, Albert. Please, don't lose it."

The boys backed out the kitchen door.

The last words they heard were mother's: "And shortly your parents and Willie will descend upon us, and I'm not sure I'm up to it!"

"Descend? What did she mean?"

"Let's ask Sally. She'll know."

"I wouldn't count on it," George said. "But it can't hurt, can it, to ask her?"

In the living room, Sally had her nose in her book about operas. She seemed peaceful and content. So they asked her what was going to descend on them when all the relatives arrived.

"Well," she said without looking up, "I'll have to give up my bedroom, and you'll have to learn some manners. I guess we're all going to descend into mother's Hell, but we'll rise again, won't we? Easter's coming, see? So go paint some eggs. You'll feel better."

He began to feel better. "Why should I be afraid of old relatives? I might like them. But what if they don't like me? Sally, what about that?"

She lifted her eyes from her book, with its bright, colorful drawings of opera stories. "They won't like you," she said. "They'll *love* you."

"Oh, that's good! And it's Easter, too. I'm going to the shed for some eggs. I can't wait. Decorating eggs, yeah, yeah."

Magnificent Easter

The old Pontiac labored toward the city, its windshield fogging over until the small rubber fan above the windshield was turned on. Slowly the window cleared. From the seat behind mother, Ben saw the familiar view of the twisting road. The dark, leafless trees with their faint hues of promised green arched before them. The Allegheny River below the Highland Park Bridge flowed over the dam that caught the river trash from the mountains in the north. At the zoo, monkeys cavorted for peanuts thrown them by children's little fingers, and tigers roared for their bloody breakfasts. Animals with unpronounceable names reeked in the morning air. The road through the zoo snaked from side to side. They turned onto Bunker Hill toward North Highland Avenue where stately old trees and statues posted as entrance guards declared that Highland Park was worthy of respect. There were finely dressed families on the path to the reservoir. Easter bonnets pinned to fancy hairstyles still had to be held in place by gloved hands. Children struggling in their shiny new shoes followed their parents. The churches along North Highland Avenue were Episcopal palaces, and a Presbyterian skyscraper soared heavenward, its gothic beauty funded by the enormous wealth of the Mellon family. Mellon's "fire escape" it was called. Along the avenue they went, rocking slowly on the streetcar tracks and passing lesser churches. And then the church they sought appeared: magnificent Sacred Heart. They found a parking spot on Shady Avenue, many blocks from the church.

"Look, look, you can just see its gothic architecture in the distance, above those trees," mother said. "And there's some Norman, too, I think. I'm not sure, but wouldn't it be wonderful? It was not unusual for European churches, which were sometimes built over many centuries, to have different architectural styles inside and out. Let's hurry. But first, Albert, I hope you can find our car after Mass."

Sally interrupted to say that the different styles of architecture reminded her of father's closet, which contained a mix of fashion styles from many eras, including old stumpy ties with odd geometric designs, and one tie in particular, which had a fire extinguisher emblazoned on it. There were baggy slacks that had never seen a dry cleaner's shop, and tropical white suits and jackets, badly yellowed now, from his courtship days with mother in the Caribbean. Did Sally haunt closets for secrets of past lives, Ben wondered? What was in his closet besides games and picture puzzles?

Mother said, "Sacred Heart has the city's longest nave—that's a fancy word for an aisle— it makes you think of "navy," doesn't it? Nothing skimpy or stumpy or baggy would do for Father Coakley, who dreamed for years of building this church. However, come to think of it, a fine church is like a fire extinguisher that fights the devil, don't you think? Mellon had his fire escape. Father Coakley travelled through England and France, seeking inspiration for Sacred Heart. He was especially fond of the Durham Cathedral."

Albert observed that Father Coakley might also have been inspired by the wealth of Pittsburgh's industrial tycoons.

"Well, yes, this was done in great industrial cities. Andrew Carnegie himself contributed to St. Paul's Cathedral, and he was not a Catholic. Churches, libraries, and museums were all the same to him, for each in its own way lifted the spirits and brightened the souls of mankind. Even Mr. Heinz, of pickle-and-ketchup fame, gave generously to build the Heinz Chapel on Pitt's campus. I hope we can visit it today just to stand inside and see the beautiful, tall, stained-glass windows transform the chapel's interior into a magical sea of blue light. The beautiful stained-glass windows of the city's magnificent churches shamed the grimy city, with its wretched smokestacks and dark mining tunnels."

Sally, who could be bossy, said that it didn't make a lot of sense for the Carnegies and Scaifes to pollute the air with coal dust and soot and turn noon into night, or to foul rivers, and then somehow redeem themselves by building monuments to spiritual purity.

Very nicely put," Albert said. "I've been all through the northern industrial cities of England, and let me tell you, the stench of poverty and the appalling blankets of smoke and soot would drive any man to flee, if it were possible, to the green hills of Virginia or Pennsylvania."

"Is that why you like cows and pigs," George asked.

"Agriculture is natural and pure. Man was not made to mine for coal or tin," he answered.

"Except," Sally said, "there would have to be *some* tin for the Tin Woodsman."

"So, Sally dear, you see both sides of the argument. Steel mills and coal mines are necessary for progress, and wealth from mills and mines builds beautiful churches, and tin is mined—I'm not sure where—to dress a character from Oz," mother added.

"I think Sally is turning into a Socialist, don't you?" Albert asked.

"Oh, Albert, Sally is much too young to be a Socialist, aren't you dear?"

"You see," Albert said, drifting into reverie, "my father was a medical doctor for a bauxite company in British Guiana. He supported corporate wealth and treated victims of mine accidents. And Willie was a manager of a paper company in India, where great wealth was amassed at the expense of half-naked coolie laborers. So, Sally, when our guests come to visit, please don't irritate them with Socialist claptrap."

"This is Easter Sunday, not a political rally," mother said, "and here's the beautiful church on a beautiful early spring morning."

"Would it meet with your approval if I were to say that today, the twenty-fifth of March, was once New Year's Day a few centuries ago? How fitting, don't you think, that Easter falls on the New Year?" Albert was pleased with himself.

"I approve," Cecilia said, "but this is today. I just can't live within two calendars at one time. Still, it's fine to understand that change happens, and this is my springtime of change." She looked at Albert with her biggest smile, bigger than he remembered. "Thank you for the thought."

Parishioners were gathered by the front steps. They seemed happy and joyful. Women and girls were draped in new spring dresses and suits, a rainbow of colors and textures, with unique broad-brimmed hats crowned by raised veils and delicate feathers. White gloves were stretched to the elbows. Little girls wore Mary Jane shoes and sailor hats with ribbons dangling down their backs. Little patent leather purses dangled casually from their gloved fingers. Fathers and sons had sharp trouser creases and bright white shirts with contemporary hand-painted ties bunched uncomfortably at the throat. Grandmothers wore shades of lavender and purple. Beneath their conservative hats were waves of blued hair. They talked in choked voices about absent husbands who always loved Easter Mass, but were a little too ill to attend, or whispered about recent funerals. They leaned affectionately toward one another to hear the whispers. They were being very brave and happy.

Mother said she wished she could have travelled to Vatican City for the Holy Year Jubilee last year.

"All it takes is money," she said bitterly.

"But the crowds would have been awful, don't you think?" Albert asked gently.

"I guess I shouldn't complain," she said. "I would be perfectly happy living here, in Shadyside, and sitting in my favorite pew at Sunday Mass. I want this so much, and I want the children in these modern schools. For these things I would gladly trade Vatican City and the beautiful basilica."

"Would you even sell your soul?" he wondered.

"Yes, I think so. It would be for a very great cause!"

Then they laughed at the thought of selling one's soul so that the children could live in a splendid parish and be educated by nuns in fine Roman Catholic schools.

"I wonder what G. K. Chesterton would have to say about that!" Albert asked. "Come to think of it," he added, "that Chesterton fellow was really rather nuts. Didn't he say that living in a family is like living in a fairy tale? What rot!"

Sally said that she didn't see anything wrong with it.

Let's go in," mother said, coaxing them forward. "But first, take a deep breath!"

The church was magnificent. The long aisle led them past tall stained-glass windows and decorated columns supporting a high roof. The woodwork of the ceiling reminded him of the large hold of an ancient ship upended above them, perhaps the Bark of Saint Peter. The brilliant rose window, enormous and graceful, seemed kaleidoscopic, the most perfect pattern frozen forever far above. Lights and candles on the altar reflected in rich tapestries of white and gold on each side of the altar. A jewel-encrusted cross hung above the altar, the light playing on the red and blue jewels and precious glass shapes. They walked to the altar rail to see the huge inlaid map of the world on the spacious floor. How pale, he thought, how pale was Saint Victor's on the slag hill in Bairdford.

Choir stalls flanked the aisle before the altar. The organist played rich polyphonic Easter hymns which filled the church. The first four pews on the gospel side of the church were empty. Mother explained that they were for the nuns of the parish. They would come in a long procession from the convent, two-by-two, and file into those pews, the senior nuns in front. An extra respectful hush would accompany their entry.

Cecilia selected a pew near the front of the church from which they could all see the drama and ceremonies of the Solemn High Mass. The choir men and boys filed to their seats while singing a joyous Easter hymn beginning, oddly, with what sounded like the words "fold napkin." In cassocks and surplices, with large black bows at their throats, the boys' choir took their seats on the Epistle side, while the men's choir was seated on the Gospel side facing the boys. The organist directed the choir using large mirrors behind the boys so the men could follow his directions.

Three priests, royally robed, with a host of acolytes and altar boys, began a processional up the side aisle and then down the long center aisle. Incense filled the air.

Cecilia followed the Mass in her large missal, its pages swollen with Mass cards, reminders of the many funerals of loved ones she had attended. She also had copies of her favorite prayers tucked between the pages. On the left of each page were the Latin prayers; on the right were the English translations. She knew the Mass by heart, but there was something profoundly satisfying in holding the book that held saints' pictures with prayers for the deceased on the reverse side. The Mass was both uplifting and sad for her. Sometimes he held her missal and turned the pages looking for cards he had not seen before. Some were very old with names of German relatives close and distant. He found a short shopping list that she had slipped between the pages. She would not remove it—it belonged.

On that late March morning the spring sun filtered through the windows in hues of red, blue, and green, staining the aisle and the lower walls. They knelt, stood, genuflected, and sat at assigned moments, with signals from an altar bell and the priest's outstretched arms. The elderly parishioners sat quietly, but made small gestures of kneeling, and that was reverence, too. The Communion lines were led by the nuns. A fourth priest assisted the three celebrants, all of them moving up and down the wide Communion rail with altar boys holding patens under communicants' chins. When Mass ended with the words *Ite Missa Est*, the stately recessional began. The choir and celebrants, as though in a royal pageant, passed up the central aisle and down the side aisle. When the long procession ended, the nuns rose, genuflected, and filed two-by-two past the side altar toward the convent. But two nuns remained seated in the first row.

Cecilia studied the two nuns, who turned to look at her family. One of the nuns smiled happily and waved her hand.

"It's Sister Thecla," mother said, putting her hands together. "Come, everyone, let's move up to see her."

Sister Thecla walked with a happy step toward them, her hands outstretched.

"Cecilia! Cecilia!" she called. "Oh it's so good to see you again after such a long time."

She embraced Cecilia there in the aisle.

"And here is Albert," Sister Thecla said, as she shook his hand in both of hers, a genuine welcome. "You are just as distinguished today as you were when we first met."

Albert had a big smile. He enjoyed Sister Thecla's ecclesiastical flirting.

Turning to the children, she said, "You probably don't remember me, but I remember you." She squeezed their shoulders. "My, aren't you all strong," she said.

"Now, I want you to meet my travelling companion from Seton Hill. This is Sister Mary Robert, who teaches mathematics, a subject I know so little about. She taught math in the high school here for a few years. She knows this parish very well."

Sister Mary Robert was gracious in her greeting, and then she excused herself to attend to something in the convent. But they were to see her again soon ringing keys like altar bells.

"You know, the sisters at Seton Hill love to come to Sacred Heart for special occasions because it is such a beautiful church, and they know so many of the nuns here. They are all 'friends in the Lord,' as the saying goes."

"Do you think that you will be moving into the parish soon? The children would love the schools. Sally would have a brand new high school building waiting for her. I hope you have time to walk with me around the property."

"Didn't you just love Mass today," she asked, looking directly at Ben.

"Yes, sister," he said, "but I have a question."

"You do? That's wonderful."

"The choir sang a hymn that began with what sounded like the words 'fold napkin.' I wonder what that means."

"Cecilia and Albert, keep your eye on this child."

She then explained that the napkin, or face cloth, is mentioned in the writings of John the Apostle. When Jesus rose from the dead, He folded the napkin, which had covered His face, so as to say that He would soon return. It's a lovely story, but the meaning of it continues to puzzle scholars. Despite that, the story of the folded napkin found its way into songs and folk stories.

George said that he served Mass at Saint Victor, but he never saw anything like what altar boys did this morning. If he comes to Sacred Heart, he would like to be an altar boy.

"Of course. You will love being in the church and getting to know the priests. Do you mind getting out of bed at five o'clock in the morning to serve at six? Why, you look a little shocked! But you'll love it, I just know."

Albert said that George would have to walk to church on those early mornings, or trot, because he has a little trouble being on time. "And don't forget, there will be dark, cold mornings, snow, and rain." Translation: don't ask me to drive you to church, stay for the Mass, and then drive you home again.

"That's so true," sister said, "and that's why Boy Scouts are often the best servers. The Christian life is a rugged life. I believe Boy Scouts earn badges for serving Mass."

He thought that a walk around the block would be over in a few minutes, but the block was huge. Along Shady Avenue the church seemed never to stop. And then they saw the construction for the new high school. They walked along Alder Street to Emerson Street. Once again, the block was long, with the Quonset hut high school, the grammar school, and the convent, before coming to Walnut Street, where they began.

Sally asked the name of the long, gray building on Emerson Street.

"That's Hunt Armory, where political rallies are held, and trade shows, and large conventions. Soldiers train there, too. You'll see them marching on Emerson Street, but there aren't so many now because most of the soldiers are serving in Korea. The sisters welcome the quiet in the soldiers' absence, but pray daily for the end of that awful conflict. Most of the trucks, and cannons, and who knows what else, are gone. Students use Emerson Street for recess now. But it saddens the sisters when they see seventh and eighth grade boys marching behind soldiers and swinging their arms as though it were a joke. The boys are too young to understand. Surprisingly, though, the soldiers seem to enjoy it!"

"Hello, don't go. I've got the keys to the school." It was Sister Mary Robert holding up a ring of musical keys.

Even Albert, who usually settled for less, was impressed with the school, with its tidy halls, clean classrooms, positive posters here and there reminding students about the Legion of Decency and the Easter poster contest. Classrooms were bright and cheerful. High on the wall in each room was a fluorescent lamp that cast a muted blue light. The lamp killed germs.

Sister Mary Robert laughed, saying that in the old days of the

Church miracles were necessities as there was so much sickness. "Now, we turn on a switch that controls the blue light and a miracle happens with no angel dust."

"What will be next?" she wondered. "Perhaps modern science will rescue us all from diseases, like polio, which is a plague attacking children. Isn't it really awful?"

Albert said that in his opinion old F.D.R. had the right idea. Everyone pitches in a few dimes and before long polio will be defeated. Scientists are perhaps the new miracle workers, no disrespect intended.

Sister Thecla agreed with him.

"You know, Albert, you have touched upon the exact reason boys and girls must have the best education today. The three R's will always be important, the foundations of learning, but Catholic schools simply must teach the sciences, with modern labs and technology available. And I really mean that girls must become responsible, must become scientists and doctors in far greater numbers than in the past. As much as I love British literature and all the arts, I know in my heart that someday soon they will give way to science education. I can see it happening at Seton Hill, and I applaud it. Balance, that's what we need!"

"My father is a doctor, retired now, but he never encouraged us to follow in his footsteps. Willie went into the business world, I'm a photographer, and my sister, Amelia, married a merchant. None of us has done a lick of work to save the world. With all due respect to the fine British writers, and to the Irish writers, too, I feel that I am a throwback to old Victorian days. I wear a modern hat, as you can see, but that's as modern as I can be. And wait 'til my parents and Willie are here! I thought this morning of Chesterton's notion that living in a family is like living in a fairy tale. Can you believe that? A fairy tale might be fine for Snow White, but it won't teach us how to defeat the modern illnesses, whether polio, war, or naked greed."

Sister Mary Robert picked up the thought, saying that here they were, standing on Emerson Street, with Sacred Heart School on their right and Hunt Armory on their left. She paused, and then she asked whether they felt inclined to turn to the right and make a future for a new generation that might cure social ills through education and scientific study, or to the left, where the cannons are?

"I'm hungry," Sally said.

Sister Mary Robert said, half-laughing, "How we do go on! We are all hungry, I'm sure, and that is one thing that we can cure right now! Come inside for lunch. You see," she said, ringing the keys in the cool air, "I am the keeper of the keys, and the keeper of the keys can open many doors."

The convent kitchen and refectory were nearly empty, except for a few sisters who came late to breakfast, and a priest who was clearly lingering after the Solemn High Mass. They were introduced as a family. Father Kent was amusing everyone with his stories about parish life.

"There's only one place for good coffee in this parish, and that's here, in the convent. Sooner or later, priests find an excuse to come to the convent every morning. In fact, I think we would give offense by staying away. Isn't that right, sisters?"

"It is impossible for a priest to offend if all that stands between courtesy and discourtesy is a cup of Joe," said Sister Mary Robert. "I do enjoy a good cup of coffee, especially after a long Lenten fast."

Albert and Cecilia were settling in with coffee while two sisters scrambled a dozen eggs and fried a large amount of bacon. Toast came from a large contraption that took in white bread at the bottom, circulated it around heaters, and plopped the toast without ceremony any which way onto white cloths. Wonder Bread, surely. Butter was spread and marmalade was available in a large pot. Oranges from Seville, they were told, make the best marmalade.

"At Douai Abbey," Albert said, "where I was in school in England, the Benedictine priests insisted upon Spanish oranges in marmalade. It was just a very British custom."

"Speaking of a cup of Joe," Father Kent began, ignoring the sisters' rolling eyes, "have you heard the great story about Joe, a man who worked with the C.Y.O. baseball team? Well, it seems that the C.Y.O. men held a function in the church basement, something to do with giving each other awards. You know how that goes. Anyway, after the event, there was a large pot of hot coffee left over. Well, Joe decided that he and another man would carry the pot of coffee to the convent as a nice gesture of unity, and fill their urn with coffee. Joe had a way with words, as everyone who knows him would attest. An uneducated man, he made up words or corrupted them in his own way. Simple things, like 'strew it in' for 'screw it in,' or 'pit it in' for 'put it in.'" He paused to drink most of the coffee in his cup and then continued. "Anyway, so here the two men come, after dark, to ring the convent bell. A sister answered the door. Joe was beaming by now. He said something like, 'Hey sister, we got a pot of hot coffee for ya, so bring us your urinal and we'll pit it in.'"

There was genuine but embarrassed laughter in the kitchen. The two sisters, who heard the story too often, still found it funny. And, after all, it was polite to laugh when a priest told a comical story. Then there was Father Kent's story about thirteen priests in Rome. They laughed and laughed on their way to St. Peter's, their cassocks blowing in the summer sun. A woman saw them and commented on how unlucky it was for thirteen priests to travel together. Her companion said, "Don't worry about it. Thirteen is only a number. Just think of it as a Maker's dozen."

"Gotta run," Father Kent said with a broad smile. "Jeanette gets upset when the priests are late for lunch. It's nice of her to come in on Easter and prepare lunch. Must keep her happy!"

Sister Mary Robert said that there are many ways to celebrate the end of Lent and the joy of the Resurrection. Father Kent probably suffered during Lent by denying himself coffee, so it stands to reason that he was making up for a long period of self-denial.

That was when Cecilia surprised them all with her philosophical comment: "Somehow, eventually, we all get what we want in life, don't we?" Albert shook his head. "A healthy notion, perhaps true."

Ben loved the eggs, bacon, and toast with orange marmalade. But the coffee was bitter, so he put in a lot of sugar and milk. Now what, he wondered?

Sister Thecla began to speak. "You can believe what you want, of course, but I think that we meet people every day—it doesn't matter where—who are so memorable, whether they're awfully smart, or gifted performers, or just plain folks struggling to get by. There's an angel in us all."

Albert said that if Joe's story is being told again and again, perhaps even at lunch with the pastor and the priests, then Joe will make his way into American city folklore, a local hero.

Sister Thecla said that the phrase *sui generis* could describe Joe. It's a longhair's way of saying that Joe's his own man, his own person, and no one else can become Joe.

Ben, hearing *sui*, said that there's a farmer near him who calls his pigs when he wants them to come to the sty, and he just shouts "*soo-ee*" about a hundred times.

"What happens?" Sister Mary Robert asked.

"Nothing," he said. "The hogs just keep rooting in the mud."

"That's a good example of '*soo-ee generis*' if I ever heard one!" Sister Thecla laughed. "I can't wait to tell my students. Now, if Farmer Brown feeds his independent hogs the old coffee grounds, I'll bet the hogs would come running in their stiff-legged way."

Sally, the budding Socialist, asked whether Father Kent's story about Joe wasn't cruel.

Cecilia answered: "I don't believe so. Father Kent was not humiliating Joe. He was just doing what the best storytellers have always done, and that's to make us laugh or cry about people, no that's wrong, not 'people', because there's no such thing as 'people' in a great story or poem or opera or play. There are just individual human beings. Maybe we embrace them or maybe we shun them, but they are unique, they are memorable."

"Incomparable," offered Sister Robert.

"Yes," mother said. "Robots need not apply. Well, I hope that schools today aren't making everyone turn out the same, marching in their identical uniforms."

Sister Thecla said, "Come when Father Kent gives a coffee-inspired sermon. I promise you that he will make you go away glad that you are you despite all the labels you wear day-to-day, year-by-year. Forgive me for being a snob, but I happen to know from reading old texts that the word 'coffee' comes from the Arabic language. In Arabic, 'coffee' can mean 'wine.'"

"OK," Albert said, "I'll bite. Is it possible at the Last Supper that Christ drank 'coffee' from his cup?"

They all laughed at the thought, but Ben had to think about that for some time.

It was time to go. The goodbyes were long and full of promises.

They staggered on uneven sidewalks to the car on Shady Avenue.

"Albert," mother said with purpose, "while we're here, let's drive around and see what the neighborhood's like."

"I imagine there are many neighborhoods to explore within a mile's radius of the church," he said, "and I don't know one from the other. Direct me."

Following mother's directions, they drove to South Highland Avenue along Walnut Street. The streetcar tracks had a magnetic pull on the wheels. They followed the tracks, somehow stuck in them, toward Alder Street. On the corner they saw a bakery named Schmidt's, a pharmacy, a hardware store, and an ice cream shop called Poli's.

"This looks nice," mother said. "My maiden name is Schmidt."

They turned onto Ellsworth Avenue, and shortly they crossed a bridge over the train tracks. The streetcar tracks continued to make the car sway a little, which was a little dangerous because parked cars couldn't have been more than a few inches from the streetcar that ran on the line. Cecilia wondered about a tiny store simply called Kate's. Who was this Kate and what did she sell? Kisses?

"Be careful, Albert. Move to your left a little. It makes me nervous being so close to these parked cars. There. That's better."

"Look at that, the Elbow Room. Very original. Nice name for a pub if you ask me. I recall a pub named the Crooked Billet somewhere in the Cotswolds. Do you think a crooked billet could be a bent elbow?"

As they moved along, Ben saw side streets that looked narrow and dirty.

"There's Roslyn Place." Mother said that the street was paved with wood blocks. The trees along it were old. "In the summer the street is woods-like, kind of creepy, especially at night. I remember a professor who lived there. He's long dead by now. He attempted to teach me economics. I made a low grade. He said that for someone who knew so little about the Federal Reserve there could be no other outcome."

"Albert, turn right at Aiken Avenue and I'll show you where I was born and where I lived as a very little girl. There was a gardener, a pony, some chickens, and Lord knows what else."

She pointed to a large building. She said that her father had sold the house and the acres of land to Shadyside Hospital, which is now a huge place. After the sale, she said, her father built the large house on Dithridge Street.

"It's getting late, I know, but we should turn around and go up to Walnut Street, a long stretch of businesses, bars, clothes stores, and a movie theater. There are some very nice neighborhoods, all pretty old, but nice," she said.

Farther out Walnut Street they found themselves at South Highland Avenue. They made turns to the left and right, probably getting themselves lost, but something mystical was pulling Albert, something he couldn't pass up. Among the old streets he found a narrow alley.

"Well that's a silly name, isn't it—*Lamort* Place. Live here and die!"

"Albert, its name is *Lamont* Place. Like a mountain. You saw the '*n*' as an '*r*'. I think you said it on purpose, or, as Ben says, "by purposely." They had a good laugh.

"Still," he said, "*mountain*. It's one of those overreaching names for an alley with the tiny houses on the left and the countless old single-car garages on the right. Must have been named by miners. Those garages were built for Model T's. This old car might just fit, but new cars couldn't."

Mother joined in. "There's a dreary little hovel for sale, one of three brick houses joined in a row."

"Nevertheless," Albert said, "even a hovel is someone's home. Isn't it?"

"Sorry, so sorry. I didn't mean to be cruel."

They had to stop a few times because kids were playing games and darting about between parked cars, even in their Easter clothes.

"Albert, please don't run over the children," mother said, her hands clutching the dashboard.

"That's enough touring for me," Albert said. "Show me the way to the Heinz Chapel for a quick drive-by, and then we'll go home and collapse."

I'll make a pot of coffee and throw together some sandwiches for anyone who's interested. And then I'm calling it a day," Cecilia said.

"Some port wine would be nice, too," Albert said with a hopeful tone.

"Coffee, wine—wine, coffee, it's six-and-a-half to one and a dozen to, uh, oh bunk, you know what I mean."

"Sister Mary Robert would give you a gold star for mathematics," he teased.

But the exhausted family saved Heinz Chapel for another day.

Sally was nodding and George was asleep on her shoulder. The last thing Ben heard was father saying that there's nothing like fresh country air to fill one's lungs.

Mother was silent as the car bounced over familiar roads toward the mine-hollowed rolling hills of Allegheny Acres.

A noisy March rain began to fall. The windshield fogged. Albert lapsed into his private world of English memories, and his little song blended with the whirring of the small rubber fan under the drumming cold rain.

Tea with Irish Whiskey

On a warm afternoon in late spring when tulips were bright red and yellow, the boys kicked up dust on Burger Road toward the sameness of the house, the shed, and the garbage dump, which had settled nicely underground after the odd winter weather.

"Hey," George said, as if making a great discovery. "There's the car. What's he doing home so early?"

Ben answered that he may never have left for the studio to begin with.

"Nah, that's not possible." At that he stopped walking. They ate a little dust before he shouted, "I know, today's the day grandma and grandpa are coming. That's why."

They picked up their pace, forgetting for the moment the big news that school was closing a week early because of a polio scare. And, believe it or not, they would be allowed to chew gum in class during the final week when they repaired their ancient texts with library tape. On the last day of school, when report cards were handed out, they could even bring comic books to school.

At the little porch, they heard the excited voices of mother and father and the very British tones and expressions of muted excitement: "Yes, yes. Oh, right, well, we'll certainly see, don't you know, accommodations elsewhere? harrumph, yesyesyes, I would think so, wouldn't you?"

Only the screen door separated them from the quartet of voices, so they stood still and listened, unsure about entering their own house.

"But Cecilia, don't you see, Willie, in India, always had houseboys doing his work. You can't expect him to fry his own bacon every morning let alone prepare soft-boiled eggs. He is an Englishman, a bachelor, an executive, after all!"

"What other arrangements did you have in mind for Willie, I wonder?"

"The Culmerville Hotel would be ideal."

"What kind of an establishment is that for Willie?"

"You have no bees, Albert? A gentleman farmer, a squire, has hives, one or two, just because. No need to explain, I'm sure. Yes, the soft murmur of bees going about their ancient business among flowers, what could be more pleasant? Harrumph."

"The Culmerville place, eh? Well, I must instruct the cook—if there is a kitchen—on the proper manner of preparing bacon and eggs for a British gentleman who has lived in India these past twenty-five years. Why, it's a mother's duty, don't you know. Have you a cigarette, by the way, as I smoked my last on that wretched train from Washington. Thank heavens Willie is coming by air to New York, and then, I suppose, if he must, he will board a rickety train to Pittsburgh. Travelling is a form of torture, don't you know?"

So this is adult conversation, he thought, dueling voices crossing over voices, words left unsaid, primitive nasal sounds conveying displeasure, or signaling a trumping of arguments. He would have to learn to listen carefully.

"George," he asked, "what in the world's going on?"

"They're just talking, that's all,' he whispered. "We'd better go in. You go first."

"Why me?"

"Well, it's the British thing to do!"

"Harumph," Ben reasoned. "That's tommyrot. You're older, so you go first."

The screen door screeched; the rusty return spring aching with the stretch.

Mother exclaimed proudly, and probably to bury the conversation leading nowhere: "Oh, my goodness, they're home already!" She did not ask the whereabouts of Sally. "Everyone," she said, looking at the very old couple Ben had not seen for about ten years, "everyone, here are the boys!"

They said their politest "hello" and "welcome," which they had been prompted to do.

Grandma hugged them, gave them a long look through her bifocals, and exclaimed that they were strong and healthy specimens if there ever was one. She teased Ben about those winter afternoons at Ruthfred Acres when he was forced to take a nap with her.

"You just wouldn't lie still. You were just a beautiful imp bent on spoiling my little nap. Do you remember? You jumped up and down, and no promise I made would settle you down for even a second."

"Old Man," she said to grandpa, "this is the little child who greeted you at the bottom step when you were sweeping the stairs. Remember, the aborigine?"

"Oh, well, if you must, I recall the experience. I see that he holds no pointed objects in his hands, so am I to believe that he has matured beyond the provoking age of three. Hello, young man." He paused, as though puzzled. "What is that large formation on your face?" He examined Ben with his doctor's eye.

"I don't know," he said respectfully, thinking that he had gum on his cheek or a chocolate dribble on his chin.

"I believe it is a proboscis, yes indeed. I've seen them before."

"Please, Old Man, stop teasing the boy. In case you don't know," she said kindly with a gleam in her eyes, "a proboscis is just a funny name for a nose."

Mother laughed. "I think you two are even now," she said.

"Shall we have some tea, Cecilia, and some cake?" Albert asked. He had rehearsed the line. There was no tea or cake that Ben could remember.

"Right you are," Cecilia answered in the best mock-British fashion she knew. "We will have a spot, shan't we?"

"Shan't we." What could that mean?

George was studying grandpa, who had yet to say a word to him.

Boldly he asked, "Grandpa, what kind of shoes are those you're wearing."

"Young George, these are shoes made of the finest leather in a London shop frequented by His Majesty's subjects stationed in the remote colonies. Because of the tropical climate, it is healthy to have ventilation. And so, narrow strips of leather are crisscrossed over the toe, spaced just so, allowing air to circulate with each step. Very smart, wouldn't you say? Function first, followed by fashion. Try saying that ten times without a mistake!"

Ben liked grandpa. "Hey," he said to him, ready with a question about his hat, which had a tiny repair in it.

"Hay is for horses."

"Oh, yeah, but I wanted to know what that repair is in your hat."

"Firstly, it is a fedora, a soft felt hat made popular among gentlemen because some fool actor in an obscure stage play was required to wear one. It was not Clark Gable. Secondly, the repair was made by me, using a surgeon's very fine stitch. Quite something, don't you think?" He plopped the hat on his head in a Napoleon fashion and tucked his hand into his shirt over a large belly. "March on to Moscow," he ordered.

"Boys, you need to know that your grandfather was an amateur actor in medical school, before I married him, of course. Did some bright person mention tea?"

The old round dining room table, where the children did homework, was covered with a pretty tablecloth. The tea setting was attractive and new. Sugar cubes and a small pitcher of milk were placed near the teapot. There was pound cake, too, from the Clover Farm store.

"Shall I pour?" mother asked.

"How else shall we have tea?" Grandfather seemed still to be on stage.

"I hope I have done this correctly," mother said. "I always like to pour tea first and then follow with the sugar and milk. Isn't that correct?"

"Quite right, but tea chills quickly, don't you know, so may I suggest that you proceed?" Grandma could be a little sharp at times. It must be what travel does to people.

When Sally came home, she was greeted with the salutation, "Here is the senior child!" Grandma held out her arms to embrace her. "Sally, how well I remember you. I have little gifts for everyone, once our luggage arrives. You will like your gift, Sally, I am sure."

Grandpa kissed her on the cheek and patted her hand. "So," he said, "the little girl grows up and looks just like her father."

Mother said that Sally resembles the Schmidt side of the family, with the thick eyebrows, a sign of natural born intelligence. But the pouting lips come from her father. She then turned her gray eyes on Albert and grandpa. "You know," she surmised, "I've just now noted that little look of sadness on her face, which quickly disappears with her smile. Sally's going to be a star wherever she goes."

"And where might you be going, if I may ask, at your tender age?" Grandma teased her more. "Could it be that you are going to a fine high school and then on to study with the ladies of the Sacred Heart in New York?"

"I'd like that," she answered, with a nervous look at mother. "Or, I guess I could stay in Bairdford and marry a miner's son."

Grandma said in mocking distress, "May the blessed Saint Barbara, one of my favorite saints and the patron saint of miners, discourage you from this moment onward."

Grandpa said with determination that miners were fine people, very fine. "Why, in British Guiana, most of my practice was occupied with bauxite miners who had accidents at their stations. Accidents, mind you, are not their fault. Good people, good lads, you see."

Mother braved a comment. "Actually," she said, surveying the faces of Albert and the boys, "we are seriously considering a move into the city, to a wonderful parish, which has the finest schools you will find anywhere. Isn't that true, Albert?"

Albert paused, sipped his tea, put the cup quietly into its saucer, and then said, "Oh, you know, we've talked a little about it. I don't know, what with the summer coming on and the need to do something about the animals. I may decide on a beehive or two. If we all decide to swarm away, there's no telling what might happen here. That's to be considered."

Mother looked shocked. "Beehives?" She said. Then she was silent. She covered herself well. "I'm just so happy that you all are here,

that we'll have a wonderful month getting to know each other again."
She smiled bravely.

"Oh, yes," grandma chimed, "a month, five weeks, or six, we'll
have a splendid visit, won't we Old Man?"

"Well, well, we just might," he answered. "Willie will help us
decide where to retire. Now there's a boy with a head on his shoulders,
don't you think? Harumph."

Cecilia looked stricken, but she gathered her strength, fixed her
indomitable Irish-German will, and observed that tea with a spot of
Irish whiskey has a celebratory effect.

"Anyone?" she asked, half-rising from her chair. "Anyone?" Silence
followed.

"I'd like one," Ben said.

"Thank you," she answered, with a brave, kind smile, and then
settled back into her chair.

Grandma fretted about the overdue luggage.

"It will come soon," Albert said. "If it's not here within the hour,
I will drive to the station and get your bags."

Were the British obsessed with tea and luggage, not to mention
time schedules?

Mother took a deep breath and stood. She went to the kitchen.
Ben heard a few bottles knocking about. She called to him. "Please go
to the bathroom and find the little eyewash glass with red markings,
next to the boric acid. I need the glass to measure whiskey. I can't find
our real shot glass, but the other will have to do. Such is life on a farm.
Your father probably used it for the cow or the pig. Why, I don't know."

He found the glass tucked out of the way deep in the cabinet. He
remembered his father using it for what he said was a sty. Odd, he
thought. Did the pig in the sty have a sty in its eye?

Mother carried the Irish whiskey bottle—or was it a bottle of Irish
whiskey?—to the table.

"Well, well," Grandpa said, "You make a strong case for a little
pick-me-up for the tea. I would like just a drop or two. It helps with
my digestion and with my sleep."

Sally said she would like a thimbleful, just to the bottom red line
of the little glass would be fine.

Mother poured a little whiskey for Albert and grandma.

George said dryly, "I might as well," but mother passed him as she had passed Sally. Mother's dollop, a double shot, was measured to the top red line.

As the celebration continued, grandpa sang a little song he suddenly remembered from his days in medical school, something about a patient whose liver was in a flivver.

"Old Man, the children do not know what a 'flivver' is. You date yourself!"

"Why, children, a flivver is simply a very old automobile, a cheap one, with perhaps a rumble seat above the boot, if there was a boot, and a tooting horn with which to summon young ladies to accompany young men to a dance, or a swim, or some such. We thank your Mr. Ford for this imaginative vehicle."

He laughed and sang a little more, something about 'a stenographer with a stenosis'."

"What was prescribed?" mother asked, playing straight man.

"That she should take a letter three times a day," Grandpa answered, hardly able to contain himself. "Another drop, perhaps?"

The pound cake was reduced to crumbs by dinner time, and the whiskey bottle was sent to the open trash pit to serve as George's next target.

Ben began to understand the attraction of Irish whiskey: it loosened the tongue, cured indigestion, inspired old songs in old men, and saved what promised to be a bad day for Cecilia. In addition, grandma made one of her few compliments: "And a fine hostess, too." Cecilia was even surprised by the pleasures of hosting a visit by curious people from faraway places. "Maybe things will work out better than I thought," she said as she open two cans of Campbell's tomato soup and spread mayonnaise on white bread for Isaly's chipped ham brought all the way from Walnut Street in Shadyside. "I just love Shadyside," she said without amplification.

Seven of them squeezed around the table. Grandpa slurped his soup, stopping after each spoonful to dab his white mustache with a paper napkin. Grandma nibbled at her sandwich, which she studied with a knowing eye. Ben imagined hearing her say, "So this is America."

"Cecilia, this is fine," she said, "but just a half-sandwich for me. I have always had a sparrow's appetite."

Sally offered to take the other half.

"Of course, dear, as you are a growing girl who requires good nutrition."

Grandma was not just being polite. She was as much interested in what was consumed as she was in what was later passed, and how frequently, too, into the privy.

The second most embarrassing moment he owed to grandma, who asked Ben on a crowded bus in Pittsburgh, "Have you moved your bowels today?" The most embarrassing moment was answering, blush-pink, eyes fogging: "Yes."

She then looked about proudly for the approval of their fellow passengers.

When the luggage containing the little gifts arrived, grandma and grandpa were in a deep sleep in their parents' double bed. One of the men carrying the bags said, "They's light." The other man, not to be ignored, said, "Yeah, but they's a lot!"

It was strange to see the old couple climb the stairs at seven o'clock each evening while the sun was still bright. For decades in British Guiana they went to bed early, and they rose very early to do a day's work in the coolest hours of the day. The afternoon tropical heat forced them under the large ceiling fans for the rest of the day. Not even the rain gave them relief. The children had to be quiet in the evenings so their grandparents would not be awakened, but from their snoring in unison Ben did not worry about their awakening before five o'clock in the morning. And so the family spent the early summer in a comfortable temperate zone as well as an imaginary equatorial zone.

Before Willie

In the week before Uncle Willie arrived—and the talk at home was only about Uncle Willie coming from India—mother did her best to entertain, to engage, to share. Surprisingly, her plans were too grandiose: a trip to Niagara Falls, a trip to Oil City to see the first oil well, and an afternoon shopping in the city. These were rejected. Their guests had come to rest, to settle in, to take some control of domestic activities, and to parade up and down, here and there, in antiquated (grandpa's) or excessively modern, comic dress (grandma). Truly British, grandpa polished his shoes each day, removed the leather belt at night before hanging up his trousers, and rotated his three ties and two hats. He wore a vest under his suit jacket, carried a watch on a chain across his large girth, and kept his Prince Albert pipe tobacco in a small canvas sack in which he placed three or four matches. He smoked Chesterfields with dignity, sharing them with grandma after meals and during the afternoon soap operas, which they both found fascinating. But grandpa usually fell asleep early during the soap opera and Cecilia lifted his cigarette from his fingers and snuffed it out in the ashtray. Grandma had read about the new bold women's style of trousers and lace-up shoes. Convinced this was fashion's future, she stood above the steps to the driveway each afternoon in high-fitting "slacks" and a cotton shirt, posing like Katharine Hepburn waiting for her destiny, the cigarette positioned between her stained fingers, soon forgotten. "Dash," she would say, "it's gone out." Then she would light another

Chesterfield, the breeze blowing out a number of matches before she turned her back to it and tried again.

Grandpa left the house by the noisy screen door at three o'clock prepared to make the short walk down Burger Road to the Clover Farm store. Often Ben would accompany him because he bought him a Coke. Grandpa's drink was a bottle of Evervess, a carbonated water, which was excellent for his digestion. On the way back he belched three or four times. "Now that's a relief, let me tell you," he would say. "A simple remedy for a chronic malady. Simple is best."

"I hope you feel better, Old Man, and I hope you have not scandalized the boy."

"What, what, did you say? He must learn the ways of the world early, don't you know?" Then he fanned himself with his hat-of-the-day.

Mother waited and waited for the troubles to begin. She believed that grandma and grandpa conspired with Albert about ways to keep "the farm" prospering. The beehive arrived, was assembled, the bees acquired somewhere, and the queen came in the mail, ready to be installed, to take charge.

"A hive must thrive," Albert said over and over, as he blew Prince Albert smoke into the small entrance to pacify the bees. This seemed quite effective. He bought a book of directions, learned the signs of hive failure, and even talked to the bees on their morning flights to find clover somewhere in the sparse vegetation: "Damn your eyes," he protested, "not that way, you fools. Go up, onto the hill, to the farm, to the farm!"

He became dangerously familiar with the bees, trying to handle them by holding out his bare arm. He said that they were naturally peaceful creatures and very intelligent indeed. Without them, he said, we would all starve. They're peaceful missionaries doing wonderful work for mankind. They ask nothing, he believed. Their instincts were flawless. They cool their hive on hot days by rapidly moving their wings. They defend their hive when wasps or hostile bees from other hives try to raid it. He came to this conclusion: "If our government leaders studied bees and learned their practices, we would not have wars. The world would be at peace." Pleased with this discovery, he concluded that all philosophers must have been men of the earth, men of the farm. They were great poets, too, writers like Wordsworth and Shakespeare, who understood the land and the shires of England and Wales.

As Cecilia listened to him hold forth, she began to see her great plans fade. What about Shadyside and Sacred Heart School? Would she lose them for a handful of bees and a bottle of honey? What could she do in an honorable way to change his thinking? Would Willie help her? Ben heard Albert and Cecilia argue in their adopted bedroom that Sally gave up for the duration. First mother would make her pleas, and then she made a few small threats, but she was not successful: "Don't let a queen bee take over this household. What about some perspective?"

"Yes, yes," he would say. "I know how you feel, but think about . . . ."

By then Ben was asleep.

School's Out

The school year usually ended by Memorial Day, but this year students were to be given final report cards and news of promotion to the next grade a week earlier due to the polio concerns of the administration. Mother was a little unhappy with the news; father did not care one way or the other. But when it became obvious that the children could entertain their guests and help to prepare for Uncle Willie's visit, she adjusted quickly. They weren't just "under foot" like little babies. Albert left early for his photography studio in Carnegie and stayed later than usual. Ben suspected this was because he found his parents to be loving nuisances, a bit "trying." The children fed the pig, the cow, the goat, and the scratchy chickens whatever paltry food they were fond of: slop, hay, cigarette butt appetizers for Diego, and bread crumbs for the chickens, their herky-jerky movements and little skirmishes entertaining to watch. Ben decided to name them all "Sunday," because that's when he saw them without feathers, boiled or baked or fried. He looked at the platter of parts but could not take one when it was passed to him.

"The boy eats like a bird," grandma said. "Surely he should not have dessert unless he eats the chicken. In British Guiana, let me tell you, the poor children are scrawnier than your chickens, but this meal would be a banquet for them. A horrible place!"

"I did what I could to make it a better place," grandpa replied. "There is no immediate cure for poverty, dysentery, tape worms, tropical diseases, and genetic diseases."

"But wasn't Queen Victoria a carrier of some genetic hitch? Or Prince Albert? I forget which." Cecilia knew her history.

"So it was rumored," Grandpa answered. "But they were beloved by their subjects, so their genetic history was not a topic for afternoon tea. And remember, our Albert is named for His Highness. Prince Albert succumbed to typhoid, I believe, at a young age. Her Majesty, Queen Victoria, entered life-long mourning upon his death. Now that was devotion if you ask me! Hmmmph. She did not wear "slacks" as someone at the table prefers."

"Old Man, when you begin wearing skirts and dresses, I will cease wearing trousers, which, by the way, are jealously guarded by men folk. Why should only men know such comfort? Even little boys in knickers long for the day when they may wear long trousers. These are new times. Do get in step!"

Ben shared his opinion: "Baseball players wear knickers, don't they? I have a Pittsburgh Pirates uniform, and the pants are bunched just under the knees. So does George. I'm number 8. It says so on the back of the shirt."

Albert added that baseball is an old game that is full of customs he could not understand. "A fussy set of rules! Throw a ball, hit a ball, run around a square. Touch this, touch that. Slip into a base, or is it slide? And you'd dare not appear on the field without a hat. And those sissy mittens! Why, real men use their bare hands. Oh well, perhaps I should be more tolerant. This is, after all, America."

Mother laughed. "Yes, Prince Albert, your Highness, now explain that sticky thing called a wicket in the sport called cricket, by jiminy!"

"You must be born and bred British to understand and appreciate cricket. Wait until Willie comes. He will teach you all you want to know about cricket and, I'm afraid, many other things."

"For dessert, to honor your visit, I've made a special junket," mother said proudly. "Curds and more curds!"

"Could I have a red bowl of Jell-O instead?" Ben pleaded.

"Oh, nonsense," she said. "It's time you expand your tastes for food. Be brave, my son!"

Sally, who could be bossy, jeered at him: "You can't leave the table until you've finished it, so there!" She remembered that he once went on strike over lima beans. That was a long dinner.

"All right, if you're not going to eat the junket I slaved over all morning, why not just run down the road and get our mail. We should have heard something from Willie by now."

"I should think so," said grandma, a little critical of Uncle Willie's recent lapses as a letter writer.

Grandpa picked up the tone of her remark. "Oh, I wouldn't make anything of it. After all is said and done, he's on his way from India, stopping here and there. He'll need to discover the world again, won't he? All those years in backward India are beginning to tell on him, don't you see?"

"Go, go, go, please. Run like a pony express boy, thank you."

Sally said, "No grazing on the way!" By that she meant stay out of the candy section of the Clover Farm store.

There was a letter from Uncle Willie addressed to Cecilia and mailed from London. he trotted back and offered it to her.

"Well, it's about time. Not you, honey, you were very quick. But Willie."

Mother took her sharp knife and opened the blue air letter. It took three slices, like cleaning a fish. She read quietly. "Well, well, you'd never guess," she said.

Grandma said that guessing was not necessary since there was a letter in mother's hand. "Out with it, please," she begged. "When?"

"We are requested to meet Willie next Monday morning at the East Liberty station. That's sooner than I expected. It must have been raining in, let's see, a place called Golders Green, London. So off he goes by air to New York and then to us."

"Why must everything be a mystery? So, he's coming on Monday. Wonderful. We haven't seen him in years. Old Man, be nice to him. No quarreling."

"Do you think he'll bring us presents? That would be nice." Ben forgot that they just got the presents from grandma after she found them in one of her many suitcases. He got a hand-carved little horse from someone in Georgetown, British Guiana. He tried to make it stand up, but it kept falling, so he leaned it against a book, and that worked.

"We should go instantly to inspect this Culmerville Hotel. It may be brand new with twelve rooms, so I've heard, but Willie must have the brightest one. Willie deserves to be comfortable," grandma said. "By the way, where is Culmerville, if I may ask?"

"About four or five miles as the crow flies. I'll drive you and Cecilia."

Cecilia said, "How do you know so much about hotels?"

"That's where wedding receptions are held. Smile. Click."

"I will have my Evervess and then nap," Grandpa said.

"Children, kindly tidy the house, or, as they say here, 'redd up the house,' and wash the few dishes. Everyone must pitch in."

Three voices competed as they left the house.

"I'm sure his hair is white by now."

"My lady friends will adore him. They'll sit at his feet and make eyes at him. He's so wonderfully British!"

"Cecilia, I'll need your nail file again to file the points, or else the car won't start."

"Here, Albert, just keep it, for Heaven's sake. Are you sure you know where this hotel is located?"

"Of course, but if we find ourselves in Red Hot, then I'll know I've gone too far." He laughed.

"My head spins. Who, I beg to know, would ever live in a place called Red Hot?" Are you pulling our legs? Really, Albert. Let's go to inspect this mysterious hotel!"

Willie of Culmerville, Late of India

They couldn't all fit in the little old Pontiac, so Albert, grandma, and grandpa drove to the East Liberty station to meet Willie, who must have been travel-weary having come from India to New York, with brief stops in between, and then to Pittsburgh. And then he stepped off the train. There were handshakes, slaps on the back, a motherly hug, and genuine joy at seeing the long-absent son and older brother. Awaiting him on Burger Road was Cecilia, who presided over a small round table hardly large enough to hold the welcoming treats from fine shops, and teacups, saucers, cake plates, and silverware, all borrowed from Dithridge Street. The children were dressed for Sunday, but it was only Monday. They would not have to shine shoes again on the coming Saturday morning. Cecilia spent more time before her mirror than Ben ever remembered. One moment she looked pleased, but the next she looked frightened. "Please, please, please," she kept saying. "What?" they answered. "Nothing, really," she replied.

Sally revealed that mother was embarrassed to have Willie, the perfect gentleman, the premier bachelor, the retired executive, and the man of independent means, set his foot on the yellowed linoleum, look around, and have to tell the white lie, "I say, Cecilia, this is a lovely house," before he hugged her and she hugged him, and then she had to tell her little white lie, "We have all been looking forward to this moment. Welcome!" The welcome would be genuine. She was, after all, a graceful lady, poised for society, but lacking the silver, crystal, and china props that she knew as a girl and as a young woman. How many times she professed that a husband and three beautiful children were greater than gems, silver, and gold, which are cold and hard. "Isn't that true, Albert?" she would ask, and he would answer, "Why yes, of course. Why do you have to ask?" And she responded, "Well, some fine thoughts need to be expressed before they are lost in the daily clutter of speech."

"When you hear your father's car coming up the drive, I want you three to go out and meet him on the walk. I'll be here lighting a few lamps and putting on the water for tea. Now, be nice, and say the things we talked about. And, please, boys, no questions, at least not now. Sally, smile; don't forget to smile. You be the hostess for the moment. If he addresses you as 'senior child,' be cheerful and welcoming. Oh, and one more thing to remember, Uncle Willie calls his mother 'Tibbens.' I don't know why, but only he calls her that, so remember."

She paused for a little prayer: "Dear Mother of God, please let the car start without the nail file. Thank you."

The three posted themselves at the top step by the driveway. In a few minutes they saw the old Pontiac struggling as it turned from Saxonburg Road onto Burger Road. They could hear the gears grinding. Grandpa was in the front seat because getting in and out of the back seat of a two-door coupe was very difficult. George, as instructed, held the door open for him. Grandma struggled to leave the car, and Uncle Willie gave her some encouragement: "There you are, Tibbens, that's the way!"

And then Uncle Willie appeared, smiling with confidence, bouncing on his toes like a diver, and setting his fedora on his head at the right pitch. His hair was gray. His glasses twinkled in their dark frame. Sally broke the rules and shouted to mother: "Hey, mother, they're here!"

"Shush, Sally," father whispered. "Do it right."

By then Uncle Willie had climbed the steps and paused on the walk. He removed his fedora, pinched its brim between his finger and thumb, let it hang softly at his belt, looked at the house, and then said his first words: "A sort of bungalow, it would seem."

"So," he said to Ben, "you must be the child who occasionally wrote me such fascinating letters, usually beginning with, 'I am writing to you because I have nothing else to do.' I've kept them for you, and when you're a few years older, you'll enjoy hearing what you had to say about chickens, pigs, the cat that ran away, and a girl by the charming name of Annie. And I'm happy that your classmates enjoyed Peter the Python!"

"And you're George, who enjoys wood burning art, finger painting, and cowboy movies. Is all of this true? I have to rely on your mother for facts because you must have been much too busy to write me, hey?"

"Yes, sir. I also like marbles and sword fighting. I'm a musketeer when we play swords. I use a garbage can lid for a shield."

"How splendid! How French! You must demonstrate your parry and thrust for me." He feigned a fencing pose.

"And you must be dear Sally. My, what lungs you have for shouting each moment's news. So, now I understand why you like German opera. Your mother tells me that you know every opera ever written. I've a little gift for you, a recording of *Salome* by Strauss, if you're fond of gore. Oh, it's all very Biblical, you know. In fact, you may earn indulgences when you listen to it. If my luggage ever arrives and the recording is in one piece, we shall have a grand time!"

"Oh, thank you Uncle Willie. I'll be sure we have a new needle on our old machine. Wow, my own record!"

Uncle Willie had a kind smile and a nice wink he used until they were able to learn when he was being businesslike or jovial. The hinges of the screen door had been oiled in his honor, and a new spring was attached. Uncle Willie entered the house to the sound of mother's voice. She was almost singing: "Oh Willie, it has been much too long. We haven't spoken since the day Albert and I were married at St. Paul's Cathedral, and you were the best man. Remember? So much has happened in fifteen years, what with a war and all, but here you are!" They hugged and traded kisses on both cheeks. "That's how the French and the Russians greet each other," she told them.

"Cecilia, I'd hoped to take my year's leave in 1940, but the war was on in Britain, and I was persuaded to do my part by staying in India supervising workers at Harvey Brothers. Oh, what a war! And now, it doesn't look very good in Korea and China."

Mother said that they would all have a grand day, pointing to the round table, covered with splendor in his honor.

"Well," he said to George, "do you like pie?"

"Oh yeah, I love pie."

"Well, in a day or two, we'll have to make pie. Does that sound interesting?"

"You bet," George answered. "Pie is my favorite food."

Grandma and grandpa came down the stairs in their comfortable tropical clothes that matched in comfort Uncle Willie's white linen suit and light blue shirt with a maroon bow tie. His shoes were like grandpa's, but new. His fedora was plopped carelessly atop grandpa's fedora on the small table near the door, a comic sight, one hat wearing another.

The teacups and silver tinkled. Grandpa was in rare form, teasing Uncle Willie about his boyhood conduct and asking him if he had a million pounds yet. Mother had stationed a fresh bottle of Irish whiskey on the table, with the eyecup still serving as a shot glass. Grandpa held it before his left eye, his glasses hanging from his right ear. "Well," he said, in a professional voice, "after a dose of this whiskey, I'm beginning to see better already."

Grandma laughed deeply. She was fully entertained and loved the attention. Uncle Willie, probably tired from his travels, promised to take a drop up to the lowest red line. "Isn't this what American cowboys call 'redeye'?" Sally said that she'd like a slug of redeye before the roundup begins. "Might as well," said George. "Me, too."

"Tibbens, Dad, Albert, and Cecilia, I understand that I am staying in the Culmerville Hotel out in the neighborhood of provincial Red Hot. To think that I could have retired in India, in great comfort, with houseboys fetching my slippers, but instead I have come to the States to find a place to retire, perhaps in St. Petersburg, Florida."

"Uncle Willie," Ben wanted to say, "say goodbye to India and say hello to Red Hot."

Mother said that Willie would be visiting them every day and that plans for his entertainment have already been made. Albert would come for him after breakfast, and drive him on the winding roads to Allegheny Acres.

"You must take me to the hotel in the morning. I want to be sure that my directions to the kitchen staff are carried out." Grandma was going to take care of her boy, even if he had gray hair and wore bifocals.

"Tibbens, I am sure that breakfast will be fine. What harm can be done to scrambled eggs and a rasher of bacon?"

"All right, but promise to tell me if there's a complete breakdown of standards."

The welcome banquet was a great success. Mother was happy and relaxed.

"Willie, it's time I show you the property. I've tried to make a nice little farm here. See for yourself."

They all walked to the shed, grandpa, Albert, Uncle Willie, George, Sally and Ben.

"This is Bessie, and here is Diego, and these scratchers in the dirt are all named 'Sunday'." Albert was proud of his animals. Uncle Willie said that in his twenty-five years in India, he'd seen a few cows, and their names were Scrawny, Lazy, and Dopey.

"We decided not to drink the milk," father said, "but now and then we make cottage cheese and butter. I've even made some soap. Still, the quality is lacking, no doubt due to Diego's wretched odor. I would build a separate shed, but just for one goat? I may sell Diego in the end."

Sally begged him to sell Diego right away. "That's a disgusting animal," she said. "I mean, it eats cigarettes!"

"Now over here is the beehive, which is getting nicely established. We'll have honey soon. I'm trying to keep the bees happy so they won't swarm."

"Uncle Willie," Ben said, "up on the hill we play baseball. Do you like baseball?"

"I don't know much about the game. I've heard about Joe DiMaggio and Bob Feller. That's a start."

Grandpa was interested in the large pit used for disposing cans and bottles. He said that the pit would be called a kitchen midden by archaeologists, but this is 1951, so why not have a trash truck take it all away?

Sally seconded that idea, especially before they sell the house so they can move to Shadyside. The site was pretty ugly, she said.

Grandma said, "Albert, you said nothing about moving away. When did you decide this? Is our visit holding you back? Willie, did you know the family was preparing to move?"

Albert said that he and mother have discussed moving, but with animals and three acres of land, it would be hard to find a buyer.

"Land is sacred," Grandpa said, and Uncle Willie agreed. "Land is wealth, power, and position," Grandpa said. "Think twice on this."

He then said that he played King Lear in medical school. He stooped, scratched his mustache, and pretended to be blind. "Oh," he cried, "daughters mine, take not my land from me. Let the rain fall like tears on my cursed head. Cordelia, dear Cordelia, I have wronged you, alas . . . ."

"You haven't lost your touch, Dad, but if Shakespeare could hear you, he would be in tears!" Uncle Willie had a way of teasing him.

"Oh Fool," Lear said to Uncle Willie, "I would have your tongue if you were not such a beloved rogue!"

Sally said something about an opera she heard on the radio about King Lear, and George said he never heard of King Lear.

"If you paid more attention at school," she said, "And brought your books home, you might know a few things. Wait until the nuns get hold of you!"

"Nuns for you," said Uncle Willie, "But try cutting corners with Benedictine monks. Isn't that right, Albert? If you didn't study, you had your ears boxed, or worse, a whipping."

Uncle Willie and Albert were sent to England when they were eight and six to a Benedictine abbey not far from London. They stayed until they completed their studies. Their parents made brief summer visits.

Uncle Willie said that some of their teachers filled the boys' souls with the fear of God. But today, discipline is out the window along with the bath water.

Albert said that he was a successful cross-country runner, but that he was always looking over his shoulder for a distempered monk waving his cane.

"Oh, well, hrumph, one hears such stories, but what was I to do with you in British Guiana? Your mother and I agreed that a good education in England was our only choice for you. Just be happy we could afford to send you. You turned out all right, if I may say."

They had returned to the beehive on their way back to the house. Grandpa put his nose close to the little opening. He was fearless. He knew about sharp objects, of course. With his fedora he waved a few bees away.

"Are you sure these are bees, Albert? They seem awfully docile."

"Be careful, Dad, we don't want to have to call a doctor."

"I am a doctor, remember. Many are the splinters I coaxed from your skin."

Grandpa then made a sudden movement back from the hive.

"What the . . . . There's something coming up my leg. Quick, slap my leg right here, no here, no here . . . . It must be a bee that's attacking me. Oh, bollocks!"

He jumped up and down. Uncle Willie and Albert were slapping his legs with their fedoras.

"Did we get it, did we get it?" they cried.

"Get what?" said grandpa, standing in a relaxed pose, one foot ahead of the other, his fedora pushed back, Oscar-Wilde-like.

Uncle Willie laughed, and so did Albert. Had they forgotten what a tease the old actor was? Does anyone really change with age?

"Now I must caution you," grandpa said, looking at Ben, "because one of us seems to like sharp-pointed objects a little too much."

The wonderful moment ended with a scolding voice: "Old Man, act your age, please. You'll wake the devil!" Then she gave a throaty laugh and asked, "Is he up to his old tricks again? Shame, shame. Cecilia said one more Irish whiskey before she locks it up so the children can't get to it. Anyone, anyone?"

Looking over grandma's shoulder, mother was beaming. Now nothing could go wrong. Ben smiled and read that in her eyes.

"Anyone?" she asked.

Sally said that since she was so young, she would gladly wait for her turn. "Just a thimbleful," she said.

"Me too," chimed George. "Just a wee drop, OK?"

The table still held delicacies. Uncle Willie liked the tea sandwiches. He held a little triangle of minced ham and olives. "The crust seems to have gone another direction," he said, laughing. Then he poured tea and sat on the sofa, obviously happy with this visit.

"Dad," he said, "tomorrow let's talk about your plans for retirement. You and Tibbens seem to move around a bit. Searching for your Shang-ri La?"

"If we can stop aging in St. Petersburg, then that will be our Shang-ri La."

On a more serious note, Albert asked his brother whether India had lost its splendor after the British gave up their hold on the country.

"Yes, I'm afraid so, but we saw it coming years and years ago. That Orwell fellow knew what he was talking about. I was among the last of the colonials when I retired, and not a day too soon."

Grandpa said that leaving India would have been much more difficult, no doubt, if Willie had had a wife and family. Uncle Willie was silent.

"You do get my point, don't you, Willie? Or, was there a wife and family stashed away?" he asked in a jovial way.

Willie frowned. "It all depends on what you mean by 'wife and family'. Yes, there were a few connections during my stay there, but I made no proposals and received none." He showed them his ringless fingers. "Perhaps it was a mistake not to have been more solidly grounded."

Grandma and mother disguised their shock by asking Uncle Willie if he would like another tea sandwich. Mother was sure she could find one with crust.

In the silence surrounding them, mother made one last offer. "Would *anyone* like a little something more? She looked at Sally and George. *"Anyone?"*

Oh, Where Have You Been, Charming Billy?

Uncle Willie returned to the "bungalow" after his first night at the Culmerville Hotel. "Quite all right," he said.

"And the breakfast bacon, eggs, and tea?" his Tibbens asked.

"Nicely done."

Grandma smiled in approval, but frowned when he began again.

"The tea, however, was a bit too much on the American side, if you know what I mean, but I imagine that is to be expected in America!" He laughed.

Cecilia, probably wondering whether his kind criticism applied to her serving Salada tea, offered to learn how to make traditional Indian-British tea, that is, Anglo-Indian tea.

"Well, to be frank, the secret is to have someone make the tea for you, isn't that right, Tibbens?"

"That's usually true," she answered, "but not everyone has cooks and houseboys fussing around."

Grandpa entered the discussion. "Humph, so you may know that the issue isn't always how to make tea. Rather, the issue is first acquiring excellent tea. Americans are so often hurried that they settle for less than the ideal. After all," he laughed, "weren't the Americans capable of brewing their tea in the Boston Harbor?"

"Did all of your bags arrive at the hotel safely," Cecilia asked?

"Indeed. I haven't counted them, if that's what you mean."

"Just to be on the safe side . . . ." Cecilia's concern drifted off like the cigarette smoke above grandma's head.

Ben would not have heard this adult conversation if school had not been cancelled in the last week. He sensed something of a geography lesson in the remarks. If school were still going on, perhaps Uncle Willie would come to class and talk about India.

George and Sally were outside playing Robin Hood. He could hear the clashing of wooden swords on garbage can lids. He wondered whether the adults at the dining room table assumed that he was outside with the Sherwood Foresters, for, surprisingly, the conversation turned to something that had been delayed since yesterday.

"So, Willie, you had quite a life in dusty old India for twenty-five years, give or take your long holidays in England and the States. I know from my medical practice in British Guiana that colonials don't always fit in with the natives. We joined clubs, had socials, dances, and the like, and attended what were commonly called "white" churches—it didn't seem to matter which brand of religion. Did you have the same situation in India?"

Uncle Willie was silent for a few seconds. Rather than talk to discover his thoughts, he thought first, unlike Americans, who were a gabby sort. To be polite, in America, listeners discounted the first few sentences, until there was a deep breath and the real speech began. Holding anyone to the first sentence or two was probably unkind, since the speaker would often say in a peeved tone, when challenged, "That is not what I meant at all!"

Pausing to light a cigarette, which was itself a little ritual, with eyes turned up, along with the chin, as the first puff was released into the air, Uncle Willie settled into his answer. He slowly shook out the match and ended the ritual. Ben listened to Sally and George slashing each other below the window. Sally was always Robin Hood. She could be bossy.

"You've read my many letters, I believe, so you know of the various episodes I've relayed about the rainy seasons, the flooding, the famines, and the long dusty spells. There were the local clashes of these people and those people, over nothing of course, while we sat behind our walls in courtyards arguing the benefits of this gin over that gin. Occasionally one of us would climb on a chair and look over the wall for a report.

When we heard that the argument had been settled, and the opposing forces had disbanded, we knew it would be safe to go to the club for dinner, a dance, and cards."

"We know that procession, don't we, Old Man?"

"What was that song I used to sing? It was original, too." Grandpa tapped the table searching for a particular beat. "I drink the gin for the tonic within/ To calm the stomach once more/ And then play gin rummy/ And while I count cards/ The houseboy chimes in/ 'And how, sir, do you feel in the tummy'?"

"I like the houseboy's cheek," Cecilia said.

"Well, they were indispensable, and they knew it. A likeable sort."

"So," Albert said, "I imagine there were some lady friends. You did mention dancing."

"Why, yes. I imagine you want me to begin at the top of the list of female companions and dismiss the rest. All right. There was a very nice young lady who really didn't belong with the group. She was single, which might have been a sign, as they say, that something was 'up.' Since I was single, and still am, I spent some time getting to know Lydia's background, her reason for being in India, and so on. A very nice girl. Went to church. Had a soft voice. Smiled at my jokes. Could scramble an egg or two. Popular with the other gents. I was cautioned by the minister's wife to be careful in matters of the heart. Count my cards, heh? I thought I was. To quote Mr. Dickens, 'in short,' Lydia said that she was 'expecting'."

Grandpa murmured something about medical terminology.

"Well," Uncle Willie continued, "that was that. There was a boy she named Billy."

Cecilia ran her hand through Ben's thick hair and whispered that three was the best number for Robin Hood.

Making Pie

Ben was not yet out the door when he heard grandpa say, "Isn't this what life's all about?"

Uncle Willie replied, "Yes, I'm sure, but you see I can't be certain, you know. In that sense, life is about mystery, isn't it? There are no easy formulas."

As he couldn't drag his heels any slower, he turned and ran down the steps to Sally and George. He offered to be Little John.

"You're too late," Robin Hood said. "But you can be King John or the sheriff, and then we'll have to knock you around a little. Is that all right with you?"

"I'd rather be King Richard the Lion Hearted."

"Can't, he's still a prisoner somewhere in Europe."

"I'm tired of playing," George said. "What's there to eat?"

"Right now, there's nothing," he said. "We have to stay outside."

"But I'm hungry. Is there any pie in the house?"

"Lunch will be a little late, I think. There's some serious talk inside."

"What about?" Sally always needed to know everything.

"I think it's about the mystery of life. You know, big people talk. Boring."

"I wish I was still in school," Sally said.

"Not me," George said, his garbage can lid poised above his head.

"Anything would be better than this boring stuff. Nothing ever happens here. It's all talk, talk, talk!"

"Grandpa sang a silly song for us. That was fun. Want to hear it?"

"No. You'll mess it up like you always do."

"What was it about?" George asked.

"Something about British Guiana. People were drinking gin and playing cards. There was this procession."

Ben said he liked that song about looking over a four-leaf clover that he overlooked before.

Sally said, "Nuts. My favorite song is 'Smoke Gets in Your Eyes'." She began to sing it in a loud voice.

A voice from the kitchen door said, "Children, don't murder a wonderful song. Come in for lunch. Sorry, but the singing waiter's on vacation."

George was up the steps in one jump. His garbage can lid rattled down the steps and turned in a noisy circle before it settled down. "I want some pie," he shouted. "any kind of pie."

Uncle Willie laughed. "I promised you pie, didn't I? Well, after lunch we shall have pie!"

"Yippee!" George sang out.

"I had potato pie once," Ben said, looking around for approval.

Cecilia said, almost apologetically, "I've never made potato pie."

"It was at a friend's house in Bairdford on that cold day, remember?"

"Yes, but you said nothing about potato pie. Is this an episode from your other life, your secret life?" She laughed when Ben looked a little hurt.

Uncle Willie asked, "What was in that pie?"

"Potatoes, some onions, and some cheese, too. And maybe some milk. I liked the crust on top. It was great."

"Well," Cecilia added, "I'll have to consult my brand new *Betty Crocker* recipe book and see if I can top that! Now," she concluded, "you must wash your hands very well. You've been playing with a garbage can, so scrub with the Lava soap."

They all had little sandwiches and some fruit—apples and pears. Grandpa said he was walking to the Clover Leaf store for some Evervess, but he would return soon.

They looked at Uncle Willie after the table had been cleared. "Pie," Sally said.

"Yes, indeed," Uncle Willie said, and then he asked Cecilia if she had a cloth tape measure he could borrow.

She found one at the bottom of her sewing basket. "Will this do?"

"Eloquently," he replied. "Euclid thanks you. Right you are!" he said. "We shall have to make a large pie."

George looked perplexed, but Sally, always sharp, began to smile. "I know what you're doing," she told Uncle Willie.

"All right, so help me. George, Ben, watch carefully so that soon you will be able to make your own pie."

Sally held the metal tip of the tape while Uncle Willie put the roll of tape in George's hand.

"Carefully, now, George, your job is to take the tape around the table edge, we'll call that the pie crimp. When you meet Sally, she'll make a note of the reading, but, Sally, don't tell us what it is."

After dropping the tape twice, George began moving around the table. He closed his eyes while Sally wrote down the number.

"Excellent, Mr. George Washington. Outstanding."

"What's the big deal, anyway? Who cares?"

"Well, Mr. Washington, I'm surprised. Weren't you a surveyor as a young man? That would be after you cut down the cherry pie tree, or was it an apple pie tree? Thanks to you and others like you, out there splashing across brooks and sloshing through the mud, you were able to measure farms. You see, colonial Americans were fanatical about property, about possessions. 'Tell me what's mine' they cried. 'Is farmer Smith stealing my land'? Surveyors were trusted with the truth. Their word was final. They strung chains, which they measured in rods. A rod is sixteen and one-half feet. This is all about geometry, angles, shapes, and so on. So, what's the circumference of the table?"

"Uncle Willie," Sally lectured, "George doesn't pay attention at school, and he hasn't had any geometry yet. That's next year, if he's promoted."

"I *was* promoted," he cried. "I'm not a dummy."

"You have to know the formula," she said. "Do you want to know what it is?"

"I asked for pie an hour ago. So far, nothing."

Grandma, mother, and Albert looked on, smiling broadly.

"I wish grandpa could see this," mother said.

"First we find the diameter of the table. We have to run a straight line through the exact center of the table, which we'll call C, for center. We do some cross checking and where the lines cross, we have C. Hold your finger there, George. What is the diameter?"

"It's fifty inches."

Uncle Willie asked for a pencil and paper. "All right, George, multiply fifty inches by . . . ." he said, looking at Sally.

"By 3.14."

"What's 3.14?" George asked.

Sally beamed, "It's ϖ—that's the Greek letter for *p*."

George wet the pencil tip, just like Gary Cooper did in a movie he saw. He scratched his head.

"I get 157 inches, but it's probably wrong."

"Perhaps, so let's check. Let's measure the circumference with the tape again."

"It's 157 inches. Is that your secret number, Sally?"

She handed George the paper on which she had written 157.

"And so," Uncle Willie wrapped up, "If you know the diameter of a circle and multiply that number by 3.14, you find the circumference.

The screen door opened quietly. Grandpa huffed and puffed. "Did I return in the nick of time?"

"Yes, Dad, you did."

Grandpa reached into a brown bag and pulled out three lunch-sized pies sealed in wax paper. "There you are, children, you have your pie."

There was a round of applause for Uncle Willie and grandpa, too. A man of the theater, he bowed.

"A fine job of making pie, Mr. George Washington," grandma said and patted George on the back.

Uncle Willie said that in life we must always know our circumferences. Was there a life's lesson there, or did he make a pun on *circumstances*? Actually, the words are the same, aren't they? Or nearly so.

Breakfast with Uncle Willie

It was Ben's turn to be driven to the Culmerville Hotel early in the morning to have breakfast with Uncle Willie. When Cecilia and grandma had breakfast with him, they were driven to the hotel by Albert, and then back home around noon, with Uncle Willie, of course. This time, however, Albert had to go to his studio to retouch wedding negatives, a tedious job involving a fine-pointed pencil that darkened the tiny, clear dots that appear on the negative, the result of dust. "So," he said, "you and Willie will come home on the Culmerville bus. Someone at the hotel will drive you to the station. This should be a pleasant adventure."

Mother cautioned him to mind his manners. "Use the napkin properly; say 'please' and 'thank you.' Watch how Uncle Willie, the continental gentleman, holds his knife and fork. The fork will be in his left hand with the tines turned down, and the knife will be used to push food onto the back of the fork. It's an engineering feat. It's fun. But don't try it. You might hurt yourself."

Father also cautioned him. "Please, no slurping, no chewing with your mouth open, no chugging marathon drinking milk—just a sip now and then. Have something to say so he'll get to know you better. And don't ply him with questions. Leave question marks at home. You understand, of course."

Uncle Willie met them in the lobby of the hotel. He understood about the bus they would need to take. "We won't have to sit on the roof, will we, as riders do in Delhi?" he joked.

"After breakfast, I'll show you my room and show you how to tie a tie properly. Quite a plain room, but adequate. Well, I guess I could say the same thing about English breakfasts, couldn't I?" He laughed. "But we'll do better than that, I'm sure. I know how young boys love to eat."

They sat by the window, which could be distracting. Was this a test of his powers of attention? He promised himself that he would not look out the window. That would be bad manners.

"I already know the menu by heart, but you have a look and find some things you like. The eggs are good, and so are the pancakes and bacon. Orange juice is freshly squeezed, with nice pulp. The British love oranges, especially in marmalade, so, if you like toast there'll always be marmalade; it's as eternal as Gibraltar. Now, here's Mabel. You'll like her. She tells me her name means 'lovable'."

"So, this is the youngest one," Mabel said. "Your uncle is a favorite of ours, so we take care of him. What'll you have, gents?"

Uncle Willie said he'd have the usual.

"Why am I not surprised?" she answered.

"May I please have a small glass of orange juice, scrambled eggs, some bacon, and some toast?"

"Wheat, rye, or Wonder Bread," she replied, with a big grin. "Oh, I need to tell you that the orange juice comes in a nice glass, and it holds whatever the orange can afford. Maybe two oranges this morning?"

"OK, sure. Thanks," he replied, hoping he made the right answer.

Uncle Willie laughed, lit a cigarette, and promised Mabel that Ben would eat everything she brought, and then some, because he wanted to end the meal with cherry pie, which he ordered for Ben.

"Real pie or that Greek pie?"

"The real McCoy, sweet and tart," Uncle Willie answered.

"You're a big one, aren't 'cha?" Mabel chided him. "Gonna be a football player, huh?"

"In time he will achieve his natural height despite what the Culmerville Hotel feeds him!"

Mabel laughed. "You Brits are priceless, wonderful. Long live the king!"

"By king, she means George VI. She's a teaser, isn't she?" Uncle Willie observed. "It's a nice way to start the day. Takes the starch out of your shirt. We Brits have a heavy load to carry, thanks to movies with Cary Grant and a few other exports to Hollywood. Speaking of which, I'm sure you enjoy grandpa's humor. He grew up in the days of music halls in England. I wonder that he finished his medical studies. A funny thing, come to think of it, I'm only now appreciating his humorous ways. You see, I left my parents very early and went to England to study. So did your father. As I look back, if you'll allow me to meander—how do you like the orange juice, by the way?—I would have liked a better sense of family. You are lucky, you know, having a brother and a sister and two fine parents."

"I guess so," he said, "but I never stopped to think about it. I guess I thought everyone else was lucky. There's a girl at school. Her name is Annie. She lives with her mom and dad and grandma and grandpa. I guess she's lucky, too."

Meditative Uncle Willie nodded his head. "Lucky, indeed!"

He took a deep breath and began: "I have a big decision to make, you know, what with retirement and all. Should I live in St. Petersburg, or should I return to India? India is a beautiful place. I already miss it. No, let me get this right. Yes, I miss India, but I especially miss a young boy I've grown very fond of, very attached to. He's just about your age. Nice chap. Name's Billy."

"Does he go to school?"

"Of course. Dominican nuns have a school nearby. Dominican nuns are everywhere in India, like . . . like . . . ."

He lifted the shakers on the table.

"Like salt and pepper!"

"Does he like sports?"

"Yes. He likes cricket. He's quite good, too."

He lit another cigarette and set it in the ashtray. Their breakfasts arrived. Mabel had Ben's breakfast up her left arm and Uncle Willie's up her right arm. A pot dangled from her finger. "Here you go gents. Take your time. The bus won't leave without you. Here's a coffee pot, Your Majesty. Just whistle if you'd like more."

"Mabel, where's your tray today?"

"I like to keep in practice," she said, sorting out the breakfasts from her serving arms. "Plates are just a little hot. Ouch, ouch," she said, laughing at her own performance. She saluted them and left.

"Promise not to tell grandma that I like coffee for breakfast, will you?"

He swore secrecy. "I like coffee, too," he said, "but mother said coffee will stunt my growth."

"Well," he said, as he snatched a cup from the next table, "just have a sip and I'll watch you shrink. What do you say to that?"

He poured him half of a cup and nudged the sugar bowl toward him. "You look like a sugar boy."

"OK," he said. "This is good coffee."

Mabel watched him. "You bet it's good, young man. It's straight from Maxwell's house, know what I mean?" She laughed, saluted again, and left.

"It must be fun growing up in India," he said, and then he told him about his geography class.

"I guess so, but India is so large that there are many Indias. While one part suffers from famine and another part from flooding, another part fights across the border over who owns this beautiful land. And languages change every so often, and dialects change every few miles. But the people are so full of music, dance, and bright colors, and they have delicious spices they sprinkle like magic dust on fish and chicken dinners. And so many religions, superstitions, and stories about ghosts coming back to haunt their houses or their families. Families are sacred. Weddings are enormous affairs. But there's so much poverty and disease. Every day there are funerals. So, I guess you could say, all thing's considered, the bad and the good, that it's fun growing up in India, but only if you aren't poor, and only if you have an extended family. Customs are very important in India. My fear is that Billy, the youngster your age, will not have a real family without a father, without a man's influence. I know I missed my father when I was in the abbey not very far from London. I really feel it now, more so than then, probably, but feelings are feelings."

Then Uncle Willie sized up his breakfast plate of eggs and bacon, turned his fork over in his left hand, and with his knife plowed a section of scrambled eggs onto the fork. Without looking, he raised it to his mouth.

Ben hardly remembered eating. He had another splash of coffee. He tried to think of something interesting and had to avoid questions, especially the dumb ones, like "how long are you going to stay?"

Uncle Willie turned and looked out the window. It was his privilege to do so.

"There's a rustic beauty in America, especially here. It reminds me of the north of England, which, I must confess, is a rather dreadful place. Industrial, ironworks, smoke, and contrary weather. Still, I like it. Odd."

They had pie for dessert, if dessert is the correct word after breakfast.

"Pie makes the coffee go down just right, don't you think?" He laughed at his own humor.

Mabel came over to their table and surveyed the plates. "I'd say you gents had a good breakfast. Now's the time for the bus, so I've asked Tony Joe, our man of all tasks, to drive you to the station. So, who's coming to breakfast with you tomorrow? The Queen Mum?"

"In a way, yes. My niece, Sally, could fill that role nicely. We'll pop up to my room in a jiffy for my tie, and then we'll be off. Righto!"

They returned promptly to the lobby.

The hotel staff said "Cheerio" in unison. Uncle Willie gave a V for Victory sign, and then they were off in the wooden station wagon bound for the station.

"Why is he named Tony Joe?"

"Mabel, who knows everything in this hotel, told me that his mother wanted to name him Anthony, and his father wanted to name him Joseph, which, by the way, is my middle name. So they gave him both names, Anthony Joseph, but mother called him Tony and father called him Joe. So, to keep the peace, they call him both names. I sense some pride in their decision, for their son was too big in their lives for just one name. Perhaps."

He didn't ask another question, remembering his father's caution, so he just said, "But you call grandma Tibbens."

He understood the unstated question. "Oddly enough, I cannot remember when I started calling her Tibbens. I'm sure I had a reason. Why not ask her when it started?"

While the station wagon was on its way to the station, he sensed that Uncle Willie had something serious to tell him.

"Tell me what you think about my big decision. India or St. Petersburg?"

"Wow" he answered. "I guess India."

"Why, I wonder?"

"To watch Billy, grow up and to take care of him?"

"I like that answer! Yes."

And then he told him about circles.

"People within a circle, in a kind of dance, a family, whether it's large or small, can leave the circle, and so the circle shrinks. On the other hand, new people can enter and the circle grows. The thing is, and this is a constant, you must allow for passage both ways. It's not good to close the circle. The youngster Billy is in the circle, with his mother and me, and lots of classmates. It's not so hard to understand, is it?"

"I don't think so," he answered. "Billy is lucky to have a family."

"Surprising that you should say that. Intuitive, too. Well, it's luck that's hard to understand. Some seem to have it, others don't. But find as much luck as you can in life, and put it in your circle. Do you see what I'm saying?"

"I think so. If you have a circle, luck will be there in the circle."

"And if luck is not there, what are you?"

"I guess you're probably unlucky."

"I see. And if you're unlucky, what are you."

"A little lonely? A little sad?"

"And that's probably not so good, is it?"

"I guess not."

"It's not enough just to be in the circle, luck or no luck. Everyone has to fit in, to belong, to care. Perhaps the hardest of all is fitting in. Perhaps that's where Luck, with a capital L, plays a role."

Uncle Willie called him a budding philosopher. He liked that.

The little bus station was crowded. They got tickets and then sat in the first row of the bus because their trip would be brief. Many passengers were probably going into the city to find bargains in the department stores. At the first stop, people were waiting to get on. An elderly lady, travelling by herself, stood by them, while others tried to pass her towards the rear of the bus.

"Let's do this," Uncle Willie said, "out of consideration for this nice lady. Give her your seat and we'll get moving quickly. You sit on my knee for the short ride."

So he sat on his uncle's lap, but just as he got settled, he saw blonde ringlets coming up the steps of the bus. He knew they were Annie's. He was mortified when she looked right at him and smiled on her way to the rear of the bus. This was his third most embarrassing moment. This was bad luck, he said to himself. Will he ever have good luck?

Had he become for the moment Uncle Willie's Billy, bouncing on his knee in a crowded bus along an expansive, corrugated cow path where Lazy and Dopey munched on dry grass? Or would he have been happier hanging on the bus roof, he wondered, or would that have placed him outside Uncle Willie's circle? Well, red faced as he was, he knew that bouncing on an elder's knee was as old as civilization itself.

The Round Table at Dithridge Street

The little old Pontiac could never carry eight passengers. Three would have to sit on laps. The car would probably scrape the road with so much weight. So, in order for all of them to visit the aunts at Dithridge Street, mother took the children on the Culmerville bus to Pittsburgh, and from there they went by streetcar to the aunts. Their grandparents and Uncle Willie drove in with Albert. They would have a special day. Lunch would be followed by a variety of activities. Sally and Aunty Nellie, who was really a cousin, would walk to the Centre Theater to see *Gone with the Wind*. George and Ben would walk to Forbes Field to see the Pirates play the Cubs. They were promised a dollar for two bleacher seats and another dollar for popcorn and pop. Albert would drive to Squirrel Hill to explore a photography store. This would get him out of the range of the aunts for two hours in what he called his Pax Romana.

Grandpa and grandma remembered some pleasant days visiting Dithridge Street when they lived with Albert and Cecilia for a few weeks in 1941, on the run-down farm in Ruthfred Acres. Old people had a wonderful ability to pick up where they left off, even after ten years had passed. Nothing in the house had changed. There were the heavy curtains through which they passed into the library and into the music room. The dark curtains were made from theater curtain material: heavy, folded, and hanging from large metal rings. After passing through one set of curtains, there was another set through which entry into the rooms was made. The children loved hiding in the dark space between curtains, with their musty and dusty fragrance.

Grandpa admired the small library of books kept perpetually fresh and young behind beveled glass doors. The illustrated Irish fairy tales were among his favorites. He read them out loud while alone in the library, dramatic readings, with hearty laughter and comments such as "you rogue, you," and "you would be jailed today, my friend, for that misadventure!" "These illustrations are priceless."

Since the pocket doors separating the library from the music room were rarely opened, grandma chided him through the closed door in a high-pitched voice: "Do you believe everything in a book of fairy tales? Is life always lived on a stage?" Between her words she was really saying, *Will you be quiet, please? My, that's a noisy book, isn't it? Some of us want to listen to Herr Wagner's* Ring *on these old records. Some of us believe that Herr Wagner started World War Two when real people suffered greatly because of a German fairy tale.* Ben wound up the old Victrola and put on a record. It didn't matter where it was in the *Ring,* since the lyrics were in German. Grandma went on: "It's just as well that I don't understand German, since the story is so ridiculous. There's one woman named Something -*hilde* and another one named Something-*hilde*. How could you tell them apart? And dwarfs! I've never met one. But the music is sublime, and I wager that on every record I'll find that wonderful music. That's all I want. And I don't mean to start a war." The music began soulfully, rising to blissful levels where even the scratches in the recordings were memorable. "I'll just put my head back," grandma said. "Just for a minute, you understand." He tiptoed out through the heavy double curtains guarding the music room.

Uncle Willie was very fond of Aunt Frances and Aunt Alice. They were charmed by him. They sometimes teased him just for his reaction. Aunt Frances, to whom Ben gave the name Aunty Gooden when he was about two, and Aunt Alice, to whom Sally gave the name Aunty Alwa when she was a precocious one-year old, were ironic, droll, and sometimes shocking. Aunt Helen, to whom Sally gave the name Aunty N., was very formal, very scholarly. Aunt Mary's name was never altered, except when she married Harry in 1910. As the senior sister, she, too, was formal, and they all were raised in the late Victorian era.

All of them, and their youngest sister, Cecilia, sat at the dining room table, which had a large circumference. But the circle was lost when leaves were installed for major dinners.

Alice and Frances made their dresses from the same simple patterns. Only the fabric designs changed over the years. They were not twins, and they never dressed as twins. Remnants of fabrics were saved to be twisted and sewn into floor coverings next to beds. Mary and Helen wore tailored clothes that were well-preserved over the years. Blues and purples were dominant.

Grandpa and grandma, after declaring a pleasant truce in the skirmish between written fairy tales and lofty musical ones, came laughing into the dining room to join them for sandwiches, cold salad, and a large round cake. Willie praised the Rolling Rock beer. Mother had a small glass of whiskey with soda and ice. The aunts were up and down from the table bringing in more treats to tempt them with. Sally liked the Wagner music grandma was playing and said she can't wait to wind up the record player and hear passages from her recording of *Salome* on the *big* machine.

"Any time," Aunt Frances said, pulling tobacco from the tip of her tongue. She laughed at the picture of Sally following the music and discovering the gory scenes. "You do know, don't you, that Salome, after John the Baptist loses his head, actually kisses him on the lips? Ugh! How does it go? 'I have kissed your lips, Jokanaan,' or some name like that. Of course, it's all in German, which makes the violence OK. All nonsense, if you ask me."

"Sadistic, but true," grandpa observed, "But in the name of high art."

Aunt Helen, the scholar and specialist in Latin and Greek, said that German is the language of science, first of all, and glorious music, thanks to Mozart, Wagner, Bach, Brahms, and especially Beethoven, "Papa's favorite."

"Willie," Aunt Frances asked, "which language do they speak in India? Hindi?"

"Yes, and dozens more, not to mention English, of course, which the natives tend to sing more than pronounce. I've actually had to ask for a translation of my manager's English into English, believe it or not!"

"Willie," Frances asked cautiously, "do you plan to return to

India for, let's say," she paused and looked at Sally, George, and Ben, "domestic reasons?"

"Look at the clock, children. It's time you were off for baseball and the Civil War." Mother reached for her purse to find the boys a couple of dollars, and Aunty Nellie, who said very little, motioned to Sally—time to go.

Uncle Willie seems to have said something merry at the table, for laughter followed them down the hallway to the side door.

"Are you sure you won't come with us to see *Gone with the Wind*?" Aunty Nellie teased.

"I kinda think they won't," Sally said, her nose squished, "as there ain't no cowpokes init, isn' that right boys?"

Their walk to Forbes Field took them down Bellefield Avenue, across Fifth Avenue, through the campus of Pitt, past the Stephen Foster Memorial, and across Forbes Avenue. They got bleacher seats in left field where Ralph Kiner played. The Chicago Cubs were a good team. There was little doubt about the outcome of the game. The greatest hope among the fans was that Kiner would get a good pitch. He was walked so many times, and, either in frustration or out of natural ability, he struck out often. The outfield wall had been brought in thirty feet ostensibly to make room for a bullpen, but fans suspected it was done to give Kiner a better chance at home runs. Chicago got ahead quickly. The Pirates went three-up and three-down, inning after inning. There was one double play, which was exciting, but that was about all. The Cubs were just better. Without really trying very hard, the Cubs were all over the bases. The crowd thinned out after the seventh inning stretch. When the game ended, Ralph Kiner had had a perfect game—four walks. Still, it was great seeing the big man so close to them in left field. Occasionally, he looked into the bleachers and smiled. Ben smiled back, fan-to-fan.

On their way back to Dithridge, George began to wonder about Uncle Willie. "What's going on?"

"He's wants to do the right thing. Should he go back to India and be like a dad to Billy, or should he go to Florida to be a help to his parents? What would you do if you were Uncle Willie? I think he's a man in the middle."

"I guess I'd go back to India, at least for a couple of years." George was asking more than saying.

George was getting a little angry. "Do you know what Sally said? She said he *had* to go back to India and do what's right for Billy, including putting him in the best schools."

Ben was surprised by his reaction to what Sally said to George. "But why should he *have* to go? It's his choice. OK, he met a nice lady there, and they danced. And then he met the lady's son, and he gets to like the son a lot. Maybe he felt sorry for them, maybe he just wanted to do something good for them, sort of like adopting them. Know what I mean?"

George stopped. He must have counted to three to figure what to say next. And then he said: "Look, Ben, I don't know how to break this to you, but Billy is Uncle Willie's son. Didn't you know?"

"Well," he tried to say something. "OK, I didn't know. So Billy's our cousin, is that right?"

"He must be," George answered. "And he's Dad's nephew. Dad is Uncle Albert now. We need to talk to mother."

They went around to Webster Hall to get a candy bar, which they promised to share, but Ben really wasn't that interested after all.

At Dithridge, they rang twice, the signal that they were home. Cecilia opened the door. She was smiling. "Guess what, the three of you are staying overnight with me. Dad will come for us at ten tomorrow morning. He's got to get home to the cow and the bees, and who knows what else. Uncle Willie and your grandparents are driving back with your father. So, it's just the four of us for now. How do you like *that*?"

Dinner was what was left from lunch. There had been the large cake, too, and almost all of it was left for them. Ben drew a diameter through the icing with a toothpick, guessed the distance, and multiplied by 3.14. He judged the circumference of the cake to be thirty-four inches. Divided by three kids, four aunts, Cecilia, and Aunty Nellie, they each had nearly a four-inch wedge waiting, each roughly the shape of India, give or take Ceylon.

—for Sylvia Francis

Neither Beavers nor Falls

Uncle Willie's stay with them was coming to an end. Plans for his entertainment and enlightenment were trimmed somewhat, which he did not mind. There was no day trip to Niagara Falls after all. Instead, he drove with Albert to a place called Beaver Falls, where picture proofs had to be delivered to a new bride and groom. There was a lot of history in Beaver Falls, which Uncle Willie thought he would enjoy. There were episodes of Indian exploits, sites of British and French skirmishes, and industrial bravado winding down after the recent war. Then rust settled in. And the Beaver River, with its thickly wooded banks, might be entertaining. However, the real reason for Uncle Willie's accompanying Albert was to work out the details of either moving to St. Petersburg or returning to India to take up his role as protector and perhaps as Billy's dad. Ben knew this because he had heard the adult conversations the day before, conversations they could now hear if they wanted to.

Mother believed that now Uncle Willie was the man in the middle. He was being pulled back to India and he was being pulled to St. Petersburg, where his parents would probably settle for some part of their retirement, until the itch to move again might take them back to British Guiana, or to the south of England. As a single man, he could help his aging parents settle in, and he could stay nearby and live privately, but be on call when need arose. Mother divulged information that the children had not imagined. "You know," she said, "when a man wants to be present in the life of his son to help him grow into a responsible person, no one should stand in his way. Lydia would love for him to return. But there's a problem that can't be solved, a sad problem." She paused, looking for words to help them understand.

Sally said that she thought she understood. "How does Uncle Willie know for sure that he's Billy's father?"

"Oh my," mother said, half-proud and half-shocked at Sally's perception. "You really do follow those opera librettos, don't you?" She laughed. "Everyone loves a mystery, I'm sure, but in life, real life, mysteries can be downright nasty."

"How can he know that Billy's his son?" Sally wondered. "I mean, Billy's eleven, isn't he? Isn't it a little late to be asking that question?"

"I'll try to explain," mother said. "Sit on the sofa and we'll see if we can sort this out. Now, we know that doctors can perform tests by taking blood samples from mother and dad. And then the blood types are matched to see if the couple could be the child's parents. I don't know all of the facts, but I remember a soap opera—oh my, operas again—about doctors solving this identical problem for a young couple. Oddly, I think the program was *Just Plain Bill*. But I'm not sure. Suppose, though, that the doctor says the blood types aren't the ones that would have produced the child's blood type. Then the truth would be that the 'father' of the child could not be the real father of the child. Do you follow me? But, if the blood types are a perfect match, then it would appear that the father of the child could be identified. But suppose two or three men with the same blood type were friends of the woman with the child. How could the doctor know which man was really the father?"

"Couldn't they just take turns being the father?" George wondered. "I mean, I heard about famous movie stars who get married two or three times. Don't they take turns being the father or the mother?"

Sally said that was a silly idea.

"Not entirely," mother said. "You have the right idea. The children could have real fathers and adoptive fathers. Your Uncle Herbert and Aunt Agnes in Texas, adopted a little boy they named Tommy. Remember? When he grows out of his clothes, Aunt Agnes sends them to us, and you wear them to school." She smiled. "I guess you adopted Tommy's clothes!"

"So Uncle Willie could adopt Billy?" he asked.

"Yes. He's thought of doing just that."

"And couldn't he have a blood test to find out if he's . . . ."

Mother broke in to say that it was possible, but what if the test proved that Uncle Willie could *not* be Billy's real father? "He would be devastated by such news, of course, but his feelings would still be there, wouldn't they?"

"So which is better," Sally asked, "to know the truth that he's not the father, or to be a dad to Billy without having proof that he is his father?"

"Honey, your Uncle Willie has tossed and turned many nights trying to understand, hoping to learn what he must do." She paused, unsure about what to say next. But then she asked, "What would you do if you were in his place? What would you advise him to do?"

They all said they would advise him to go back to India.

"I think you may just be right," Cecilia said. "Is it because you're still children that you see things so clearly? Oh, how I envy you."

She opened a drawer and removed a folder containing Billy's picture with his mother, Lydia. "Isn't he a beautiful boy?" she asked. "I would love to bring him here to live with us, but I don't think that will ever happen."

Lydia was a pretty woman with dark hair, and Billy looked a lot like his mother, with thick dark eyebrows and dark eyes. He had a slender build. He looked undernourished.

Sally was the first to speak. "He doesn't look like Uncle Willie."

"Well, of course he's only eleven. His face will change as he gets older. I should show you your baby pictures. You might be surprised! Lydia's parents are Greek and Italian. Your grandma and grandpa are Portuguese. I'm not sure what I'm trying to say. Anyway . . . ."

Sally asked Cecilia if she was still upset that Uncle Willie, grandpa, and grandma came to visit.

"The thought of their coming this summer was very disturbing because my hope was to prepare for a move to the city, to Sacred Heart parish, and I was afraid that it would not happen. But now that they're here, I realize that I love them all very much. And I agonize over Uncle Willie's dilemma. Still, I have to work to sell the house before September and find a house in the city. I wish your father shared my dream. Maybe he does. I feel a kinship with Uncle Willie. He wants to do what's right, and so do I."

Grandma came down the stairs with a fresh cigarette glowing in the shadows. She had been napping, or trying to nap. She looked them over and said, "I was afraid I would miss the soap operas and afternoon tea, because as I lay in bed I was sure I heard a soap opera going on. Except there was no organ music, so I guess I'm in time for *Portia Faces Life.*"

Grandpa came down the stairs, his hat in hand. "I am now on my way to scale Mount Evervess," he said. "Is there a youngster who wishes to accompany me?"

George raised his hand.

Uncle Willie came into the house just in time for tea. He looked tired and worried, but when he saw his mother he cheered up. "Tea, I need some tea," he said. "Tea in a box, tea in a bag, just tea."

Mother asked him how he liked Beaver Falls. He did not hesitate to reply, "There were neither beavers nor falls."

Albert laughed when he came in. "You are correct, Willie. There were neither beavers nor falls. To this sad observation I must add, just having come from the beehive, there are no bees. They have swarmed."

Mother laughed. "Do cows, pigs, goats, and chickens ever swarm? I only ask because everything outside has been very quiet."

"On hot days, cows, pigs, goats, and chickens have been known to sleep. After tea, I'll tiptoe to the shed and then report my findings."

The house became quiet that afternoon, except for the low droning of the soap operas and the murmurs of grandma and mother. Sally disappeared to her room. Ben loafed on the sofa and slowly drifted off to sleep.

To the Rescue

In March, Ben could not have known that the visit of grandparents and Uncle Willie would fill his life with experiences that made ordinary, everyday happenings disappear like dream scenes after awakening: grandparents' snoring in the afternoon and evening; their footsteps in the kitchen by the teapot; their laughter at lunchtime; and their passionate comments during soap operas heard on the old Zenith. Uncle Willie's visits after breakfast at his hotel signaled unexpected events. Nothing was the same. He saw little of BB Bain and the Skipper kid, with his droopy nose and thin mustache—he had been held back at the Bairdford School not because he was dumb but for being in trouble so often that he would miss weeks of classes. He was exciting and surprising, but also a bad influence. He lived far back off the road on a scratch farm on the hill past the starting place for sled riding. Why Bessie struggled up the hill to root in Mrs. Skipper's garden Ben would never know. Maybe she was swarming.

Ben lived in a world of parents and relatives whose actions defined goodness. Uncle Willie's decision to return to India for Lydia and Billy seemed so correct that it was never questioned. At the hotel, he sent what he called a cable to Lydia, a brief message asking, "Are you all right, and do you need anything now, because I am making plans to return soon, and I need to know how you are."

"Well, you know," Willie said with resignation, "there are just some things that have to be done." Grandpa replied, "Yes, yes, so true, imagine not doing what is right—can't imagine that, can you?" Grandma said little, but her eyes were red from crying. Mother put her arm around her shoulders, and said that all would turn out well, that this may just be the right moment for Willie to make that great decision in life that he had postponed for years.

In preparation for Willie's trip, Albert took the family to his studio in Carnegie. He asked a neighbor to drive three of them in his car, but the man said just to take his station wagon for the day. At the studio, the camera was set up, the lights adjusted, and the posing arranged so that they all were included in a group picture for Lydia and Billy. Albert joked when he pressed the delayed release, pretending that he could not get from the camera quickly enough to be captured, was caught on film dashing in a blur and a foolish grin. "Be serious, Albert. Let Groucho Marx play the fool in a pith helmet. We are roasting under these lights," grandma chided him. But in his spirit, they found themselves waving foolishly at the camera, making big welcoming smiles, and generally enjoying themselves. Grandpa, who should have been seated, stood at the side posing like a character he had portrayed in an Oscar Wilde satire. He wore his fedora like a Hollywood gangster. There was a serious picture of grandpa, grandma, Albert, Cecilia, and Uncle Willie, which Ben snapped while wearing Albert's fedora. There would be many copies to be shared.

Uncle Willie returned to the hotel where he hoped to find a message from India waiting for him. He was anxious about the slowness of Lydia's response. But there was no message. After breakfast the next morning, he stayed in his room reading. At noon he inquired about a message, but none had been received.

"Is it possible that Lydia sent an airmail letter, which would be slow coming from such a distance?" Cecilia tried to calm him, but he became more nervous. "I had not expected this," he said.

"You are welcome to stay as long as necessary," she said, "and then some!"

When Uncle Willie returned the next morning, he held a blue airmail letter in his hand. "Lydia wrote me a week ago, but the blasted mail service was slow. I don't have good news, though."

"Can you tell us what's wrong?" grandma asked. "Surely the news can't be all bad."

"The letter is brief, probably written in haste. Billy had the sniffles when I left ten days ago. His nose bled. Doctors examined him, withheld opinions, and did the next best thing, which was to wait to see what Nature's course would be. Then the doctors said they weren't able to make a diagnosis of an underlying illness. More waiting. That's about it. Lydia put off writing, hoping for more cheerful news, but when my cable reached her, she decided to write."

They were quiet for a moment or two, until grandpa spoke. 'It's difficult to say with any certainty. The doctors are correct. However, having seen every tropical disease imaginable, and having puzzled over symptoms like these in our clinic in British Guiana, I have reason to be just a bit alarmed. More than that—suspicious. Since the Partition in India, as it is euphemistically known, many doctors retired early and returned to England or Australia and elsewhere. India was never known to be a center of progressive medicine. I strongly suspect that the doctors who left India took their skills with them, leaving behind a level of medical skill similar to that of the turn of the century. Antibiotics and sulfa are wonders, but they can't cure all illnesses."

Grandma read his commentary with more alarm than Ben imagined, for he never thought of medicine beyond cough syrup and aspirin.

"Look here," she said, "I know something about antiquated medical practice in backward countries, enough to be unkind about it. How often some poor beggar appeared in our courtyard, half-dead from this or that disease. I was something of a practical nurse, wasn't I, removing clotted bandages that had never been changed. And those voodoo practices involving some poor chicken. Horrible."

"The stuff of local fiction, I think, but with more truth than you might imagine," grandpa added.

"So what do we do?" Uncle Willie asked. "I can't just wait for updates. What must be done?"

"I think I know what you'll say next," grandma offered, "and that is to return to India, and, as they say, take charge. Use your influence, and so on. Isn't that correct?"

"Yes, Tibbens. I want to go. I must go back."

Grandma looked with telling insight at grandpa, who slowly moved his head from left to right, pondering the situation. Was he going to lighten the moment with some Oscar Wilde wit or a music hall joke?

"Willie," he said, more serious than anyone had ever heard him speak, "it would be good for you to do that, for reasons such as we have discussed on our walks through the streets of Culmerville. But more than that, and I admire you for your resolve, you must let me accompany you! I'm sure I can help with the medical case, and I can assist Billy for the better, don't you see?"

Grandma slowly nodded her assent, but her eyes filled with tears.

Cecilia, oddly silent but always respectful, said that grandma must remain with the family for as long as it takes Willie to go to India and then return with Lydia and Billy. "Yes, that's what I believe," she said triumphantly.

Albert was caught by surprise. His lips twitch before he said, "Yes, yes, that's true. Very welcome, indeed. The fresh air of our woods will strengthen Billy, and the children will teach him everything he needs to know to fit in. Yes, to fit in!"

Sally looked shocked. George looked to her for help, but she was stage struck—unheard of for Sally.

Grandpa said that a quick flight to New York and a morning at the British embassy were the first considerations. Then flights to Rome and the nearest airport in India. Three days, perhaps less.

Grandma said that they must go to Joseph Horne's for shirts. "You must look like professionals. Americans admire frayed collars, but the embassy staff would not."

Albert left the house in a determined mood. A few minutes later Ben could smell an odd smoke, one that did not signal garbage burning.

Mother brought bottles from the kitchen. She cracked ice in a towel, bringing a meat tenderizer down with strong "thunks."

"We'll begin with a walk to the Clover Farm store, telephone to the city, make arrangements for flights, and pack light bags," grandpa said.

"What's that smell?" grandma asked, annoyed by the interruption.

"Go check," mother said to Ben, a little peeved.

Out by the shed, he saw his father poking high crackling flames spitting sparks amid thick gray smoke. He walked closer. Albert waved him forward.

"Just so you know," he said, "when bees swarm, the hive's probably no good, so it's best to burn it. Smells a little like a church, doesn't it? Do you know why?"

They moved around the smoky fire as the wind changed.

"Well, it smells like Sacred Heart after the altar boy puts out all of those candles."

"Right-o," he said. "Beeswax. Just imagine that we are making an offering to the heavens above. You like that smell, don't you? Someday, maybe you'll put out candles in Sacred Heart Church."

"Ah, I guess so," he answered, cold sweat running down his back. "Gotta go tell mother what's burning."

"I'll be in soon. Did I hear mother cracking ice?"

"She's beating the ice cubes with a hammer. I think she's a little upset."

"So it goes, so it goes. I'll be in soon."

Mother was sad to hear that the hive was burning, but, she said, it was for the best. "The bees weren't really happy here after all, and so they left. There's that old saying, 'You can't go home again.' I guess it's true for bees, too."

"Is there any ice left?" Ben asked.

"Not much. Ice tends to disappear quickly in a crisis. Ices-crisis—she smiled. Well . . . you can use what's left in my glass. There's a drop of smoky Irish whiskey left in it. I wouldn't blame you if you went on a bender."

"But aren't you happy that grandpa and Uncle Willie are going to India to rescue Billy?"

"Yes, of course. I suppose you could say that I am devastatingly happy."

"That's good, isn't it?"

"Yes, yes, yes. All happiness is good in the end. Remember that."

"Maybe Billy will come back with grandpa and Uncle Willie. Would you like that?"

"Yes, yes," she said, wiping a tea spill from the counter, "but everything depends on *back where?*"

Listing Without His Cane

Everything developed so quickly that Ben could not put the fragments together: the burning of the beehive; the drop or two of Irish whiskey; Sally's gloomy face (how she wanted change and then dreaded it when it came); and George's begging that they play Robin Hood. But, as Ben told him, Robin Hood was not herself today and, in fact, no one was very merry in Sherwood Forest. Uncle Willie, Albert, and grandpa walked slowly to the Clover Farm store to make a phone call and drink Everess. Grandpa's stride was theatrical, a main player stepping from the wings into the middle of a major scene. Grandma lamented that the Old Man was reliving his youthful days in medicine, a bad sign, she thought. "I hope they run out of nickels early," grandma said, dreading the phone calls they were to make. "He may have conquered Everess, it's true, but he needs two naps a day and reminders to take his medicine."

Cecilia had recovered from yesterday. Sensing changes in the wind, she said: "Well, I understand Willie's returning to India, which was his decision days ago. But granddad's volunteering to accompany him seems like a rash decision. Don't you agree, children?"

Ben didn't think mother saw them on the sofa, patiently waiting for inspiration to do something other than sit on the sofa. Sally edged her pointing finger toward the cover of an Oz book, and George looked longingly at the old Zenith radio, which he often played with because it was a powerful radio once upon a time and could pick up ships' broadcasts and programs from around the world. He claimed to have listened to radio talk on a battleship. "What did they say?" Ben asked, but George dodged the question by saying that the men were talking in a foreign language, like German, for instance.

Cecilia observed that it's quite unlikely Germany still had battleships. "Remember the war," she said. "Their ships are at the bottom of the sea, right?"

Sally said that George was listening to ghost talk. "Brrrr," she said.

"Why do their ships have to be sunk?" George wanted to know. "They could be used as museums, couldn't they?"

"I imagine so, but the privilege of deciding what's a museum belongs to the victors. *Our* ships become museums."

Ben asked, "Do you remember that big ship we saw in Pittsburgh a few weeks after my birthday about five years ago? Bigger than a whale. We went in October, I remember, because the trees under Mt. Washington were all red and yellow. Anyway, it was fun. There was a long line of people waiting to get on the ship, even a lot of women. I looked at the big hats they were wearing. It could have been Easter!"

"Dressing up to tour a Navy vessel is perfectly acceptable. My guess is the women dressed for dinner afterward rather than to inspect that odd-looking captured Japanese airplane on board. And, don't forget, it was a Sunday."

"It was so neat! We saw that Japanese plane, and then what was the most fun was walking through that dark room, it was so big, like being in a movie, and there were palm trees and monkeys and bird sounds and it felt like a jungle."

Sally added dryly that it was a regular Japanese Sherwood Forest.

"Or it was supposed to be one of those islands that Japan fought so hard to keep," mother said.

"Anyway," Ben said, "it was so neat. And just when my eyes get used to the dark, I hear something snap. I look up. I see a man with a gun in a palm tree. His face's covered with some kind of paint. Brown and yellow, I think. It's a Japanese soldier, aiming his rifle at me! I try to shout, but my throat's dry."

"I doubt it. Probably a U.S. Marine, don't you think? And that's when you pulled my skirt."

"Did I?"

"Brave soldier," George snapped.

"I think it was an LSMFT back from service."

"Mother," Sally corrected her, "LSMFT stands for 'Lucky Strike Means Fine Tobacco.'"

"Oh my, but I smoke Chesterfields," she laughed. "Then it must have been LST."

"What does that mean?" George wanted to know.

"I have no idea. Ask your father when he comes back."

Ben said, "It's something about landing tanks, I think."

"Now I remember," mother said. "The ship was built near Pittsburgh, so it was a homecoming after the war, like salmon returning to their place of birth. Spell it *b-i-r-t-h* or *b-e-r-t-h*. Take your choice." Cecilia loved to play with words.

Grandma enjoyed the discussion. "Time for tea, isn't it?"

"Is it that late? Where are they? I am shaking with worry," mother said. "I need some tea and something a little stronger, too."

Sally said that she could use a nip.

George laughed. "If she's going to have a wee drop, so will I."

"You are impossible when you're bored."

Grandma brought some peace. "It's wonderful to have children in the house. I wish that Willie and Albert had not gone off to England at such an early age, but what were we supposed to do? I often wonder whether I missed the best years of my life."

"Go look," mother told Ben.

He stood by the window for a minute, and then he saw them walking very slowly up the road. It seemed clear that Uncle Willie and Albert were adjusting their pace for grandpa, who seemed to list from left to right. He had not taken his cane.

"They're coming," he reported.

Grandpa labored up the stairs to the bedroom. Mother said what they all were thinking. "Your grandpa is eighty. He should not be cavorting around the globe, from Pittsburgh to India. What a journey— to New York, and London, and Paris, and Rome, and Cairo, and then a long haul across the ocean to India. He would be an absolute wreck when he arrived."

Uncle Willie said that it was a hard decision to tell grandpa that he needed to stay behind. In addition, it was ironic that the doctor did not have the necessary inoculations to enter India. Every imaginable disease awaited him, and he had no natural immunities. But Uncle Willie had been exposed to every virus and many bacteria known to man.

Coming into the little house, grandpa went slowly up the stairs. After a respectful stay to allow time for what must be said about him, he returned to the little circle. Grandma knew what to say: "Have a bracing cup of tea," she said to him. "It will sustain you."

"Well, all right, if I must, but I feel bad about not pitching in to help."

Uncle Willie promised to send airmail letters every day to report on Billy's progress. He would take the photographs with him to cheer up Billy, to show him a family that wished him a quick recovery. Ben suggested that they send some coloring books and crayons and a few comic books.

"As this is my last night at the hotel, I should take little gifts to the nice people taking care of me. I know I'll be teased and hugged, but that's all right."

Albert had breakfast with him the next day. He said that Uncle Willie was hugged, kissed, teased, serenaded, "hip-hip-hoorayed," and "jolly-good-fellowed." Mabel said, "Your Highness, this will always be your table and throne."

Tony Joe packed Willie's bags in the back seat and in "the boot." He said, "Now I've heard everything! The boot."

"Cheerio," they called while waving goodbye. And then he was gone.

Noah's Ark

After a long week of waiting, two letters from India arrived on the same day. The first letter opened was the first written. Uncle Willie said he was exhausted by his many flights. He spent a day in London to recuperate and to meet with his banker. He said that he was happy to be back in India and that Lydia and Billy were as well as could be expected under the circumstances. Billy enjoyed the comical photographs, the comic books, and the coloring books. The radio was his constant companion. The doctors told Uncle Willie that progress was being made, but that the diagnosis was a difficult one to make because Billy had an infection usually found in older males. It seems that Billy had been disobedient one day when he and other children decided to swim in a local pond that was known to be unsanitary. This fact was withheld from the doctors by Billy, who was afraid he would be punished.

"Well, he was punished, wasn't he? Some toxic biological agent had entered his nasal mucous, settled down, and began to reproduce. There was no immunity to this microscopic intruder." Grandpa said that Willie was being most diplomatic in his commentary, for the "toxic agent" was no doubt a fungus that settled in the nose and perhaps the eyes, set up shop, and started a large family. In India this was very commonplace in adults who worked along rivers or near farm ponds in which animal dung was deposited. The risk was well known, but economic realities applied and the adults took their chances. Grandpa said he would write to Willie and ask for scientific data to confirm his long-distance diagnosis. Was there recent flooding, he wanted to know, and did the boys on their lark lazily sip the water, perhaps?

The second letter, written two days later, repeated most of what was said in the first letter, but in an abridged manner. The big news, which filled the letter, was that Uncle Willie doubted that he would return to the States "anytime soon." Upon the advice of Barclays Bank and Merrill Lynch, he knew that returning to the States now could cause his monthly income to decline. And, most unfortunately, national political unrest was growing in the enormous democratic republic. Viceroy Mountbatten's exodus from India so soon after the Partition did not help the situation. If only the viceroy had stayed in India longer. His actions had invoked Churchill's ire. It was a mess. "Wait and see" was now Uncle Willie's motto.

"Well, the important news is that Billy's on the road to recovery," mother said.

"Not quite yet, I fear" grandpa said. "If it's what I suspect, surgery must be performed. But let's hope that nothing else has happened to his system. It will take some effort to rid the body of this nasty fungus, but surgery is usually very effective."

Grandma said that she and grandpa must soon make plans for their trip to Florida. "Albert and Cecilia have important decisions to make," she said. "The summer has passed too quickly. When school resumes . . . ."

But she didn't finish the sentence. The topic was too painful for Cecilia. What grandma didn't know was that it was also becoming too painful for Ben, who knew that moving to the city was a source of contention for his parents. They all knew mother's position—move to Sacred Heart parish. But Albert was reluctant to say what he deeply felt—stay here and live close to nature, with or without animals. He used the animals to bargain with mother. "I'll get rid of the blasted beasts if you insist. Someone will buy them, or take them off my hands as a favor. I know that much. Cecilia, surely this will satisfy you!" Ben heard his plea while he was lying in bed at night, unable to sleep. And he heard Cecilia say, in what context he was not sure, "If it weren't for the children, I would put my hat on and leave!" Her words had the force of an ultimatum—surrender your position and sign the treaty.

The rest of the summer was lackluster. Games did not interest him. BB Bain and their other buddies seemed to stay away, except for Ned, a stuffy boy who came to the door and asked to see the doctor. Grandpa heard him and called from the dining room: "come, the doctor is in." Ben invited Ned to come in. Grandpa said, "You don't sound very good. Have you swallowed a small frog, or are you wearing your father's false teeth?"

"My throat hurts really bad," Ned whined.

"Open wide," grandpa said, taking a small flashlight out of his vest pocket. "Let's have a little daylight down there. Well, well, as I suspected, you have a case of summer tonsillitis. Not a nice thing that. I can't give you anything for the pain, except aspirin, with your parent's permission, but I would get to your family doctor immediately. You may have to have the tonsils removed. And your adenoids, to boot."

Ned struggled to say thanks.

Grandpa wrote a few words on a pad and said, "Give this to your parents, all right? They'll take care of you."

"OK, thanks." Ned was anxious to leave. He turned toward the door.

"You'll have a sore throat for a day or two, but you can calm that down with big dishes of vanilla ice cream. But don't accept pineapple juice if it's offered you. No, bargain for ice cream."

"OK, thanks a lot, sir," Ned croaked. Even in pain he was a model of politeness. Ben understood then why during baseball games Ned made sure that no one was standing close to him when he swung the bat. "Move back a little," he'd say. He was a polite batter.

Ben told Ned that he wouldn't feel much pain. Just sleep and be waited on by your mom. Ned shook his head in agreement and left the house, but looking pretty sad despite the encouragement.

Still the doctor, grandfather said, "While I have my little torch, let me look at your throat." He opened wide, knowing the diagnosis already. "You have no tonsils. What have you done with them?"

"They were taken out when I was six."

"Smart decision, I'm sure."

Grandma had watched the performance from the first step. "Old

Man, the boy's 'thank you' was amply polite. He did not ask for an encore about ice cream."

"But life is full of encores. Why, every morning when I get out of bed, that's an encore, isn't it?"

"Would you like to inspect my throat, too," she asked, in jest.

"No need, no need," grandpa answered. "I have sufficient evidence of the healthy condition of your throat."

They stayed up past their usual bedtime to talk with Albert and Cecilia. Ben listened quietly to the radio. Grandpa and grandma shared their anxiety about moving to Florida without Uncle Willie being there with them. They needed his encouragement, at least until they were certain that they liked Florida. If they moved again, they said, they would locate themselves in Barbados.

He turned the radio volume down even lower when Cecilia said that they were welcome to stay for however long they wished. "I have enjoyed your visit so much. I can't imagine you're leaving us, even though you feel you must."

"Bless you, Cecilia. I would accept your offer without hesitation, but you and Albert and the children may be selling the house. Having the children with us has been so wonderful. I know I've said this to you many times, but what I regret most about my life was *not* having Albert and Willie at home with me, to grow up there. They were off with the monks in England much too soon. Now, as I look at your children, I long to live those years again, when we were young, when the boys were the ages of your children. Now I'm being selfish, I know, but this is my wish."

Grandpa said to grandma, "My dear, this is an encore I would gladly give you, but, alas, the show must go on."

"That's so kind of you, Sylvester, perhaps the kindest thing you've said to me in years. Thank you!"

In their weeks with them at Allegheny Acres, grandma never called him Sylvester until that night.

The children were not asked how they felt about moving, or about grandma and grandpa staying on, perhaps through Christmas. When Ben asked George how he felt, he just shrugged his shoulders. Sally said that she wanted to have her own bedroom again, but not so much that she couldn't wait until Christmas, or whenever. Ben asked her what "whenever" meant, and she said, "You know, maybe until Easter or Memorial Day. Why do you always have to have precise answers?"

"A few years ago, remember, we had a big argument about what 'a few' means." And you said it means seven. So, a few peanuts meant seven peanuts. George thought 'a few' meant about twelve. So don't complain when I want to know exactly what 'whenever' means."

To this, she answered in a bored voice, "Whatever."

It was that kind of a summer.

Precisely, Ben needed to know what was going to happen. If he had his way, they would give the animals away, burn the shed and the coop, and stay where they were: on a farm that wasn't a farm. When he had the courage, he asked mother what they were going to do. "We'll see," she answered. So he asked his father, "What are we going to do?" He answered, "Do about *what*?" Ben answered, "You know." "Oh that," he said, "We'll see."

After that, he let himself be convinced that they would stay. There *would* be geography, arithmetic, sliding down the hill to the outhouse on the ice, clapping erasers, hauling coal and water, marbles, egg sandwiches at lunch, Miss Miller's violin, grammar, art, and so much more. And there *would* be Annie, too. Absolutely.

The third letter came a week later. Billy seemed to be doing very well after the surgery on the lining of his nose. "Poor boy! But there will be a happy ending here, I just know," Cecilia said at the Sunday dinner table. They were enjoying meatloaf, boiled potatoes, and well-educated Harvard beets. Oddly, and thankfully, there was no Sunday chicken on this Sunday. Even chickens need a day off. After dinner, Ben went to count the chickens. The number he came back with was zero. Then he knew that somewhere up on the hill, or back by the skating pond, the chickens had found a new owner. King Midas would miss the daily fresh eggs in the slop trough.

On Monday afternoon, a truck backed into the driveway. The motor idled. He watched as Bessie was led to a long ramp and up onto the truck. Bessie was bawling as loud as she did weeks earlier when her heifer was sold. Then the male goat, Diego, with its comical beard, followed the same path. There was no longer a Snowball to keep him company. Finally, the deposed King Midas was pulled and shoved from the pen, snorting madly, and with great difficulty he was all but lifted into the truck. So, this was Albert's Noah's Ark. Ben couldn't shake that thought.

Albert muttered a few words; one of them was "luck," perhaps "good luck," or "better luck than I had." This was a moment of defeat for him, but he took it as well as could be expected. The driver shifted gears. The truck lurched forward. Ben could hear twelve cloven hooves sliding in straw on the bed of the truck. He sensed that the drive would be very short. The truck turned onto Saxonburg Road and disappeared.

Grandpa, grandma, and mother tried to console Albert with words of wisdom: "It's for the best," and "they'll put on weight and be happy." Grandpa said a funny thing about the two happiest days in a farmer's life—the day he buys a pig and the day he gives it away. Mild laughter followed.

Out of kindness, Cecilia waited until Tuesday to announce quietly that in a month or so another truck would come to take their furniture to the city, but she wasn't quite sure where in the city the furniture would be delivered. "Your father and I will be looking for a place. Surely there's a three thousand dollar palace for sale. Wish us luck."

Fire and Smoke

"Boys, you and Sally had better settle your affairs soon. No time for moping and feeling sorry for yourselves. We're going to move, soon."

Sally said that she understood. George said moving away was not such a big deal. Ben said that he would miss the country life, the school, and his friends. "But you're the youngest," mother said. "You feel so much because you're young. Don't ever deny those feelings. Accept them."

"We are close to finding a place in the city, within walking distance of Sacred Heart. No more school busses, or standing in the rain or snow waiting for your bus. No more stinky outhouses and potbellied stoves stinking of coal. You saw Sacred Heart School last spring. Was there anything more beautiful? You will be able to ride the streetcar to Dithridge Street, ice skate on Saturdays at the Duquesne Gardens, go to the museum and library, and there are five movie theaters in East Liberty. Just think!"

Despite mother's pep talk, he felt empty, lost, and even betrayed. Grandpa and grandma tried to cheer him up. Uncle Willie's letters were full of support for their moving. "This will not be your last move," he said. "There will be others full of promise and enchantment."

Uncle Willie was happy in India. He would soon marry Lydia. Leaning on table lamps or stuck in the edges of mirrors were pictures of his new family.

Ben missed him terribly. What was it about him that made him feel this way? He could not say. His grandparents were now family members as far as he was concerned, all of them in the circle. But moving to the city did not include them. No, they would live by themselves, alone, in Florida. How could they accept this? "Will we ever see them again?" he asked.

"Of course we will," Cecilia assured him. "They're coming back next spring for their fiftieth wedding anniversary. Uncle Willie and his family are invited, too. We'll all gather at Dithridge Street again for a splendid time, with cake, ice cream, and games."

Ben walked in the woods when he felt sad and sat by the edge of the pond where he had skated in another season, another time. He thought of Annie. He realized that he'd never said more than a few words to her. He'd hoped to be a little braver when school began.

He even missed the animals, which surprised him. The shed looked forlorn. He offered to help his father burn it, along with the squat little coop. "All in time," Albert said. "We'll get to it. Hold your horses."

They waited for news of the new house, but mother said in a cautionary voice, "Oh, I promise you it won't be *new.*"

"But I need to know the address because I need to forward my comic book subscriptions."

"Which ones? *Archie, Nancy,* and *Blondie?*"

"And *Red Ryder,* too."

"When did that happen?"

"You gave it to me for Christmas."

"How could I have forgotten?" she said.

"Everything will fall into place in a short while. We've made an offer on a house? Isn't that exciting?"

"I guess, but you don't sound excited."

"And a nice couple is interested in this house. I think they're serious about it."

"Do they have kids?"

"Yes. Older."

Days passed. Meals were sometimes early, sometimes late. Leftovers were a steady fare. When the hot days and blinding light were too much, Ben settled in the basement to look through boxes that had to be taped shut. A pile of boxes near the door had to be carried to the dump beyond the shed to be burned.

The day of the burn came quickly, a clear day with no rain promised. When the boxes were piled and the water hose uncoiled, Albert poured gasoline he had siphoned from his car. With a twisted newspaper burning in his hand, he waited until the exact right time. "Stand back!" Then he tossed the flaming paper onto the boxes that had been soaked with gas. They watched the fire build and stepped back when it really blazed. What was in the boxes he did not know. Just junk, he was told, yellow papers, old clothes, and other stuff. His job was to hold the hose, to be ready just in case the fire got too big. They kept moving back from the growing flames.

"Aim the water at the base of the fire, not at the top of the flames," Albert ordered. "That's it. Keep it coming."

Mother was drawn from the house at the sight of the climbing flames. "Do you think this is wise, Albert? I don't want to stir up the volunteer fireman on a Tuesday afternoon. They're all at work, I'm sure."

"Guess what it would have cost to have had this junk trucked away. Why have we kept this stuff so along?"

"Many of the boxes are filled with your discarded photographs and old negatives. We brought them with us when we moved. Remember?"

"I must not have missed them. I don't remember."

"George is carrying new boxes for the fire. What should he do with them?"

"Stand back, that's what. Aim the water at the base and keep it going."

"Albert, if the fire truck comes, I'm going in the shed with Diego and hide."

"You forget, Cecilia, Diego is gone."

"Oh, that's right. I hope he's happy, wherever he is. I hope we'll be happy wherever we'll be."

Tires crunched on the driveway. They scarcely heard them with the roaring of the fire. Two men got out of the truck cab. They left the doors open and walked slowly toward them. Were they firemen?

"Oh Albert, look what you've done."

"It's nothing. I gave them the animals. They're not the fire patrol."

The men were polite. They seemed to understand that what must be done must be done.

"How do?" the elder man said. "Hate moving day myself. Nice fire you got going."

"There's more. Wait until the shed goes, and the coop. Any advice on how to do it?"

"If it was me, I'd break the shed up and burn the boards a few at a time. Control. That's what you need. I got crowbars and hammers if you need them."

"How are the animals faring?"

"Good. Eatin' a lot and fittin' in with the others. We just swang by when we seen smoke. Need a hand with them boxes there? I'd advise emptyin' 'em first and then burnin' 'em. Got a rake handy, with a long handle?" Ben dropped the hose, soaking himself in the process, and then ran to the basement. He found the rake and ran back with it.

Mother called to him: "Don't run! There are sharp points, and I don't want you falling."

Behind him came grandma in slacks and grandpa with his cane, but without his tie. They were dressed for the country. Their cigarettes were tipped with polite little ashes.

"I'm Rick, by the way. Let me have that rake. Watch out for the sparks."

Ben picked up the squirming hose with its narrow red streak on the side, like a snake he thought. He aimed it while Rick squatted low, turned his face, and drove the fork into the base of the fire.

"Just givin' it some oxygen is all. Fires need oxygen, just like people."

When he couldn't stand any more heat, Rick crouched lower and backed away.

"Now Vernon here can tell you all about fire. He was a volunteer fireman, but he had an accident. Tell 'em, Vern."

"I slipped down a wet ladder from the second floor of a house last year. Banged my leg bad. The doc said to stay off ladders, so I had to quit."

"Hey, Vern. You didn't quit the firemen's dances, did you? He likes to hang around the station. More hopping than dancing!"

Drunk from the flames, they stared for the longest time into the bright heat. Grandma and grandpa came closer, also mesmerized. After fifteen minutes, Rick said, "Well, Al, looks like you got the job under control. Let me and Vern know when the shed's goin' up."

George brought the last of the boxes. Ben carried two chairs from the kitchen table for grandma and grandpa. The little family sat silently watching the drama of the fire. In half an hour the boxes were all gone, but the smoke lingered as the cool evening settled over Burger Road. Grandpa struggled to stand. He stirred the ashes with his cane and solemnly pronounced them dead.

"Come on Back . . . Come on Back"

In what certainly was a dream, Ben heard a voice calling out an order: "Come on back." Still half-asleep, he thought he was calling out to Uncle Willie and his grandparents. Was it me calling them back, he asked himself. He needed them. Then it began again, "Come on back."

He struggled across the little room, half-awake, half-dreaming. From the window he looked down on a strange man walking behind a huge truck, his arms extended and hands waving. "Come on back . . . come on back," he called to the driver, who inched his way in reverse.

He was awake now; the dream, if it was ever a dream, had ended. This was the day he dreaded.

The movers were early. Cecilia and Albert scurried about on the first floor. They were surprised, too. "They're here. They're here," mother cried out.

"Yes, because we asked them to come, didn't we, and we're paying them to move us. Right?"

"I'll wake the children. They'll be surprised. We need to fold their army cots and sheets. We'll need the sheets for tonight, their first night in the new house."

"The very *old* new house, to be sure," he said as kindly as he could.

"Oh, I hope they like it, I hope, I hope."

"What's to like, Cecilia? It's old, it's been vacant for months, and it's damp, dusty, and perpetually dark, despite its narrow windows. I have major improvements to make, starting with new copper pipes to the bathroom and kitchen. We'll need tile for the floors and space heaters for at least four rooms. The coal furnace is defunct."

"If it's too much to move in today, we can stay at Dithridge Street for a week or two while you work."

"I wish the new owners were willing to wait a month before taking possession so I could get the work done."

"But we might have lost the sale," mother said.

"True."

The children had bowls of cereal for breakfast. Just about everything in the kitchen had been wrapped in newspaper and packed in boxes. Mother was frantically emptying the refrigerator. "We can't take any of this stuff," she said. She spooned ice cream into the sink and then the dark raspberry Jell-O, which made a sucking sound when it was plopped over the drain. Ice cubes were wrenched from trays.

"I should have done all of this yesterday, but I was so tired. I'm exhausted still," mother said. "Do what you can to help," she told the children, "or just stay out of everyone's way."

"I can't find my red guns, my pistols. They were in a box, and I can't find it." Ben was a little anguished about this.

"Why in a box?" mother asked mechanically.

"I was hiding them from George."

"Oh, well, they'll come back, they'll show up. Nothing is ever *really* hidden."

"Well, they could have been in a box that got burned."

"If that's the case, they're not red any more. They'd be smoky-black by now."

"I could go poke in the ashes out back."

"Oh, don't. I'm sure they'll show up when we unpack. Oh, I dread unpacking! And, in case you didn't know it, *revolver*, a fancy word for pistol, means "come back," just like those revolving doors you played in a few years ago when we were in town. Remember? You would waltz around and around behind the glass, and you wouldn't come out until I reached into the opening and pulled you out. Remember? Now make yourself scarce for a while. Now *I'm* going in circles."

He went outside to watch the men loading what now looked like very old furniture that oddly seemed to lose its value when visible in true sunlight. Some veneer was curling. He was pretty sure then that they were a poor family, a happy but poor family. They were really no different from their neighbors, he thought, who escaped from the city Depression twenty years earlier. The only local noble villagers were the Snyders, who made money through coal years before. Mother parodied the voices she heard at church functions, saying, "Oh, look, there goes Thelma! She's one of the Snyders from Snyder's Corner."

The living and dining rooms were emptied quickly. The linoleum was still new where furniture was once placed, and faded, even worn through, where the traffic patterns were. The thin coat of paint that covered the walls had faded, too. Old colors bled through. Without Cecilia's pictures that gave character to the walls—a canal scene from Venice with the Bridge of Sighs and a picture of Ireland's Saint Brigid—the walls were marked and pitted from years of "decorating."

"Anything else go?" one of the men asked. "We still got room."

"We'll take care of the little things that are left. So, we'll meet you at the house on Lamont Place in about an hour."

And so, after three hours of work, off they went, their heavy truck inching along the driveway and onto Burger Road. Left behind were the kitchen appliances, which were already ancient, but the new owners wanted to keep them if only for a few weeks. At the new house there was an old refrigerator Albert got for a few dollars. The kitchen range was also an antique. "We must get something better as soon as possible," mother said. "We've allowed ourselves to be rushed into the sale. That may have been a mistake. We hardly had a chance to say goodbye to your parents. I am so sorry for that. I hope I can make it up to them somehow. Still, they seem happy in Florida. So far away."

After a quick check of the rooms, which were now bare and ugly, mother shuddered. "Did we do the right thing?" she asked herself.

"Albert, are we paying the movers for the job or by the hour? If it's by the hour, I hope they don't decide to stop and have lunch somewhere along the way."

"We agreed to pay them by the hour. If they stop for coffee and a sandwich, who could blame them? Getting furniture into Lamont Place is going to be more difficult than moving it out of this house. There's that steep, narrow stairway to navigate to the second floor, and little turning room on top. They'll be tired when they finish, so I expect they'll want to wrap everything up and get home for dinner, don't you think?"

Mother was tired, but there was no place to collapse. Everything had gone. "Albert, I will never move again," she said, as though taking an oath.

I know, I know," he said. "But look on the bright side. We'll be just where you've wanted us to be for the last three years." His voice was a little acidic.

"True, but only partially true. I had dreamed of a white house with a blue roof and a little garden for lettuce, peas, and . . . oh, I can't think, those little red things that you have to pull out of the ground."

"Radishes."

"But our new front yard is so tiny, and the backyard has to be used for hanging the wash, so there's no room for a garden there. Well, I'll adjust. I can't do another lick of work. Let's just go," she said.

"But what about the sink, there's stuff melting?" Ben said.

"I just don't care. It will be gone soon. The new owners won't be here for hours. So just forget the sink. Mrs. What's-her-name, you know, Mrs. Thing, will understand if there's a little mess to be washed away. No harm done."

So, it was all over. He went to the kitchen for the last time. What he had loved about it was the memory of mother stirring cocoa early on a winter morning, and the cupboard filled with wonderful soups. But the cupboard was bare. The clots of red Jell-O in the sink had shifted this way and that until the dregs of the little freezer were glazed in reddish-pink. This was his last image of the home where he had found such happiness. His father masked his sorrow as Ben hid his. Both felt the ache of small failure. Nothing would be the same again. It was goodbye for keeps. How he wished he could come on back someday. Was there no magic in his Honeymoon Express? But like the bees, like the animals, their stay had ended. What would his future be on the little narrow alley, in the new school, day after day, night after night? He felt hot tears on his face.

"Hurry, hurry, hurry," Cecilia called from the car. "We've got to go! Be brave! And always remember, even in sadness there is joy. Believe me! The poets have said it's so."

One last look at the kitchen, which now seemed to tilt a little, and then he left in a slow march toward whatever came next.

"Hop in the back. Make room for Sir Galahad. That's it. Off we go. We are on our way. Life begins anew!"

Mother turned around to see him. She smiled with her lips, but not with her eyes. "You'll have a wonderful time, I promise you. Life is full of surprises and adventures, too many to count, and they're just waiting for you. Think of the friends you'll make. Oh, you are a lucky boy! *A lucky boy.*"

The road over Coal Mine Hill rolled beneath them. From the rear window Ben watched his world recede. Albert, his fury contained, struggled with the gearshift as the aged Pontiac crept up and up the hill, shuddering and whining up the steep road, high above the jaundiced sulfur ponds and over the deep, dark mine buried below—Ned's graveyard.

And so it was.

Part Two

"All Aboard!"

The call of the conductor moments before the train leaves the station.

Part Two of *Home at Last* originally appeared as *Lucky Jack!* in 2014, a publication of iUniverse. The current version of *Lucky Jack!* has been changed significantly in order to be included in *Home at Last*.

Adrift (1953)

In the eighteen months since Ben's family drove away from their bungalow on Burger Road, Cecilia struggled to grasp her elusive dream of Shadyside near her beloved church; Albert quietly remembered with sadness his lost hope for what John Milton called "fresh woods and pastures new": his failure with the animals and the bees that now lived in the barns or hives of strangers; George could not make sense of city life, but he had an angry, ironic pal named Tom, a young artist, and between them they struggled to figure out what they believed life was about; and Sally, whose life was as operatic as the Met performances from New York every Saturday, walked off the stage at the new high school with this prize and that prize, including the promise that she would attend a fine college near New York City. A promise, yes, but one without the necessary funds. Cecilia's quiet lament was this—how long, Lord, until our future is happy and secure, and when will I know the answer, please? I want a happy home! And I want to *be* at home. And if I could still have my little adventures . . . .

Ben spent days, weeks, and months searching for his rural friends from the Bairdford School—were they in the row ahead of him at Sacred Heart School; weren't those Eddie's ears poking out under his dark hair; wasn't that Skipper's horsey snort on Emerson Street at recess: and wasn't that pretty girl at the lunch table his beloved Annie, curls longer and eyes as blue as he remembered? And why were these tricks being played on him? Why did he dream of these lost faces night after night? He wandered aimlessly through the streets of East Liberty and Shadyside searching for something, anything, anyone? Students in his grade knew each another, but there was no room yet for him in their circles. And so he wandered. Keep moving, he thought.

Afternoons he came home to an empty house, a dark place, where he gasped for breath and shook his head in disbelief. "What has happened to me?" he thought over and over. His father was silent for days, and the work to make the house livable was as final as any work Albert ever attempted—new copper pipes, brown and black floor tiles, and a cheap carpet for the living room. Cecilia, eager to have the world she once knew as a young woman, found pictures for the walls, but driving nails to hang them made the old plaster crumble. Is this prophetic, she wondered? And so the pictures both hid the broken plaster and brought her peace when they hung on sticky hooks that sooner or later pulled away from the cold, damp walls. Ben heard them fall when he was in his bed. "What are we doing here?" This was his final thought before falling asleep to confront his dreams.

Cecilia knew he was miserable. She watched him slouching down the alley on his way to school. "George! Go walk with Ben, please. Talk to him!" What she really asked for was some magical event that would brighten him, make him smile, make him eat his dinner with more enthusiasm. Albert was not concerned. His favorite word was *adjust*. "Give him time to adjust. He's a boy. Boys know how to adjust."

"Albert, forget the Benedictine monks for a moment. What kind of *adjusting* did they offer you and Willie when you were boys? Our son needs someone to *adjust* with, another boy, a friend, someone who *knows* his new world, who'll take him in, don't you see?"

"Cecilia, we're talking about two different words. You mean something very active, something with a *spark*. I mean that he need's *time*. That's all."

"It's been well over a year now, and last winter he loafed in the house, and last spring he went out to explore, and he came back soaking wet from rain. Remember? It's a miracle he didn't get pneumonia. He's growing up, getting taller. And he's looking at girls. Have you noticed? I've asked my sisters to make novenas for him. They're very devout; they love the children, you know."

"If he's looking at girls, then he *is* adjusting. I should probably have "the talk" with the boys. I don't know what to say about birds and bees, but I'll have a talk with the boys."

"Thank you, Albert. That would be kind of you. They'll remember the birds and the bees, even if they've swarmed!" She had a good laugh. "You can't blame John Milton for this, can you? Lycidas, the shepherd, loved his cloak of blue. Remember?" Albert seemed to brighten somewhat.

Albert pointed his nose toward the kitchen. "Do I hear the tea kettle?"

"I wish Willie and your parents were here to join us. I miss them so."

"As do I," the proper Englishman responded. "But Willie and Lydia are married now, with an impetuous boy, too. They have a life of their own in India, at least until they relocate to Barbados or Hong Kong! God knows."

The Talk

Albert chose a time after Mass on a Sunday in May to inform his sons about the mysteries of women and girls, something he knew little about. He had never had a talk with his own father, the doctor, or with Willie, the former bachelor-rajah of India. But he would carry off his mission with typical British aplomb. So the boys, still dressed for church, postponed their Sunday adventures to hear what their father had to say.

"Now, you know," Albert began, "that as we grow older and begin to notice that the girls we sometimes teased and fought with on the playground, and called some pretty bad names, like 'piano legs' or 'four eyes,' are getting rather pretty (he almost said 'pretty pretty'), and so, being young men, which you are now, you linger and look, not quite sure just what to say or do."

Ben broke in with the news that the nuns at Sacred Heart are teaching the students how to dance. "You know, square dancing. Not much touching. We square dance in the front of the classroom. Then we learned how to hold the girl's hand, and we put our arm around them, because it's a *dance*, see."

Albert, grateful for the break that allowed him to group his thoughts, replied to the boys, who nodded their head up and down as though they heard a distant music: "Good, good, good. I enjoy dancing. The exercise is good. I always try to follow the steps, *one*-two-three, *one*-two-three, *one*-two-three, and then I imagine *other* steps, other possibilities, such as crossing my right foot over my left foot and back again between the beats. He demonstrated between the two beds. Inspiration. Exercise. Try it, especially in a polka. At wedding receptions there's always polka music, and when your mother comes with me to Tarentum or Carnegie, when I'm taking pictures, we polka. You'll see!"

George said that he has a girlfriend who dances with some of the other girls because boys won't try dancing. Why is that? He wondered whether he should get another girlfriend, one who doesn't dance. Albert was silent.

Ben wondered how a boy got another girlfriend. Furthermore, why would he want a new one? For him, there was only Annie; there was no one else. If only he had talked to Annie, if only he had signed his name on the Valentine card he dropped on Annie's desk when she was not looking. She must have many signed "from a secret admirer." The correct spelling of *admirer* should have been the only tip she needed to see *his* bespectacled face in the large red heart with the silver arrow piercing it.

Albert gathered his thoughts slowly, as a European man normally would: "Well, to continue, I want you to understand that women— girls—are very special, all beautiful in their own way. Young men must shield them from ruffians, must escort them to the door, and must refrain from barnyard language, what Shakespeare called 'country matters,' if you follow me."

George bobbed his head. Ben gave his father's comments a puzzled, quizzical look. What are "country matters" anyway?

Albert was relieved. "We'll talk again, soon. Just think about what I've said." He almost ended with "cheerio," but thought better of it.

The House Where Ben Lived

Ben lived in a row house, built in 1882, on the narrow alley named Lamont Place. This was a two-storied sliver of a row house with colonial redbrick and a flat roof. The three row houses were once occupied by steelworkers at mill furnaces along the rivers, the rippling river and the low sky above glowing red against the night clouds. There were eight windows in the house, but only his front bedroom windows faced east. The morning sun was intrusive; it was so bright that Albert placed sets of negatives along the sills. Beneath each negative was proof paper. Very slowly, shapes began to appear on the paper in salmon-pink hues—brides, grooms, dancing maids of honor, and very proud parents of couples married in churches, hotel ballrooms, or fire stations in blighted towns north of the city: Curtisville, Culmerville, and Red Hot (if such a crossroads even existed). Rooms were narrow, dank, and musty. The cellar's rotund coal furnace had been banked forever years before. But long before it expired, its ashes were carried into the front and backyards, spread around with a rake, and left to be crushed by time and footsteps into something like topsoil where only weeds and grapes could grow. A tiny vineyard appealed to Albert —a miniature farm in the city. In place of the furnace, there were three gas space heaters upstairs and one downstairs. Though the heaters were vented through old chimneys, Cecilia lamented their make-shift efficiency: "Albert," she said, day and night, "are we all about to be asphyxiated before blessed spring arrives?" He replied, night and day, "Why, in rural Ireland and Highland Scotland, farmers would come from far-and-wee to warm themselves in this cheery home." Cecilia could detect something acidic in his reply. When the temperature on the alley fell below zero in January and February, the family lived in two climates—tropical, with bright blue-orange flames in four rooms, and arctic cold in the other rooms.

Across the alley was an old barn used long ago to shelter horses and carriages, but now it was occupied by two roofers with the fanciful name of *Valentine Bros.* (The name made Ben remember Annie, *his* Valentine!) When the large sliding door was open, the inside was dark, even when a light or two burned. He could not see the brothers, but he was confident their eyes were watching him. Once, as he swung (*swang*, the memorable form of the verb in Allegheny Acres) his leg boldly over the bike seat to set out on some mission, one of the brothers called out of the dark in a haunted voice, "go git 'em cowboy!" After that, when their door was open, he walked his bike up the street and out of range of that voice. Then, beyond their view, he ran hard, put his left foot on the pedal and heaved himself over the saddle, a gallant cowboy, the Kid, racing toward Elwood Street, to issue justice from the imaginary barrels of Red Fire (which were lost forever, ghost-gray in a dump somewhere or at the bottom of some creek).

He was therefore happier outside the house, (if *happy* was the accurate, convenient word). The kids along the alley played football, hide-and-seek, and bunt-baseball, whose bases were so close together that home runs were common. Pretty girls twirled their laundry-line ropes and sang their skipping songs. But they stopped to let him pass through their games without an offer to join them.

He never kissed a girl on Lamont Place. He never danced on Lamont Place. Why? Perhaps because the Great Tempter lived elsewhere, on the street of roses. And it was there that he almost learned to kiss and dance. And *almost* was close enough (allowing for the condition of his romantic heart). For he lived within parentheses and was almost invisible. Almost.

The Great Tempter

On a hazy, pungent summer day in 1953, when Ben was thirteen, he woke at ten o'clock in a suffocating, sunbaked bedroom filled with dreamy shadows. He was home alone. George had already "made" his bed by pulling his sheet over the mattress. His pillow was on the floor. Dust on the gray marble mantelpiece was etched by the random coins that Ben slid into his pocket every day. "Never leave the house without some money in your pocket," was his mother's advice. She had left for her social work agency much earlier. His father was in Carnegie breathing acrid chemicals in his darkroom where negatives hung from clothespins. Sally was shopping somewhere with a friend.

He opened George's junk drawer, a small one at the top of an old dresser. His junk told a lot about him. He had brass knuckles that were never used and he had a Bowie knife in a leather sheath. They might prove useful in the gritty city of tough boys. They threw the knife at the inside of the closet door. If their aim was good, the knife quivered in the dry wood before falling to the floor. Mother would have been angry had she known this. In the junk drawer there were also dried cigars, a can of lighter fluid, and half of a Mickey Spillane paperback called *I, the Jury.* His friend Tom had the other half. That way each read half of the novel and then they traded. "Hurry up," they'd say to each other. Before closing George's drawer, he borrowed a cigarette. Then he climbed goat-like down the steep, ladder-like steps to the kitchen. "Baa–aa–aa," cried the hungry goat.

In the kitchen there were remnants of breakfasts taken on the run—watery margarine, discarded toast crusts with teeth marks, a frying pan with whitening grease, and dishes to wash. The rule that summer was simple: last up cleans up. He fried three strips of limp bacon and made toast in a flop-eared toaster bought with Depression era Wilson condensed milk labels. The margarine was not for him, though, for he spread real butter on the toast (he bought sticks of butter with his paper route money). After eating at the sink (he never sat down) he washed the dishes and leaned them like false teeth to dry. Sacred Heart's calendar of saints hung by the back door—the halo-joined twins, Saints Peter and Paul, watched over his August adventures. Eighth grade would come, but there was still time for challenges in the afternoon, and especially at night, when he and Jack prowled and howled down dark alleyways and climbed onto garage roofs to see the night spread before them.

After breakfast he played 45 rpm records in the little dining room. *Our Lady of Fatima* was fine to hear every morning. He liked the words "we come on bended knee." Then, while he played highlights from *Carmen*, he felt the house shake. The front door had burst open, the doorknob digging into the powdery wall plaster. George had returned.

"Forgot my smokes," he said.

"Why bother? There are only three left in the pack."

"There were four last night."

"I subtracted one from the pack."

He laughed. "Why don't you smoke your own?"

"I have to save some for Jack."

"Oh, that bum. OK." George mimicked Tom's voice, but he had yet to perfect the guttural laugh following his witty jabs.

George jumped up the stairs two at a time, wrenched his junk drawer open, and was down again in a second or two. Toreador music stirred the stale air. George, waiting for his moment of truth, sighted down his Toledo steel blade. Now! *El Toro* didn't have a chance. The drama was over in a second!

"*Olé!*" he cried, slamming the door on his way out, shaking the picture of the Bridge of Sighs, a memory of Venice hanging over the sofa. This bridge was the famous passage from the Doge's palace to the prison where Casanova was once an inmate. A betrayed husband probably had the great lover arrested. But Cecilia liked to think that Casanova was released from his cell—with the Doge's apology—to scores of applauding masked Venetian virgins, wives, widows, and grandmothers, all costumed in fine silk. In fact, however, Casanova is believed to have escaped from prison by being spirited off the island in a getaway gondola. After fleeing, though, he would have needed an assortment of masks, a powdered wig, a bag of gold coins, a bath, a shave, and a suit of new silk clothes. Appearance was everything in the Most Serene Republic of Venice.

"Actually," Cecilia often said, "there's a Bridge of Sighs in town, connecting the soot-covered courthouse with the jail, but no gondolas, no masks. Just streetcars. Our Bridge of Sighs was built when *Pittsburgh* was spelled *Pittsburg*, you see. Did you know that?" she teased.

By the time he was halfway through a Spike Jones record, something about tea-for-two and a secluded rendezvous, the phone rang in the tiny, dark living room, with its scant Danish Modern furniture. Only one person called in the morning. It was Jack.

Enter Jack

He had met Jack at altar boy practice. "Hey," Jack said, "can you help me with this Latin?" But all the help in the world could not make Jack say the words. He either forgot the words or he just muffed them. Why did Jack want to be an altar boy? He wasn't cut out for the role, that's for sure, but he had to respect Jack's motives. Without so much as an apology, Jack explained: "If I get to be an altar boy, see, I get to serve at weddings, right, and when I do the groom gives money to the servers, right? I figure five dollars a pop. For that I'd learn Latin, I'd learn Greek!" Ben told him that older boys got the Saturday weddings. But new boys got the funerals on school days, so they were excused from one or two periods, depending on whether it was a quick funeral Mass for someone unknown or a High Mass for a celebrity. There was even a trip to the cemetery in a Cadillac if the deceased was a celebrity. But zero-dollars "a pop."

"I'm so sorry," said the nun in charge. "It was good of you to want to be an altar boy. Jack, I know your sweet mother, and I think you are a wonderful reflection of her devotion. Please, why don't you try the choir? You have a lovely voice." Jack's voice was changing, comically, as is so often the case. It would have been just like Jack to clown around at choir practice. He was a devil of a clown, as Ben was beginning to learn.

But Jack became his friend, and that's what counted. Besides, as he soon learned, Jack was the ticket to Roslyn Place, where three lovely girls lived: Jenny, Becky, and Abby.

Jack was disappointed. He would not get rich as an altar boy. He was done in by the Latin language. What he called the *wedding gigs* were most often served by Robert, a tall, pompadoured, pale-skinned kid, who was known by all to be pompous and arrogant. But Jack liked Ben, his tutor, and so he invited him to his house. In true Pittsburghese, a language Jack knew well, he said "kam-on-doun ma house." His mother would have none of that kind of talking, but Jack slipped sometimes, and sometimes he slipped just for the laugh.

He rode his bike to Jack's house. He heard Jack's raucous laugh coming from behind a fence next door. "*Ha-ha--hehe. . .my old man ran outta gas. . .so there we was next to a saloon.*" Jack loved saloons, Ben was to learn; he loved anything dank, dark, and smelly, "like an armpit," he crooned. "Let me see your cellar," he insisted, already dancing on the top step and staring into the dark, pungent basement.

Jack could be bold, too. Once with Abby, whose yard he was in, he saw the slight dusting of white-blonde hair on her arms. Jack liked to tickle-tease the arm hair, until Abby cried, "Stop it, Jackie!" But she loved his attention. Jack had nerve. Ben could never have touched her like that.

Then Jack ran to an old apple tree in the yard, reached for a low branch, and swung back and forth, his knees drawn up to his chest. A circus scene. He scratched his chin like a monkey. What would have come next on his program will never be known for Abby's Papa put his face in the screened kitchen window and called her into the house. "Abigail," he said in a deep southern voice from *Gone with the Wind*, "I am about to drip coffee, and we wish to begin lunch." He added cynically, "I am reasonably certain that Jackie and his friend will come by again later in the afternoon."

"*Oui, oui*, Papa, I'm coming right away." And off she skipped.

Abby was in love with New Orleans. She easily dropped French Creole phrases, just for the effect. Jack's reaction was to drop from the tree and announce to all who listened: "All ze gurls in France ze wears tizu-paper pants."

His days often began with a call from Jack: "Hey, come on up," Ben said, knowing Jack wouldn't. "We'll go do something."

On the rare visit, Jack preferred to wait for him on the street, sitting on his old, black skinny-wheel bike. "Your house is always empty," he said, "like somebody died there."

He wondered whether Jack could hear Spike Jones over the phone. Then he asked the question that was most on his mind: "Is Jenny on her porch?" He loved the idea of sitting on the porch and playing games with Jenny and being entertained by her pretty voice and smart chatter.

"Nah, but she will be. Trust me. So, come on down."

"I'm almost there!"

There was Roslyn Place, a dead-end street paved with wooden blocks. It was a little elegant street where professors, businessmen, and public servants lived behind redbrick walls and ivy-covered windows. The house was almost beyond the reach of Jack's impoverished father. "Hey, if my dad doesn't pay the rent this month, we'll have to move to Homewood," Jack lamented. He appreciated the value of money, especially Ben's, which he borrowed a-dime-at-a-time for ice cream. Jack never had his own cigarettes because he knew Ben carried a pack of Old Gold in his shirt pocket. When Jack wanted a smoke, which was often, he would joust with Sir Galahad of Ye Olde Allegheny Acres. He usually gave in, turned over an Old Gold, and watched Sir Jack calm down in a haze of smoke.

There was also the little street on which three beautiful girls lived. Jack saw them every day. They knew him; they understood him. He loved them all. They were his "trinity." "I love them all and in that order!"

Jack's house was larger than Ben's, more ornate and architecturally advanced despite its having been squeezed onto the end of the street. Behind the house were train tracks that ran to Pennsylvania Station a few miles away. Jack's house was a rental property, nothing more. The furniture was old and soft; a playpen was never folded and stored, even though the new baby was weeks away from delivery. Dishes usually went unwashed until the evening. Two piles of clothes were heaped on the dining room floor, one coming fresh from the dryer and the other going, eventually, to the big washing machine in the little laundry room. Clean clothes were picked from the clean pile, which got smaller as the other pile grew taller. Conditions in Jack's bedroom mirrored the domestic disarray downstairs. Reach under the bunk bed for a comic book and out would roll dust balls and retired Sunday socks.

Large windows lit the bedroom. Jack's shades were rarely drawn because no one could really see into the bedroom unless passengers zipping by on the trains were prepared to take a look. The front windows of his house were guarded by old sycamore trees.

Ben loved life there. Life was lived quickly. Motion was constant. Jack's dad seldom relaxed, even when working crossword puzzles. His pencil twitched above the little squares like a bird's beak while he considered the frustrating options. Then he would make stenographic notes around the borders of the paper, either words being considered or interesting snatches of conversations and baby patter around him. He liked to talk about his army service as a stenographer. His spelling skills had not deteriorated, which often happened to stenographers when they turned sounds into curious shapes, like carpenters' shavings, a curl here and a curl there.

In the Dark Closet

Becky and Jenny were quiet and serious. They followed the rules. They tucked themselves in beds before lightning bugs began courting in the trees outside their windows. During the day, however, when they were in the mood for annoying company, they invited Ben and Jack to their porch to play cards, or on long afternoons to play endless games of Monopoly. While Jack raced around the board at his usual speed, he amused the girls with tales of his exploits. It just seemed to Jack that they needed a little excitement. They were a good audience, so good, in fact, that the boys sometimes had trouble inventing encores.

They would reveal their night's plans and boast about where they would rove—to the chilly county morgue or to their dark hiding space on the support high above the tracks under the Aiken Avenue Bridge. The cars and trucks rumbling above them drowned their voices as they sang and shouted in their private world. Jack dramatized the exploits he had planned, which would require police chases in the runty neighborhoods they prowled, like Pierce Street, which had tough gangs. Jack told the girls about Frankenstein wine, his own vintage made with iced cherry Coke and Ben's Old Golds. "Just take a deep drag," he said, "then blow through the straw and watch the smoke come out above the rim of the glass." He crossed his eyes and puffed his cheeks.

"That sounds awful!" they would say. "Tell us more! We can keep secrets." This was the response Jack had hoped for.

Then Ben revealed that once Jack ordered a cherry-vanilla

Skyscraper cone at Isaly's in Shadyside, but he did not pay for it from his shallow pockets. "Where'd my money go? I got a hole in my pocket! I'll pay you tomorrow," he shouted. The injustice of it—his ice cream melting under the fat thumb of the frustrated soda jerker. Ben enjoyed the drama as he sculpted with his tongue the chocolate almond fudge delight he had just paid for. Jack loved an audience, and Ben encouraged his dramatics. "Gimme a dime. You got it. Hurry up. I'll pay you back." Ben delayed, which prompted more begging. "You had dinner at my house on Sunday! A lousy dime is all." Finally, he gave him a dime. Jack's hand was already sticky from the cone he had wrenched from the soda jerk's fist by peeling back his thumb. He laughed and laughed his way out of Isaly's clinical brightness into the enveloping dark of the Pittsburgh night.

"Oh, Jackie," Jenny said, her forehead wet with perspiration, "your eyes just dance all over the place. But are you ever serious?"

Well, Jack was not only a mad searcher of fun. He was also a thoughtful guy. Often, when it rained at night, they'd sit under a small decorative awning at the Shadyside Hardware smoking Old Golds one after another and shooting the butts on the wet sidewalk. Jack talked about his view of the world, one without funny-named nuns spanking the hands of naughty boys with rulers too short to hurt, or high school Brothers punching bad boys silly for mouthing off. He was good, but only to a point. He actually thought about the *Baltimore Catechism,* which he called the *Catch-icism.* If Satan was so bad, he'd say, don't forget that he was always Saint Lucifer on the Devil's calendar, a being to be reckoned with. "Find the *thrills* of life," he'd say, blowing plumes of smoke and squinting in a trance while women wearing plastic boots and gossamer scarves hurried past them toward the dry safety of their cars.

What's it all about if not mystery, he'd say. Satan's everywhere, watching. He's in the room when we play spin-the-bottle (Coke bottles spin best), and in the dark closet full of coats, umbrellas, and boots. Abby, or Jenny, or Becky giggled between heavy winter coats with their pockets of forgotten small change and broken cigarettes. So, you'd have to find her, the lucky one, among empty hangers ringing a jazzy tune, find her and then try to kiss her in the dark. Find her lips and kiss her before you passed out from excitement and lack of oxygen. That's what

Jack wanted! And then he'd burst out of the closet into the shaded light, gasping for air while awe-struck eyes followed his twisting dance steps, the waltz he didn't know he knew: *one*-two-three . . . *one*-two-three . . . polka *step,* polka *step.*

A short minute later, one of the girls, the lucky one, would come out, her hands on her lips, a joyful shame, and her smile so wide. Crouching a little, she then covered her whole face to muffle her laugh. She might say something witty: "Oh, boy, it was hotter in there than a Saturday confessional!"

The Coke bottle began its rounds again—searching, searching.

"When you close your eyes in the closet, it's like a sunset," Jack rhapsodized, "red, purple, green, blue, and orange, all mixed and stirred, like you see at sunset over the railroad tracks." What Satan could do with sun and clouds wasn't mentioned in the *Catechism,* you can bet, but Jack knew the power. He'd say the power and the glory of Saint Lucifer should not be forgotten when the pungent incense reaches the back of church, just before the priest turns to the congregation and intones, *Ite Missa est.* That was Latin Jack could understand. It was enough! Mass is over! Shuffle out into the daylight. Watch the cars touring around the block, drivers searching for parking spaces before the next Mass. Ebb and flow, give-and-take. Walk the narrow line. The bacon and pancakes await him! Go in Peace, but go quickly. Where he found this profundity was a mystery as much to Jack as to Ben. Some are just gifted, that's all.

When the rain on the awning stopped, Jack stretched his long legs and squinted toward Isaly's blinding neon lights that buzzed like flies at a sticky devils' hubbub.

"Let's go," he said, while searching his tight pockets for a dime. "Coffee time. Let's go!"

As if he needed any!

At the Yellow Wheel Saloon

Jack's dad brushed with fame and fortune in an odd way, but one that never enriched him, like the time he happened to bump into Gene Kelly at the Enright and spilled Coke on the dancer's brightly polished shoes. This was before Gene Kelly was famous, when he was just another hoofer on the Enright stage. As far as Jack was concerned, this bump with the famous dancer signified that his dad was drawn to richness and greatness which would someday present themselves at the ever-open front door. He waited and waited.

Jack enjoyed his dad's company, bragging whenever he could about what a great amateur boxer his dad was in Golden Glove days. But the Depression and the war teamed up to take his few riches away. In its place he found himself surrounded by many children, a tolerant and cheerful wife, and the landlord with his hand extended in months that were just too short. Jack covered for him when debtors called. He answered the phone claiming to be a cowboy, a potato farmer, or a detective. "Ain't here, friend." "Gone fishin'," or "Drivin' a rig in Iowa." Jack had a good time. He'd tell his dad, "Hey, today you were fighting a bull in Wyoming," or "Start packing, we're moving to Homewood." Then they would crouch like boxers and throw soft punches. "Careful there, Sluggo, I was a Golden Gloves champ, almost pro. Take *that* and *that!*"

His dad drove an ancient Chrysler with four doors and a little parlor in the back with room to stretch out and smoke a cigarette in comfort.

He joked that Al Capone once owned it, or that Bogart had one just like it. In fact, maybe this *was* Bogey's. Filling the gas tank was unheard of. "I don't even know how deep it is," his dad said," but when I pump a buck's worth on payday, I hear gurgles and echoes. Sounds like a river at the bottom of a canyon. Guess what, Sluggo, your quarter allowance goes in the tank first. Catch me if you can next week. I might be on the road, or cheating at poker in Vegas."

That was the summer Ben became a car thief.

While Jack's dad slept in the living room watching TV boxing matches, he helped Jack ease that big old Chrysler out of its parking spot on Ellsworth Avenue so they could dash about town.

"Just collecting my allowance," Jack said, with an eye on the gas gauge, which was already on E. Jack was actually better than his dad at figuring just when the gas needle went too far past E. This was a skill he developed out of necessity. If he let the needle go too far, he would run out of gas some distance from the Ellsworth parking space by the streetcar tracks. That meant he would have to borrow a quarter, or, if he was broke, look for pop bottles to cash in for the two-cent deposit. When he had raised about a quarter, he would have to decide just how much gas he needed to buy to get him home with the needle almost on E. Too much gas meant driving around the block at thirty in low gear for five minutes. And then he had to worry about losing his parking place. How could he explain to his dad on Sunday morning why the car was not in its usual spot, especially with his mom and the kids dressed for church and ready to pile in the Chrysler that was not there? And so Jack got the car back where it should be, with the needle on E, if he was lucky. But sometimes he wasn't.

When luck betrayed him, Jack did everything he could to trick his dad. Sometimes he was allowed to run ahead and start the car, which ran at its best when the monster of an engine was hot. Jack pushed on the starter button to wake up the engine; gas sucked into the carburetor, and blue smoke spewed from the tail pipe. Then he dropped the clutch and lurched forward into the space that had fortunately been cleared for him. If he was unlucky, and the space ahead of him was taken, he had to bluff that he had backed the car all by himself just so his mother, who was expecting a baby soon, did not have to walk very far. And off they would go, rocking to-and-fro over the slippery streetcar tracks to Mass at Saint Paul's Cathedral. Breathless, they arrived, hardly late at all. Jack's mom would probably pray for more money and a little girl. Jack would pray for luck, which wasn't really about money. No, it was about getting away with things he'd otherwise have to pay for.

Jack rehearsed the plans for Saturday night's adventure. "You be English and I'll be a dumb German kid. You talk the bartender into giving us free Cokes and tell him all about you being a kid from England without any money, just a bob or two, and the banks are closed. I'll grunt and look stupid and grin. Talk like an Englishman, with lots of *cheerio* and *I say, my good man.* Ben could do this well. His dad's whole family spoke with a perfect British accent.

Jack parked the Chrysler a block from the Yellow Wheel Saloon, which streetcar conductors visited when they were thirsty or needed to make a quick trip to the loo. They stopped their streetcars right in front of the saloon, tilted their ventilated caps rakishly like movie combat pilots did, hoisted their cash box from the floor, and bounced down the steps and into the bar. Conductors chatted with the bartender about aching bladders and pointed back toward the loo. After they returned to the bar, they emptied their Cokes and slid the bottles back to the bartender on their way to the door, their yellow streetcars ready for yet another lap around the dark city.

Jack cheered him on—"Go on! Go on! Just like we planned. Free Cokes. This'll be great. Best ever. You are great, man, great. Free Cokes. Go on!"

He led Jack into the Yellow Wheel Saloon. There were no customers; it was a slow Saturday night. And so the saloon became their stage. Ben held his hand behind him, and Jack took it in his. He grunted and then made some eerie *m* and *n* sounds.

The bartender put down a polishing rag and moved to the front of the bar. "You boys lost or something? Can't find your mommy? Got a load in your pants?" He snickered down the bar into the dark corner where his partner was wiping tables. "Rock, these boys a couple of your kids outta your past? Fall behind on the mortgage to your last ex-wife?"

Rock said that if you closed your eyes and threw a stone in Brooklyn, chances were one out of three you'd hit one of his kids from his sailor-boy days.

"What're the odds in this burg, Rock, about one out of four?"

"Petey, just ask these kids what they want. They want their bottles warmed, or what?"

Ben pulled Jack to the bar, cleared his throat, and said, "I beg your pardon, sir, but I have just arrived in the city from London, England, with my distant cousin, Ludwig, who cannot speak English. He actually cannot speak at all. In a bombing raid some ten years ago, in Dresden, he was shocked and deafened. He has not uttered a word since that day. Doctors say that Ludwig has suffered damaged nerves, and we are here to consult with specialists at Children's Hospital. My parents are staying at Webster Hall. I am just entertaining Ludwig on a walk, and we have come so far that we are thirsty. I was wondering, my good man, whether you would give us bottles of that famous beverage we hear so much about. I believe its proper name is Coca-Cola. I would gladly pay for them, but you see I have only British currency and the banks are not open."

Petey just stared in disbelief, his jaw slack. Then he collected his thoughts and called to Rock, who was listening to him and watching Jack bounce from one foot to the other. "Hey Rock, was you ever in a place called Dresden that they bombed back in the war? Your rubber ducky ever dock there, 'cause I think one of your little stones just showed up looking for daddy and a handout for Cokes?"

"Could be," Rock said. "I'll have to check my diary. Just give the kids Cokes. Give 'em a thrill. When's the last time *we* had a thrill, huh?"

The bartender handed them sweaty bottles of what he called virgin Coke, and told them to strike a blow for liberty. Ben showed Ludwig how to drink from the bottle. Ludwig sucked in air, trapping his tongue in the opening, and crossed his eyes. He made satisfied *m* and *n* sounds, his eyes popping with Teutonic glee.

"Shoulda put a nipple on it." The bartenders laughed. "You say Ludwig ain't said a word in ten years? What's he speak, German or English, or nothing? Hey Rock, you ever hear somebody talk in nothing? 'Zat how you and your new ex-wife talked?"

Ben got bolder. "Actually, he was shocked by the bombs before he ever said anything. He was not yet two at the time. The doctors say that nothing like this has ever happened before. Ludwig's parents died in the bombing. Ever since then he has been with my family, and we all speak English."

Rock called down the bar. "If that ain't a puzzle for the medics, what is? Hey Petey, think of the bill for that house call!"

"Yeah, yeah," said Petey, "just think, old Ludwig there's gonna make some girl a good husband someday. Can't say the wrong thing, and can't complain when the department store bills come in the mail."

"You boys like them Cokes? What d'ya say, Ludwig? They got anything like that in good ol' Dresden? Have another, boys, on the house." He slid two wet bottles across the bar. They raised them to their lips, tilted back their heads while continuing to stare at Petey, and swallowed the pop in three noisy gulps.

When Ben had regained his breath he said, "I cannot thank you enough for your kindness. I know that if Ludwig could speak he would also express his gratitude."

He began to make moves to go, but Ludwig held him in place with a strong grip. Ludwig started to make strange word-like sounds. His lips came together as if to kiss, and out came a breathy *p* followed by *z* and an *r*. *Pleasure?*

"My God in Heaven, I think Ludwig wants to speak."

"Get this, Rock. A deef-and-dumb kid comes to Pittsburgh, drinks two Cokes on the house, and starts talkin' ten years after the bombs dropped. Only in America's all I can say."

"*Ahh pe*," Ludwig strained.

"What's he saying?" Rock asked. He started to move up the bar to hear for himself.

Ben pleaded, "Ludwig, do not get so excited. If you can hear me, please do not do anything bad." He knew what Jack was capable of when he had an audience.

"Kid's a crooner, a real Sinatra, ain't he Rock? Be on *Hit Parade* next week."

"*Yah ors*." Ludwig's eyes sparkled; his lips hissed with *pzr*. *Pleasure?* He bounced from one foot to another and squeezed Ben's hand tighter.

"Hey Petey, call the *Press*. Tell 'em we got a scoop. German kid finds his tongue in the Yellow Wheel Saloon."

Ludwig's face was ablaze with excitement. More sounds came through his lip-drool: "*Ah pe yah ors.*"

"He *is* going to speak," he prompted Ludwig. "After ten years of silence he's going to speak!"

Ludwig's scarlet face leaned over the bar into the bartender's face. They were nose-to-nose. In a primitive pitch as though from a madhouse, Ludwig screamed, "*Up yours, sailor!*" Ben tried to pull Ludwig away from the bar, but he was frozen there. His insane laughter would not stop. The two men reached under the bar for the bat and the phone. But Lucky Ludwig would not budge.

"Let's get outta here, Jack, or we're goners."

With his free left hand, Jack swept the four bottles into the cradle of his arm. He started to move for the door, the bottles rolling in his folded arm. He still held Ben's hand and would not let go. The laughter erupted again. Jack's eyes were glassy with tears. He swung around to run, forgetting that his left leg was wrapped around a bar stool. He lurched to keep his balance. He scrambled and kicked the stool away while at the same time he rescued three of the bottles. Ben dragged him to the door, but Jack stopped. The bartender came closer with his bat. On his face was a knowing grin. He had been had by two bratty kids. Rock was crying tears on the bar and trying to say this was the best night he ever remembered, but his round mouth could only gulp air. He *had* had a thrill!

Jack blocked the doorway until the very last second.

Two couples, probably early moviegoers, tried to come in but they quickly turned and left. The women were a little frightened and Ben felt bad about that. It wasn't in their script.

Petey mocked a savage attack with the bat, its fat end twitching and ready to strike. They exploded through the doorway at the last second, in their wake loud screaming laughter and a Coke bottle bouncing and spinning on the tile floor.

A faded yellow trolley ground to a halt. Sparks fell in the dark from the wires above. Out limped a tired conductor, his hat vainly slipped back on his bald head, his dented money box hanging from his index finger. Ben thought he was after them for crossing dangerously in his path. The rails were slippery from the evening dew, but they escaped, their voices hoarse from strain and laughter. Back in the mob getaway car they romped to the nearest gas station to barter their two bottles for a splash of gas.

A Sunday Morning Scold

On the next morning Jack was running late for the ten o'clock Mass at Saint Paul's. He would never be on time. His dad called a commonplace warning up the stairs: "Jack, you're late."

Jack answered as he always did: "How late?"

"You're maximo late," his dad called up the stairs. "Motivate yourself to Mass and meet us afterward to ride back. After the last Gospel, Dithridge Street side. Don't be too conspicuous."

Jack's dad ushered the rest of the family out the door and up the short street to his mob-boss Chrysler. He wondered out loud whether the car was a little farther down the street than he remembered parking it. Ben stayed with them to help with the kids.

The gas needle was perilously close to E. Or was it actually on E? Jack had bought a dime's worth of Sunoco on his way home from the Yellow Wheel Saloon. Deposit money from the bottles helped, and he had two dimes left to his name, one dime for the streetcar he would have to ride to church. He wished they had bought more gas.

He was afraid the morning would end badly, but he never dreamed how badly.

Jack's dad pulled out over the streetcar tracks and cobblestones for the five-minute drive. With some good coasting on the downhill slant he would be OK, and maybe he could find 32.9 cents for a gallon to get them home. He could slip a quarter from the collection envelope with a drawing of the Lamb of God stamped on it. And Ben had some change, too, if he needed it.

A few blocks from home the motor sputtered and died. Jack's dad pulled the lumbering car to the curb and heard the tires squeak against the concrete. The next trolley could squeeze by, its bell madly ringing a Sunday morning scold.

It was too far to walk to church and still a long trek home with petulant and portable children. And his wife expecting soon.

"John," she said in controlled frustration, "this is getting to be a regular occurrence on Sunday morning. I'm absolutely humiliated by this."

"Some of your legendary bacon and eggs with biscuits will set us all right," he answered. "I'll send Jack to Walnut Street for a can of gas."

"There's more to it than gas, John!"

A 75 Wilkinsburg via East Liberty streetcar came thundering down the avenue, bell clanging, sparks flying from the wires. The conductor's Sunday hat was pitched back, his bejeweled fingers sparkling their own fire. He wore a wide grin masking a silent laugh. The streetcar rocked and the sparks flew, and sand jumped from the rails just for show. It was crowded with Cathedral parishioners on the last run for Mass.

"Here comes the Last Collection," shouted Jack's dad.

In the window of the streetcar's folding front door, Jack's face pressed to the glass, framed like some important saint's painting. Last on, first off. His hair was still wet. He had a sheepish grin as he held up two nicotine-stained fingers in a V for Victory for his stranded family.

"I hope Jack remembers to bring a bulletin home," his mom said in a tired voice as she shifted Bobby on her hip and took a deep breath for the long walk home. "Men," she said, loud enough to hear, "I wonder if they're worth the fuss. Someday, may God's purpose become clear to me!" she prayed.

Ben lifted one of the twins and carried her halfway, and then he lifted the other twin for the remainder of the walk. He had no idea kids could be so heavy. They were like bags of cement. Jerry rode on his dad's shoulders. And then Jack's mom stopped for a moment, put Bobby on the sidewalk, and called to her husband about something happening. Diaper leak, probably. Or open pin. But her look of fear said that something more had happened. Still, they trekked on, slower now. Ben wished that Jack had been with them to carry Bobby. He began to feel guilty about what was happening.

An hour later, still dressed for church with her Sunday hat tipped back in a subtle protest, Jack's mom scrambled eggs with cheese while Jack's brother tried not to burn the toast. Biscuits turned golden brown in the oven and would soak up butter on Jack's plate in a few minutes.

She insisted that she was fine. "Probably just a stitch that old pregnant ladies get." But from her posture he knew she was being brave. She leaned on the counter, elbows carrying her weight, and, with her eye on the old clock, he knew she longed for a rest on the soft sofa.

Jack's dad studied the *Press*, certain that he was a crossword puzzle winner from last Sunday. He was not.

"This crossword puzzle contest is a fraud," he announced, as he had every Sunday, yet he still mailed his entry each Monday on the way to work.

"I need a three-letter word for 'annoying group.' A little help, dear, if we're going to get rich. It begins with *m*."

"I know," she volunteered. "It has to be *men*."

"Doesn't fit!"

"Oh yes it does," she replied. "It *always* fits."

"Here comes Jackie!" one of the kids shouted.

The screen door winced as Jack pulled it open.

"And there go the eggs," she answered. "The boy inhales them."

"That's because you're such a great cook," Jack's dad answered. "And you look terrific in your bonnet. Never take it off!"

"Jackie, did you bring me a bulletin?"

"I forgot. Honest, I just forgot."

"I need the bulletin; it lists who's being buried and who's getting married."

"How can you tell the difference?" Jack's dad asked. He was in high spirits.

His mom said, "Not in front of the children," and Jack said that he got it, and little Jerry, with his mouth full of eggs, mumbled proudly, "I got it, too!"

"Life's a puzzle, Jackie. You might as well know it. What's a five-letter word for food? It begins and ends with a *t*. It could be *treat*. It could be *trout*."

Jack looked at the Sunday breakfast on the kitchen table. "How about *toast?*"

"It fits."

Then Jack asked Ben, the paperboy, if he had secret access to the *Press* puzzle answers. He gave the knowing grin of a jester. They were told to get a quart of gas. "The can's in the trunk. The car's where you last saw it. Enjoy your walk."

"Why is it always me who gets stuck with the can?"

"Think about it while you walk, and, by the way, no smoking with gas on your hands."

"I don't smoke," cried Jack. Why are you always picking on me?"

"Life's a puzzle. Tell me when you find the answer."

Ben told Jack that something serious had happened that morning, but he couldn't say what it was. But it was more than a hunch. Jack looked at him with fear in his eyes. Last night was so long ago, so long ago.

King Kong—Danger Everywhere

Jack had heard that there was a great shoe they should buy, called King Kong—dull black with orange threading. And Jack wanted a pair. He begged his mother for early birthday money and promised he would not be late for Mass ever again. Her eyebrows rose as she reached for her battered purse and found a few bills. He was out the door and on his bike, bald tires slipping on the wet wooden blocks. She silently supplied the "thank you" and "you're welcome." Ben followed, a little embarrassed.

He did not have enough money, so he told Jack to come with him to collect from a few of his customers on Fifth Avenue. They rode their bikes, each trying to cut the other off. It was a longer trip than it should have been, but the playful bumping was worth it.

Ben went up and down the apartment halls, but only a few customers answered his knock. He began to raise some money but was still a little short. Then he heard the piano on the third floor. Jack didn't like climbing steps but he followed him. Byron Janis was home with his grand piano chasing Liszt or Chopin melodies with dazzling speed and precision. He tapped on the door during a pause in the music. When the door opened, he appeared in a T-shirt, baggy slacks, and white socks, chewing away as he always did on some favorite fruit or nuts.

"You always seem to find me," he said with some difficulty. "But after today you'll have to collect from my parents at the store."

Ben asked whether he was going away on a trip.

"Indeed," he answered. "I have to be on a tour in Europe—Amsterdam, Milan, Vienna, Budapest, and some other places, but not exactly in that order. "Do you know where Amsterdam is?" he asked.

He said he had an idea.

"The Dutch," he hinted.

"Oh, yeah, Dutch Boy paint, and then there's Dutch cleanser. The boy with his finger in the dike."

"Do you know where New Amsterdam is?"

He refrained from saying next to Old Amsterdam.

"Well, just so you know, it's in New York City. Remember the governor with the peg leg? He was the boss there in the seventeenth century. Ever hear of Rip Van Winkle at school? Or Sleepy Hollow?"

He laughed and said not to worry. He dug in his pocket, handed over the cash, smiled, and closed the door. The piano began slowly, soft and meditative, a little mournful, in a sad lament, but quickly it raced up and down the scales. Searching, searching. Up and down. Jack sat on the top step, blocking his path.

"Hey, Jack, it's *shoe time*," he shouted. "Let's go."

"Not yet, OK, just a minute. I never heard anything like this."

"If you could run that fast," he joked, "you'd never be late for school or church."

"Right," he said in a distant voice. "Never late, but really early. I wouldn't like that."

Energy restored, Jack romped down the stairs, singing snatches about "rainbows" and "rain drops."

On Frankstown Avenue near Penn in East Liberty there was an Army-Navy store that supplied the neighborhood with helmets, canteens, uniform stripes for all the branches, socks the color of split pea soup, and rows of brown boots, their tongues hanging out, panting for the next war —Korea was at peace. On the second floor by the window over the Frankstown Avenue was a contemporary shoe department. It was hot and stuffy, smelling of fresh leather and polish, the smell of school starting. The salesman measured them and then picked up two boxes in the back.

"Try these on, boys, the real McCoy. Tell your moms I left room to grow. Genuine King Kong shoes. Only place in Pittsburgh you can get 'em."

Jack removed his brogues, which had done service on his Pap-Pap's feet for many years. He had painted the old boots with stove-black paint.

"They look ready for the museum," Ben said.

"They came with Pap-Pap from Ireland," he replied, "before I was born. Now they fit me just right."

The salesman took the old brogues by the laces and respectfully laid them out in the King Kong box; Jack stood for a long time before the mirror.

"Neat," he said. He tucked the box under his arm, paid the cashier, compared the King Kongs on their feet, and stumbled slightly onto the sidewalk.

"Having trouble?" Ben asked. "Pap-Pap could break them in for you." They walked the bikes down Penn Avenue to the five-and-ten store. It would have been a shame not to wander the aisles there. Without discussion they moved to the toy section. A feeling in the gut told Ben that he could never forget this place, with its cheap gun-and-holster sets, tiny fire engines, miniature soldiers still fighting in Germany and Italy, trick handcuffs, and picture puzzles of Death Valley and the Grand Canyon. Young enough to look but too old to buy. With reverence, they moved on to turtles, their distinctive odor reminding Ben of the many turtles that passed through his fingers to ashen graves in the backyard.

"I'm going to buy Jerry a turtle," Jack said, "because the last one died. It was named Howdy."

He studied the little turtles in their tank and found one that was just right, with its dark green shell and yellow-and-red lines along its head.

"That's it," he said, and lifted it out with a little net hanging on the tank. Nearby were small boxes with wire carry handles, like ones used in Chinese takeout places.

"What's his name?" Ben asked.

"Let's call him Doody."

Inside the box was damp moss. He dropped the turtle onto the moss, closed the lid, and wandered around for other sights. When he was satisfied that his brother would be pleased, he paid for Doody. And then they went onto the street where their bikes still leaned against the stone wall. The King Kong box was tightly fastened to Jack's handlebars. Ben's box was in his basket. Jack's basket was at home, a tiny basket no larger than a loaf of bread.

Ben suddenly winced in pain from a powerful numbing punch to his shoulder. There had been a knuckle in that punch. A knuckle sandwich. That meant Big Hank was out on probation again. His favorite greeting was a knuckle-punch to the arm. Having settled some debt with him, he turned to Jack.

"So, what you got in the little box? Let me see. Some fudge I could eat?"

Jack stared him down. "It's only a turtle. Do you eat turtles, Henry?"

"Call me Big Hank or I'll kick your butt all over the place."

While Jack was tall and lanky with very long arms, Big Hank was huge in the shoulders and biceps. But the most startling part of his body was a huge set of hands that turned into gigantic fists and sharp knuckles. Nature had equipped him for a sad and short life. His father died on D-Day, a random victim of German machine guns. His mother, a really nice lady, let Big Hank roam the streets. She did not complain when juvenile court judges told her it was time to give Big Hank a rest in the home for juveniles called Thorn Hill.

Jack's dad had passed feinting and dodging tricks to his first born. In a fighter's stance, with elbows by his side and sturdy legs under him, he was a regular palisade of defense. Swing all you want, you couldn't get through the fortress of sticks that was his body.

Polite jabs would not hurt Big Hank. A tank or cannon would do that, or a bayonet from Frankstown Avenue. Jack's first thought was to talk himself out of trouble, but his smart patter, "Oh, yeah," and "Says who?" was met with, "Turtle Boy's going to feel some pain." Big Hank slammed Jack into the store wall. Jack's fair skin turned red. The old scars on his head came out under the thin blond hair. He made a boxer's pose with a rounded back and bent knees. He circled and limbered his arms. Smiling, Big Hank stumbled in with two stunning punches to the shoulder. Jack twisted Big Hank's arm, slid his right leg behind him, toppling him to the sidewalk. Big Hank rolled into a parking meter and climbed the pole for balance. He was mad, his knuckles bleeding, his jeans torn.

Witty Jack said, "Hey, Big Hank, old buddy, better put a nickel in the meter 'cause that's all the time I'm gonna need to make you say *uncle.*"

Big Hank shouted back, "Laugh all you want, Turtle Boy, 'cause I'm gonna crack your shell and make soup with you, see!"

Why, he wondered, was Big Hank making this friendly meeting such a big event? Was he high on Thorn Hill posturing?

A crowd was gathering: retirees, widows, a few school kids holding twisted paper bags with pencils poking out, and nuns from the convent out in pairs, buying whatever nuns needed. Big Hank, standing again, beat his huge fists on Jack's shoulders. But Jack's long arms fastened around broad-chested Big Hank's middle. His arms and fists were now of little use. He was losing his breath in the bear hug, his head pushed up and back by Jack's skull. He made the mistake of using breath to threaten Jack—"Gonna murderize you, you're a gonner, TB!" Jack took him to the sidewalk again with a tripping motion. Then Jack's long skinny legs were tightened like a vise around Big Hank's head, the knuckle-knobs of his knees digging into his scarlet and white ears. He tried to pry the legs apart, but Jack turned in clockwise circles on his left hip, propelling himself with his King Kongs, now badly lacerated on the sidewalk, which glittered in the afternoon sun. Big Hank had to follow his turns like a shadow.

"Time's almost up, Big Hank."

More people had gathered. They said things like, "Beats TV wrestling, that phony stuff with dance steps and all." "I think I saw this guy in the last Olympics. Now that's real wrestlin'." "Make him puke and he'll quit." There were peacemakers among the crowd. "Boys, boys, boys stop this instant. Nothing can be gained by fighting. Let him go!" The kids with the pencils began beating each other with the eraser-tipped ends. No one paid them any attention to them. Then the older of the pair of nuns stepped through the crowd, as nuns can do, and poked Jack hard with the sharp end of her umbrella.

"John," she said, "I know you and your beautiful mother. This demonstration is regrettable." Then she rotated her umbrella, holding it by the pointed end while tapping Jack with the crook handle. How true was the familiar adage that anything in a nun's hand is a potential weapon? Sixth graders remembered Sister Propella swinging her heavy rosary furiously before some startled boy's face, his perfect pompadour wave mussed by the wind that could have lifted a bomber into the air. "I want you at Confession on Saturday, do you understand?" Each word was punctuated by the tapping umbrella. "Now get up!" The younger, lesser nun, whose habit had not acquired the sheen that comes with age and experience, deferred to her superior's technique for making peace. She murmured to those near her that God is not being served by this barbaric conduct.

"What's the world coming to?" asked an old lady with a badly scratched and scarred wooden cane. "Why, my late husband would have taken these boys behind the outhouse for a lesson or two!"

Jack released his knees. He struggled to stand. Big Hank, tipsier than Jack, but more theatrical, rolled away and bounced to his feet, and then did a little foot work that said, "I didn't feel nothin', punk!" Turned to face Jack, he stumbled backward toward Frankstown Avenue, staring down his arms in disbelief that they had failed him. How was that possible?

"Catch you later, Turtle Boy, when there ain't no nuns crying for ya," was his parting shot.

"Sure thing, Big Hank. Gimme a call later, big guy."

A Glancing Blow

They mounted up and made their way through the crowd on the sidewalks of Penn Avenue and on to South Highland, Ellsworth, and Roslyn Place. Jack would have explaining to do about the scarred new shoes and the blood on his elbows. But he delayed his mother's angry reaction by stopping on Ellsworth at a favorite hangout called Kate's, a tiny wedge of a store above the train tracks and by the pedestrian bridge over them. He removed the King Kongs and replaced them with the boots from Ireland. He was careful with Doody in his dark, damp box.

"It shouldn't have been that way. Big Hank never loses, never quits. I want to go down to the tracks and sit awhile before I go home," he said, "because I need to figure out what to do about all of this."

Not far from his house, they slid down the embankment to the tracks. The tracks were surrounded by piles of shifting, sharp, gray rocks about the size of eggs. They sometimes pitched them at bottles dropped there by winos at night. Jack put Doody on a railroad tie, which was the only level place. Across the double tracks were smaller boys loafing away the afternoon. But one of them got the idea to toss stones toward Jack and Ben. They were too far away to hit them, or so it seemed. Jack would normally have returned fire, but not today. He stood up to get a look at the boys. Probably Pierce Street kids just practicing.

"So, what do you want to do?" Ben asked. "I should be starting my paper route by now."

Jack turned to answer, and in that moment a rock arching over the

173

tracks in a lazy lob came toward Jack's head. *"Duck!"* The rock scraped across Jack's head and continued on its new orbit. Blood began to run across his forehead and into his eye. He turned around twice, doubled over in pain, and fell on the sharp rocks. He might have passed out from the shock but he recovered enough to ask Ben how bad it was.

"I can't tell. There's just blood."

He took off his T-shirt, wrapped it tightly over his head, and tied a knot under his chin. "What'll I do?" he cried. "My mom'll murder me!" Ben said that Jack had to go home, which was fairly close by. In fact, he may have to go to the Shadyside Hospital emergency room for stitches. The boys across the track had fled. Jack dumped his bike near the sidewalk. "Get it later," he said. Up on the sidewalk Ben pushed his bike and tried to reassure Jack that he was doing fine. He staggered some, stopping a few times to muster his will to stagger home to a scolding he did not want to hear.

"Where's Doody?" he shouted. A vein on his forehead throbbed. "Go back! Get him quick!"

He was relieved he didn't have to face Jack's mom and explain what happened. Jack would make up a good story. This was his gift. Ben ran around back to the wall above the tracks where they loafed on dull evenings. He dropped to the muddy path beside the tracks and then climbed the shifting rocks to the rails. He ran and jumped along the track toward Doody. He couldn't see the box for a few seconds, and then it was there, next to the silver track. But, to his horror, the ground began to vibrate and the tracks quivered. Around a curve a roaring steam engine plunged, coughing ugly gray smoke. The engineer blew an emergency whistle like Morse code, but simplified for morons: "Get off the tracks, you fool, I can't stop this engine. Get off!"

He fell down the rocky slope into the muddy path. He could never reach Doody in time. Impossible. But the vibrations began to move the container, and a rush of wind pushed by the train caused the little package to fall and bounce. In a second he saw the engineer's red mouth screaming from his window, words like *stupid* and *jerk*. Still rolling, he was mortified. Humiliated. How could he explain the burning scratches and cuts on his arms and face? Should he tell the truth that he almost died trying to save Doody, a little turtle? Would he have been a hero or a fool? Was this all about Doody or Jack? Or Death?

The long train raced by him, frozen there, sprawled on his stomach. What a stunt! The caboose finally passed, its back door open to a black interior, jeering at him and wagging its arrogant tail. The gust from the train blew the moss out of sight, and the box, filled with air like a parachute, rode in the currents above him. Doody had to be among the rocks, but where? He was afraid to take a step, so he crouched low and scanned the area for the dark, green shell. But the rocks were so filled with shadows from the afternoon sun that he could not see Doody. He felt hopeless. Should he mark the spot with a wine bottle and ask Jack to come back to help him? Suddenly, he saw a slight movement. It came from the underside of Doody's shell, which was the color of dry grass. His little feet were moving like oars, his head secure in the shell. He lifted him with his index finger and thumb, and cupped his little body in his hand.

He righted Jack's scrawny bike for the walk home. There was an odd sensation in his left hand where Doody scratched in protest, and under his right hand the bike wobbled like an unsteady, newborn colt. The bike was better ridden than pushed, oddly enough, and with that insight and the sense of hope and satisfaction the pathetic menagerie of gorilla shoes, an itinerant turtle, and a shaky colt inched its way toward Jack and whatever came next.

What Came Next— Domestic Sunshine

Jack had an inch-long scrape on the top of his head, for the rock had just glanced off his hard skull. The bleeding was dramatic, but after his mom's careful treatment he was able to rest in bed and doze during the day. True, he had been grounded for three days but he could watch TV, sit on the wall by the tracks, talk on the phone whenever he could get the line, eat anything in the refrigerator that pleased him, and, on the final day of being grounded, he could even make requests, not like the request of the condemned man, but like that of the hero whose slightest hint was a command—"I sure could eat some fried chicken and mashed potatoes," he said weakly, and within the hour plates were delivered to him by bewildered brothers who had not seen so much of Jack since they were born.

His mom had shaved what little blond hair there was around the wound. She then treated it with Vaseline and gauze; on top of this she stretched two Band-Aids positioned like railway ties. She padded this bandage with more gauze, placed three strips of white tape over it, and then, having built a small mound, she put three balls of cotton above the odd bandage for cushioning just in case Jerry and Bobby wrestled with Jack too forcefully. Jack asked to see the finished product. His mother held a mirror over his head where a halo would normally be. He looked into that mirror with her small makeup mirror, moving it up and down until he found the reflection in the larger mirror. He had fun doing this. He asked his mom to move the mirror as he moved his so he could see into his ear. That's when she said, "Oh, Jackie, for a grounded kid who is still recovering from a dangerous blow to the head, you sure do know how to play the devil with me."

The three pretty girls, Abby, Becky, and Jenny, were invited in to see him. He gave a good account of the attack, telling them that he had skillfully dodged the hail of rocks thrown at him by juvenile delinquents escaped from Thorn Hill, but the one rock he did not see bounced off his noggin and knocked him out for five minutes. Blood ran down his face and his back; he could not see anything. And, when a train came rushing at him, he forced himself to consciousness; in the last second he managed to crawl to safety. It was a convincing performance.

"Oh, Jackie," they said, "it must have been awful, just awful. Were you wearing your Saint Christopher medal when it happened?"

Jack said, "No, I gave the medal to my dad to hang on the car mirror because he needed it more than I did."

Jack's mom interrupted him: "But you had your rosary in your jeans pocket. I found it when I did the wash."

Jack just looked at her and said, "I did?"

The audience ended then, and Jack promised to visit the girls soon; he was sure they'd want to see his scar while it was fresh and rosy. The girls squealed in disgust and delight. The screen door banged shut with finality.

Jack opened up to Ben in their long talks during his recovery. He said that his mom was even more remarkable than he ever knew. She treated him with such kindness. She invited him to sit with her during soap operas when she should have been ironing. Ben saw this kindness on an afternoon before he began his paper route. The little TV's blue-gray light; the slow scrolling of its screen; the hum of the aged speaker; the hot iron scenting the room with clean heat; all impressed him with domestic happiness. The refrigerator was only a few steps away; the afternoon's green light filtered through the old sycamore trees; birds squabbled, and dogs moaned behind someone's fence. Yes, all confirmed that he was in the best place any boy could hope for.

She was his sainted mother. At first Jack asked her many questions about the soaps. While his questions irritated her, she was soon asking him questions about what they watched.

"Jackie, why do I dislike that handsome man? What's he going to do to Beatrice? He's selfish and devilish, but so are many characters in the program. Why? What do you think?"

"Well," Jack began, "just look at his mustache. It tells everything about him. It's dark, hangs below his lip, and makes me think of a chimney sweeper, like the one I saw in some old movie at midnight. It's so thick. When he kissed her, I thought she would be hurt, but maybe he was the one who was hurt, I guess, because, after he kissed her, he used his thumbs to comb the mustache. I dunno."

"So, the man's hiding something; maybe he's afraid that love will hurt him. He's insecure and wants to destroy anyone who gets too close to him and his dark secret."

Jack said he didn't know what the secret was. Jack had trouble with secrets.

"Well, Jackie, I don't want to put ideas in your head at your impressionable age, and you really should be out playing and *not* seeing what bad things some adults do to each other on these programs. I'll just say that the man with the mustache, whose name, by the way, is Raoul, knows that Beatrice has inherited some money, a lot of money, and he wants to marry her, and then he'll probably run off with her money to Brazil. We'll have to wait and see."

"OK," he said, "but why Brazil?"

She thought a few seconds. "Well, there are dark jungles and uncharted rivers. The land is full of mystery. If I wanted to disappear, I would go to Brazil, or somewhere like it. Anyway, it's just a story."

She looked at him oddly when he said, "I'll bet there are mysterious men in Brazil with black mustaches, too." Jack said that if he ever runs away, it would be to Wilmerding because his dad could pick him up when he called. His dad knew Wilmerding like the back of his hand.

Mom sighed. "Oh Jackie, you have a way of distracting me, and look at that pile of ironing that's beginning to dry out. Hit the switch."

And then she stunned the boys with the news: "By the way, school will start two weeks late this year, on September 8."

Jack jumped with pleasure. "Why is that?" he said. "Why?"

She looked worried. "There's another polio scare." And then she told Jack it was time to go upstairs and rest. He bounced up the stairs two at a time, but on the landing he remembered and slowly climbed like an old man to the top. Ben left for his paper route, but all the while he imagined Jack stretched out on the cool lower bunk, asking himself whether life could get any better, squeezing his eyes tight in the sunny room and falling into a deep sleep, deeper than an old man would know, and full of dreams, perhaps of sitting with his buddy atop a flat-roofed garage in the dark, waiting for an audience to pass by, and then beginning the chorus of, "Oh, oh, oh, no, nooo, oh, please, nooo. Oh yes, yes." The knowing audience of passersby laughed. "Hey, get a new act, will you. I've heard this one before. Sweet dreams!" Or he might dream of sights he'd seen through cracks in window shades he visited at night on certain streets in Shadyside, in narrow passageways between the crowded houses. Oh, it's great to be Jack, flat on his back on the cool mattress, listening for the call to dinner of Swiss steak, potatoes, onions, and parsnips in thick gravy.

Lash LaRue Meets Red Ranger

Jack lived for the moment, a-second-at-a-time. He could be sentimental, but never nostalgic. God gave him eyes in front, not in back, he said. A vision was an instantaneous appreciation of now, like a camera's click catches not the past or the future, but now. It was nearly impossible to keep up with Jack. Just when you thought you had, he would already be off somewhere else. He saw sharply in bright light as well as in darkness. Shadows revealed substances to him. He liked the shadows. "The Shadow knows!" he would say when a doubter questioned him.

And so he loved the near-darkness of the movie theater, snug in his plush seat with its odor of the inside of a slipper. And when the projector began to throw odd shapes on the screen, and as the sound track dragged itself awake, Jack took what sounded like his last breath, a deep one, and was not heard again. And when the lights slowly came up for intermission he sat erect and shouted, "What happened?" Then he'd settle back in the toasty-warm contour of the velour seat and take in the next show. One after another, double bills became double-double bills.

On Saturday mornings he couldn't wait for the movies to open. Twenty-two cents got him in and nothing short of fire or earthquake would get him out. The Sheridan Square, the Regent, the Enright, the Liberty, and the Cameraphone all competed for his patronage on Saturdays. But he avoided the Triangle, a sinister gang hangout on Frankstown Avenue. Jack went to the movie that had the best matinee giveaways, such as wagons and bikes. It was the bike that he coveted most and he found a way to increase his chance of winning in a most cunning way. He secretly borrowed a handful of quarters from his little brothers' piggy banks, sometimes five or six quarters, depending on their stash. His brothers got quarters every Sunday if they were good during the week. It became Jack's job to keep them good or to cover for them if necessary. His own Sunday quarter for church rarely tinkled in the brass collection plate. When his mom noticed, he'd say that he was saving it for the second collection, for missionaries in Africa. So often, however, there was no second collection. Jack had a keen sense of missionary needs. And so the quarters accumulated, hidden away in his junk drawer only to reappear on Saturday.

On the typical Saturday he was among the first in the lobby. Kids came in full of excitement, each clutching a pink or yellow or blue ticket with a number on it. For each raffle the ticket color changed. You couldn't cheat, but you could be cagey. In a friendly way, Jack would approach a kid, usually younger by a grade at school.

"Hey," he'd say, "buy your ticket? You ain't gonna win anyway, sell me your ticket. I'll give you a quarter for it. That's five Hershey bars, kid, one for each day of the week, see, in your lunch bucket."

The kid would say no, he had a good chance of winning.

Jack said, "Here, let me see your number, give me your ticket, I'll give it right back." The kid, sensing something magical in Jack's prophetic powers, gave him the ticket, and Jack pressed a quarter into the kid's sweaty palm. "Hang onto my quarter for me," he said in a trustworthy voice. Then he'd hold the ticket before the light, study it, and begin to hand it back. Then sadly he revealed his finding: "This number is so low you'll never win. This ticket is just about worthless, trust me."

The kid rubbed the quarter between his thumb and index finger. It began to feel good.

Jack held the ticket out and said, "OK, if you don't believe me. Take the worthless ticket and give me my quarter back."

"Wait," said the kid, "you can have it and I'll keep the quarter," which was halfway to his pocket.

"OK with me," Jack said. "You know how to drive a hard bargain!" The drama often ended this way. But on a bad Saturday, when parents or big brothers got involved, he went outside where the line was very long and said to a kid up front, "Hey, mind letting me in? I gotta buy a bunch of tickets for my brothers and sisters who are stuck in traffic, OK?" The boldness and confidence worked to get him to the mouse hole at the window where he'd buy as many tickets as he had quarters for. They would get to their seats just as the lights were going down.

When Jack was no longer grounded, Ben sat with him on Saturday morning in the Enright, clutching his one raffle ticket while Jack held seven or eight. The matinee prize was exactly what Jack waited for—a glorious blazing-red and-chrome Schwinn with whitewall tires, mirrors on the handlebar, a light at the center, chrome shocks above the front wheel, Roadmaster brakes, a horn button in a nicely swollen red panel between two sturdy metal bars in front of the seat, reflectors, and streamers.

Jack chewed his fingernails through the first western, *Outlaw Country*, starring Lash LaRue playing double roles: he's Lash, an honest marshal, and he's his twin brother, the Frontier Phantom, an outlaw with a conscience. The one brother cracks the whip of justice, the other smokes small cigars. Ben thought the most memorable line of dialogue was Frontier's response to Lash's placing him under arrest: "Don't be a fool, Lash!" Lash, of course, could never be a fool. Why would Frontier think Lash could ever be one? Should the lines perhaps have been reversed? Ben knew that he himself would be Lash, just as he was Roy Rogers and the Durango Kid; Jack would have to be his errant twin, the deep philosopher—the Catechism Kid. Even the three pretty girls would agree with Ben. But there is a happy ending typical of those films—Frontier wisely listens to Lash and decides to reform and even spend some time in jail. Forgiveness granted. And so, with a crack of the whip, the Louisiana cowboy, with a day's dark beard and a voice of slow vowels, rights the wrongs in his family and on the silver screen as well. The Enright was purified for the ritual granting of a red Schwinn bike to one lucky boy.

Then the lights came on. The manager danced onto the stage followed by not one but two ushers pushing the model red Schwinn into the spotlight. What a shout the kids made! The manager held a microphone on a long-tangled cord that he straightened with lazy jump-rope twirls.

He laughed. "Hello boys and girls, or should I say hello toys and curls? Hey, do we have any twins in the audience?"

Everyone laughed. The manager said that the tickets in the basket matched all of the tickets held by the kids, and one lucky ticket was going to be drawn in just a minute, but before chaos broke out, he needed to say that if a girl wins, there's a twin bike with all of the features, except that the horn was in the frame that ran at an angle toward the ground. Girls should not have to ride boys' bikes. The winner would receive a special letter to the Sears manager on North Highland Avenue. Have your dad drive you there and the bike will be placed in his car. "How does that sound, guys and gals?"

Jack began bouncing in his seat. This was his moment.

"Our senior usher, Tony, will reach into the basket and pick the winning ticket. The lucky winner should call out a cheer and run down the aisle to the stage."

Tony removed his jacket, as he had been coached to do, rolled up his sleeve, showed an empty hand to the kids, closed his eyes, and pulled one ticket from the basket. He held it high in triumph before handing it to the manager.

"The lucky number is 7-3-6-2, that's 7-3-6-2."

He had a huge grin, but the audience was silent, and then there was murmuring like kids make when the last bell rings in the morning and the teacher's not in the classroom. What could it mean? Did anybody see Mrs. So-and-So? Jack began going through his tickets. Not the first one. He dropped it on the floor. Or the second or the third, but when he saw the number 7362 on the fourth ticket, he let out a piercing shout. "I got it! That's *my* number!"

In an instant he was scampering across the kneecaps of the boys and girls to his left. Hands waving in the air, he bounced onto the stage. The manager shook his hand with vigor. The kids groaned.

"Here it is," Jack cried, "my ticket!"

"Well boys and girls, the manager spoke into the microphone, let's confirm that the ticket says 7-3-6-2." He held it before him and slowly read each number. More groans followed. "Let's see who our winner is. Please tell us your name, young man." Jack seized the microphone, which had a surprising similarity to an Isaly's Skyscraper ice cream cone. The manager struggled, but he had to give it up, and Jack held the microphone to his lips.

"My name's Jack," he cried. "I just want to thank my mom and dad for making all this possible, and my little brothers, too, for their part."

He put the Sears envelope in his back pocket. There was a prompted applause as Jack ran up the aisle and entered his row, saying politely, "excuse me." The lights were already low; the next movie began with crackles and spider marks shaking on the screen. He settled back, but he was so excited that he hardly saw the movie, a Durango Kid western called *Laramie*. When the lights came up, he asked what happened. Ben told him that the good guy in the white hat won. Black-hatted men were evil, and so they always lost the girl or the stagecoach gold. Life was about winning and losing. For the first time, this was not a double-double bill. The envelope for the manager at Sears felt like a rock in his pocket. Time to go home and beg his dad for a ride to Sears.

On the walk home Jack asked what he should call the bike. Names assured ownership. He tried on a few, but none fit. Naming a bike was harder than naming a turtle. Streetcars rumbled past; pretty girls sauntered on the sidewalk; a sleepy dog sniffed Jack's King Kongs, yawned, and went back to his nap. Ben came up with a name he liked. It captured the color and the purpose of the bike; it promised masculine adventures.

"What name?" he asked.

Ben paused for a moment of reverence. The name would be "Red Ranger."

"Yes!" he shouted. "That's it. I love it!" He gave him a pal's punch right over Big Hank's, which was a dull yellow now. "Thanks!"

Interlude I: Remembering, Not Dreaming

The extended vacation of two weeks promised more adventures, more benign howling from rooftops, skirmishes on sidewalks, and little plays of deception, like getting free Cokes or free tickets to the movies on Penn Avenue. There was an auto show at the Armory, too, that they planned to sneak into through the coal chute by sliding down the tall pile of coal. But none of this was to be.

The extended vacation was just a lonely time for Jack; he could not leave his house. The polio scare frightened his parents. They knew that if polio was out there, Jack would find it. So, he was grounded for his own good. Also, the advanced pregnancy of his mother made her depend on Jack because she began to develop complications. She was told not to climb stairs or lift laundry baskets. She slept on the first-floor sofa; she watched soap operas. She was certain that so much time spent watching inane television was sinful, especially with Jack at her side witnessing her addiction. Still, she called her son a good companion, her redeeming angel. "And if I should happen to fall asleep, you will tell me what I missed, won't you?"

They all knew the warnings about polio. Elderly relatives had their special advice. Do not swim in yellow polluted streams made by coal mine run-off. Do not exert yourself in sports. Stay out of drafts. Get lots of sleep. Avoid crowds, like those at Saturday morning movies. Read books, visit libraries and museums. Keep up with your studies.

Talk with elderly friends and relatives. Sip milkshakes slowly to avoid dangerous headaches. Report headaches, leg cramps, and back pain to your parents. Do not kiss girls. Wash hands over and over. Do not touch doorknobs you do not know. Stay out of phone booths. Stay away from public urinals. Keep a prayerful attitude. Be a Boy Scout at heart and follow the *Catechism* on all matters pertaining to carnal excesses. And do your best to be positive and cheerful with younger brothers and sisters.

The highlight of Ben's day was delivering the Pittsburgh *Press* up and down apartment halls on Shadyside's Fifth Avenue. Each day presented different collective aromas, culminating on Friday afternoon with pungent sauerkraut, fried fish, and spice-laden meals he could not even imagine. If food equaled life, then the apartments were fully alive, even without Byron Janis' piano music in the background. It troubled him that school would open soon with lessons doubled up, shortened lunch periods, and, he was afraid, empty desks of students hospitalized, in iron lungs, or already in physical therapy. Football players would look lost in their new game jerseys, with no practices to go to and no games on Friday nights.

Dreams of adventure were replaced by odd memories. There was a vivid scene six or seven years earlier in another part of the city. His sister's bike, a girl's bike, a huge, heavy thing made of prewar steel, was available when she was away and sometimes he would straddle the bike but not sit on the seat, which was set too high for him. He got bold enough to stand up on the pedals and coast down the block. If he fell, he found a way to avoid being embarrassed. He would get up, walk around the bike and then kneel by the sprocket, which he pretended to fix.

In the house the radio played the afternoon soap operas, which Cecilia listened to with her good ear. She knew every detail of *Just Plain Bill* and *Stella Dallas*. Then news broke right in the middle of a program. Roosevelt had died.

Cecilia cried, gasping for air. "Oh, no," was all she could say. She covered her face with her hands.

Ben ran to his sister's bike, straddled it, pedaled some, but moved quickly up the sidewalk calling out the news: "Roosevelt is dead. Roosevelt is dead!"

A block from home a woman stood in her yard admiring the lilac bushes, which had survived the winter storms. They were covered with beautiful bunches of purple flowers. She was smoking a long cigarette, in public. She wore high-belted slacks. "Roosevelt is dead," he recited.

"Boy," she called to him. The smoke came from her mouth and nose, her head tipped back for the full pleasure of the moment. She removed a speck of tobacco from her tongue with her fingers. "Boy," she demanded, "which *one?*"

How foolish! He thought there was one Roosevelt, but there was another, and her name was Eleanor. This was one of many insights he began collecting from his earliest years—for most people trials come before errors. But not for him. Errors came first and then came the trials. He should have recognized then that he was too introspective, too scrupulous, a busybody, and a nuisance. In the next few years he pictured himself as the inside-out boy—too busy figuring out the little disasters of yesterday to live the renewal of now, of today. Yes, FDR was gone, but Eleanor lived. (Cecilia believed that Eleanor was a little too "pink" for her tastes, and added something about Russia.)

Sometime later, an unusual moment happened one evening when Cecilia came home with a book in her bag, not a library book, for there was no plastic cover. He picked up the book from her reading pile and studied the title—*The End of My Life*. What does this mean, he asked her, because if someone says his life ended then he must be dead? Cecilia had no answer. All she said was that Aunty Gooden was given the book as a gift.

"Look," she said, "the author has a beautiful name—Vance Bourjaily. Sounds *very* French to me. Wouldn't you agree?"

"*Oui, oui,*" he answered.

Cecilia laughed. "Your Aunty Gooden passed it on with the caution that it was one of those new books that were in bookstores, books about the Second World War."

"Are you really going to read it?" he asked.

"Probably," she answered, "but I have a novel by Willa Cather that comes first."

"Well," he said, "if a dead man tells the story, let me know."

"You don't actually have to die to be dead," she said. "There are many deaths in a person's life, but then life returns. When my father died, I thought I had died, too, and for months I was in a dark depression, but then slowly I began to feel life around me, reawakening my spirits. I was very young then. That's what the title suggests to me, but you're too young to understand something like a temporary death."

Two weeks later, she told him that it was a sensitive story with a young narrator, an ambulance driver in Italy during the war. One day, while showing off, he risked a pretty nurse's life and she was killed by a German bullet. The young man felt such guilt; he felt that he was also dead. He was old enough to feel this death, but not experienced enough to forgive himself. He did not know how to escape from the prison of his past, from guilt. (Ben worried that *he* was escaping from his past and that the sorrow he felt about Annie was lost to him now.) It must be terrifying to have those thoughts of life ending just when life was beginning in earnest. (Was his life just beginning in earnest?) Then she tried to cheer him up by saying that the character's nickname was Skinner.

Cecilia finished her thoughts: "Maybe the author was telling readers that in life there are many skins we can live in *if* we have forgiveness and hope. At least that's what I think," she said. "And that's all that matters to me."

(That would fit, he said to himself, thinking of Peter the Python's skin rolled in a shoebox and of Annie's holding the snake's head.)

Old Man Brooks

Jack was still helping his mom while making his case for a weekend out of the house. Ben wandered around to familiar places, one of them being the corner of Alder and South Highland. There he talked to an old man who used to live on his street until his two sisters-in-law forced him out. This was shortly after the death of his second wife. He settled in a room on the corner of Alder and South Highland. Sometimes Ben visited him; they had soup for lunch and talked about his past on the railroad and even the rail-side romances that came his way.

On sunny, warm days, he stationed himself on the corner to be entertained by the women coming from the bakery, Giant Eagle, or the drug store. They bought Menzi's milk and ice cream at Poli's. They'd hurry home before the ice cream melted. Old Man Brooks stood in the warm sunlight though his lips, a feint lavender-blue, belonged more to an Arctic explorer. He wore a straw hat with a band of dark brown, a dress shirt and saucy bow tie, blue trousers pulled above his pot belly, and high, laced boots from another era. A rubber bag was strapped to his leg under the baggy pants.

"My plumbing quit on me," he said.

He made the best of street-corner chatter with the women passing by for his personal review. This was probably the last pleasure he had in his long life.

Ben told him about the polio scare and school being closed for two weeks.

"Nothing for me to worry about," he said, and added that old men are a fearless lot. "Death. I've seen death," he said. "I nursed my wife for a year before she died, did everything, including diapers and baths. She was brave, but she knew it was the end. Old people are ready, so what's there to be afraid of?" But he was still angry that he lost his little house on Lamont Place to "them two rum-hounds" he had for sisters-in-law. Sometimes the tipsy sisters struggled up the alley, shoulder-to-shoulder, propping themselves up, their hennaed hair bobbing left and right above tight scowls.

What interested him most were the "nice young things," the "sweet pieces," and "the cuties" on his corner. These were widows and lonely women with their bags of milk and bread, a few oranges, and tea bags. To Ben's eyes they were not beauties. Jenny, Becky, and Abby *were* beauties. These tired and stooped grandmothers were frequently dressed in remnants of long ago, in out-of-fashion dresses rescued from Goodwill. But how they brightened when Old Man Brooks held them lightly by their elbows, smiled, and told them they looked beautiful. He courted his sweeties to the curb, helped them with the step down, and, as they minced hurried steps to the far curb, he raised his hand in an old man's salute, fingers loose and wayward.

He'd turn to him and say, "What a sweet piece! What a cutie!" And then, before long, he lifted his gold retiree's watch from a little pocket, said that a train was due to pass beneath the South Highland Avenue Bridge, and so off he went to stand in the engine smoke or the diesel fumes, perhaps thinking about his fifty years of coupling cars, tossing Depression-era thugs from empty cars, and entertaining the pretty girls at stops and layovers along the way.

On Probation

He couldn't understand Old Man Brooks' passion for beautiful women, whatever their age. He asked himself, "When will I have my own evidence of passion? Was there a library book that would tell all?" Should he ask his brother, who, by the way, took turns falling in love with Abby and Becky? To his great surprise, he learned everything he needed to know about love from Jenny on a brilliant afternoon below the sun-penetrated trees on Roslyn Place. Even in shade he squinted behind sunglasses, for he had just been to the eye doctor for a new prescription in time for the new school year. Cecilia was a social worker helping partially sighted children to live normal lives, to stay in school, to prosper with learning aids such as Talking Book recordings. She knew just about every ophthalmologist in the city and she insisted that he have drops in his eyes. These drops dilated his pupils for a very long week. He could not read. Movies were out of the question, but he still went to them and suffered silently. The screen was so bright he had to shut his eyes. Leaving the darkened theater, his head throbbing, he stumbled blindly into the brilliant daylight on Penn Avenue. He had to be led home down dark, damp alleys where the sun never shone. The streetcar tracks sparkled, their images remaining with him for hours.

He spent most of the long days on Jenny's porch trying to play Hearts or Monopoly. Because he could not read the cards, thanks to that doctor and his potent drops, Jenny read his cards. On long, rainy afternoons, paying little attention to the rules of Monopoly, she slid his car around the board. Along the way, she paid his fines and bought him properties from his dwindling stack of bills. But he was so happy! He secretly adored her. He was happily lost in the labyrinth of love as well as on the Monopoly board. (Traitor, he accused himself, thinking of Annie, the guilty voice from deep below. How long could he continue to live in guilty, blinding parentheses?)

Jenny studied him with her dark, inquiring eyes. "How can you look at me without seeing me?"

"I had these stupid drops in my eyes, and I can't see anything up close," he whined.

She laughed her throaty laugh. "Well," she asked, not quite believing me, "what do I look like when you can't see me?"

He missed a few turns since he was stuck in jail. In fact, she may have placed him in jail just so she could ask her surprising question. He thought for a moment.

"Well, you have dark hair, and really dark eyes ('uh-huh'), and your eyes and hair shine."

He could only imagine the tip of her tongue exploring the chipped tooth, her lips wet, and her head tilted in expectation, but ready for a throaty laugh. "You have a small scar, or mark, right over your nose ('uh-huh'), and your blouse is light pink. You have something that looks like a string of pearls, but they could be shells. You have a very tiny spot right above your lip ('uh-huh'), probably a freckle, and sometimes you wear earrings. I think you and Abby have silver ones. Maybe you just trade them back and forth. Let's see, what else? Oh, yeah, there's another dark spot, right under your Adam's apple."

Jenny broke in with the news that girls don't have Adam's apples. "Only men do. Men look so funny when they talk. I like to watch their Adam's apples bob around. They think I'm laughing at something they said, but I'm not. I'm laughing at their funny Adam's apples!"

"Where was I?" he continued.

"In jail," she answered.

"Oh, yes, your arms are covered with tiny brown hair that makes your skin look real white. You never wear nail polish, and your wristwatch is stopped at a little after eleven o'clock. You don't seem to care what time it is, but you always know when it's time for lunch, or time to take your brother to the bakery. What kid wants to go to a bakery—unless it's to get the ticket from the machine? That's all I'd go to a bakery for."

"What about my ears?"

He was stuck by that question, so he told her that they were just ears, like anybody's ears.

"No, they're not," she replied with conviction. "Can't you see that I had my ears *pierced?*"

She turned her face left and right to let him examine her ears. "Huh? See."

He pretended he could see what must have been swollen and reddened ear lobes. He blundered on.

"Did it hurt?" He wrinkled his nose to show that he felt her pain.

"Not much. Abby did it this morning with a big hot needle, a cork, and ice cubes. She has an aunt who's a nurse. She taught her how to do it."

"I'd never let her near me with a hot needle!"

"Be honest, now," she said, shifting topics with ease. "Do you think I'm pretty?"

"Sure," he answered, feeling a body-long tingle at having said what he always believed.

"How pretty am I?"

"Oh, you are really, really pretty!" And in an instant of great invention he added, "And you have a pretty name, too."

"In case you didn't know, I'm named for a poem! Really, I am. I'm not Jennifer—there're tons of *them*—I'm Jenny, Jenny, Jenny. So there!"

"But how can you be named for a poem?" He thought about a poem. "Do you mean like 'Mary had a little lamb' or something like that?"

"Yes and no. Mary may have had a little lamb, but Jenny had a *kiss!* My dad liked this poem and so he convinced my mom to name me Jenny. The poem starts: 'Jenny kissed me when we met.' I forget the rest."

In the brief silence following Jenny's revelation, he heard the sound of a hushed, wet kiss.

His heart jumped. Could Jenny hear *that?*

"When we play spin-the-bottle, why are you in such a hurry to get out of the closet? People talk, you know. Your brother was in the closet with Abby for five minutes the last time, and Jackie spent even more time with her making all kinds of indecent kissing noises. Ugh!"

"Jack is Jack," he said, "so who knows? But my brother's in high school, so that's why he's there so long. Also, I think Abby and Jackie are just playing a trick on my brother, that's all."

"So," Jenny asked with a tone of finality, allowing him one chance before she unlocked his jail cell, "in what other ways am I pretty?"

He told her he liked the way she laughed, and that her voice was deep and husky. "How do you do that, anyway?" He paused. He was still in jail. He added that she has soft skin and eyelashes that curled like a movie star's.

"Which one?" she asked.

"Uh, I'd say Bette Davis, maybe Eva Marie Saint."

"Eva Marie Saint!" she threw back at him. "You are so wrong. Eva Marie Saint and I have nothing in common! Try Ava Gardner, and you'd be so right." Then, with a sigh, she picked up his racing car, which had been impounded for the last ten minutes. He was going to get out of jail.

"Are you just making this up?" she asked. "How do I know you're telling the truth? You joke around a lot, you and Jack. You two are terrible some times. All the time! Aren't you ever serious? You two would find a way to have fun at a funeral!" Still holding his jalopy, she asked with an undertone of danger, a Bette Davis kind of danger, "Do you think Abby's pretty?"

"I don't know," he said. He couldn't fall into that trap.

Jenny said, "I've watched you with Abby. You just stare at her. That's rude. And you almost never talk to her."

He found an exit: "She's OK, but she's different in lots of ways. There's the southern accent. And she's so tall that I have to look up at her, and most of the time she stands on the top step. I feel like a shrimp. I wouldn't know what to do with her in the closet if the bottle ever stopped at me. Funny, it never does. Does she like Jack more? And why don't my brother and Jack ever know where they stand with her? How does she do that?"

"I'm not telling," she answered.

"Am I out of jail yet?"

She considered his question. "On probation," she ruled. "Just barely."

Was There Sunshine
Behind the Cloud?

On Love's probation! A wonderful redundancy. While Jack sat on Red Ranger and decided whether or not he would ever ride his red, gleaming steed, Ben began wandering again. He was a myopic boy with new glasses bouncing on his sweaty nose. Now, so close to 20/20 vision, his vision restored many days after the doctor's drops, he saw for the first time the brilliant sharp outline of every leaf on every oak and maple, every blade of grass, and even the sharp outline of smoke spiraling and mesmerizing from his mouth and nose. Summer love opened up the world. He regarded the least significant details as fresh discoveries. Love enlarged him. Love made him—interesting. He stopped his annoying whining and complaining. He talked to his parents and maiden aunts. He even stopped biting his nails. There was an extra bounce in his step when he delivered the *Press*. He smiled and looked for good in people. Ever-perceptive Jack called him a *goony bird*.

When he went into the Maryland Pharmacy to read Classic comic books, the girls he last saw in May looked up, if only for a second. One whispered to her friend, "There he is again." Love forced him to the movies, to the enchantment of westerns with Roy Rogers and John Wayne. (He made a wonderful mistake, though, when he saw *All Quiet on the Western Front*, which he expected to be about cowboys. It was the strangest movie he had ever seen, with its comic book words telling him what German soldiers were saying in their trenches.) *Bowery*

Boys naturalism in the New York slums was real to him; he had only
to look around him in East Liberty to realize that Jack, Big Hank, and
he were the East Liberty Boys, thriving in back alleys or on rooftops
like nephews of King Kong. His chest expanded; his ears warmed and
flushed. The confessional became a stranger to him. He gladly gave
Sir Jack many Old Golds and Zippo lights and shiny Roosevelt dimes.

Big Hank rode his wobbly bike with Jack and Ben up and down
streets Ben never knew existed. Big Hank in the Big City was no longer
a menace. On Summerlea Street, Big Hank led his pals in a screeching
chorus à la Johnnie Ray in front of the house belonging to the man who
wrote the popular song about a tearful Dear John: *Cry*. But it wasn't just
the lyrics they loved: *If your sweetheart sends a letter of goodbye . . . .* It was
the exaggerated stutter in and between the words, a kind of hiccupy,
jazzy improvisation. They invented their own lyrics—"When-n-n ya
he-ear-ear the din-din-dinner bellll, slaw-slaw-ber lak-lak a dawg!"
They loved the way they made simple words fall apart and join again,
magically—their own shorthand, a vowel here, a consonant there,
sliding along on saliva toward private meaning. One had to belong to
sing along. Ben *belonged*.

And off they rode, Jack on his comic wreck of a bike, and Big Hank,
too big for his green menace, with its rusty chain and bald tires, and
Ben on a no-name bike painted church-door red by his father, who
used a brush left over from his spotty restoration of their alley home.
Big Hank led them up narrow streets, through unlocked gates that led
to backyards and other streets and alleys, some unpaved, dead-ended,
or too steep for bike brakes. They slid sideways down these cliff-like
streets and alleys. They passed through empty lots piled with the refuse
from derelict construction sites. They caught their breath for fifteen
minutes on Orr Street in the Lower Hill District, in front of number 73.
"Dumb address," Big Hank said. "A house needs three numbers, don't
it?" A pretty, ragged girl shouted, "Hi Big Hank! *Where've you been?*"

Big Hank was a good guy after all, their safety force, their tank
leading troops across all terrains. Sir Jack and Ben were the Fort Knox
of Roosevelt dimes; Big Hank was the Fort Knox of heavy armor. He
defied all order, as when he pumped his magical bike through busy
intersections, his arms outstretched and his huge hands waving *stop* to

cross traffic. "Follow me!" he cried. And then, just as quickly as he had appeared by their side coasting down Walnut Street hill, he mysteriously disappeared up or down some little-known path, or through someone's backyard where white sheets billowed like sails over blue water.

Was that cloud passing in front of the sun promising something awful to their unprotected selves, lost as they often were on streets that Big Hank alone knew how to navigate?

Among the Dinosaurs

After Ben's little conversations with Old Man Brooks, he was not comforted about the polio scare, nor did he feel any healthier. So the advice to talk to old people as an antidote to polio was a sentimental nicety, but nothing more. Then, on Saturday morning, after Jack called to say that he had the day off, Ben suggested that they visit the Carnegie Museum. Perhaps there they would find protection from the mysterious disease. The museum, a massive fortress on Forbes Avenue in Oakland, was Andrew Carnegie's gift to the city, but, according to Cecilia, behind his generous profusion was an old man's desire for expiation after exploiting thousands of unprotected workers at his steel mill along the river. "My father used to see Mr. Carnegie driving about in his carriage," Cecilia added proudly. He gave libraries and pipe organs to cities and towns across the country. Having little education himself, he decided that books, schools, and devotion to God were necessary for the multitudes to be lifted to higher stations in life.

The museum in Oakland was midnight-black from around-the-clock furnace smoke that fell like a blanket over the city. For generations the noon sky above the city was darkened by Mr. Carnegie's smoke. Drivers squinted to see, their headlights burning at noon. Streetlights remained on for days at a time. Businessmen, riding in trains past what would much later become Jack's house, wore white shirts to their offices. The train's smoke and cinders came in open windows, soiling the shirts. Once in the city, however, the men changed into fresh white shirts and sent the gray-black shirts they arrived in to the Chinese laundry.

Aunt Frances told Ben that Mr. Carnegie ordered that he be buried in the Sleepy Hollow Cemetery, an hour's drive from New York City. She had visited his grave, among others, during that time when rubbing gravestones was in vogue. She added that a large Celtic cross was stationed in the pure air at the entrance to his gravesite grounds. And ringing the half acre were graves of his most loyal servants. He believed that these common folks were entitled to climb the stairs to Heaven along with their master. Close by the Carnegie burial site, a mighty Rockefeller slept in a massive mausoleum. And a famous labor leader was buried nearby in a tidy plot marked with a commoner's simple stone.

But the grave she truly revered belonged to Washington Irving, who had asked that the cemetery be named Sleepy Hollow, the setting of his famous tale, *The Legend of Sleepy Hollow.* (Ben remembered his love for the Headless Horseman and his crayon paintings of that very cemetery, where the dead don't die.) Irving's gravestone (not the original one, unfortunately, as so many pieces were chipped off by his many followers) is a pilgrimage site for many, and the small flags next to it commemorate his service in the War of 1812, and his diplomatic service. Aunt Frances was full of surprises. "Remember the famous line of verse Longfellow wrote soon after Irving died? You don't? Well, it went like this: 'How sweet a life was his; how sweet a death!'" She puffed on her Bugler home-rolled cigarette, her eyes to the ceiling, and concluded her thought: "Believe that if you want, but I'm pretty sure death is not sweet. It's just balderdash!" And then he watched her sweet smile that signified she bore no animosity toward Mr. Longfellow. "Ask a librarian for Irving's book since they don't have much to do anyway."

She closed her little lecture by saying that American history is better learned in colonial cemeteries than in history classes taught by nuns who never crossed the Allegheny Mountains. "Next to cemeteries," she said, "visit the Carnegie Museum, which is really nothing more than a cemetery with a library and a dining room." So he and Jack did.

The sky darkened as a storm approached. The thunder echoed in the high-ceilinged marble passages leading to the Hall of Dinosaurs, which was stuffy with years of dust on rib cages and arched reptilian backs of unpronounceable monsters with their huge tails and long ferocious teeth. A guard slept near the entrance. Ben thought of the wonderful children's library in another wing of the building where he once discovered the fascinating books he carried back and forth every Saturday morning a few years before. Jack liked the echo in the hall. He tested it with strange sounds like those made by demented men he saw in movies. The guard stirred. Jack said that the dinosaurs' backbones and ribs reminded him of the chicken backs he had at Sunday dinners. He was always late for dinner, and only the backs were left. Even the wings were gone. Did dinosaurs have wishbones, he wondered, as he leaned backward under the rib cage above him to answer his question. The guard stirred again. Jack broke into a song set to the music of *The Eyes of Texas*, but the eyes belonged not to cowboys but to the guard wearing a badge. "Don't, Jack, you'll get us thrown out and we just got here. And it's still raining."

"Well, well," said an old man of fifty or sixty, who suddenly appeared. "I see that you enjoy animal relics. Very good! And now a question for you bright boys. I wonder if you know what *pudenda* means. No? Need a hint, hmmm?" His eyes were moist and his lips were wet. His smile, if it was a smile, was an open mouth with his curled tongue resting on his lower lip. He turned the point of his wet umbrella on the marble floor. His raincoat was spotted with water.

Jack hesitated, and then he replied in a confident voice, "It's what you have to do. Our teacher uses it all the time."

"Is your teacher pretty," the man asked with the odd smile.

Jack said, "We can only see her face."

"And her hands, too," Ben added. "She's a nun."

"Ah-ha, ah-ha. The good sisters," he said. "They do cover just about the entire anatomy, do they not?" The guard approached, his fingers under his broad belt. The man with the umbrella patted Ben on the back of his hand as though he were an uncle, and offered to see them again under the dinosaur skeletons. He turned and melted away. There was a small pool of water where he once stood. As they left the Hall of Dinosaurs, Ben saw the guard settling himself into the rest of his restful shift, a day's work nearly done.

Down the long stairs they made something of a racket. Jack sang, "The eyes of watchmen are upon us," but no guard was in sight. Ben told him about the children's library.

"Let's go in and find a dictionary so we can figure out what that word means. Maybe it's a magic word." They saw a huge dictionary on a pedestal near the door.

"OK, so what was that word again?" Jack thought for a second before suggesting that it was *produda*.

He looked it up, but there was no word like that.

"How about *proental?*"

"How do you spell it?"

He said *p-r-e-w-e-n-t-i-l*. That's it!"

Nothing. He tried again, totally lost and ridiculous. He closed the dictionary, which nearly fell on the floor. He learned that these big *Webster's* were not meant to be closed tight, and a rocking pedestal did not help matters.

"What do we do now?" Jack asked, looking around for the possibilities the children's library offered him. He liked the low tables and the tiny chairs, the pictures of dragons and winged horses around the ceiling, and, most of all, a sign pointing toward the dining room. "You got any money?"

"Wait, first, let's ask that librarian. She's not doing anything."

"You ask," he said, "I'm not."

A nice lady about Jack's mom's age seemed pleased to see them. He asked her if she could help them find a word, something that means "things you have to do."

"Well," she said, studying him a few seconds, "could the word possibly be *pudenda?*"

"Yeah, that's it." Jack was excited. "This lady knows everything."

"Actually," she said kindly, "the word meaning 'what needs to be done' is *agenda*. It's a Latin word. Have you studied Latin yet?"

He said that he was an altar boy at Sacred Heart and that he knew some Latin, but he didn't know what it meant.

"Excuse me for just a second," she said, reaching for her phone. She called someone, and what she said so distinctly was, "Mr. P is in the building. Could you check into it?" She returned, asking them, "Are there any books you would like to take home?" Ben asked about *The Legend of Sleepy Hollow.* "Good choice," she said, leading them to a shelf along the wall. She was pleased because the book was on the shelf, a nicely illustrated one, but, she said proudly, "Once Halloween comes, all of the copies are usually checked out." They thanked her, but before they left the room, Ben placed the thin book on a low table where a young reader would find it.

There wasn't time for the dining room. The paper route waited, the stack of papers protected from rain under thick layers of old papers. Jack decided that they should dash across Forbes and up Bellefield to Fifth where they would take the 75 to his stop. But other lines ran on those tracks, the 73 and 76, which would not be for them. They rushed in the freezing rain past Pitt's great lawns bordering the longest block in the city. Heinz Chapel was almost hidden in the mist, its tall pillars of blue stained-glass windows still beautiful in the afternoon's fading light. Since they were already soaked, Jack stopped. He had decided that they should walk until they spied a streetcar headed their way. And then one came along, perhaps a 75, so they ran as fast as they could to meet the streetcar, a 75, too, just in time to slip through the double door. Ben paid a dime for Jack, who was already in the rear of the nearly-empty car. He was sprawled on the back cushions. He looked like a robber baron settled in his private car. They rocked along the tracks at a lazy pace. The ceiling lights blinked. Rain came in the open windows with a rush of chilled air.

Jack was shivering in his wet clothes, and so was he. "I'm freezing in here," he said. "Mom'll be real mad at me for running so fast and getting drenched. So much for polio prevention. I'll never be allowed out again. Can you be double grounded?" he wondered.

At his stop, a sodden Jack left the streetcar and jogged home, probably concocting an artful story about getting caught in a sudden downpour for which he was not in any way to be held responsible.

Ben got off at Spahr Street, by Kate's and Henry's Pie Shop, two of his favorite places (it was Henry himself who taught him the difference between an orange bottle of pop and a bottle of orange pop). At home he dried himself, borrowed a hat from his father's collection, and put on boots that George wore once, and only once, expensive ones charged to Cecilia's account at Kaufmann's just so he could stay dry on a short trip home. She was angry for days.

His bundle of papers, always a small one on Saturdays, was surprisingly dry. Up and down the stairs he raced, sweating through his heavy clothes, and then down Maryland Avenue to the drug store. There was a pinball machine that consumed his nickels one-at-a-time. And then, out of nickels, he walked home, exhausted and worried.

Jack called that night with the news that he was in fact double-grounded, a phrase his mom had never heard. "Am I double grounded?" he asked, and she replied, "Well, yes, I imagine you are." She ordered him upstairs for a long hot shower, tossed warm wrinkled clothes up to the landing, ordered him to wear them without protest, and ordered him down to the living room to lie under a blanket until his dad came home.

"Don't say a word about what you did until your father is here," she cautioned. "I want him to have the raw experience of your fascinating conduct today. I will make you a large cup of strong Irish tea, and you will drink it right down," she said. The tea was served. Into the tea she had poured a generous dollop of Irish whiskey for medication. He drank a second cup, also with a wee drop, and even tried for a third cup, so he would really get better quickly, but he was denied this request. Stretched out in the wrinkled slacks and a thick flannel cowboy shirt from the bottom of the pile, the winter collection, Jack waited for his father and story time. Groggy with grog, he slept.

All of this happened while Ben delivered papers in the rain, soaked with sweat and aching from the run to the streetcar. There was no whiskey waiting for him, Irish or domestic, because his father began marking the bottle with deep scratches in the glass. He suspected someone was snitching his whiskey. He was right, for after school George and Tom, his cynical artist friend, each had a shot, but what their father did not know is that George had replaced the cheap whiskey, called Kinsey, with shots of water, so the level never went down. (Unlike Jack's Chrysler, the whiskey never reached the level of E.) Tom invented a song for the occasion: "Georgie, Georgie, Albert's son, stole the Kinsey and away he run."

When the whiskey had no calming, warming effect, Albert cursed the makers of Kinsey in his most perfect Queen's English: "Damn their eyes!" Ben knew what alcohol could do from two of his own experiences. The first time, a few years earlier, involved dropping a raw egg into a wide glass of cheap wine and drinking it down in a single, smooth, endless gulp. Albert nodded approvingly. "Good for the digestion," he boasted. Ben felt ill for hours. The second time was on a Holy Day of Obligation, a cold November day. As there was no school, he read *Blondie* and *Nancy* comic books in the morning while drinking a glass of Albert's cheap wine. When he began to feel strange, he went outside and bounced a basketball, which was really a soccer ball Albert gave to the boys. He did not know the difference between soccer and basketball. Ben bounced the ball and tried to throw it into a bottomless fruit basket nailed to the phone pole across the street. The pole appeared to move. A little tipsy, he opened the door to the enclosed porch with some difficulty and went immediately to the sofa, a cheap Danish Modern with skinny, comfortless cushions. He slept for an hour, and then he returned to his comic books.

Later, he realized that alcohol defines people, whether for good or bad, sharpens their images in memory, fairly or unfairly, and bathes them in a mist, whether Irish or Scotch, so that the characters remembered are lifted to a low pedestal in the mind's private garden. There is wonder on their faces, a determination, and a satisfaction. Jack's grandfather greets him at the hedged entrance of this imaginary garden. Rarely did Ben see him in daylight, and he never knew where the old man slept in Jack's house. Sometimes they met him in the night streets coming from his favorite establishment, *This and That*, on Walnut Street. Pap-Pap was lit from within by the whiskey he'd consumed before walking his odd walk back to his bed. He straightened out the sidewalks the best he could.

A Promotion in Rank

Jack called the next morning to tell Ben what was happening at home after his big stir at the museum. Ben listened passively, asked a few questions, and commented, "You're kidding. Tell me that again!" Oddly, Jack became introspective. He said that they never should have stolen his dad's car. What if there were an emergency, and what if there was no car on Ellsworth Avenue? What if they were in an accident? Or if the police stopped them? He went on and on with cases like these. Ben got worried. Was it really Jack at the other end of the line? There would be no more car heists. Jack's dad was staying close to home now, and the car had a good supply of gas for the short ride to the hospital. Jack was allowed to sit on his bright, red bike, and he could go to Jenny's porch in the afternoon. His mother would depend on her "good squire" to do many of her chores. He seemed relieved.

"But Jack, what did you tell your mom and dad about the museum, getting soaked in the rain, and the cold streetcar ride?"

This was his preposterous story, his masterful creation. First, the setting: he was ordered to rest on the sofa. The blanket was so hot on top of his winter clothes, but he had to be a martyr about it. And then, when his dad finally came home, Jack told his story. He said that they had been safe in the library from the titanic storm raging in Oakland. Foolishly or not, when there was a momentary lull in the rain and wind, they gambled. They dashed toward Fifth Avenue for the streetcar, but the blinding rain and wind came on, taking them completely by surprise. Drivers stopped in the middle of the street, their wipers useless; umbrellas turned inside out; papers flew from people's arms. A few seconds later and they would have been unable to squeeze onto the 75. So many people ahead of them were crowding on, pushing and shoving. The people didn't care whether it was a 73, 75, or 76. Whatever it was, it was their lifeboat. They pushed their way on, politely locking elbows so they would not be separated. The conductor shouted to stranded would-be passengers, "That's it. No more room." He rang each passenger on board by jerking the lanyard above him. There must have been a hundred piercing bells, one after another, so fast that their ears continued to ring for minutes. This was a punishing kind of streetcar bookkeeping. Jack doubted that people even dropped dimes into the box. He did, of course. Such confusion occurred when passengers discovered that they were on the wrong streetcar, but getting off made no sense because the streetcar following was no doubt packed like a sardine can. Jack swore that a special edition of the Press would surely be rushed into print with a story about this fateful afternoon of flooding and stranded women and children clinging for their lives to the sturdy ginkgo trees on Bellefield Avenue.

Of course, as might be expected, there were heroes as well as goats aboard. A woman, looking much like his mom, was in the final days of pregnancy, but no one stood to give her a seat. Jack, soaked to the bone, politely asked a teenage kid to stand up and be a gentleman so a lady could sit, but this goofy kid just smiled, crossed his eyes at Jack, and raised his hand. He was wearing one extended finger on his fist. An older man prevented enraged Jack from acting out his anger. The man grabbed that fist and jerked the kid out of the seat, throwing the whole row of standees into a sudden near fall. The lady said, "Thank you very much," and squeezed into the narrow space the skinny kid had just occupied. A few cheers rose from the sodden masses.

Jack's dad was impressed. He was proud of his noble and chivalric son. He reached over Sir Jack's head and kindly touched the pink scar of late. He said in regal pleasure, "Another chevron has been earned, Jack, and so you have been promoted in rank. Responsibilities are assigned with the higher rank. What's for dinner, I wonder?"

He was smart to leave out the dictionary man with the gutter tongue, but Ben had to say to him, "Jack, nothing you said was true. Your dad thinks you were a hero. Your mom must have been furious with you. Didn't she say anything?"

Jack said that she tried to say something, but her mouth was locked open for a minute.

And then she excused Jack; otherwise, there would have been a fight on the day before his birthday. "Mercifully, August is almost over," she said. A cake mix was at the ready in the kitchen, and a can of double-chocolate icing was on a shelf. Jack knew this this because he always inspected his prospects for each birthday. All she said then was, "It's all the soap operas I let him watch. Tonight's dinner is frozen in the fridge. You can have your choice of spaghetti or lasagna. Think it over." He already had the prematurely-old King Kong shoes. The best he could hope for would be a parole for an afternoon. Ben had planted the idea that they would go to the zoo to see the monkeys. Wouldn't that be almost like going to the museum? Jack decided to float the request after dinner.

His mother looked hard at his dad, then focused on the ceiling light, and said the happy words, "Jack, or should I call you Raoul, it will be OK to visit monkeys, provided you do not end up in a cage with a banana squashed in your hand. Ouch! John, the baby just kicked. It's probably another boy!"

Lingering questions disturbed Ben. Was it the higher rank that brought on Jack's remorse, his sense of responsibility, his feeling of guilt? And he wondered where *he* fit in Jack's scheme of things.

Life at the Round Table

Jack had a small family birthday party in the evening of September the first. But his mom promised him she would "do it right," and, once the weather turned cold, invite Jack's friends to a *real* party. That evening Ben went to Dithridge Street with his parents for some TV and conversation. The large house had always intrigued him, with its promise of hidden spaces behind the built-in bookcases. The old books behind glass doors were wonderful to examine for unusual pictures and exotic stories of fairyland Ireland, Norwegian trolls, and Arthurian knights with long shining swords. Illustrated Hans Christian Andersen tales in volumes scented with age were collectors' items. A complete and uniform collection of Dickens' works occupied the center shelf, just low enough for children's hands to reach them.

The dining room was huge, with a great circular walnut table in the center, graceful buffet, and crystal cupboards with beveled glass doors that were locked tight. Above the furniture was a large oil painting called *Hudson River with Dutch Cottage*, which Ben studied so often when he was younger, either for the pleasure itself or during long dinners followed by cigarette smoke that gathered above the table in the crystal chandelier. The yellow-orange cottage stood alone, slathered with enormous green bushes attached to huge roots at the corners as if to lift the fairy-tale building into the blue sky.

Almost as an afterthought a black-and-white television was squeezed into a corner. Atop the TV set was a control box that allowed the roof antenna to turn in every direction to find the best reception. Ben believed that by turning the antenna to the north he could find Canadian TV. He'd often heard newscaster John Cameron Swayze's signature greeting, "And a good evening to you," before he reported the news. But he failed in his search. Thinking that the TV was as nimble as the old Zenith radio on Burger Road, the radio that found German ships at sea, he assumed that the TV antenna could at least find Toronto. "And a good evening to you, too" he responded to kind Mr. Swayze. And then he pulled out a chair and joined his family at the round table.

Albert, Cecilia, and Ben sat at the table with his aunts, Mary, Helen, Alice, and Frances. A longstanding favorite boarder, Mr. McGee, sat with them like a member of the family. Mother informed the gathering that the children were not in school yet because of the polio outbreak, which, as they would remember, was not nearly as severe as last summer's. She looked at Ben for a response, and so he said that he was doing some things with Jack, like going to the museum and the library. They all thought that was good.

"Tomorrow I'm going to the zoo with Jack to see the monkeys." There was silence. Mother said, "Well, that would *not* be a very good idea. You see, monkeys are dirty animals that bite and spit at people and, excuse my frankness, they throw feces for enjoyment. Do you understand? I would think that the zoo should be closed until winter."

Aunt Helen said that Cecilia was right about this. "Find something else to do that will be safer. You wouldn't want to expose yourself and your friend to contagion."

Aunt Frances, always off topic, said that she remembered those awful Gibraltar monkeys jumping on tourists' backs demanding bananas and apples. Or were they apes? Who knows? Who cares? Mondays, Wednesdays, Fridays: monkeys. Tuesdays, Thursdays, Saturdays: apes. Ugh!"

Then the pest broke in: "What about Sundays?"

Aunt Mary, in the small silence he had created, looked at him with her kind eyes. "On Sundays," she said, "I listen for the seven forty-five bells, and when the last one is silent, I gather my hat, umbrella, and missal, and walk to church."

Aunt Frances regained the floor in the even longer silence. "Now, as you know, I love animals, dogs especially, but I would never befriend a monkey or an ape. And, Cecilia, you remember that awful donkey I was persuaded to ride in Jerusalem? I went back to that hotel and bathed for the longest time. But first, I had to wait an eternity for the hot water. Those awful hotels! Holy Land or not, I won't ever go back there. Whatever did Mr. Innocent, Mark Twain, see in it?

"Frances," Cecilia said, "Twain ridiculed, berated, and satirized the Old World. I'm sure he waited for hot water, too, don't you think?"

Aunt Frances took a long draw on her Bugler self-rolled cigarette, which almost went out during her long aside. She looked at her glass of beer. "I enjoy Miller beer in the evening, don't you? And I *don't* have to wait for it, either." She took a slow sip, and then she smiled angelically.

Albert, usually very silent in the home of his sisters-in-law, said that he saw monkeys in the wild when he lived in British Guiana. "They were good for nothing in my opinion."

Aunt Mary, the eldest of the group, brought peace to what she thought was a minor insurrection: "I don't wish any monkey any harm. Live and let live."

Mother smiled, rolled her eyes, and said, "Well, since we are talking of polio and monkeys in the same breath, I'll tell you something that might surprise you, so please do not repeat what I have to say. This is for young ears, actually." She looked at him patiently.

"Polio has been getting attention in the newspapers, and so parents are very cautious. They don't know what to do. Should they impose a family quarantine? It was beginning to be known that a team of Pittsburgh doctors was working around the clock to find the cause and cure of polio. Could there be a vaccine, an inoculation? Would it be safe? On a hill above Oakland, in the Municipal Hospital for Contagious Diseases, there are research labs in the basement, and there are many monkeys used in experiments."

She continued. "On the floors above the labs are hundreds of boys and girls with various types of the disease. Children who can't breathe on their own are kept alive in iron lung machines. For many children hospitalization lasts for months. Brothers and sisters suffering with polio are separated: boys on one floor, girls on another. They never see each other. Family members are not permitted to visit. Now, this is not such an old hospital, but the ventilation is poor. The summer air is warm and damp. Windows are opened in the afternoons to cool the patients. A doctor told me the pitiful story of a little girl who struggled to lift her arm to point to the window. She asked politely, 'What is that bad smell coming in the window?' A nurse answered her in a cheerful tone, 'Oh, those are the monkeys that didn't make it!'" Beer glasses were raised and lowered around the table. Mr. McGee looked at his watch only to discover that he was not wearing one.

Aunt Frances said that, upon further reflection, these monkeys, no matter how dirty, were heroic. Why doesn't someone make a statue to honor them? Is it their fault they're primates? I know," she continued, "that a few are sacrificed for the good of mankind, but it saddens me to think of it!"

Aunt Alice, who was always silent when any controversy arose, felt obliged to add to the discussion. She said that the dentist she works with in the public schools told her that scores of laboratory monkeys are disposed of every week. Monkeys do not get polio in their natural setting, but in the lab they can be infected, or so she was told. "I guess," she added, "that the more monkeys they sacrifice the quicker the cure will come. Oh my, these summers are just awful. What a summer! Frightening polio! It changes everything. It drains the joy out of life. Let the winter descend for all I care. Let it stay until there's a cure." She almost cried.

Cecilia begged for an answer to the question: "When will this awful disease be cured? We have children! We cannot just wait! How soon?"

Albert, lifting his glass in agreement, complained that everywhere he turned someone was begging for dimes to cure polio. "March of Dimes, March of Dimes! It's beginning to wear me out."

"Oh, Albert, don't be such a grouch about it," Cecilia said. "Just carry some dimes in your pocket, for Heaven's sake." She lifted her glass to him as if in a toast, and he made a small gesture in return. Ben grew to understand the codes and the silences around the table.

The conversation turned to another subject, and it was for these moments that he really came along. Aunt Frances, the daring sister who announced in a punctuated silence that she was no stranger to love, claimed that a wealthy elderly man and his girlfriend were necking one night in Schenley Park. *Girlfriend* was a code word for *naughty woman.* Well, apparently there was much-too-much *amour* in the car, and the man had a horrible heart attack. He died, as they say, on the spot! Frances concluded, "The doctor wrote on the death certificate that the cause of death was Cadillac arrest!"

Nervous laughter followed rapid glances from person to person, and the humor was judged to be perfectly fine. After all, Ben's fourteenth birthday was two weeks away. The laughter became a roar. Mr. McGee had tears in his eyes he was so amused. A few seconds of savory silence followed before respectful eyes turned to Aunt Mary, the senior sister who had lost her young husband to the flu of 1918, as well as her considerable inheritance in the thirties, thanks to her team of financial advisors, Messrs. Dunne, Wendt & Gonne, who fumbled her fortune.

"Oh my," she said, "it seems you can't do much these days without an automobile, can you?" More laughter followed. She was pleased to have caused such merriment. It showed in her modest smile.

Mr. P is in the Building

Jack loved zoos. He liked the pouncing and swinging animals and their foul smells. But snakes were not his favorite. They just stank, and then about once a year they might move. He had no patience for them, but he admired their laziness. Elephants and giraffes provided little entertainment. Why? He said they looked like big buildings. Birds, no matter how exotic or plain, were stupid for not flying away. But zebras were a mystery. Were they white-on-black or black-on-white? He studied them. Was that their defense, confusing the lions that eyed them from a distance? Big game animals were just pathetic, just lazing away the day, waiting for keepers to toss them large chunks of raw meat, which they approached in bored, shiftless motion, sniffing and licking the unpursued prey. But apes, gorillas, orangutans, chimps, and all kinds of monkeys, whether large or pocket-sized, turned Jack into the pith-helmeted hunters he admired in the movie *King Solomon's Mines*. And when Ben suggested that they see monkeys on the day after his birthday, Jack assumed they would be going to the zoo. "Jack," he began nervously, "my parents and my aunts told me some things last night that made me change my mind. I'm sorry, but I can't go to the zoo. Too dangerous. A health hazard. Your mom would be pretty angry about a trip to the zoo if she knew what I heard last night. But, not to worry, I'm still taking you to a monkey place."

They picked up speed on the turn from Ellsworth to Bayard Street. They passed Pitt property that was once a huge, sunken field used to bury construction junk when the Cathedral of Learning was being built. As they neared his aunts' large Victorian house, with three Russian wolfhounds pacing in the side yard, Jack became suspicious.

"You going in to see those scary dogs? Are there monkeys there, too?"

Ben did not answer him because they heard a commanding voice behind them. "Hey, you jerks, wait up for Pete's sake!" It was Big Hank. "Where're you two squirts goin'?" They pulled off to the curb. "What's new Mr. Kazoo? What's new Turtle Boy?"

Big Hank gave Ben the nickname Mr. Kazoo after Ben told him that he played the kazoo in the first grade band. Rather, he tried to play it. The teacher kept telling him, "Don't blow into it. Just hum." But he couldn't get the hang of it, so she gave him a triangle to play. "I just couldn't get the rhythm, or I'd forget when to tap it. It's a boring instrument."

"I know your pain," he said. "With me, it's whistling. Could never do it."

And that's how Ben became Mr. Kazoo. Could've been worse.

Big Hank asked Jack, "Where's that fancy bike you won?"

Jack said that the bike's so new he didn't want to wreck it or have it stolen.

"Know what you mean, because I hate new things. New shoes? Hey, I scrape them on the pavement. New shirt? Hey, I ride my bike over it in a puddle, pop a button, make it old fast."

"So, Big Hank, where're you headed?" He was in a quiet mood.

"To see my mom. She works up by the hospitals in a doctor's office. I need a handful of aspirin for this stupid headache." Ben asked whether he had plans for after that, and Big Hank said, "sleep all day."

They pedaled ahead for a few blocks, silently, until Big Hank, returning briefly to his old self, made a death-defying turn into oncoming traffic, his big mitts stretched out, commanding traffic to stop. He pumped hard down the steep hill, too steep for his puny brakes. They held their breath, listening for a loud crash and pedestrian screams. Then they breathed again. He was safe.

Somewhere ahead was an ugly, tall Depression-era building. As the building rose, the new floors were set back and then set back again. The top floor looked like a turret. At night, the building had the outline of a boxy Christmas tree, with square windows for lights. A veneer of Mr. Carnegie's smoke had already begun to claim the building, and, as they would soon learn, the back of the building was already blackened by a putrid pall where the incinerator vented.

A steep flight of steps led to the main entrance. Climb, climb, climb. That's all one did in this section of Oakland. The long pull from Fifth Avenue up Darrah Street, past an intersection, then up again to a street that earned its name: Terrace Street. At the intersection of Darrah and Terrace was this drab building, with the setbacks that reminded Ben of the Dutch cottage on the Hudson. They stopped to stare at the front of the building. He felt nervous watching Jack trying to make sense of the promise of monkeys.

"Where are the monkeys?"

"Honest," he said, "the monkeys are here. You just can't see them."

They were standing before the massive Municipal Hospital for Contagious Diseases.

"But I came to see them," he complained.

"Jack, just think of them as a mystery, like we learned in Catechism class. A mystery is about the unseen that we accept as a matter of faith. Faith, Jack."

Jack dismissed that piety as stupid. "If I can't see or hear or touch or taste or smell or steal something, then there's nothing. It's not that I can't *pretend* that something exists when I know it doesn't really exist. A mystery? They're to be solved, like in the Charlie Chan movies. I know Chan will solve the mystery. What's in that building that I can't see or taste or touch or hear or smell? Huh? Answer me that, Mr. Know-it-All!"

"All right. What's in the building? I'll tell you." He looked at Jack's sad eyes. "Jack, Mr. P is in the building."

"Well, that's a big help," he said. "Isn't that what the librarian said on the phone when we tried to find out the meaning of that word? What was it? *Pendoofus?*"

"Jack, this is another Mr. P."

"Like Mr. Peanut?" he said sarcastically. Ben was sorry that he got them into this situation.

"Jack," he said, "Mr. Polio is in the building."

Well, he just about exploded.

"What are you talking about? Tell me!" he insisted.

Ben felt lost, out of his depth, but he tried. He told Jack that this was the hospital children came to when they got polio. This was where doctors took care of kids in a special way, and this is where lots of doctors are trying to find a cure for polio, or to prevent polio with vaccinations.

"So," Jack's voice choked, "we rode here so I could see for myself that polio is real? That it's not about talking to old people or going to museums? It's about coming right here? *This* is safer than a zoo?" He reached into his jeans pockets. He pulled out two handfuls of peanuts, some still in their shells. He smiled, almost laughed. "Mom gave these to me this morning. I packed my pockets with them. She said, 'Here Jackie, take these and share them with your cousins.'" He seemed pleased. "So, where're these monkeys? I want to throw 'em peanuts."

"The monkeys are in the building, lots of them. They're in cages, just like at the Highland Park Zoo. Let's go in and ask someone if we can give peanuts to the monkeys."

They opened the heavy doors. So far so good. In a small, drab lobby, a woman sat behind a little desk. She looked at the boys with curiosity in her eyes.

"Hi," Ben said. "My friend and I have come from Shadyside. We were told that there are monkeys here, and we wanted to give them these peanuts."

Jack showed her the dusty contents of his hands. "Some got smashed," he said.

"Oh, my, you are just so kind to think of us," the nice lady said. The name on her badge was Janet. "But I'm just a volunteer, and I don't have much to do with the monkeys. But let me do this. I'll take the peanuts." She looked for a place to put them. "Here," she said, lifting a large ashtray from a desk behind her. "Just put them in here and I'll ask one of the lab technicians to take them downstairs. I know the monkeys are well fed; the technicians spoil them with bananas from home. Once a monkey always a monkey," she said with a sad tone of regret.

Jack asked if the monkeys had names.

"I think so," she answered, "the little ones, probably, the favorites."

Jack was very interested in naming animals. He asked if they could name two of them.

"Oh, why yes, that would be very nice, I think. It's very kind of you to do that." Just then, a woman dressed in white walked by the desk. Janet said to her, "Caroline, these nice boys have come all the way from Shadyside to make a little gift of peanuts for our monkeys. See?" She pointed to the pile in the ashtray.

Caroline said that there is always a need for kindness, especially in these trying times. "Sure, I'll make a point of taking your peanuts downstairs."

"Can we go with you, just to watch?" Jack asked. She smiled, her eyes filling with tears.

"I wish I could take you, but these are such special monkeys that only a few people can touch them. They are very important monkeys, you understand."

"We want to give them names," Jack said. "Can we do that?" Caroline looked at the things on Janet's little desk. She pointed to index cards.

"These will work, won't they Janet, honey?" she said. "Write the names on these cards, and I'll make sure they're attached to cages." Jack filled out a card, choosing the name *Lucky Jack.*

"I like this name," she said. "We all can use a little luck, even our friends the monkeys."

She glanced privately at Janet. On his card Ben printed *Big Hank.*

"Thank you," she said, "I'll see that one of the larger monkeys gets this name. You are such creative boys! Like Adam in Eden, right Janet? Well!"

In the silence that followed, and in the eyes of the good women, they knew that their next word had to be *goodbye.* They waved back to them as they left the lobby. They raced down the steps two at a time, exhilarated by their accomplishments.

"All right!" Jack yelled over his shoulder. "That was great!"

"Yeah. That was great," Ben said, relieved of worry. Behind the building they rested their bikes against a low wall. Sitting on the wall, kicking their feet before them like they were resting by a swimming pool, Ben looked up at the chimney, which sent waves of heat above the building. The brickwork below the chimney was almost black. It was the saddest sight. When they noticed the curious smell, Jack asked about it. Ben looked at the dozens of windows behind which boys and girls slept in the afternoon. Windows were being pulled shut as though on command. Ben told him the stink was nothing, nothing at all. "This is Pittsburgh, isn't it? When doesn't the air stink in the Smoky City?"

They returned by Bayard Street, but Ben said they should turn up Craig Street by the King Edward apartments. They stopped at Indovina's Italian grocery, which sold the best cherries in town. Ben bought two bags, and in no time they were eating cherries while steering with their elbows. Some cherries were sweet, some were sour, and some were soft. They rode along, spitting cherry pits to the left and right, pinging them off car roofs or in their spokes. Around and around the pits would fly, like marbles in a casino game, and then they scattered under the humming tires of cars racing past them in the afternoon sun.

Turning the Calendar Page

When the phone rang the next morning, its ring seemed odd, even ominous. Ben was in the kitchen looking at the calendar. The adventures of late August under the watchful eyes of Saints Peter and Paul had come and gone. On September 3, a sad Thursday, the day following his trip to the Municipal Hospital, he found a new saint in the kitchen. Mother had turned the calendar page. Saint Helena, with a magnificent cross, stared at him as he cooked bacon. Her sad eyes followed him to the refrigerator for the butter, and then to the toaster, which was beginning to smoke. He had been caught having breakfast. She had found him out just as she had found the True Cross centuries earlier. Was she Heaven's special investigator sent to discover yesterday's lies and deceit? Was the cross in her hands reserved for him? "Here," she seemed to say, "wear this!" There was no escaping guilt. It was already in his soul. He did not need a nun prodding him with her umbrella to know that he was in trouble. The ringing stopped; the record needle click-clicked in code that said "all gone, all gone."

Jack called again. His first words on that morning came as a blow to the body: "Big Hank's in the hospital. He's real sick. His mother thinks it's polio. Mom's crying. Come down. I'll tell you more."

His mouth was dry and his stomach churned. Why Big Hank? What had he done to deserve this? He was strong, bold, fearless, a street kid without much luck. If he got sick, why didn't they? They spent time with him, did many forbidden things, risked all, but he got sick. And hadn't he paid many installments of his debt at Thorn Hill?

On his way to Jack's house by backstreets, he thought about Big Hank. He remembered one night a month before, a night when Big Hank stood alone against three kids near the tracks. He had leaned his bike against the wall of a little store near Pierce Street where he often stopped for candy, pop, cigarettes, chips, and magazines, paying for some items while liberating others. Infamous Pierce Street amounted to a row of brick houses slammed together by builders who did not have to live there. The architectural effect was one of sinister fear. Rumor had it that the city prowl cars drove down the street at high speed with doors locked. Big Hank was drawn to places like this.

Three Pierce Street kids blocked the door of the little store. "You ain't goin' in here, man. You bad news."

Well, that was an invitation for Big Hank to negotiate: "It's a free country, runt. Move or I'll toss you over that railing."

"You and what army?" said Slam.

Negotiations having failed, Slam the Man began pushing Big Hank. The next biggest boy circled quickly to disorient him. The smallest boy, probably new to these rituals, just watched, but crouched like he might jump in, too. Jack and Ben stood back in the dark.

Jack shouted, "Hey, Big Hank, take it easy on these kids, they look undernourished and stupid." Slam the Man found himself in a headlock. Big Hank circled quickly; the kid could do nothing to break the hold. The smallest kid began shadow boxing. The middle kid foolishly tried to jump Big Hank, but Jack pinned him down on the pavement. "It ain't fair to pile on, guy."

The shadow boxer felt foolish by then, so Ben asked him his name, just to make him feel good. "My name Leroy," he boasted. "It mean *king*."

Big Hank, triumphant, set the very dizzy Slam the Man free. Then he walked through the doorway into the neon brightness; Jack and Ben followed him. The three kids were mouthing off, making fatal promises if they ever see these boys in their neighborhood again. Big Hank popped Jack on the shoulder and faked a jab to Ben's stomach. After he bought potato chips and Cokes, he left the store, but he could not find his bike. The three kids were gone. Jack and Ben saw their bikes in the dark, beyond the light's circle.

"What'd they do with my bike, the jerks?" He looked onto the tracks and behind the garbage cans. And then he saw it. The three kids had forced the bike upright between the three iron fence rails. It was woven into the rails and all but nailed in place. He didn't get angry. He studied the railing and the bike. Then he decided how to remove it by turning the handlebars and taking the seat off. The pedals were the hardest to disengage. With his enormous strength, he lifted, pushed, and pulled. "It's comin'. It's comin'." Ben expected to hear metal snap under his force, but it didn't. When the odd bike was finally free, it rested on the top railing. He had threaded his bike through the rails, moving it up slowly, like he was solving a Chinese puzzle. He straightened the handlebars, replaced the seat, and reattached the rusty chain. Jack gave him the bag of chips and Cokes.

"Take it easy, Big Hank. Next time you need help just whistle."

"Never could whistle," he answered. "But I'll keep tryin'."

Ben thought that if Big Hank ever met those kids again, they'd spend an hour sitting on that railing laughing like old buddies. And so, off he went into the young night to do whatever Big Hank does.

Ben imagined him at Thorn Hill, reuniting with guards and cafeteria workers, telling stories about the outside, checking on the recent graduates, and chiding the new kids for their foolish ways. He reminded him of Jack's heretical portrait of Saint Lucifer, part light, part darkness, Good Thief, Bad Thief, an awesome force to be respected. Guilt and guile, side by side.

Big Hank

Jack and his mom were in the living room. Brothers and sisters, unaware of the tragedy, ran up and down the stairs yelling in their annoying high-pitched voices. "No, you can't." "I can too dance! Wanna watch me?"

Ben could tell that Jack's mom had been crying. She twisted a dish towel in her hands. Jack studied her for some signal—what to say, what to do. "Jesus, Mary, and Joseph," she sobbed, the Irish woman's prayer. "When Hank's mother called this morning, I expected her to ask how I was doing with my situation. She's nice that way. I just said to her, 'Hello, Yvonne, my, it's good to hear your voice.' Then she began to cry, deep sobs, and I knew her call could only be about Big Hank. Had he fallen, been hit by a car, been arrested, you know, things like that. Oh, no. Nothing so simple. She told me everything in a systematic way, despite her grief. Here's what happened. A mother would never forget her words."

"When Yvonne came home last night after work, she looked for Hank, but she couldn't find him, that is, until she went to his bedroom. And there he was, spread out on that bed that hardly fits him. His eyes were open and he was terrorized. A small pile of aspirins was under the table lamp, the only light in the room. She'd given him aspirins that morning in her office because he had a headache. Actually, she thought he just made that up as an excuse to drop by. Usually, he asked for a few dollars. And that was all there was. She asked Hank was he all right.

His answer was, 'I don't think so. I can't move. My throat's sore. My voice sounds weird.'

"Well, she called the doctor she works for, and he said he'd be right over. Dr. Crane arrived after what seemed an eternity to Yvonne. He examined Hank and then asked him to smile, and he did, but only the left side of his lips turned up. The right side drooped. Then Dr. Crane took a card from his shirt pocket, one of the face cards, put it on Hank's stomach, and propped it up with his fingers. 'Hank, I know you like to play cards, so tell me what card you see here on your stomach. Lift with your elbows if you'd like.' He couldn't lift his head and shoulders or prop himself up. Then the doctor gave him a reassuring pat on his hand, signaled Yvonne into the kitchen, and said, 'It could be polio, but I can't be absolutely sure until tests are made. It could be something else, too. Maybe he fell and hurt his spine. You know how that goes.' Then he made a phone call, requested an ambulance, which came right away, and they took him to the hospital. But Yvonne couldn't go with him. That's the rule. Then, early this morning, a social worker called from the hospital; she said that a nurse needed to talk with her about Hank. And that's how she learned it was polio, for certain."

Jack's mom said that she wanted to go to Yvonne's apartment to be of some comfort, but in her condition that was not to be. And then she began to grill them about Big Hank, about where he had been, and who had been with him, and what was he doing, God knows where.

"When did you see Hank last?"

Jack answered quickly, "Yesterday morning."

His mom replied, "What? He went to the zoo with you?"

"No, mom, up by Darrah Street. He was on his way to see his mother, that's all."

"But his mother works way up on that hill in Oakland, near the hospitals. What were you doing there when the zoo's in the other direction?"

"We were just cruising around seeing what's going on, you know. I still had the peanuts in my pockets. I gave them to the monkeys later. Honest! He left us, and we didn't see him again. He said that he was going to sleep all day. Oh, there's something else."

His mom raised her eyebrows and said, "Oh, this better be good!"

224

"Well, we went behind this big building and sat on the wall there, just to rest before heading back. We got hungry, so on the way back we bought some cherries."

Ben said, "We saw Hank a few days earlier on Penn Avenue, the day Jack bought the turtle. Hank gave us a friendly punch or two, and then he wrestled a little with Jack the way they sometimes do. But Hank wasn't himself. He should have pinned Jack and then let him go, like always. But he couldn't do it, and Jack had him down. Then this nun showed up and bawled him out for causing a scene in public. So Jack let him go, and Hank walked away. He looked at his arms and flexed his muscles, like he couldn't believe they had lost their strength. I don't know where his bike was; he was walking toward Frankstown Avenue. Maybe to a movie at the Triangle. Could he have been sick then?"

"Jesus, Mary, and Joseph," she cried, tears coming again. "Jackie, if he was sick, and you two were rolling around in the dirt, and a nun had to talk sense to you, do you know what that means? Kids give other kids germs. How could you have been so irresponsible?" She snapped the towel at Jack. "Where is your father? He needs to be here."

Jack said that his dad was re-parking the car, which was too far down on Ellsworth.

"Where's Pap-Pap?" asked Jack, perhaps wanting to show that adults were important to him, or else to change the subject.

"He's probably in bed, sleeping." Then she finished the sentence, "it off."

Interlude II: Saturdays

On the next Saturday, his favorite day of the week, winter or summer, Ben pulled his noisy wagon to the Giant Eagle on the corner of South Highland and Alder while his mother walked beside him planning her week's menu. "Let's do lamb chops and roasted chicken this week. I need a bottle of BV for Sunday's beef roast. It makes good gravy. How are we on toilet paper?" They walked up and down the aisles. He pushed a cart that soon filled with food and supplies for the week. Each week was the same, unless a major holiday had arrived. He squeezed the bags into the wagon, which was parked outside the store. He began pulling, being careful of sharp turns, which usually upended the wagon. At curbs, mother lifted the back of the wagon and set it down in the street. Old Man Brooks was not at the corner on Saturdays in the summer. There were just too many cuties to attend to. Instead, he observed them from his narrow window. Saturday and Sunday were his days of rest.

Every Saturday afternoon, like a scene in a play, Kate left Kate's to follow the route of her *Sun-Telegraph* paperboy. She collected from her customers on Lamont Place in a cheerful manner, speaking in a sprightly British accent, though she was born only a few blocks away. It was great seeing her on the street.

A trusting woman, Kate gave customers a generous line of credit. So many times Ben watched her total purchases on tan grocery bags. She would transfer the total to a tall ledger by the cash register. Customers trusted her, too. They settled their bills whenever they could. The boys never swiped anything from Kate. One step down from the counter was a door connecting with her brother's shoe-repair store. On Saturday afternoons, when Kate was out collecting, he kept the door open and dealt with Kate's customers as well as his own. Wearing a canvas apron smeared with brown and black polish, he sliced small amounts of bologna for customers. "Just tell Kate forty-nine cents next time," he told them, or whatever the amount was. That's how simple it was at Kate's.

On this particular Saturday, mother and Ben talked about Big Hank, his mother's sadness, and the uncertainty of his future. He would not be in school for weeks, perhaps months. He was not much of a student to begin with, and losing half a grade was the same as missing the year. And he was too big to be held back a year. Parents would probably complain about him. This was not a good start of Ben's Saturday. The atmosphere was solemn.

Georgie-Georgie-Albert's-son was reassembling the old Health-Mor vacuum sweeper when they got home with the grocery wagon. This was his brother's only Saturday chore. But before running the sweeper, with its shrill, deafening motor, he gave it a Saturday tune-up. After he vacuumed, dust settled for the rest of the day, only to be stirred again next Saturday, and so on. Then there was the laundry machine, which chugged and chugged in the basement. Although it was a new machine, it was just an antiquated model with a dangerous wringer that was positioned over a slate tub. A long shifting rod controlled filling and emptying the machine. Wash, wring, rinse, wring, load a basket, carry the basket to the little backyard, pin the clothes to four lines stretched across three narrow backyards, raise the lines with bending poles, look at the sky, interpret the clouds, and do the next load, and so on. A heavy Saturday rain was known as the second rinse. Cecilia's long complaint about the antiquated washing machine was lost on Albert.

He replied, "You asked for a new washer, so I bought you a new washer!"

"Oh, Albert, I didn't mean a machine that was designed during the Spanish-American War for Irish washerwomen to struggle with while the mistress of the manor shopped in Gimbels or Horne's. I meant an automatic machine and, God willing, a dryer. Spend a dime or two and save me time. Oh, Lord, I am grateful that we don't have a mangle to burn my fingers and the sheets on. Clean wrinkles are just perfect."

Ben pitched in to help her: "Jack's mom washes for a family of eight, almost nine, and she has a great big washer and a dryer. And, she's Irish!"

"That's what I call curb-side diplomacy!" she replied with a laugh. "Now, run off and deliver your papers to the rich and famous."

"Did I tell you that Byron Janis is on a tour in big cities over in Europe? Now that's famous."

Mother was a little hard of hearing. "Who, *who?*" she asked.

But he was almost out the door. "Later," he called.

She answered him in kitchen-German, *"Raus mit euch!"* Out with you! This was the favorite command she shouted at the overfed cat that rubbed her ankles and purred by the stove in the kitchen of their little country bungalow in Allegheny Acres. Mother was a modern woman with a modern pressure cooker that often threatened to explode. "Keep the cat out, please!" she would cry. "I don't want to scald it." (This was the cat that ran away, and no wonder.) Then she called out, "Albert, why did you buy me this pressure cooker, which I'll never understand, and there's no instruction book!"

"It was on sale," he said. "And it prepares healthful meals. It saves all the vitamins."

"It might," she continued, "if you like your dinner on the ceiling."

That was Allegheny Acres.

At the end of the day on Saturday, Albert and Cecilia often went to the Elbow Room on Ellsworth Avenue to have some time away and to taste something better than the cheap beer he bought by the case every month. Ben was asleep by the time they returned in the gray Studebaker. Sunday morning papers had to be delivered very early to avoid customer complaints—so said the second-place Paperboy of the Year for 1953.

Dancing

Sunday papers were especially heavy with so many ads for Labor Day sales. This was the last opportunity tardy parents had to buy school clothes, pencils, and lunch boxes for their kids. Sending them to school on Tuesday unprepared, unwashed, undraped, and uninspired would start nuns thinking about vocational education in high school for the lower rung of students in the parish. Saint Joseph was a carpenter, they would say, a noble profession, and the world sorely needs electricians and plumbers to rebuild the rotting cities after the long war. Why, just look around you, they would say. Nuns weren't the only ones to sanctify Labor Day. No. Cigar-chewing politicians were watching from open convertibles streaming down Fifth Avenue. They assessed their chances for reelection, smiling broadly with pink cheeks and yellow teeth, happily surveying democracy at work, ward-by-ward.

There was some news gathered by Yvonne's doctor friends. They reported that Big Hank was still very weak, still in pain, and struggling to breathe. He might have to be placed in an iron lung, which would allow his chest muscles a chance to rest. There was guarded hope that he would escape paralysis, but for now he struggled with body motion. "Smile?" the doctors asked him, but he would respond with the same grotesque half-smile, half-frown. "Excellent," the doctors would say.

His mother was understandably upset to learn that Hank's old green bicycle, the sign of his former vigor, had been stolen from behind the tall hedge next to the apartment. He used to ram the bike as far into the hedge as he could each night, and it was waiting for him to dislodge with a violent jerking motion the next day. The only hope for justice was that the thief would wreck it and then limp away, knees bloody and a finger broken.

Ben went to Jack's for his mother's famous breakfast. Now she moved slowly in the kitchen and her movements were measured by frequent pauses. Attending Mass was out of the question, and so the old Chrysler just leaned against the curb collecting road dust and tree sap. The twins, Sarah and Susan, and the little boys, Jerry and Bobby, sensed the change—no rambunctious teasing of Jack at the breakfast table; instead, a quiet Jack who used to love being teased. And their father's crossword puzzle left undone. Change was in the air. He sensed it, too, uncomfortable and disconnected as he sat there.

And then, as breakfast ended, in came the lovely fresh-from-church Becky, beautiful, radiant, and pure. He wished that *she* would place him on probation. The touch of rouge and lipstick was magical. He maneuvered closer for a breath of her perfume, something mildly lilac, a simple scent. Springtime in September. She had come to babysit for an hour so Jack's mom could rest on the soft sofa, with her knees drawn up to contain her large belly, while her feet were tucked between the sofa pillows for traction.

Becky kicked off her new loafers, with room to grow, and slid them into a corner. It was so natural, so at home, a gesture he had never seen before. In her pretty white socks she tip-toed to the clean laundry pile, which was deeper than usual, and held out her hands. She clicked her fingers in a nice rhythm.

"Who would like to dance?" she asked, and the little girls hopped over and put their hands in hers.

"Bobby and Jerry, don't just stare. Come over here and dance with us."

Ben was afraid she would invite him to dance, but she didn't. Sometimes she could be a little bossy.

The boys pushed and shoved, but eventually they understood that they were to hold hands and move up and down.

"Ring around the laundry, ring around the laundry," they sang, with Becky leading. They danced in one direction and then returned.

Becky had a natural spring in her step, light enough for the twins to follow. The boys loved falling onto the clean laundry pile. Up they bounced to rejoin the merry circle, which welcomed them with a whoop of pleasure. It was a pretty sight, twice in one direction and twice in reverse, with singing about running around the mountain looking for the sheep, or swaying like rowers in small boats on a choppy sea: "Don't stand up in the rocking boat, the rocking boat, or we'll all fall in." Then the boys fell into the laundry pile and squealed, Bobby burrowing into the pile and hiding, only to jump up with glee. Jack's mom laughed; her stomach began to sway. She held it with her hands when she wasn't clapping in rhythm. And then they all danced to the other clothes pile, which was also large, but less fluffy because of the weight of stretched, damp fabric. The song continued, but changed: "Daddy's gonna holler, needs a clean collar. Don't fall in 'less you have a dollar."

Jerry sang, "I got a dollar," and fell into the dank laundry. "Oh Jerry, you are brave," called his mom, red-faced with laughter.

He had never seen such a joyful and spontaneous dance before. Around and around they turned, the twins' curls growing longer with perspiration and the merry-go-round pull: love's shorthand, a curl here, a curl there. Jack sat beaming with pleasure.

And then a strange thing happened. An old man appeared quietly. He was unshaven, white hair was poking in all directions, and his trousers looked like a working man's after a hard day. He wore yellowing socks that came within an inch of his long johns, which were visible either because the trousers were too short or the waist was just riding too high. Jack greeted him: "Pap-Pap, show us how to dance the jig." The old man, sleeping below the floor, must have been awakened into a strange world, reminiscent of his youth in Ireland. He was the softly swaying man returning from *This and That* in the green-black night. In an instant he began to dance what Jack called a jig, even though there was no pipe and tabor to give him a rhythm. The rhythm must have been within him. He must have listened to it often in his private and isolated world.

"Don't stop, Jerome! I love to watch you dance," called out Maureen, his daughter-in-law. Becky and the children, Jack and Ben, and his mom clapped and clapped. Pap-Pap was spryer that Ben ever expected. After he stopped, he asked, "Is there by any chance a cup of hot coffee for a hard-working turf cutter?" They all laughed. Then the silence fell like pennies into a well, with a moment of expectation and glances toward Jack's mom, who was moving oddly.

"Sarah and Susan, each take a leg and pull me around to sit and get my bearings. There, that's better," she sighed. "Jerry, run upstairs and tell your father it's time to back his old car down the street and load me in for a ride to Shadyside Hospital! You better help him with the message, Jackie! Or just say that mom said, 'It's time.'"

Becky and Ben helped her stand. They each handed her a shoe. She could just squeeze into them. He looked at Becky and smiled. While slipping into her new loafers, she smiled back, but he knew she was worried. Those words, "it's time," are frightening in their brevity.

Red Ranger, Red Ranger

Jack's dad pulled his old car forward to Ellsworth Avenue. The trip to the Shadyside Hospital maternity wing would normally take only two minutes, but, at his cautious speed, five minutes might be more accurate. After they left, a formal calm settled over the household. Becky was good with the children. Pap-Pap went out for a Sunday stroll. Jack uncovered Red Ranger, now unchained, and then he checked the tires, the headlight, and the anemic horn. He straddled the seat, leaned over the handlebars, and rolled the bike back and forth on the narrow porch.

Abby and Jenny came over to say hello and offer their help. Abby's mother had already promised to stay with the children in the evenings while Jack's dad visited in the hospital. Neighbors would deliver dinners for two weeks. Names for boys and girls were discussed. A diaper service, a friend's gift, was on notice for the baby's birth. The wait would not be long. This would be Maureen's sixth child. She was a strong woman, but she was almost forty-one.

Becky and Jenny took over laundry duties, tossing load after load into the old Maytag while the dryer churned noisily for most of the day. Freshly dried clothes were bunched on the sofa. Family members who could follow orders had to find their clothes and either place them in drawers or on the growing pile for ironing. Socks, unmatched or hole-drilled, were forbidden on that pile. Some clothes had no takers. "Who owns this ragged pair of shorts? Anyone? No? Ragbag, ragbag, here's some more junk fresh from the floor." Pap-Pap's long johns caused much laughter. "Yuck, what are these?" "Weird." "What's this escape hatch, anyway?" "Let's run them through another wash!"

Music and song made the work fun. By suppertime, the floor in the dining room was revealed for the first time in months. Jack collected a few items that no longer fit him. Many were as transparent as tissue. He had no school clothes. He had hoped to find something nice to wear; Tuesday would be dress-up day. Well, he would improvise, make a fashion statement, and be the Beau Brummell of eighth grade. Then, miraculously, Jenny tossed him a shirt from his dad's pile. "This is yours. I've seen you wear it," she said mechanically without looking at him. Well, it was and it wasn't. Actually, the large shirt belonged to Big Hank, on loan like a library book, but now overdue, with a missing button and wheel stains still visible down the back. It was dull yellow with large butterfly wings down the front. Would Big Hank miss the shirt? Would it still fit him? Was his mother searching for it? Jack told him he'd keep it to remind him of Big Hank, who was to stay in the hospital for months, perhaps until Christmas. Who knew?

Jack pulled Ben aside and said in Henry Fonda's voice of noble suffering, "Since my closet is almost empty, it's safe to say that my wardrobe is very limited. So, I might need some help on Tuesday, especially since my mom won't be here to wake me up. Good chap, could you come down early and make sure that I get up and then help me dress for my public?" He would ask his dad for a ride to Sears, if that was possible, to buy some sale clothes. Otherwise, he'd try to find some of his dad's clothes that fit, but he just had an old suit and some ragged Arrow shirts. In fact, the shirts were probably in the ragbag already, ordered there by decisive Becky.

When the persistent ringing of the phone broke the domestic peace, Jack was quick to answer it. He listened, said something in a mumble, and dropped the receiver onto the cradle. For the last hour he had expected to hear his dad's voice with happy news that he was a brother again and that mom was fine. He looked at Ben and said in a quiet voice, "Nothing, still waiting. Let's walk over to the hospital and see what's going on."

"Are we allowed to go into the hospital?" he asked.

Jack said that the doors are never locked. "Let's go."

They walked toward South Aiken Avenue. They saw debris gathered where the old Chrysler had been parked for days: cigarette packs, dry leaves, a matchbook, yellowing newspaper, and trash like that. After crossing the bridge, Jack became meditative. They sat on a stone step and were silent. Ben looked at the hospital and remembered that his mother's father used to own the grounds on which it was built. He had a large house—there were many children—a pony barn and a gardener's shed. He named the house *Sans-Souci*, a popular estate name in the nineteenth century. The French name meant *without care*. He bought the property because it was situated above the railway station. Stairs led to a platform below, and so he could travel to the city and be in his office in about twenty minutes. Cecilia and her sisters loved life in their home in the country along dusty Centre Avenue. After the hospital association bought the property, their father built the house on Dithridge Street at the corner of Bayard Street where the strange, long-legged Russian wolfhounds prowled behind a fence.

Jack reached into Ben's shirt pocket for a cigarette and held it between his teeth, his way of asking for a light. He was pondering something deep, or else he would have wrestled for a smoke. He said that when little Bobby was born, there was some adjusting necessary. Bedrooms were changed, his mom needed help with just about everything, and Jack, the first born, was elected to perform many tasks. Now, with a new baby coming, he saw an end to Roslyn Place. "Hello, Homewood," he said. "Hello, stupid school. Rats! Now I'll need to get a job, maybe as a pin boy at some smoky bowling alley, with sharp-edged, rubber-ringed duckpins bouncing around my head, or tenpins fracturing my shins. Is that a future, my future? Sweaty and stunned all the time?"

"You could have your portrait painted: *Youth with Gutter Ball.*"

"Yeah, that's about right, and yours would be *Altar Boy with Old Golds.*"

"And Big Hank, what would his picture be called? *Angry Boy Searches for Bike on Pierce Street?*"

Jack thought about it.

There was a telling pause. "Do you think he'll ever ride a bike again?" Ben asked.

"He has to. He's Big Hank, so he has to!" Jack said, flicking his cigarette butt into the street.

"How can you be so sure?"

Jack stood, brushed himself off, and settled the matter: "The Shadow knows!"

They entered the hospital through the first door they saw. They walked down long corridors until they found a carpeted lobby. Jack asked a lady behind a counter where his mother was. She said she would call the directory. She made two calls, but no luck. "Are you sure your mother's in the hospital?" she asked.

"She's having a baby."

"OK," she said, and made a third call. "Found her," she said cheerfully, and listened to a voice somewhere in the building. This took a minute while Jack paced the floor. "Thank you," she said. "I'll tell him."

"Is she all right?" Jack asked.

"Let me tell you what I learned from a nurse in obstetrics. That's where mothers have babies. First, I want to tell you that you have a beautiful new sister, and she's just fine, crying her lungs out and kicking like a colt. Don't you just love it? I'm so happy for you."

"That's great news! A girl! I can't believe it. When can I see her and my mom?"

"Well," she said, "I have to tell you something else. You see, your mother had a complication; the doctors here felt it would be best to transport her to Magee Women's Hospital. She was taken there by ambulance. I suggest that you go home and wait for your father to call. I assure you, he will call."

"But what's wrong? She was fine when she left."

"Your father should be the one to tell you. Wait for him to call. That's my best advice."

"Jack, the lady's right. Let's head home. There may be news waiting for you."

They jogged across the bridge. Jack was murmuring things Ben could not understand.

He ran up the porch steps and into the house. He said to Becky,

"Mom had a baby girl. But she had complications that I thought had gone away, so they sent her to Magee. That's where I'm going now."

"Oh Jackie, be careful," Becky pleaded.

Ben followed him out the door. Jack pulled Red Ranger off the porch, threw his leg over the saddle, and went flying up the street.

"I'll follow you," he yelled. "It's down near Forbes."

In the twilight on Sunday night Jack raced faster than he had ever seen him go, crisscrossing the car tracks and jumping to the sidewalk to get by stopped cars. He had learned a few moves from Big Hank, but not the safest. He rode the devil out of Red Ranger. He turned on the light and followed its narrow beam. Ben followed the light, too; otherwise, he would have lost him. Gawkers on the sidewalk shouted, "Slow down you nut. Nothing's that important!" But they did not know Jack. When he reached top speed, he sat back and coasted for a few seconds to get his breath, and then he pumped furiously again. On his old wreck of a bike he would have crashed, or the bike would have disintegrated. Not even the devil's blacksmith could have mended it. Ben had reached his limit; he couldn't keep up, but he saw Jack's light weaving left and right. On Fifth Jack flew, turned down Bellefield, and then took a shortcut across the broad Pitt campus, even down the stairs, the bike bucking like a rodeo horse. The dark brooding museum was behind him. Forbes Field was to his left.

In the crazy moment it takes to see an entire scenario develop, Ben remembered sitting with Jack in the bleachers of Forbes Field for a double-header on another Sunday. Jack had a way of picking events that best displayed his spirit, even if the event was accidental. It happened that a Hollywood film crew came out to left field between games and set up cameras and microphones aimed at the crowded bleachers. The fans were directed to jump and cheer, and then they were directed to shout "boo." These scenes were used in the movie *Angels in the Outfield*. They paid twenty-two cents to get into a lot of movie theaters just to find themselves, their star-studded selves. Jack said, "There we are! Hey, I look great, but you look stupid." Well, the truth is that they had been sitting in the highest row, too far back to be recognized in the movie. They were throwaway extras. But Ralph Kiner obliged them by hitting a homer, and *that* was in the movie. Some Sunday!

What he needed for Jack now was one of those angels, one who could ride on the back fender and whisper sense in his ear: "Slow down. You cannot change Fate. You have a beautiful baby sister. Trust the doctors. Have Faith." That angel would sound like Ben. But who could say that there wasn't already an angel with singed wings and sooty face saying, "I'll get you there, but for Pete's sake, you're not in Ireland. Get in the *right* lane. Blow that silly horn of yours. And don't forget what you think about *give-and-take* and pretty girls in the dark closet. Excitement, thrills, dancing, that's what you're all about! Don't let anyone take that away from you!"

Horns blared. Closer and closer he moved to the hospital. Nothing would stop him. When Ben finally caught up to him, Jack was hiding Red Ranger under a tall hedge. "What am I gonna do?" he shouted. "This isn't happening! I'm sorry! I'm sorry I didn't put more gas in the tank. I thought there would be enough." He appeared to be incoherent, but Ben suddenly knew what he meant. On that Sunday, seemingly ages ago, when Ben walked back to the house holding Sarah and Susan, Jack's mom lifted the toddler, Bobby. Then he remembered that she put him down and clutched her side. "John," she called. "Something happened."

Talking in the Dark

"Jack, what are you talking about? The car ran out of gas. OK. You didn't put enough gas in. OK. I think you knew that when you told me that it was a mistake to sneak off with the car that night. But on that Sunday, when you saw all of us on the sidewalk, stranded, your streetcar was long gone by the time your mom picked up Bobby. You were probably making eyes at that girl with the plaid ribbons in the back of the church. Right? I mean, you did go to church, didn't you?"

"No. I was over in Webster Hall, waiting for Mass to end. That's why I didn't have the stupid bulletin. So what. I just couldn't pretend that everything was all right. I sat on the couch and ate a candy bar. People went by. They seemed so happy to be there. I wish I could have been happy, too."

"Even so, how could you know about your mom's lifting Bobby? I didn't tell you. Only your mom and dad knew that she felt something. You can't blame yourself because she did the most natural thing, you know, like carrying a tired kid. Who told you about it, anyway?"

"Dad did. When he called. He was at Shadyside Hospital. He never said anything about Magee."

"OK, he just called with an update. He wasn't accusing you of doing wrong. That was your conscience you were listening to."

"Yeah," he said, "I see what you're saying. My conscience. But I should never have been late for Mass. I should have been in the car, and then *I* would have carried Bobby. That's all I hear myself saying anymore—'I should have, I should have,' instead of, 'I need those, I need that, give me more, make me happy.'"

"You should wait until your dad comes home with news about your mom. We already know the baby's healthy. That's good for a start, isn't it?"

"But we're here, right now, and they're up there behind one of those windows. What's wrong with going up?"

"To begin," he said as kindly as he could, "you are sweaty and filthy. Your shirt has holes in it. You look kind of mean right now, in the dark. Guess what you would look like in those bright rooms? You're underage to visit. Then there's me. What would I do up there but look silly. Right? Anything your dad says to you I would have to pretend I didn't hear."

Jack was silent, considering his next move.

"And, Jack," he said in a reasonable voice, "what if you ask a thousand questions about your mom, like where do babies come from, and how do they get there, and how do they know when it's time to come out? Do you think your dad would give you answers?"

Jack laughed. "Dad's never without words, you know, so I think he'd say *something*."

"When you were racing down Fifth a few minutes ago, I wanted to yell, '*Stop*. Turn around.' But you were too far ahead of me to hear. This was a mistake coming here. We could both be in the emergency room right now, being treated for multiple stupidities. That's all your parents need to deal with."

"Right, I wish I could be as good as you. You know everything." He paused, bursting to finally say it: "We're here now. I've got to see my dad, to see what he thinks, to learn about my mom. And that's final!"

Jack walked into the hospital, squinted with night vision in the neon brightness, and looked for help. Ben followed him, squinting so hard his glasses almost fell off.

There always seems to be a nice lady at a counter willing to help. That's what he liked about hospitals. In no time they were rising in an elevator to the surgery floor where Jack would meet his dad. And there he was, his shoulders slumped. He was studying an abstract painting on the wall; his back was to them. But Jack must have been reflected in the picture's glass, because his dad turned toward them. "Jack! What are you doing here? The two of you at this hour?" He was smiling. It might have been the light that made Ben see this: Jack's dad had tears in his eyes. For the first time ever he saw him hug Jack and pat his sweaty back, a long hug.

Jack's voice sort of gurgled in the hug. "I just wanted to be here to see how everybody is. It's great news about a baby girl!"

"Jack, you can begin by calling her by her name, Patricia. She'll be here soon to be with her mom. She's already been baptized by the Shadyside Hospital chaplain, Father Demeter."

Ben wondered why it was necessary to baptize a healthy baby in the hospital, but nothing more was said about it.

"Jack, you need to know about mother. She's just down the hall recovering from what the doctor called surgical repair. She's still out like a light, which is good, because she's going to have a lot of pain for a few days. She'll stay in this hospital."

Ben couldn't hold it any longer. He wanted to assure them both that she would be fine. "Hey, know what?" he blurted, "I was born in this hospital, and look at me, I'm OK!"

Jack's dad laughed. "Really?" he asked with a smile. "That's good enough for me!"

Jack said he needed a second opinion on that one.

Jack had to ask, "What went wrong? Why did she have to come here if she had a healthy baby?" His voice cracked. Ben thought Jack might pass out.

"Just to be safe, just to get top doctors to make her insides right, that's why. Look, I won't kid you, the doctors at Shadyside told me that she has a serious problem, that the loss of blood was great. Jackie, are you OK? For Pete's sake, sit down. Lower your head. There you go!"

Ben sat, too.

"You probably don't know much about having babies, and why should you? You're just fourteen. Give it a year. Biology class in high school awaits. For that matter, I know next to nothing about babies. I just try to make enough money to pay for them," he laughed.

Jack looked up. "Does this mean we're moving to Homewood?"

"Only if you have a burning desire to, and only if your mother wants to. Jack, what does Homewood have to do with having a baby? So, where was I? Oh, your mother has had a few babies, hasn't she, including twins. That means that her insides were pretty stressed—the doctor's word for it—and she's forty. When we get a little older, the old muscles don't do what they used to do. Pushing them too hard can tear a muscle. That's what happened."

He saw Ben move on his chair by the door. "Maybe I'm saying too much."

"Was it my fault? Was it because of something I did . . . or didn't do?" Jack asked as though these were his final words on Earth.

His dad pursed his lips, loosened his tie, and, looking straight at Jack, he said to him, "The answer to your question is 'no.' Jack, life's a mystery. Let me know when you solve it!"

Jack's eye's clouded, wet with tears. He was choking with gratitude and love. "I think I'm beginning to solve the puzzle, but I need a little more time. Like fifty years."

"A good idea to start early on that puzzle. Now, here's something else you will want to know. I only tell you this because your mom's going to have a long recuperation, and I don't want you getting impatient with her."

"I promise, I won't do that," Jack said with determination.

"Good! You'll change diapers and walk Patricia at night so I can sleep? Right? Now some not-so-good news, but it turns out fine. There was a pretty big growth. This came as a great surprise to the doctors. It was removed." He paused in reflection.

"Dad, are you all right?" Jack said these words slowly, fearful of the answer.

His dad smiled, but he did not answer Jack's question. Instead, he looked him in the eye and said: "So, Jack, you have permission to spoil Patricia as much as you can, to take good care of her, and to be the big brother. OK?"

"I'll do it. I promise. Can I drop out of school, too?"

They all laughed. A nurse shushed them, but she was smiling. She had been listening. "Your little Patricia is now in our nursery. She was just brought over by a nurse and a careful volunteer driver. Her first ride in a Cadillac! And tomorrow she will be reunited with her mother at breakfast time. And to think that my mother told me I should be a secretary. But I said 'no, no, no' to that idea. I was going to become a nurse, I told her, and now maybe you can see why! So, you fine gentlemen can just go home and say a few prayers for Maureen and Patricia, because right now everything checks out just fine!"

Dressing Jack

On Labor Day Ben served Mass at eight o'clock with a new kid, who, like Jack, couldn't pronounce the Latin responses. He carried him when he faltered. The organist raced the music, pushing the priest to a record twenty-minute Mass in black vestments. During the week the masses were all about the dead, and they happened to be quick Masses because long prayers were skipped.

A handful of old women came to Communion. They put out their tongues and squeezed their eyes shut. The Host was light on their tongues, which were not sensitive at their age, so the priest had to say as distinctly as he respectfully could, in Latin, "This is the body of Christ." That was the signal to pull in the tongue and struggle off their knees. He liked the old people. They knew they were cramming for their finals, and they did this with dignity. Some stayed for the next Mass. Those who came early for the six o'clock Mass waited at the heavy doors that were not unlocked until a quarter-to-six. They showed the sacristan angry faces under their babushkas, especially on rainy days and in the winter. Ben imagined this little drama was performed in every church in the city.

He tried to think of the day before and of the strange evening with Jack. But those hours seemed so unreal, so far removed. Still, there was a wild excitement: imagining self-portraits; Jack racing through the darkening streets; the good news about the baby and her mother; the emotions of Jack and his dad; and Jack's passionate vows on the way home, at a slow speed, the dim light shining on the mist. He swore that he would never let his family down; that he would give Patricia every free moment; that his mom would never lift anything heavier than a teacup; and that his dad's car was forever immune to theft. And he would be a very good friend to Big Hank when he comes home.

On Tuesday morning, school finally started. Ben got up early to serve the six o'clock Mass. Then he walked to Jack's house and got there by seven. The shaded street was cool, fragrant, and damp. The wooden bricks were slippery. Just as he reached the end of the street, Jenny and Becky were leaving for school. They were so close together they might have been locked at their elbows. Jenny saw him and called his name.

"Wait, wait, wait," she said as she ran up the stairs to the house. In a few seconds she was skipping down the steps and running toward him.

"Here," she said, holding out her closed hand, squeezed tight. "This is for you, for good luck."

He held out his hand. He closed his eyes, which she said he had to do, and then he felt her hold his hand. She pressed something small and warm onto his palm, closed his fingers, and squeezed his hand for a few seconds. "For good luck," she repeated. And then she turned to join her sister for the walk to school. When he opened his hand, he saw the Monopoly jalopy. His heart was flying. He closed his fingers and squeezed them tight. Then he raised his hand and said, "Thank you!" She smiled, and off they went. He stood there, stunned. A thought came to him: luck's tokens are best kept warm; he'd never known anyone to carry an ice cube for good luck.

What luck would he have dressing Jack this morning? He doubted that his dad could raise Jack from his warm bed the way his mom could. It takes practice. The door was open, as it usually was in summer, and even in winter. He just walked in and shouted "hello." Jack's dad was in the kitchen looking for plates and bowls. The children were all advising him, pointing to some of the cupboards and to the refrigerator. "Hello there," he answered. "There's a chance Jack might still be in bed."

"I'll check him out," he said. Jack was still in bed, immovable. There would be no toast for him this morning.

"Get up. You're way late." Slowly his leg and foot explored the air and then touched the worn carpet. His small pile of clean laundry was still under the open window. Ben raked through it for underwear, a sad exercise in futility.

"Where are your shorts and undershirt?"

"I'm wearin' 'em," he said.

He mumbled, "I'll have to skip my morning prayers and last night's prayers, my shower, my toast, and my homework, too."

"Wake up, Jack, school starts today. You don't have any homework, unless you promised some last June and never did it."

"I don't? I didn't," he replied, a little too cryptic to sort out. "What'll I wear today?"

For Jack this would be a comic game to hide the fact that he was unprepared to dress for the first day of school. Ben began to play the game by looking out the window overlooking the street. What could he see through the sycamore trees? "Let's see," he pondered. "What's Dickie Day wearing? OK, Dickie's starting down his porch steps. He's holding his streetcar pass between his teeth and pulling his belt tight." Of course, there was no Dickie.

"Well, what's he got on? What's he wearing?"

"It looks to me like he's wearing a pale blue knit shirt with two buttons—a gaucho shirt—and he's wearing light pink slacks with blue stitching and dark pink pocket flaps."

"Do I have anything exactly like that?" he said more than asked. Hey, what's a gaucho shirt?"

"It's like a golf shirt."

"What's a gaucho?" he asked.

"I don't know. Maybe some cowboy."

Hangers banged emptily against one another and scratched like chalk on the blackboard. Nothing like that.

"Are his pants pegged?"

"Nuns don't allow pegged pants, Jack. You know that. Next year, if you decide to go to high school, you can peg your pants and comb your hair back in a DA."

Funny, Jack knew about the DA. Just walk behind a duck and look at its feathers.

"Yeah. Sure. So, what else is Dickie wearing?"

"Well, it's hard to see, but it looks like he's holding up his pink slacks with a green lizard belt, pulled real tight, and new spade shoes. Black ones. And a first-day-of-school-to-impress-the-nuns tie. You know, the one with the hand-painted picture the Last Supper, painted sideways, you know, like an Indian totem pole. It's tan, with all those pink faces and black beards, with those twenty-six dark eyes looking around the corner at *you*, Sir Jack, the original sinner."

"Me? Hey, I'm Mr. Innocent. Do I have anything like that in here?" Hangers scraped in the empty closet.

"Here," he said, "wear these limp jeans, and this faded yellow shirt with butterfly wings. OK? Now we're getting somewhere here."

"What about socks? What's Dickie wearing?"

"Jack, he's almost out of sight." He got on his knees and put his head out the window. "They're argyles, red, black, and yellow ones. OK?"

"I don't have any like that, do I?"

"Swipe socks from your dad and let's go. It's late!"

Jack jumped down the stairs and slid into the kitchen. He swiped a triangle of toast from his dad's plate. "Got you!" he teased. His dad slopped tea on the *Post-Gazette*.

"See ya later, I'm late. Say 'hi' to mom and little Patty Cake for me."

Outside, Red Ranger was once again covered with the tarp. Jack patted the bike under the covering. "Good boy, good boy!" he said.

"Hey," he laughed, "if Dickie goes anywhere near Pierce Street in that clown suit you put him in, he won't last long enough to have *his* last supper. Who was he supposed to be, anyway, Red Skelton? You play a very mean game with a box of crayons!"

"I just got tired of his usual uniform. You know, the jeans and Boy Scout shirt."

Then, in a serious tone, Jack said, "Thanks for your help. You know, it's so hard to get good help these days."

"Take a look at this," he said. "Jenny just gave it to me for good luck."

"Maybe you'll need it, Mr. Kazoo. Abby told me that Becky told her that Jenny said you would make a better husband, but that *my* eyes sparkle!"

Then he said that he expected Jenny that evening to help with the kids. "She'll have one of those good luck charms for me, want to bet? Probably that ol' top hat." He did a fair imitation of Fred Astaire.

"Let me know," he said.

And in the early morning sun on the first day of school, under the old trees, Jack put his face close to Ben's, his eyes wide open, his feet still dancing, and shouted with his old spirit, "Cast your eyeballs on these sparkling peepers and cry!"

Interlude III: Waiting Is the Longest Season

Once school started on that Tuesday, Ben soon realized how locked up he was by schedules: serving Mass at six, being in his seat by the last bell, fasting for First Fridays, having doughnuts and hot chocolate in the cafeteria after the Mass, delivering the *Press*, and doing afternoon homework while listening to radio dramas for kids, such as *Sergeant Preston of the Yukon*, which had a beautiful musical theme that set a mood of deep snow far in the north. Also on his mind were thoughts about Jack's mom and Patricia, and Big Hank, way up on that hill in Oakland, waiting, waiting, waiting, that long stretch of emptiness, on his back, no visitors, stuck there for what might be months. Was there polio in the Yukon? The polio scare was all but over. Little was said or written about it. What had happened over the summer was called Fate. When would the cure come?

The nuns got on with the joys of learning. The younger and more playful ones had a special sentiment for the boys and girls whom God had spared. Curiously, the nuns reduced prayer time, shortened the rosary each morning to one decade, and assigned the remaining four decades for homework. The first two weeks of school were dedicated to reviewing what was forgotten over the summer, and so they played some nice games to help them remember: Spelling Bees are Buzzing; Grammar Challenges us Every Day; Geography is All About Us; and Whatever Happened to Long Division after He Left Town? Even the nuns played, sometimes making educated mistakes to catch the class off-guard.

"Did you know," Sister wrote on the board: *its' a sin to see forbidden movies?"*

A teacher's pet shouted, "I know, Sister, you should have said *it is a sin,* right?" She ran to the board, which was allowed, and wrote *it is.*

Sister said, "What do you all think about this? Did I make a mistake? If I did, then *whomever* corrects it gets this holy card of a mystery saint."

"Sister! *whoever* would be correct!"

"Very good, Theresa. I'm giving you a holy card of Saint Joan of Arc. It's lovely!"

An eager girl said, "I got it. There aren't any forbidden movies. There are only condemned movies." There was a big smile on her face. She wanted a holy card, too, probably to earn her some praise at home.

"An interesting thought, Denise," Sister said, "but is this really a lesson on mortal sins or on Grammar's Daily Challenges?"

"Oh, oh, oh, oh," yelled Donnie. "You should have said *its a sin,* because sin is a serious subject." He wrote his correction on the board.

"You are so very close, Donnie, that I am awarding you a holy card of, let me see, Saint Albert the Great. Now, has anybody else found another solution?"

"I have one!"

"Well, Danny, write it on the board for us to see."

Danny ran to the board and picked up the chalk. He paused. "I forget," he said. "Whoops."

Danny was the clown who forgot a lot of things.

"Philip, I know you can correct the mistake."

"Well, what do I get if I do?" He was a tease.

"Philip, I think I am ashamed of you. But since we are in a playful mood, I'll give you a holy card of the mystery saint. See," she said, holding the card for all to see. "The face of this holy martyr seems to say that he can understand you, Philip." They all laughed, but the girls thought the body stuck with a bunch of arrows was pretty disgusting.

Philip added the holy card to his growing collection. He was that smart. This was not a card he would ever trade, not for Saint Peter or all the Apostles. He wrote on the board *it's a sin*. The chalk snapped in two when he scraped an elaborate apostrophe for the contraction.

"Someday, Philip, I predict that you will have the resolve of your saint-of-the-day, Saint Sebastian!"

In Geography they played Stump the Teacher with Sister Maris Stella.

"Sister, where is Yellowstone?" She knew.

"Sister, what's the name of the big river in Egypt?" She knew.

"Sister, what state has a beehive for a symbol?"

"Oh, my, Danny, I think you stumped the teacher! What is the answer?"

"Utah," he said proudly. "I was there this summer."

"Then you deserve a holy card of, let me see, Saint Barbara the Generous, the patron saint of miners. She must have liked dark, dirty places! And, she is so generous that she protects us from explosions, like they sometimes have in coal mines. She is a busy bee!"

"Now," she began, "I have a question for the boys. Ready? Her eyes scanned the class. They sat on the edges of their seats. If Saint Barbara were to come back to life, which could happen, you know, if it's God's will, what kind of car do you think she would drive?"

What a question! Some boys shouted "Ford" and others shouted "Chevy." "No way, Fords are better that Chevys." This went on for a minute.

Sister Maris Stella held up her hands like a traffic cop to stop the shouting. "Sorry, boys, but she would drive a Mercury. And here's why. Saint Barbara is the patron of miners, as I've said, and way down deep in a mine in Europe miners were looking for heavy rocks that mercury comes from. Many miners died at an early age because of mercury poison. Don't touch mercury! Well, way down under the earth, in this mine, there's a shrine of Saint Barbara, and the miners pray to her for protection. And in gold mines in Brazil, too, there is her statue, her shrine." Then she told the "ladies" in the class that when the day comes—she tapped her ring finger—be sure to thank Saint Barbara, who must have worked very hard. So, I think she would drive a Mercury! A gold Mercury! They all laughed.

As much fun as this was, he felt the time passing and the season changing. He had his fourteenth birthday, which was quietly celebrated amid elderly relatives at Dithridge Street. He was still waiting for Jack's after-the-fact birthday party.

During the first week of October, Jack told him a surprising story. He said that he had been called to the principal's office to talk to Sister Rosemary, a tall, thin nun, whose authority was never questioned. Jack said that Sister Rosemary asked him about the "altercation" he had had with a fellow on Penn Avenue some weeks earlier. He remembered everything they said:

"Do you remember my tapping you with the tip of my umbrella?" she asked him. "I said that I knew you, John, and your wonderful mother."

"Yes, Sister."

"Well, I hope there has been no further disgraceful conduct."

"No, Sister."

"John, your mother and I go back quite a few years. We were schoolmates. When I told her that I was joining the order of the Sisters of Charity, she said, 'Oh, no, no,' and then, 'oh, yes, yes!' The words 'no' and 'yes' meant the same thing. She knew my heart and I knew hers. I requested the name Rosemary for my religious life; it was my maternal grandmother's name, and the superiors granted my request. My name before Rosemary was Patricia. Do you think it's a coincidence that your little sister and I have the same name?"

"No, Sister."

"I was honored when your mother told me the baby's name. As you are the oldest brother, ever-watchful over your sister, I think you should know how the name was chosen. Just as I will watch over you in the eighth grade, you will watch over little Patricia. How does that sound to you?"

"Very nice, Sister. Thank you!"

"Oh," she said, touching his head, "I see that the scar is healed nicely. Do all boys have such rough-and-tumble experiences?"

"I guess so, Sister. Sometimes."

"And what has become of the young man on the sidewalk? Where does he go to school?"

"He goes to Liberty School, Sister, but he's not in school now because he got real sick."

"That is so sad. What happened to him?"

"He's in the hospital. He got polio."

"Oh, dear Lord. How very, very sad. He will be in my prayers, and all of the Sisters will pray for him. I had hoped that we would escape this awful disease."

October was pumpkin-orange and red and gold in the trees. The calendar saint for the month was Saint Edward the Confessor. Wearing his crown and showing a sad but holy expression, Saint Edward reminded him of his sister's old Halloween costume of a knight's armor, made of cardboard and painted silver by his father. There was a red cross on the breastplate.

Ben was too old to wear a Halloween costume. But Jack, Abby, and Ben walked behind the twins and the boys as they went door-to-door. Abby dressed up like an elongated Raggedy Ann, but only because she was going to a party later on. Jack had a great time talking the twins into sharing their candy with him. The boys were too smart to give Jack anything, except loose pieces of popcorn and Bazooka bubble gum, which was too hard to bother chewing.

Thanksgiving was brown-black, the color of the empty trees after a rain. The calendar saint for the month was Cecilia, the musical saint for whom his mother was named. There was a Thanksgiving feast at Dithridge Street. His aunts were joined by his uncle and aunt from Green Tree. Uncle Erhard was politeness itself, lighting the ladies' cigarettes, pouring wine, and agreeing with everyone. "You don't say," was his frequent response. He wore his famous brown cardigan with leather buttons.

Christmas would soon be green and red on a snowy white background. There would be joyful lamps strung along the city streets in shades of a darkened rainbow.

And during all of this time Jack's mom grew stronger; Patricia would smile when prompted; and Big Hank was slowly recovering. Jack and Ben took some credit for making him feel better. They decided to write him a letter. The trouble was that they had next to nothing to tell him, for life was just so dull. Was dullness their future? They did not know how to cheer him up. He surprised them by writing back: "Hay you bums!" His handwriting was shaky. The letter was short because he was still weak. He had nothing to say, either.

Jack asked a painful question. "What are we going to do when Big Hank comes home?" This was not a trick question.

"What'll we do, Mr. Kazoo? What'll we do?"

Crescent City Blues

One evening after Thanksgiving, Ben went to Jack's house to hear what Big Hank's mother had to say about his slow recovery. Of course, her reason for the visit was to see the baby and to ask how Jack's mom was progressing. But when she was asked about Big Hank, she bit her lower lip for a few seconds, sipped some tea, and said that he has been a brave boy. Some doctors and nurses gave her pieces of information. "It's like making a picture puzzle," she said, "one piece at a time." Her story continued. "Hank has been hospitalized for nearly ten weeks. When he left in the ambulance, he could not move. Breathing was difficult. There was talk of an iron lung, but he struggled to breathe and swallow on his own. He's made progress. The doctors hope that he will have a full recovery, but, even so, he would be weak for a long time. Therapy helps. The nurses really like Hank. They said he's really a comical kid once you get to know him. I could have told them that! And he's a fighter."

"Yvonne, that's such good news. I am so happy for you both."

Then little Bobby joined the two adults on the sofa, knee-to-knee. He worked his way through the knees like a country kid among the lambs, touching them as he counted, "One, two, free, ten."

"Very good," said a pleased mother while turning her eyes to Yvonne.

"If he continues on this steady path, there's a real possibility he'll be home for Christmas. But what would he come home to? I would be at work every day. The apartment is not a very pleasant place. What if he fell? The doctor said that falling would be one of the worst things that could happen. We have no relatives in town. Hank's father, Fred, died on that D-Day beach. But Fred's brother, Ronald, lives near New Orleans. He works at one of the hospitals there. He wants us to move to New Orleans, to the warm climate. Hank could get strong, have therapy, and not have to worry about snow and ice and these hills in Pittsburgh. Uncle Ronald's a nice man, a very giving man. And Aunt Queenie is wonderful. I am very tempted to accept his invitation. But Hank would fight it, I just know! This is his home."

"He'll listen to you, he'll listen to reason, I'm sure."

"I hope you're right, Maureen. It's just so hard because I can't see him." She began to cry.

"Jackie," his mom asked, "you'll both help, won't you? When the time comes, that is?"

They said they would. Did she mean help by trying to lift his spirits, or by visiting him in the apartment? They both shook their heads "yes."

"It would be a great help," Yvonne said, "if you could move a little of the furniture to the basement, and cheer up his room with a coat of paint and some curtains. Do you think you can do this?"

"Of course they can," said Jack's mom. "I'll pack a lunch for them. Perhaps Abby, Jenny, and Becky can put their heads together about decorating. Jackie, it's about work, not a party."

Jerry, Bobby, and the savvy little twins shouted with joy at the word "party."

"Not that kind of a party, children. But I'll make sandwiches for you, too. How does that sound?"

"All right!" Jerry reminded her that he doesn't like crusts. Yvonne wiped her eyes. Her spirits lifted. "Won't it be wonderful when he sees the changes?"

"Yvonne, I like the idea of moving to New Orleans, which would be a fresh start for both of you. Hank would have a man to guide him, and you would be invited to all of those famous parties New Orleans is known for."

"Oh, I'm so glad we had a chance to talk. I feel so much better now.

But it's getting late. I've got to run," Yvonne said in a lighter, happier voice.

"Boys, be gentlemen and walk with Yvonne so she gets home safely. And if the spirit moves you, stop at Isaly's to warm yourself. I'll have split pea soup for you when you get back."

"Could you make that tomato soup?" Jack asked.

"Of course, Mr. Spoiled, tomato soup it will be." She laughed.

A Wish the Day Would Never End

Ben was happy to hear from Jack that his parents were having a triple-header party on Saturday afternoon: first, a gathering of friends and relatives to welcome Patricia into the family; second, to mark Jack's fading fourteenth birthday; and third, to celebrate Pap-Pap's seventieth birthday. Jack cleaned the house, relocating the growing piles of laundry to his bedroom, which he now shared with Jerry, who claimed the lower bunk over Jack's mild protest.

There was a large square cake measuring thirty-by-thirty inches, and three-inches deep, with chocolate icing half-an-inch thick. One corner decoration was of an angelic child with a halo. What could this possible mean? Maybe it was a cartoon of Sir Jack's haloed head. Close by was an outline of undulating baptismal water below a Cross. In another were fourteen candles arranged in a big grin. *That* would be Jack. Above the grin was the outline of a black top hat with sunbursts radiating from it. And there was another scene—an Irish harp with musical notes over a patch of four-leaf clover, and above that was a leprechaun's gold-buckled tall hat. Coffee and tea steamed in the kitchen. Bottles of soft drinks floated in a tub of ice. Little sandwiches challenged Jack's appetite, but he had been cautioned by his mom: "Birthday Boy or not, you are limited to three tea sandwiches."

The house filled up quickly with friends and relatives. Abby, Jenny, and Becky looked fine. This was a celebration that would not be forgotten. Pap-Pap was dressed in an oddly-fashioned gray suit, a nearly-white shirt, and a bright green tie, freshly pressed. The tie's lining made a shiny pattern to match the dark green decorative harp. His brogues had been polished.

"Jerome," his daughter-in-law announced, "you are the most handsome man in the house. By the way, this is not a backward compliment to my husband. Since he looks exactly like you, I think we have a natural tie."

Jack wore new clothes that for once fit him: jeans, blue shirt, and a comic brown tie Ben gave him from his father's never-never collection. It was wide, like the ties worn by sleepy Robert Mitchum in his black-and-white cop films that ran as second features. The popcorn sellers loved him because, when the movie began, there was considerable movement to the lobby. The tie was decorated with a large fire extinguisher. Below the image was the brand name: Ex-Pyre.

Becky laughed when she saw the tie. "Jackie, are you going to cool things down for us today?" Even though it was December, the front door was open, yet the house was still warm.

Yvonne came from the kitchen. She held a cigarette that she had probably just lit from the front burner, an old habit of hers. She looked happy and pleased to be there. Jack's mom was seated in an overstuffed chair. Pillows surrounded her. She said the pillows were Jack's idea. He was so protective these days. Before she could rise, with help, of course, the wedged pillows, like doorstops, would first have to be removed.

There was a woman standing beside the chair, her hand on the shoulder of Jack's mom. She was slender; her hair was brushed back. Her skirt hung above old-lady black shoes, and her blouse was light blue. On the lapel was a gold cross. At first Ben thought she was a nurse from Magee. She caught him staring, smiled, tilted back her head in a good laugh, and then called him by name. His instant response was, "Good morning, Sister Rosemary!" Everyone laughed. She might just as well have been standing in front of the classroom.

Sister Rosemary came to the center of the room. She moved slowly, her expression now quite serious. She said that she must make a few remarks before the cutting of the cake, which, she said, would call for the most astute gerrymandering. She began:

"This is a bittersweet moment, a true Advent moment if ever there was one. Maureen, if I begin to cry, let me go on, please. You understand! First, I want to welcome little Patricia, my namesake, into such a lovely family." She looked kindly at Jack. *"As you probably know, Patricia was baptized a few minutes after she was born. Such a healthy, pink, robust child would normally be presented in the baptistery after noon Mass, with a few other fidgety babies dressed in lace finery. But this did not happen. A knowing nurse left the delivery room and signaled an attendant to call the chaplain, Father Demeter. You see, in His wisdom, which I have spent many years trying to understand, God sent Maureen and John not one child but two children on that afternoon. Father Demeter baptized beautiful Patricia. John told him that the name Patrick had been chosen if the baby should be a boy. The tiny baby, the little Saint, was baptized Patrick and ushered into the Kingdom of God. Now, I have gone on too long. Thank you for your kindness and understanding. Thank you."*

Moved to tears by Sister Rosemary's beautiful words, Ben began to understand what he had heard in the hospital waiting room. He felt guilt rising in his body, and he thought to himself: "I'm not a family member; it was foolish to have been there at this private family moment, when Jack should have learned of the twins."

Jenny and Becky whispered something to each other. They probably knew about the twins but would not tell a soul. There were tears in the room. Jack stood like a statue of himself.

After the nodding of knowing heads, the tears, the sad smiles, there were hugs and kisses shared by family and friends. It had been the bittersweet moment Sister Rosemary spoke of.

And there was news. Big Hank was coming home! This was Yvonne's bittersweet moment.

"May I?" she asked Maureen.

"Oh, please, please, everyone, listen to Yvonne!"

"John and Maureen, whatever can I say? God bless you all."

She paused for a few moments, and then began:

"Henry will be home by Christmas. What a wonderful gift. As you probably know, I have not seen or spoken to him for nearly four months. We write, and I send him crafts and magazines to pass the time. The doctors told me that he

will need to continue his therapy once he comes home, and this includes periodic time in a whirlpool. I don't know where I can find one, but we'll see. He will still have to spend lots of time in bed. He is weak but in good spirits. Now he'll have to listen to me!" Everyone laughed. "He knows that after a day or two at home we'll be driven by my brother-in-law to New Orleans where we will live in a nice warm climate—no snow, no hills. Actually, I guess there is a hill in a big park—Monkey Hill. A perfect name! It was made to show people what a hill looks like. Children love it, so they say. If he's happy in New Orleans, we'll stay. But if he wants to come back, and if the doctors approve, then we will be back."

There was muted, reverent applause.

"We want what's best for you and Hank," said Maureen. "Privately, if I may, I would love to see him again racing up and down the streets on his bicycle." Quickly, she covered her mouth, remembering too late that the bike had been stolen. "I think it's time to cut the cake, don't you agree?" she said.

The twins held little paper plates while Becky and Jenny tried to cut democratic pieces of cake. The baptism icing of the haloed child was not disturbed. Ben understood why.

Coffee bubbled in the pot. And tea, some with a drop of whiskey from Ireland, some without, was quietly negotiated. Jack made sure that Sister Rosemary had a few drops to settle her spirits. Bobby and Jerry tussled over who got the cake's rich, colorful leprechaun's hat and the musical notes by the harp.

"Happy Birthday, Pap-Pap. Happy Birthday, Jerome! Happy Birthday, Grandpa! Happy birthday, Jack!" called a small chorus of family and guests. "And bless Patrick and Patricia!"

Jack's dad said, "Jackie, isn't it comforting to know that when you're seventy you'll be the handsomest man in the room!"

Quiet settled. The mood shifted in the room. Cool refreshing air came through the open front door. On the floor was a crazy pattern of sunlight cast through battered and bent venetian blinds.

Jenny was standing next to Ben, or, more correctly, he was standing next to Jenny. She was beautiful. He could see in her features and gestures something of Becky, nearly two years older and almost an adult.

"So," Jenny asked, "have you been having good luck?"

"Lots and lots of good luck," he answered.

"I think Patricia and Patrick are perfect names."

"Jenny, did you know? I didn't."

"Yes. This morning I brought the cake. I lifted the lid to take a peek. I saw it, and I knew. Jack's mom looked at me. I was crying. She knew I knew. She just put her arms around me and gave me a hug. She said, 'It happens, honey. Honey, it happens.'"

Ben wanted to hug her, too, but all he could do was ask whether Patrick and Patricia have middle names.

"I would bet on it," she answered, "because names are protectors."

"What's your middle name?" he asked.

"I'm not telling you unless you tell me your middle name first."

"I don't like mine, so I never say it out loud."

"OK, then whisper it in my ear," she said, pulling back the pretty brown hair from her cheek. "Go ahead."

Then she sat on the arm of the overstuffed chair while Jack's mom was in the kitchen settling a territorial dispute.

He bent down, took off his glasses, and stuffed them in a pocket, while wishing he had a long middle name with many syllables. He studied her ear, which was absolutely beautiful. There was a tiny blue earring. Ben took a big breath and whispered, "My middle name is Cyril." He drew out the hushed sound of *s* and the liquid sounds of *r* and *l*. His lips might have brushed her ear. He felt her laugh. He expected a smart slap on his cheek, but there was none. Then, she turned his ear toward her mouth. She whispered in his ear, which tickled and tingled at the nearness of her mouth and the warmth of her breath: "My middle name is Pauline. Do you have any more names?"

He was happy to be alive.

"Yes!" he whispered slowly. "I have more names. I am Ben Cyril Warren. So there!"

Jenny turned his face to hers and said in Ava Gardner's sultry voice, "Benedict Cyril Warren, you are a *mouthful!*"

Jack called them. Whispers ended.

"Take a deep breath," Jack teased, "and let's get some of that cake, unless you're too cozy there!"

The children had been back again and again for ever-smaller

pieces of the disappearing cake, but they could not be denied on this glorious afternoon. Jack drank hot coffee in a tiny cup from his mother's prized china set she got for almost nothing at the Giant Eagle. Pap–Pap corrected his coffee with wee drops of whiskey to fortify himself for the day. The twins played hand-clapping games and sang a kind of nursery rhyme. Then they spilled on the floor in laughter. Jenny and Becky looked on with a sense of happy sadness. Windows were raised to get a cross breeze. Jack's mom looked exhausted, but she was so happy, too.

A voice in the kitchen called out, "There's more! Come and get it."

But all too soon, late autumn twilight settled on the street. He and Jack were asked to walk with the girls to escort Yvonne safely to her apartment.

On their way, Jack told him that he just learned that his mom had twins. His parents held back the information, uncertain about whether he should be told. But he had to know. Sister Rosemary, a distant cousin of Maureen, said that through baptism Patrick was a family member. A saint. And he must be recognized.

Abby was talking excitedly to Yvonne, probably about New Orleans, where everything was French. She was more animated and happier than Ben had ever seen her. Yvonne put her arm around her and they shared a long laugh. They all hugged Yvonne at the apartment steps, and said how much they wanted to see Hank when he returns.

On the way back, the three girls were so giddy that, with their arms around each other's waist, they swung their hips and sang a spirited song. Abby raised her left hand as though she were holding an umbrella on Rue Bourbon. "Second line," she sang out. Jenny and Becky joined her, and in a few seconds the girls were dancing joyfully, twisting and turning, raising and lowering their make-believe umbrellas. They tipped imaginary hats left and right. Jack raised his imaginary twirling umbrella, signaled for Ben to join him, tipping his top hat to imaginary strollers, and so they waltzed to the dancing girls and joined the merriment on a Saturday sidewalk in Shadyside.

Ranger Rouge

When Big Hank returned a few days later, there was no band to greet him, no puffy Santa Claus tethered in the brown grass, and no special ramp built for him to reach the porch. He was spread out in the back seat of Uncle Ronald's Ford with a comforter and pillows to protect him. He looked out the windows at the evening scenes but he saw only reflected lights and bare tree tops. Ben guessed that Big Hank felt terror in his muscles and nerves. But he was home. The walls of his room were not freshly painted, and the drab window was not brightened by a Woolworth curtain with a pretty design. Yvonne did not have time for decorating, but the boys rearranged furniture, stacked some of it in the basement, and gave a few odd pieces to the Salvation Army. Uncle Ronald wanted to return to New Orleans as quickly as possible, but the trip would be spread over three days. They would reach home two days before Christmas Eve.

The recovery would require rest in bed, an exercise regime, a special diet, and medication. Although he had regained his ability to walk, he was still unsteady on his feet. He favored his right side. He had his old smile back, which was very encouraging, but Ben wondered what he would smile about. His darkest emotion was anger—why did this happen to him?

The daily hospital routine of bed rest, small talk with boys in his room, and occasional whirlpool treatment depressed him. He worked the puzzles his mother sent and he tried to make model airplanes.

Other dexterity games were required, even as simple as drawing birds and small animals, which he then colored with crayons. He drew pictures of his green bike, the fronts of houses he liked, and comic book characters, such as Dick Tracy and Mutt and Jeff. He talked about the doctors who came every morning, testing him, joking a little, and then moving on accompanied by two nurses in starched uniforms. He vividly remembered a visit by the chief doctor and researcher, Jonas Salk, who was greatly revered. Dr. Salk said to him and to the others in the room that the menace of polio must be defeated very soon, and that his research team was talented and dedicated. "It will happen," he told Big Hank. "You have my word!" He touched each of the boys as he passed through the room.

Hank said that New Orleans might as well be on the moon as far as he was concerned. He learned that he would be surrounded by stupid flat spaces; and stupid rain would fall every day in the summer. But hurricanes excited him. They are all named for girls, Ben told him, names like Abigail, Becky, and so on. "Let 'em blow," he said. "I can take 'em!" Uncle Ronald did his best to tell him about the banana trees, the live oaks, the spacious parks, and the Mississippi River, which, you could say, begins in Pittsburgh. But the odd thing is that the river's surface is many feet above your head because of the levies built to hold the river in its course. "If there's a flood, wear an inner tube and bob around until someone comes to get you."

"Yeah, I'd like that," he said.

The history of New Orleans did not interest him: the Civil War, slavery, Mardi Gras, cotton and sugar mills, the Old Mint, and so on. But when he learned that coffee in New Orleans was like no other coffee in the world, he made his first funny remark: "I'm bringing the biggest cup there is, and I'm drinking coffee all day long!" He could not grasp the idea of chicory coffee. "Why ruin a good thing with a weed?" As a kid with a Pittsburgh accent, he could speak like a native in the district known as the Irish Channel. People there might just as well be from Rankin or Etna. "Bring on them micks, I'm ready!" he cried. "And don't forget them streetcars," he said. "I'll ride 'em all over town." He knew nothing about jazz, but they bet he would love it. How could he not? Maybe he could play an instrument at school; a wind instrument might build back his throat and chest muscles. But the fear was that if all he could blow was *toot*, he would be too impatient to continue.

At first, they thought of asking Abby to talk to him about New Orleans, but they knew she could not understand what makes Big Hank the kid he is. But she could learn, and perhaps she could visit him during Mardi Gras next year. He needed to connect with people he knew, so they gave him stamps for post cards and challenged him to find the most bizarre ones he could. They asked for cards of 'gators pulling the bikini bottoms from pretty girls in the bayou. They did not know what a bayou was. All he had to write was, "Hay you bums." They would understand.

Ben bought as many Classic comic books as there were in the narrow corner of Kate's little store. There were comic books on Dickens, Dumas, Twain, and Stevenson, as well as thrilling stories with ship wrecks, French Revolution guillotines, American Revolution spies, painted Indians, and spooky ghosts. *The Corsican Brothers* was a favorite story about brothers feeling each other's pain. He saw Big Hank as one of the brothers rather than as one of the musketeers. Big Hank picked out a comic, looked it over, and declared, "This is pretty heavy stuff! Love the drawings."

The day of departure came. Yvonne made a nest in the back seat with makeshift blinds covering the windows so that he could sleep. Abby, Jenny, and Becky made muffins and cookies. Jack's mom sent apples, oranges, and pears for the trip. Sister Rosemary had the nuns praying for the travelers day and night. A Saint Christopher medal was pinned under the visor by the map that would direct them over the long trip.

Early on the Sunday before Christmas, the boys rode bikes to the apartment to help load the trailer and deliver the box of baked goods and fruit. Jack rode Red Ranger. They found Big Hank drinking coffee and eating toast. The toaster and coffee pot were the final kitchen items to be loaded. Awaiting them in New Orleans were new beds, one with a hard mattress for Big Hank.

They joked about all the school he would have to miss, teased him about the southern belles just waiting for him, and promised that they would try to visit him in June. Abby had already exchanged addresses with Yvonne so that at Mardi Gras they could get together and pal around, wear masks, and watch the solemn Indians in their elaborate, feathered costumes turning revelers' heads in the French Quarter.

Jack supervised the loading. He kept a space open in the center of the trailer for last minute items, whatever they might be. There was not much to load. The job was quickly completed. Uncle Ronald signaled thumbs up to Jack as soon as Big Hank struggled into the back seat and Yvonne covered him in the freezing car. "Let's roll," Uncle Ronald called out. "Time's a-wasting!" As if on cue, Jack pushed Red Ranger behind the trailer. He took spools of red and white ribbons from his jacket pockets. He wrapped white ribbon around the cross bar and red ribbon around the handlebar. He let some ribbons dangle. Then he tucked an envelope into the front spokes, pushing it down as far as he could toward the axle. He gave Red Ranger a ceremonial lift. Nothing clumsy would do. He slid the bike into the opening he had reserved for it, looked at what he had done, and then swung the doors closed. He snapped the big padlock and pulled it to make sure it was locked.

The Ford and its trailer slowly moved into the street, with waving of hands and dabbing of tears inside and outside. Ben and Jack just stared at the little caravan until it turned onto Walnut Street, the street Big Hank loved above all.

Almost There

All Jack could say was, "Let's go. Right, let's go to Isaly's for hot chocolate."

"And maybe a smoke, too," Ben added.

After hot chocolate and Old Golds, Jack walked while Ben pushed his church-door-red bike toward Roslyn Place. The weather was changing. Snow began to fall, hesitant, tentative snow. It blurred his vision as flakes melted behind his lenses. He was reminded of the calendar for November, with the picture of Saint Cecilia, patron of music. His mother had not turned the page to December, to Saint Lucy, whose time was running out. He took his glasses off and wiped the lenses. Jack was hunched over, lost in reflection. Snow fell more heavily. It appeared to be rising, disengaged, and hesitant.

"Hey Jack," Ben said, a little sorry to break the silence of this odd moment. "Is that your mom's coffee I smell?"

"It's *my* coffee," he said, laughing. "The whole pot! If you want some, you'll have to wrestle me for it!" He pushed Ben with his shoulder. "Well," he added thoughtfully, "maybe one cup. I feel generous today!"

"Why did you do it? Do your parents know you gave your bike to Big Hank?"

"They know, and they said it was a kind thing to do for Big Hank. And it made me feel good. They'll find it in the trailer. What could be better?"

"You said it! Hey, wish I could go in with you for a cup of that coffee, but I have to serve Mass in an hour. This is the last Sunday of Advent. Christmas is Friday. See you, Santa. Gotta go!"

"I'll call you later," he said. "You can help us decorate our scrawny tree—dad's big bargain."

Big Hank was gone. Ben doubted that he would return to the city he loved. Somehow, for reasons that were not entirely clear to him, he felt that New Orleans would cast a spell on Big Hank, that he would come to own the city's dark corners, back alleys, and misty river banks. And hills? He could tell them some things about hills! He was a tough kid with a kind smile, a forgiving kid. Ben would miss him.

And Jack? He would be busy with his baby sister. He would climb stairs for his mother, feed Doody his dinner of dried flies, and be awarded more chevrons for work well done. But would he follow his parents' path—love, marriage, many children, and happy, manageable poverty?

Knowing that summer would come too quickly with its recurring threat of disease, Ben wrapped the cold morning air around himself for comfort.

The uncommon snow rose before him, a fitting image in an uncertain, tipsy world. What would his place be, he wondered—this altar boy with Old Golds, this paperboy in the Sunday dark before dawn?

He pumped hard up the hill toward Kate's, sometimes slipping on the tracks. His glasses were wet with melted snow. He tucked them into a pocket and took a chance he could see the way without them. It really wasn't so bad. The soft blur surrounding him like a quilt; he was a voyager in a white world, familiar and unfamiliar. The rounded edges of the Monopoly jalopy pressed into his thigh. It felt good. Yes! He would find Fate wherever he loafed, and when he did, he would shake him by his ears and shout, "Lazy loafer! Where have you been? Don't you know? I want good luck and happiness!"

Mother had left him a note saying that his father was at the studio rushing a Christmas order. She drove with him as far as Green Tree to visit her brother and sister-in-law. Green Tree, but no Christmas tree yet. Sally and George would return from shopping by six, unless the snow piled up.

He served Mass at a side altar for an Ethiopian Franciscan friar. It appeared to him that the world the friar left behind (but would soon return to) was a happy place just in need of a little help from America. In fact, it was an arid land of deserts and terrible mountains. But Ethiopian coffee was the finest, the Franciscan said. "I miss it so!" Ben wasn't sure whether he missed the coffee or the country.

"Where is Ethiopia?" he asked him.

"Well, come with me," he said, leading him to the main altar. He was still dressed in his vestments for Mass.

With respect, they walked around the huge inlaid world map on the floor of the main altar.

"This is Africa, is it not, the second continent of seven? And this is the Horn of Africa, on the east coast, and the horn includes the enormous and ancient country of Ethiopia where Christianity flourished in ancient days. See how large it is? Now, after the last world war, and after the Italian army was routed in 1941, there is great poverty. And great pride, I must add. I am in America visiting parishes, begging for money to build a church, a clinic, and a school. That will be my message in this morning's sermon. A special collection will be taken during Mass. Franciscans have always been beggars of God."

"It must be very hot and dusty there," Ben said. "Look, there's the equator."

"You are indeed correct, but here, in Pittsburgh, the snowflakes bite like pesky desert insects, and I have to borrow a winter coat from your pastor, and I wear shoes, not sandals, when I travel about."

"Where will you go next?"

"I will travel by train to New York City to ask for money in a number of churches. My first visit will be to Greenwich Village, to Saint Anthony of Padua, a Franciscan parish. I will reside there, off and on, for a few weeks. Wish me blessed luck!"

They walked behind the altar to the sacristy.

"I should also add," he began to say, "that I have been invited to walk in the procession with the cardinal and bishops in Saint Patrick's on Christmas morning. Afterwards, I will happily spend the rest of the day in Harlem in a food kitchen. There will be Ethiopian coffee there, I am sure! So, life is balanced. Saint Francis of Assisi was a great teacher.

From Harlem I travel north to New Haven. And then back to Saint Anthony. Such an exciting life I lead!"

Ben reached under his cassock to his pocket for some money given him by his customers. These were his Christmas tips.

"Father, please take this. I hope it helps."

He gave him ten dollars in wrinkled ones.

"You are very kind and generous, my friend."

Then, after receiving his blessing, he tore off the surplice and cassock, pulled on his old winter coat, and ran home in the snow. He felt good about what he had done.

Jack called at noon. "Hey, tree time! Where've you been?"

"Ethiopia."

"Yeah, sure," he said. "Get on down for sausage, bacon, pancakes, scrambled eggs, hot, hot coffee, and sweet rolls that Jenny's bringing. She'll be here, too, Mr. Kazoo. So slide on down!"

Yes! Slide down the alley, slide down Ellsworth Avenue's sidewalks, covered in deepening snow. King Kongs worn smooth, snow piling on the black toes, a twist, a turn, a backward glide, arms out like a skater's, running, sliding, big breaths, the cold afternoon air up my sleeves and all the way down to the bottom of my lungs. That's it!

"Hey, save me a place next to Jenny, OK?"

"Dream on, dream on," he said. "Think it's Christmas or something?"

"I'm almost there!"

"Time's a-wasting," he said.

"I'm almost there!" he said with a laugh.

And then he was.

Buffet

Snow covered the slippery wood pavement blocks. At the end of the little street, Jack's house beckoned with its inviting light in each window. The old screen door was open, its spring long ago sprung by kids hanging on its flimsy frame. The sounds and aromas from the kitchen were splendid. But as Ben held the door open under the spell of the breakfast awaiting him, he heard quick steps, and then Jenny slipped under his arm, turning her eyes up and smiling. Flakes of snow in her hair and little pink jewels in her ears were highlighted through the steam forming on his glasses. She held a bakery box by one of its strings. So trusting, he thought. A bright little laugh and she was in. He looked over his shoulder at the afternoon shadows on this last Sunday before Christmas. He closed the screen door slowly behind him.

Jack waved him toward the Christmas tree, already decorated at the bottom by sticky fingers of little brothers. After breakfast, older, experienced fingers would hide bare spots around the tree with falls of tinsel and bunches of old glass balls of green, purple, blue, and red that tricked the eye by simple magic.

"This is a French breakfast—or is it lunch? Anyway, mom calls it a 'buffet.' Dad calls it 'mess on the carpet.' Oh, he said *mess* in the army means *chow*. You get in a line, he said, which we don't have right now, take a plate, fill it with what you want, and then get a glass of juice, if you want, and then find a place to sit. Any place! See, the twins are sitting on the steps and having a great time. Older people, they get chairs. You and me sit on the floor, cross our legs, and try to balance the plate and eat at the same time! There's Jenny and the gang; they're using their skirts like table clothes. Lucky girls, huh? They just know what to do. The twins think they're at a picnic."

Jack was so proud; he went on and on. Ben ate with an odd sensation of lifting the fork from his knees to his mouth and trying not to drop anything while trying to agree with Jack at the same time. And knowing that the girls were watching and laughing at them. Scrambled eggs have a special gravity. Some parts slide off the fork, others don't. You just take your chances, like in life. Bacon's a finger food. The twins ate their bacon that way. They crossed their eyes to watch their progress.

"What you have to do for old people is help them get up from their chairs. Give 'em a hand and pull, see? I mean old women. Old men you don't have to help, unless they have a cane. Just hand them the cane. Oh, if you want more food, you try to get up while holding your plate. I can't do it, but maybe you can. If not, it's OK to take a piece of bacon from someone close to you, like you. Thanks."

He took a piece of bacon from Ben's plate and spoke over the mouthful. "You see, you need to load your plate just like you did; then you don't have to go back. It's a trick you learn."

He saw Abby and Jenny smiling at Jack. They held out their plates to him.

"No," Jack insisted. "You never take anything from a girl's plate. That's uncouth. Manners are all about being couth," he said, lifting his little finger and coaxing the coffee cup to his lips. The girls rolled in laughter. So did the twins.

"So that's a buffet, in case you ever go to France. I think the word works in Ethiopia, too, if you can find it on a map."

A few minutes later, Jenny came to Ben with a fresh cup of coffee.

"This is for you, Cyril, to top off that big breakfast."

She had remembered his middle name. "Just whisper," he begged.

"It's good to the last drop," she said. "I'll bet you didn't know that!"

He lifted his coffee in a toast: "To Lucky Jack," he said, taking a sip.

And Jenny whispered to him: "Oh, Cyril, it's Christmas. We're all very lucky, aren't we? Count yourself lucky, too. I do."

Jack tapped his cup against Ben's. "Hey, me too," Jenny said with her deep laugh, so they tapped cups again.

From the corner of his eye he saw the outlines of Jack's mom and dad and Pap-Pap, all drinking Irish coffee. Patricia let out a plaintive sigh. They all laughed. "I guess she can't wait for Christmas, too," Jack told them.

Ben thought of Big Hank, probably somewhere in Ohio by now, pointed south toward New Orleans for Christmas with his new family. He thought of Red Ranger and its promise of joy for that unlucky boy. He thought of Jenny standing next to him, a great thought. And he thought of the incredible summer and their adventures. Would he ever live such a life again, so magical, so miraculous? Jack's dad always said life's a mystery, some big, some small. Ben remembered him struggling with the mysterious *Press* crossword puzzles that were seldom solved for the large cash prizes: is it *pool* or *fool* when both words seemed right? *Stare* or *spare?* He sometimes spoke in riddles, and he scribbled the hieroglyphs of shorthand. Ben wondered, did he know Jack's trick with the gas needle that perpetually seemed to rest on E? Jack's dad was kind, witty, easily amused by nonsense, and loyal to all. He never asked Ben, wryly or not, "Young bespectacled boy, don't you have a home of your own?"

In this little reflection on that amazing afternoon, He began to grasp something of the meaning of life's mystery. It seemed to him that mystery was not to be feared. He needed to let mystery draw him in, encircle him, befriend him, embolden him.

He felt Jenny's lips by his ear. "Hey, Cyril," she whispered, "you seem to be fading out. Did you know your eyes were closed?"

"I was just thinking about something."

"Well, think about this, Mr. Kazoo, all of us kids are going to walk in the snow. You know, slip and slide! You coming, deep thinker?"

"Yep! Uh-huh!"

"So, you're coming with us, right?"

He whispered in her ear: "Yes, yes, and yes."

"Do you like my pink earrings?"

"Oh, yes."

"They glow in the dark? Want to see them do that?" She laughed.

He closed his eyes tight. "I can see them!"

She slapped his arm. "Oh, you and Jackie! Between the two of you, I don't know who's crazier." She shook her "naughty" finger at Jack across the room, and he faked an ashamed pose.

"Come on," she said, pulling his sleeve. "Let's go!"

They left the bright, warm house, with its aromas, chatter, and laughter, and stepped into the embracing cold, the snow sifting through branches of old wintery trees against a darkening December sky. His glasses fogged in the cold air. And then he realized that he and Jack were targets for snowballs, which arced softly from the girls' gloved fingers.

"You two have been naughty and not nice," Becky said, and the others agreed with a larger volley. They twisted and shouted in mock pain. The battle ensued until Becky shouted, "Truce! Abby lost her shoe in the snow."

They circled, searching for her shoe. Jack and Ben spent more time watching her one-legged hop-hopping than they did searching for the shoe. Then Jenny and Becky put their arms around Abby and they all danced. Girls always seem to know what to do.

"Hey, you two wallflowers, come on and dance. Come to the hop!"

They hopped over to the girls and hopped up and down.

"Bunny Rabbit comes at Easter, you know," Jack announced, and then led a line right back to his steps and through the waiting door. Abby took off her one shoe and said she needed a taste of hot coffee or she'd freeze. Jack tossed her a towel to wrap her legs in. His mother laughed. "Well done, Jackie, but next time maybe you could step over to a lady in distress, bow, and then deliver the towel."

Jack answered, "My work is not done here. I must round up a posse to search for a missing shoe, and we must finish the task by the stroke of midnight."

His mother knew Jack too well. "No such thing, Jackie. First the dishes and then the mighty task."

The girls began washing dishes; their sleeves were rolled up. They made a game of the suds. This would be a long chore.

Ben stood next to Jenny to dry the dishes. Jack clowned with Abby about the sloppy slippers his mother gave her to wear. They kept falling off. Becky kept order in the kitchen. "Organize, girls. Organize!"

"Hey, Jenny," he said, "I think you lost an earring in the snow."

"I know, Cyril. But I'm not worried; it glows in the dark. Remember? It'll be fun searching. Want to help me?"

"Oh, yes," he said. "I love searches. You can count on me!"

"But not until after the dishes, or Becky will crown me."

An hour later, in the growing dark, they tip-toed through the snow, which had stopped falling. Around they went, looking for a tiny glow under a snowflake. They talked and talked. Jenny asked him why Jack gave his bike to Big Hank. "We were surprised, but then you never know what he's going to do next. And there is always a *next* with Jackie!"

"I'm not sure," he answered, "but I think something happened this summer that changed him. He's more thoughtful than before, and Big Hank's going far away. Maybe it was just kindness."

"My mom told me that if a person doesn't learn kindness by the age of eleven or twelve, there's not much hope for them. You, by the way, Cyril, are kind. Quiet and kind. The best kind of kind. And you *are* deep, you know, in a nice way. Maybe, just maybe, Jackie changed because of you. Of course, I haven't a clue what you two do all day, so I shouldn't guess about it."

Kind, quiet, deep? Maybe. Take risks and chances? Probably not.

"So, how did you get earrings that glow in the dark?"

"My brother got them as a prize in a box of cereal, and he gave them to me. You just squeeze them on the ear."

"Oh, yeah. I get you. I sent away for a prize a long time ago. It was a Lone Ranger Atomic Bomb ring. Mother made me eat the whole box of KIX before I could have the box top."

"That was deep of you," she laughed.

"You take this little red cap off the back of the bomb, go into a dark closet, hold the bomb to your eye, wait, and then the bomb begins to flash little bright lights. It doesn't make any noise, just flashes like fireworks. I'm going to keep it for a long time."

"Do you remember the closet from last summer? Abby told me that she and Jackie saw some lights."

"I heard."

"Cyril, what do you think about this earring? Is it worth freezing my ears off for it? I don't think so, do you?"

Then she removed her glove and touched her ear that was glimmering in the dark.

"Here, this is for you. One earring's not much good, but since you like things that sparkle in the dark, why don't you keep it for a long time, too? I wish it could be a red bike with a silly horn, but this is the best I can do. Please accept it, and no speeches."

He kept that little treasure in the sunlight, and at night he watched it glow brightly, as it did for many years.

They went squinting and blinking into Jack's house.

"Any luck," he asked.

"No, you've got all the luck, Jackie. Sprinkle a little on us, OK? Spread a little around."

Ben saw in his eyes that Jack was moved by what Jenny said, and she said it with such feeling.

"Gotta go," Ben said. "Gotta slip and slide back to my house and see what's happening there." In a home of his own. And so he said thanks to Jack and Jenny for the great day, and to Jack's mom and dad for the great buffet.

"Not staying to help decorate the tree?" Jack teased.

"I've got one waiting for me at home," he said, "if my dad remembered to buy one, if there were any left."

That was Roslyn Place, his second home, long ago, in the summer and fall, a time of joy, excitement, and sadness, a magical time compressed softly and kindly in memory.

—for Gerald Levin

⚜

Home in the Dark

He glided home on the snowy sidewalks, a skier without his skis. So tired. Maybe he should catch a streetcar. No. Probably not. Walking is good, but sliding is better. He got on the streetcar tracks, wet and slippery, and glided as on skates up Ellsworth Avenue to Kate's. Henry's Pie Shop window was bright, but a single pumpkin pie was all he saw on a green background. Tipsy with fatigue, he forced himself to jog up Lamont Place where exhausted old cars, parked tightly to the curb, tilted this way and that in their end-of-life infirmities. They were robed in a chalky white pall in the dim moonlight. On the porch was a short-needle tree wrapped in twine. Already beginning to turn yellow, the tree was steeped in exotic incense. The warped door pushed open with a muffled cry of wood-on-wood.

Someone was busy in the kitchen.

"*Olé,* I'm home!" No answer. It would be his mother, who was a little hard of hearing. He'd have to say it louder. "Hey, I'm home!"

Fussing in the kitchen stopped. Mother looked around the doorway, smiled, and asked, "Did you see the tree?"

"Yes, I like it. Lucky dad could find one so late."

She sang a little song. It began: "Your shoes are soaked. They're squishing."

Mother could always hear what she wanted to hear. Over the years she taught him to listen for music in the ordinary. She sang old, familiar songs in the kitchen.

He climbed the alpine steps, foot-heavy with soaking shoes. This had been a long day: the overstuffed Sunday newspapers digging into his shoulder in the bloated bag he carried; Big Hank's farewell—he wished him good coffee in a large pot, and happy miles on the big red bike; the Ethiopian priest from far away, with such confidence in the holiness of charity; Jack's celebrated buffet, with so many friends and little Patty Cake's happy laugh; snowballs and dancing on Roslyn Place, the wooden pavements under the snow; and skating home on the 75 Wilkinsburg via East Liberty tracks, happy and exhausted.

He put on dry clothes, some belonging to him and some to George. He felt their sleepy warmth. Just for a few minutes he stretched out on the bed, lights off, and quiet in the street below. The Valentine Bros. were far away, perhaps resting in Florida. Would it be wrong to sleep for a few minutes? Mother would call when dinner was ready. Or would she let him sleep until morning? That would be nice. Between dinner and dreams, he would choose dreams.

On the dusty mantelpiece was Jenny's pink earring. As his eyes grew accustomed to the dark, the earring began to glow a little, and then more, like the evening star. He thought:

"If I dream, make it a dream of today, a dream of faces—Jack's laughter; Big Hank's sad eyes; Jenny's smile just before she whispered Cyril; *and mother's face tilted to present her good ear. That would be good. That would be very good."*

And so the dreamer dreamed in the warm dark, lit only by the tiny glow of distant Venus on the mantelpiece.

Truth in Wine

In the little kitchen, Cecilia turned the lamb chops again just to breathe the rich flavor that brought back a fleeting moment from a happy past. Albert was out in the snow somewhere. Sally and George seemed lost somewhere, moving in their own orbits. George was probably in Tom's cynical orbit wobbling comically around Shadyside. She wished they would come home.

She called up the steep stairs: "Dinner's ready. It's just the two of us tonight. Come down, chop-chop." He didn't hear her, she thought, and she was not climbing those steep stairs to wake him. He missed a nice pun, too. "Would you come to the table if I had a wonderful potato pie for you, with onions and a *delicious* golden crust?" She sounded a little peevish and was sorry.

She sat in the hard chair at the table, feeling the blues of the long winter Sunday. A few days until Christmas and yet, she asked, where is the joy? Where is the happiness she was so certain of? She believed there was joy even in disappointment and sadness. She told Ben there was, and she had said that the poets said it was so—Joy, the Daughter of Elysium, had silenced the noise of chaos in Beethoven's Ninth. There it was!

Still, she thought, I don't have my Nativity crèche for the dining room mantel. It had fallen a year earlier in a crash when the mantel itself fell. Albert had never attached the mantel to the wall. There were frequent warnings: do not lean on the mantel because it is not fastened in place. Albert did not always finish his projects. In the fall of the

Nativity crèche Cecilia lost the head of a camel, a wing of her favorite angel, and the head of one of the Magi. She remembered the animals that met their separate fates on the little farm: King Midas, Diego, Snowball, the Sunday chickens, and the big cow, Bossier, or was she called Bessie? Oh, Albert! We dropped that crèche, too. Sorry. I think it's my fault.

"But I will make it right. I will make it work," she said aloud in the hollow house. And she meant it. She would keep this promise. She pulled her best robe about her and dangled a quilted slipper from her foot.

She poured a small glass of Albert's cheap red wine into an odd glass, once a votive candle cup, purple, dented and twisted, light-catching in the candle world of the sanctuary. Probably a sin to use it like this, a venial sin, like so many she stored up for Saturday confessions. The sugary wine tasted good next to the rich lamb chop. She might as well have Ben's chop rather than let it go to waste. So she did.

It had been a long winter day, and so she rested as well as she could on the comfortless Danish sofa. Perhaps Denmark's Prince Hamlet would find some comfort on the thin cushions far away in his stone castle. Hamlet reminded her of Tom, George's ironic friend, and Tom, strangely, looked remarkably like Jack, Ben's friend. They were both tall and skinny, loosely jointed, quick to laugh, and sometimes they shadowboxed—throwing punches into the air just to make a point or to get a laugh. They had Nordic blond hair, almost transparent, and through the cropped hair their scalps were obvious—Jack's with scars, Tom's smooth.

Ben appears to have had a nice day, coming home in the dark as he did with his jeans soaked to the knees and his squishy shoes weighted with water. Since Mass—the last she saw of him was at the side altar—he had been busy, she knew, with a boy he called Big Hank, a victim of polio, who was being driven slowly to New Orleans to begin a new life. And then he was at Jack's house for most of the day. There was the new baby. She knew Ben would tell her about their exploits if he decided to wake up and come down for dinner. Otherwise, tomorrow. *Bonne nuit,* my lucky Ben, and *sweet dreams!*

Surprised that her thoughts turned again to Tom, she saw him as an unusual boy—this Hamlet. Tom was a little disconnected. He comfortably kept a distance, even when he was clowning about—on his knees mocking Henri de Toulouse-Lautrec in that new movie, *Moulin Rouge*. Tom, on his knees, crossing the carpet, crying "Henri, Henri!" A bit mean and insensitive, like so much humor since the war. Surely he knew from the movie that Toulouse-Lautrec suffered from a congenital bone disease that had shortened and crippled his legs. The parents were first cousins. It happens! No laughing matter there. She had a sudden but fleeting thought of Big Hank's sorrowful passage to New Orleans.

And there were Tom's paintings, which were dark and abstract, more background than foreground. He hadn't found his subject yet. The paintings on canvas had no real center; they were too serious for a youth of fifteen. What they needed was his genuine humor, if only he would release it more often. She loved to think of Tom's artwork on, of all things, a pair of bloated boxing gloves! Now where did he ever find *those*? He had painted a truck on each glove, one red and the other yellow. Construction dump trucks. Nicely done. And below each truck was some wording. When she put the gloves almost to her nose she could read the tiny messages. One glove said *stay back* while the other said *six feet*. She loved that in Tom.

She paused for another sip of Albert's candy-sweet wine, with its hints of chocolate and cherry beneath the top note of Concord grape. She was surprised to detect just a hint of Burger Road beeswax, perhaps a last "Amen" from the votive cup. And then in a further mood of fancy—where this winter evening was definitely careening—she dreamed up a scene of Friday night boxing on TV—Tom in black shorts and a sweeping black cape blazoned with his dump trucks. Bowing politely to the prince-pugilist and pointing a skinny finger, the Master of Ceremonies proclaimed—*in this corner, from Copenhagen, the Danish Shadow, Kid Dumper!* How like the Tom she was beginning to know: crawling across the living room floor shouting the artist's name while laughing with himself, laughing *inward* it seemed. Tom would be good for George, but, she wondered, for how many rounds, for how many orbits?

She was startled to hear a sound from above. Was Ben awake? What if he were to see her in this state? On those steep stairs, sleepwalking, no doubt, after his long day, he would certainly tumble! She listened with her good ear. Silence. The wind, no doubt. Or else the house was haunted.

Again, she sipped the potent wine from the votive cup that held more than she had ever guessed. She felt warm and cozy in her robe and slippers. In the wine there was an ounce of truth: sometimes she needed to be alone, to think, to puzzle out answers to questions that sometimes frightened her—Was Albert right about Ben? Had he found a friend, a sweetheart, a connection? Was he adjusting, growing up to be happy in the little alley house? Had she done the right thing about the move from the pathetic little farm: Albert's fresh woods and pastures new? Well, she realized, what's done is done—not a bad philosophy to struggle on with. It could sustain one. Cecilia believed that the mysteries of life *can* be solved—the deep secrets—whether portrayed in hieroglyphics or tea leaves or laboratory microscopes.

Strong in her belief, she laughed, a happy laugh, as she remembered herself tethered to Bessie, or was it Bossier, on Burger Road hill that summer afternoon. She had prayed in peasant French for a safe descent. *Merde*, she remembered. She had indeed carried on.

The lamb chops were perfect, just right. Why can't all life be so simple? She held the purple cup before her reading lamp, as though making a toast, and turned it in the lamp's glow with two fingers. She had enjoyed her private nip. And then, remembering all that was good in her little world, and accepting what she could of its mysteries, she began to hum the music of her favorite Christmas carol, *Joy to the World*. She smiled to herself, first with her lips and then with her bright eyes. *To bed*, she said, *to bed, there's knocking at the gate*. Day is done. She scaled the fearsome steps and, indeed, went to bed.

A Moonlight Fantasia

The clock by Cecilia's bed is wound tight and set for 7:00 a.m., on Monday, December 21, 1953. She thinks she detects with her bad ear the very Germanic tick-tock of the seconds passing. She thinks of her father and his beloved Beethoven. She sees Beethoven's metronome moving hypnotically, left-right, right-left, tick-tock tick-tock. In her reverie, her hearing is perfect. She sees the metronome shape of Beethoven's tombstone. She hears herself laugh. Just listen, Papa would say to the child, his beloved Cecilia, whom he named for the patron saint of music. She imagines the music rising over the scratchy static on the old wind-up Victrola at Dithridge Street. Can you just hear the music's beat? With two good ears, she believes she still hears the music's beat. Yes, Papa, she whispers.

But now, the tick-tock clock's numbers are invisible because its glow is in eclipse. Some nights, but rarely, the single sliver of a window admits for a few minutes a glimpse of moonlight. This is not one of those nights. Her reverie's a quasi-dream, perhaps, wherein deep, hidden memories and yesterday's trials seem logically entwined. The justice of dreams, she thinks. She loves the rare but beautiful dramas created in a dream mood, in a weightless moment when she becomes so in love with her life, a life remembered, sculpted, and treasured. She thinks of Albert, who has no reserve of batteries for her clock's light— why have a drawer full of adjunct batteries just so they can peter out before you need them? Albert, you have just described the U.S. Senate.

Maybe the Supreme Court. Please, be respectful. Actually, he replies, I had in mind the House of Lords, where the rule states that at least one-third of the wigged members must stay alive in a session and wake frequently to shout *hear! hear!* Cecilia loves these games, which are seldom played now, but in reverie they are fresh, even new. Now, in a flash, the reverie modulates as Cecilia stands at the bottom of the perilously steep stairs and calls out, *Albert, can you hear-hear me? Al-bert, Yoo-hoo!* Silence. A trick of time makes her think—Ben, Sally, and George are out doing what they usually do: Ben is exploring the known Universe with Jack and Big Hank, the Marco Polo of Shadyside; George is spinning around backstreets in Tom's father's old Ford, probably without permission; and Sally is buying shoes in town. How she goes through shoes! Wooden shoes might just be what Sally needs to tiptoe through our tulip patch. And then—perhaps she is really asleep—Cecilia hears a familiar three-note Urban Lamont Sonata a study in cacophony—she knows, of course, that three notes are sufficient for Beethoven to make magical music—the startling scrape of the iron gate on the flagstone walk that frightens cats into trees; followed by the yawning spring's crescendo on the porch door; followed by the shattering yelp of the door against the jam, which swells or shrinks in barometric precision. Since it is summer, the mode is to swell. Push hard. Albert, much younger now, has come home. Albert, where have you been? I've been calling for you. What's that in the bag? He smiles his rare smile. It is a little something for you from Poli's, our neighborhood purveyor of homemade ice cream. A whole pint. The flavor of the week: mint chocolate chip. Oh, Albert, how wonderful. She dreams that she is dreaming. No more tripe, promise me. Let me spoon some for us now. I am so excited. Lately, you are so full of surprises. I love surprises. Here's a generous dish for you, Mister Hunter-Gatherer. Now it's soft, a sign of quality. Would you like me to pour you a cup of freshly brewed coffee? Oh, good. It is very hot. Don't burn yourself. What I like to do is put a dollop of ice cream in the coffee. That cools it and enriches the coffee at the same time. I am reminded, said Albert in his British cadence, of a little cafe in Amsterdam, a place to smoke questionable weeds and to sip coffee. The waitress asked me in a pretty Dutch version of English if I would like my coffee "korrected." I almost answered, well, what's wrong with it in the first place, but I showed restraint. Why, yes, I said. Into the cup she poured a little brandy. Noo is it korrect, she said. And she was absolutely right. In the spirit of Amsterdam, I sometimes pour a wee drop of whiskey into my coffee. Cecilia said, Albert, it is time for you to learn the truth: your bottles of Kinsey have been corrected. You didn't know that, did you? Well, here's the story. Now please show restraint. Tom and George used to sip your whiskey after school, on the sly, of course, and they replaced what they drank with Pittsburgh tap water, which has its own distinctive flavor and hue, somewhere between iodine and rust. I am sure they were just being considerate. They have since taken the oath. I know you cursed the distillers of cheap Kinsey. Now, perhaps, you owe them an apology. Whatever the tension, it is now time for release—ice cream and coffee on a summer morning in July, her favorite month. And when we're finished, do you know what? We're going to walk slowly together in the sunlight to Poli's. We're going to sit in a booth, the one all carved with lovers' sweet little lies—HP + AN, BT + OY. Do you think these couples are still together? Albert said he has never seen a minus sign in their calculations. Well, we will each have a large dish of the ice cream of the week and cups of their good coffee. If you insist, Albert said, I agree to this adventure you've charted—we will stroll through the alley, preposterously named Lamont Place, and onto Alder Street on our way to South Highland Avenue, to the very corner where Old Man Brooks likes to stand, his blue eyes bright, his paunch of a stomach proudly displayed and boasting a gold watch chain, and his fingers moving in so many ways to accentuate his little love songs for the lavender-haired ladies. A streetcar will ring its merry bell, and we'll be seated in the booth. If you don't mind my saying so, there's a parallel between this booth and the ancient coronation chair in Westminster Abbey. That famous old pew is covered with hieroglyphic scratches, perhaps love messages, and so forth, as though it were a tippler's seat in a Bristol pub. Mabel comes to take their order. Mabel, from the Culmerville Hotel? Well, sweethearts, she sings, and what can I bring to you this morning? We would each like to have a large bowl of mint chocolate chip ice cream with big spoons and hot coffee on the side. I'll have it in a jiff, sweethearts, but first, tell me, is this a first date for you both? And would you by chance have a handsome bachelor brother? Willie be coming? She chuckles as she pivots toward the ice cream freezer. They eat shyly and sip quietly. Dutch treat? Albert, since you've been to Holland and know all about the Dutch and their dikes, I think you should pay the check, and I'll put a tip down just because. We must do this again. Perhaps we'll carve *our* initials inside a heart—that's what we did when I was a teenager, and that was only a few years ago. Well, a little more. Time melts faster than the mint chocolate chip ice cream. I'll ask a favor of you, Mister Lord of the Manor. Please go next door to Schmidt's bakery for a loaf of white bread, sliced, of course. I'm off for home to call my sisters before I forget. Their phone number is MAflower 3813. They get moody when I make them wait. Ta-ta and cheerio. Mr. Brooks dances over the pavement with her and says that he has wonderful conversations with Ben, a bright boy for sure. Thank you. We all miss you on the alley. We're so sorry you had to move. Me too. It was them three rum hounds I had for sisters-in-law who pulled a legal trick and got my house after my dear wife passed away. My home! So we've heard. Be of good cheer. Goodbye for now. Albert comes home with bread in a white wrapper tied in bakery twine, but it is wheat bread. I thought you said you wanted *wheat*. What will the children say about wheat bread? Cecilia has an answer. You are only half-wrong. Look up *wheat* in Webster's and you will find that long ago *wheat* meant *white,* I think. Actually, I am quite sure. Albert, you live a charmed life. Sally will say who cares, and George will ask is it any good, and Ben, why he'll take a slice and sniff it, like he does everything. Remember, at the dinner table at Dithridge Street he sniffed a fine holiday knife blade, and we all roared laughing? Yes, I remember. I am glad you do; isn't memory wonderful! Memories are dreams and dreams are memories. All is forgiven in them. Cecilia's joyful spirit is released and floats to tranquil infinity. Why, I'd be at a loss, as in the silences between movements of the great music of Papa's beloved Beethoven, that great timekeeper, and, like me, Beethoven was a little hard of hearing, too. Tomorrow night, or the next, or the next—I'm not Mister Walt Whitman's Learned Astronomer—there will be a moon, if only for an hour! Albert, I will wake you when it comes, and if I don't, you wake me. I know it sounds silly, but I feel the need of a moon. Is that wrong? I do not think so, Albert replies: I wish you a moon, so there! Oh, she thinks, anything in a dream is possible for little girls and youthful matrons. If only for a moment.

—for John W. Francis

C Major, I'm Home

At 7:00 a.m., with a scent of dusty snow from the window propped open with Albert's wooden shoe, the foolish little clock makes its shivering sound and Cecilia opens her bright eyes to the morning light gathering timidly in the window. (And later, in the afternoon, when she sees the pale, almost transparent full moon descending in the winter sky over Carnegie and Green Tree—a satisfactory matinee performance by this understudy moon—she will smile and breathe deeply the damp bracing air.) For now, though, she stretches, listens for any sound of others disturbed by the alarm, and then cautiously sits up in bed to plan her Monday: no laundry, no chores, no shopping—only helping her partially-sighted boys and girls to stay in traditional schools where they receive special attention. She has a wonderful sense that it will indeed be a good day, a nice day, perhaps a little misty. Ben will be very hungry and bursting with stories of yesterday's exploits. Her intuition tells her that something splendid happened to him. She can hardly wait to hear him at dinner. And so, she begins her little morning rituals. The coffee pot rattles over the blue flame, wonderful coffee. She says "good morning" to Saint Cecilia—held over from November—and cautions her that she must leave the kitchen in ten days to make a place for January's mystery calendar saint. She tells her that sadly nothing on earth is eternal—"I know you will understand."

As for me, she thinks, she remembers Papa coming home from the city, the front door opening, and his baritone voice singing out: *C major,*

I'm home! C major, his favorite key, the key of light and grandeur and heroism, was his code for the "key" to the happy home.

And if Albert hears her small song, her Matins prayer, she does not mind at all. *C major,* she whispers in the cold, damp kitchen.

She is home, in her own home, and she thinks of the past year in her tiny, too-hot, too-cold, plaster-crumbling alley home with all its scrapes and bites. She thinks of her oft-distant Albert, remote in his darkroom; and quiet, mysterious George; and bright Sally; and Ben, her searcher, her adventurer, her storyteller. Yes, she believes sublimely, deliciously, home is an estate of mind, and she *is* home. At last.

The coffeepot's contained fury rocks above blue flames as Albert begins his descent on the steep stairs. He loses his ancient carpet slippers with each step. "Dash it all," he mutters, poking about with his toes for the errant slipper. "Dash it all." Cecilia listens. "Albert, would you like a cup of fresh coffee?" He thinks, and then asks, "Did you make tea?" She rolls her eyes toward heaven. She says to herself, "Mr. Maxwell has a house, that's true, but I'm on an alley I'll call home. That's it, I guess. That's it. Find happiness where you can. It's there waiting for you." The weak morning light brightens the little kitchen window. "That's it," she says. "Albert will have coffee this morning, like it or not. That's it." Adventures await her. No time for tea today. No tea-for-two. Just life's little adventures—*petites aventures.* "Lord help me," she prays, and then she turns to Albert who wears one slipper and holds the mate in his hand. "Albert, please drive me to work today, or I will be late. That would be so nice." Albert says that he will, and he does so. On the way she spies the teasing moon behind a misty curtain of treetops—a good omen, a lucky, sweet charm. "Don't look now, Albert, but the moon is coming up over the trees. That's odd, don't you think? The moon should be golden, not milky white—full or not full. Sorry if I sound like the Learned Astronomer. Anyhow, I feel very good now. Quite happy. I just know that something wonderful is about to happen for all of us. It's coming."

"Well, you are a moon person, and you have had your wish. I'm a sun person; with my camera I write with the sun—photo-graph, right?"

"Yes. So, between us, we cover the day: you've got the sun and I've got the moon."

"That just leaves the stars and the planets. What about them?"

Cecilia thinks for a moment. "We're here, on Craig Street, and I'm on time for work. If I do a good job with my partially-sighted boys and girls, they will someday, or should I say some *night*, see beyond my moon to the brightest stars, the constellations, and the planets, especially Venus. So, my answer to your question is this: the stars and planets belong to my boys and girls. It is what I wish for them. I know it's a great reach. But wouldn't that be some adventure! That would be my gift."

Albert replies, "A man's reach should exceed his grasp. . ... Is this where I should say 'Amen'?"

"That would be very nice, thank you."

"Then I say Amen and Amen."

"And now, back to Earth please. Albert, do let Ben sleep as long as he wants. Don't let him be distracted. I'd like to have a little talk with him when I get home. We'll have baked chicken for dinner, and baked potatoes. Something special, don't you think?"

"Well, I had a little talk with him a few months ago. Remember—about girls and such?"

"Yes, he told me. I think he understands everything now—about *what* I'm not sure. But I'm pretty sure that Jack told him a few things, too. Jack's gems, I call them."

Albert laughed. "Since you are now already late, let me add something more. How do you manage to talk so well with Ben, and with Sally and George?"

"Without being aware of it, I've developed a way of listening that puts me at an advantage, especially since the children came along. Maybe it's magic, who knows?"

Albert seems at an impasse, as though he never really knew this Cecilia. He surprised himself by saying, "I remember that you told me years ago that you once danced with the magician Houdini. Was that really true?"

"Did I tell you that? Yes, it's true. Actually, no, not quite. The truth is, when I was twenty, I went to some charity shindig at Carnegie Hall, and Houdini was very much present. He was a star! It so happened that the nice but clumsy fellow I was dancing with—one of those eternal, dizzying waltzes—bumped into Houdini and some society lady or other. It was then that the Great Houdini's magical powers must have been imparted to me. A few days later, I told the priest in confession that I thought it was a sin, perhaps only a venial sin, to touch a magician, for the Church has no place for magic. He said that it was nothing of the kind, that I was just being scrupulous."

"What happened then?"

"Father Price paused, and then he said, 'Cecilia, do not dwell on such little, idle matters when the world is filled with unexplained wonders. Have adventures. Be yourself.'"

"'Father, forgive me,' I replied, rather boldly at that, "'but how do you know my name? I'm puzzled.'"

"And what did he say? Did he give you absolution?"

"I really don't remember saying penance. Maybe I forgot to! But before he closed the slide he distinctly said in English, in a very teasing voice, too: 'Call it a miracle, or call it magical, but let it be a source of wonder for all the years to come. Go in Peace.'"

"A wonderful story. How could you keep secret about it for so long?"

"I don't know. But I have a way of listening to Ben that he responds to so well. Because I lost hearing in one ear when I was a little girl, I frequently asked my friends to please repeat what they said. Later, I learned to pause before responding, a little trick of mine, so that I could study their faces, a forgivable impudence even for a girl with impaired hearing. Therefore, I had time to know, even intuit, what the speaker was really saying. And our Ben reveals so much about himself!"

Albert nodded in agreement.

"Buy each of the children a little gift, just from you, and I'll wrap them for under the tree, the one leaning on the porch, hint-hint."

"What would I buy? Should I sit on Santa's lap?" They laughed at the thought.

For Sally, a pretty leather bookmark; for George, a hunting knife that opens and closes, but not too sharp or too long; for Ben, three View Master discs. He likes to look at the world in three dimensions. He told me he loves to because it's like cheating, but he said it's not his fault. Very insightful. So, why not pictures of some exotic places, like Dublin, or Rome, or Istanbul."

"Or India?"

"Perfect. Yes!"

"Now I'm really late. Oh, well. . .."

"Go in Peace," said Albert. "And be careful about bumping into people today. Choose carefully."

"I will. Yesterday was wonderful. Today is young, but I feel something, and it feels good. I can't wait to get home to *la casa*. I can't wait."

"Snow tonight."

"That will be wonderful! If you can, don't stay in Carnegie too late."

"I'll race home for dinner. Keep a light on for me."

"Will the moon do? And tiny Venus, too?"

"Yes and yes, in your honor, but the sun is mine tomorrow."

"Of course. You're a photographer. You write with the sun. *Adiós, Apollo.*"

"*Ciao!*"

Cecilia, a happy wife and mother, climbed the steps to her office at the Association for the Blind. She heard the machines trembling on the third floor, and she breathed in the fragrance of straw being shaped and sewn into brooms by visually impaired men and women. She was reminded of Burger Road in the fall and of the lowly animals pictured in the Christmas stables of paintings and frescos. She had come a long way, never dreaming (but always a dreamer) that one day she would have this lovely life.

A frustrated retired country gentleman, Albert drove the pointed nose of his gray Studebaker along the river valleys of Carnegie, where families perched on hillside towns and river banks came proudly for their yearly portraits. Sometimes Albert looked down his nose at the masses of compliant, scrubby men on the sidewalk without seeing his own shadow among them.

Sally, George, and Ben continued to grow, as the markings on the door to the cellar will attest. Their futures were assured in the safe and secure 1950's, when coffee was a nickel, hamburgers were a quarter, and Isaly's tall cones were a dime. Nothing seemed to change. Jack would laugh and joke around for years to come. The three lovely girls of Roslyn Place would be there to please and tease the boys. Big Hank, behind his devil's mask, would plunge his red bicycle through the French Quarter celebrants on Mardi Gras.

Tom, the young artist, Cecilia's Danish Dumper, wrecked the family Ford on Fifth Avenue when the car jumped the little lip of a curb and smashed into a sturdy old tree. He limped rather proudly long after the bone mended.

★ ★ ★ ★ ★

And so it was in the timeless mosaic world of Ben, Albert, Jack, and Cecilia, our keen-eyed dreamers who savored life's subtle moments under the spinning sun—a time of happiness found or sadly lost like swarming bees. And on the rare evenings when the sky was clear of smoke and clouds, Cecilia asked Albert to drive with her to Highland Park, where lovers "park and spark" along the circling road beneath the reservoirs. She quoted her sister Mary: "You just can't do much without an automobile these days." Then she searched the darkening sky, the crowded stage of heaven with its dramas divided into lunar acts—such mythology, such gods, such poetry, such music, and such dancing—a tango, a waltz, a second line—round and round. Around and around, like Ben's Honeymoon Express, an endless circle of delight. "A ridiculous toy," she said with a laugh. "Whoever dreamed that up was a cynical man, don't you think?"

"Well, perhaps. Or else he was rabidly optimistic." Cecilia was amused.

The next station? Why, yes, it's just around the bend.

Afterword

On April 12, 1955, Ben delivered the *Press* up and down apartment halls on Fifth Avenue and on the pretty streets of Shadyside. He made sure to place each paper with the bold headline showing. The headline read: **"Polio Is Conquered**.*"* Ten years earlier, to the very day, President Franklin Delano Roosevelt passed away. He was the major force behind conquering polio, the disease that had attacked him as a young man.

Thanks to Dr. Jonas Salk and the many scientists who labored so long to develop the vaccine that ended the polio epidemics. And thanks to the faithful who persevered, day after day, during those many long and fearful summers.